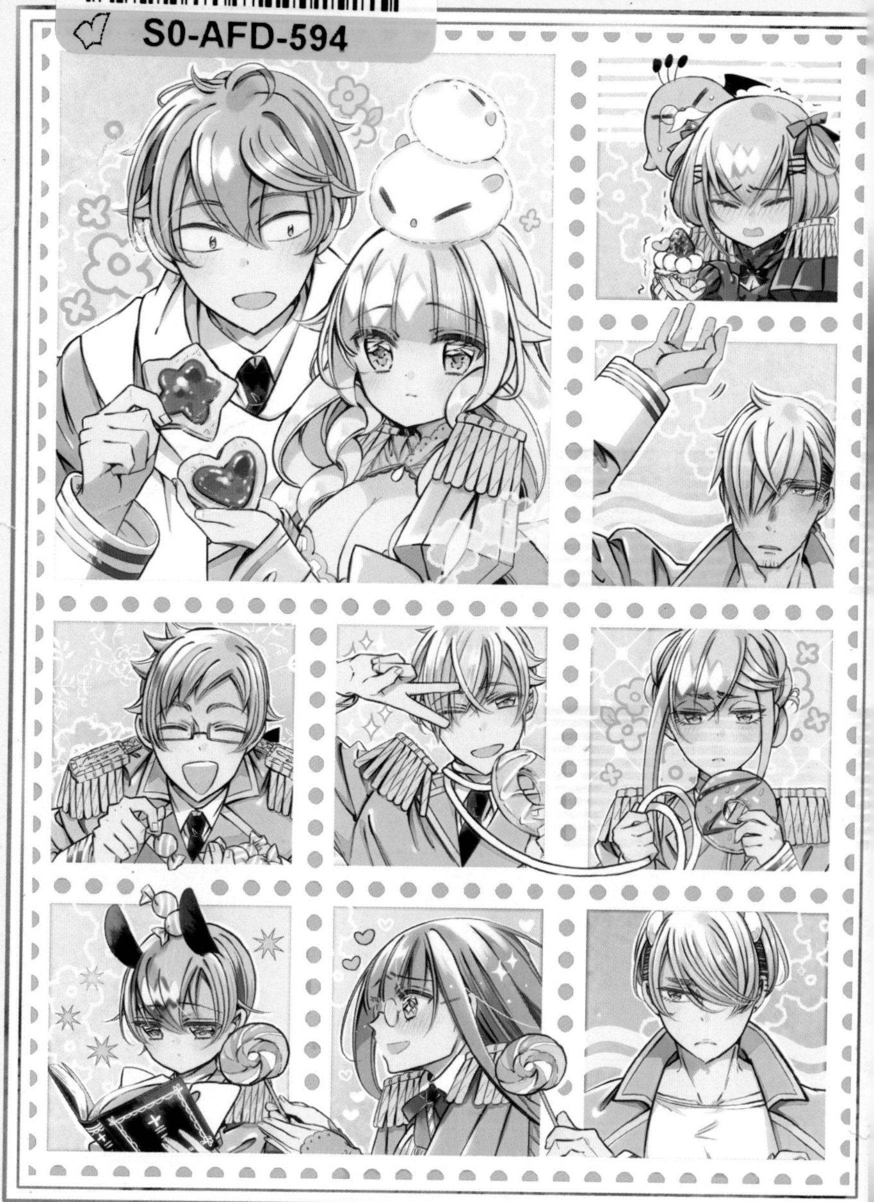

As Miss Beelzebub Likes, Volume 9

matoba

As Miss
Beelzebub
Likes

page ——— Chapter **57**
003

page ——— Chapter **58**
033

page ——— Chapter **59**
073

page ——— Chapter **60**
101

page ——— Chapter **61**
125

contents

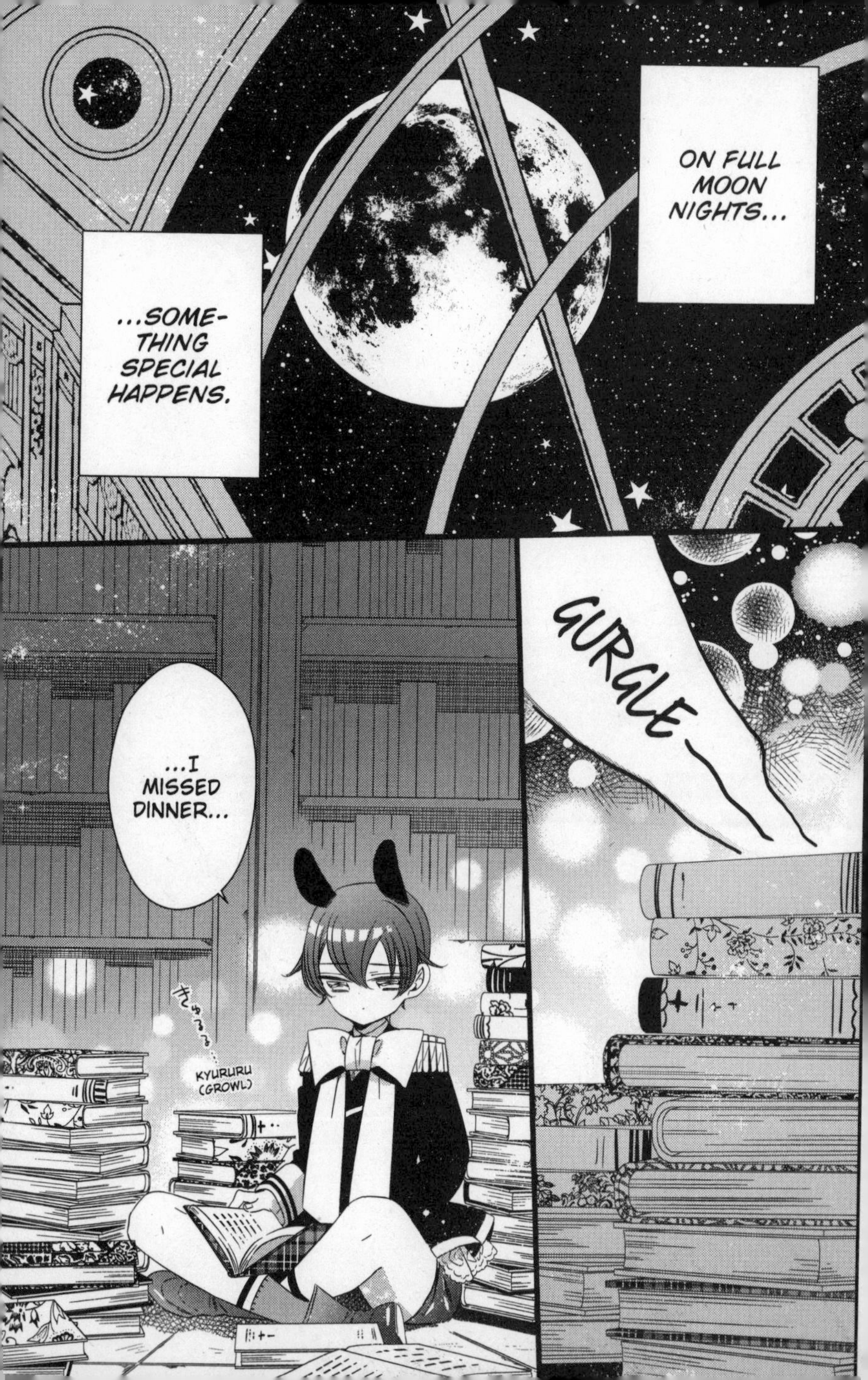
ON FULL MOON NIGHTS...
...SOME-THING SPECIAL HAPPENS.
GURGLE—
...I MISSED DINNER...
きゅるる…
KYURURU (GROWL)

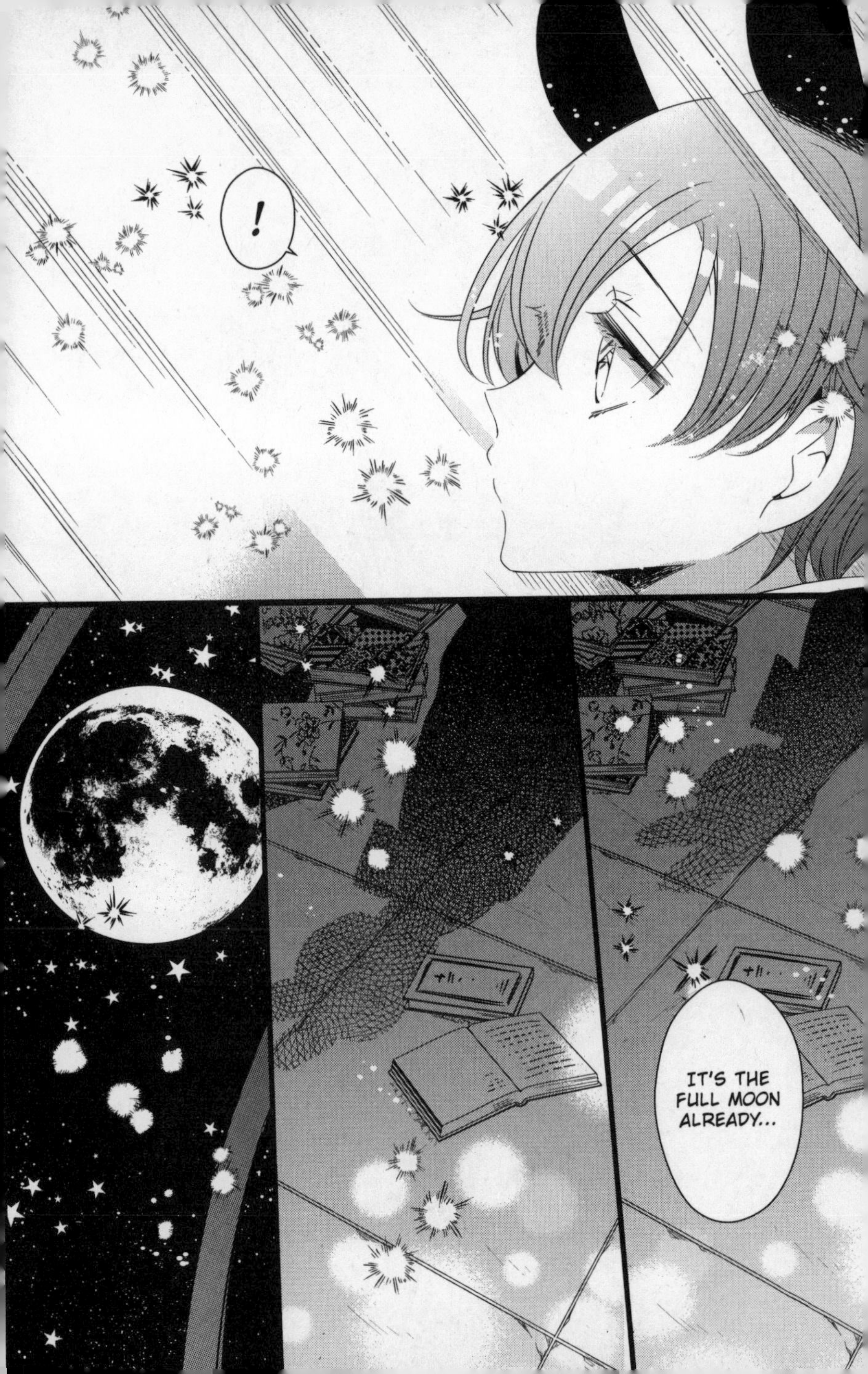
!
IT'S THE FULL MOON ALREADY...

CHAPTER 57

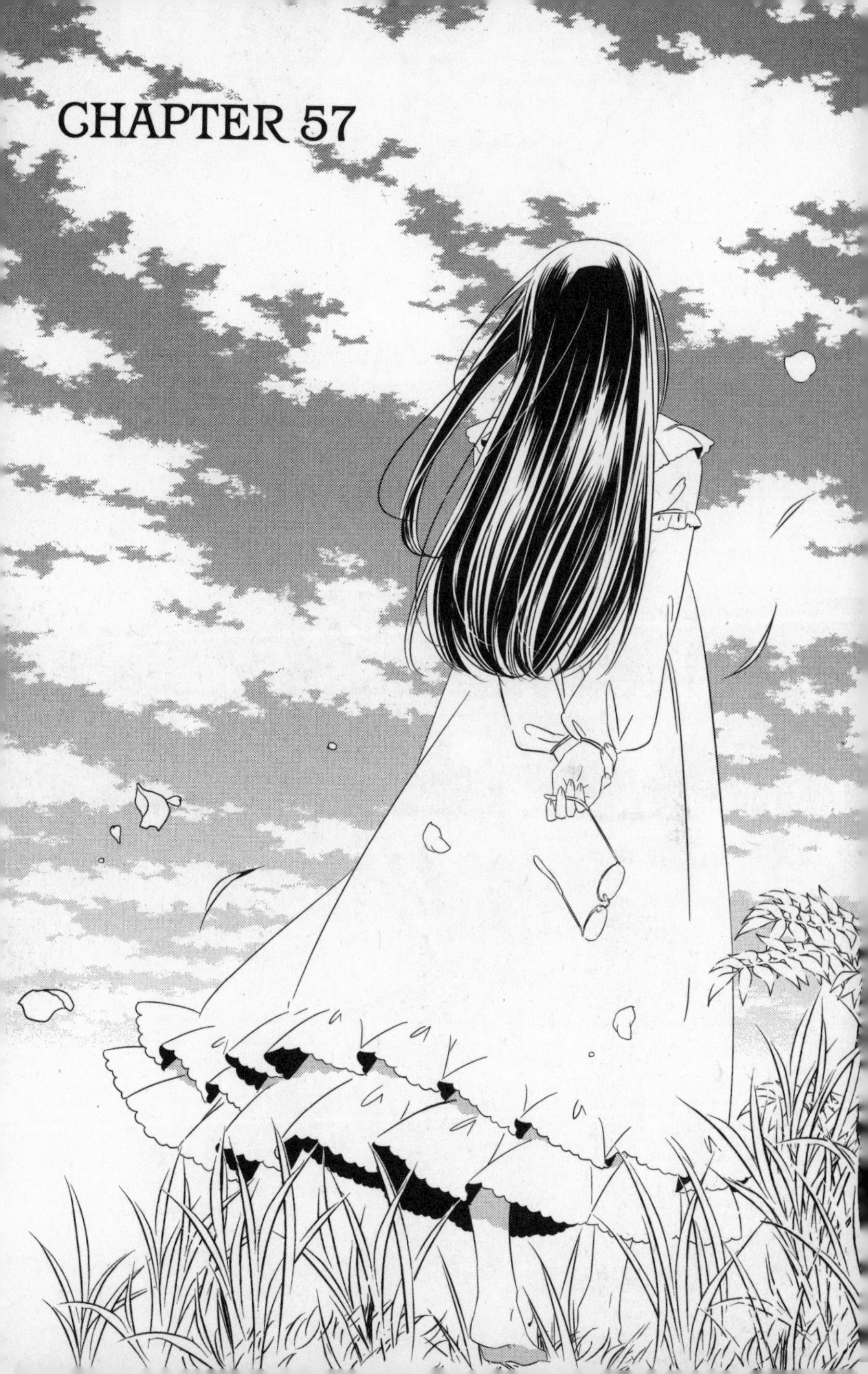

HEADLONG RUSH

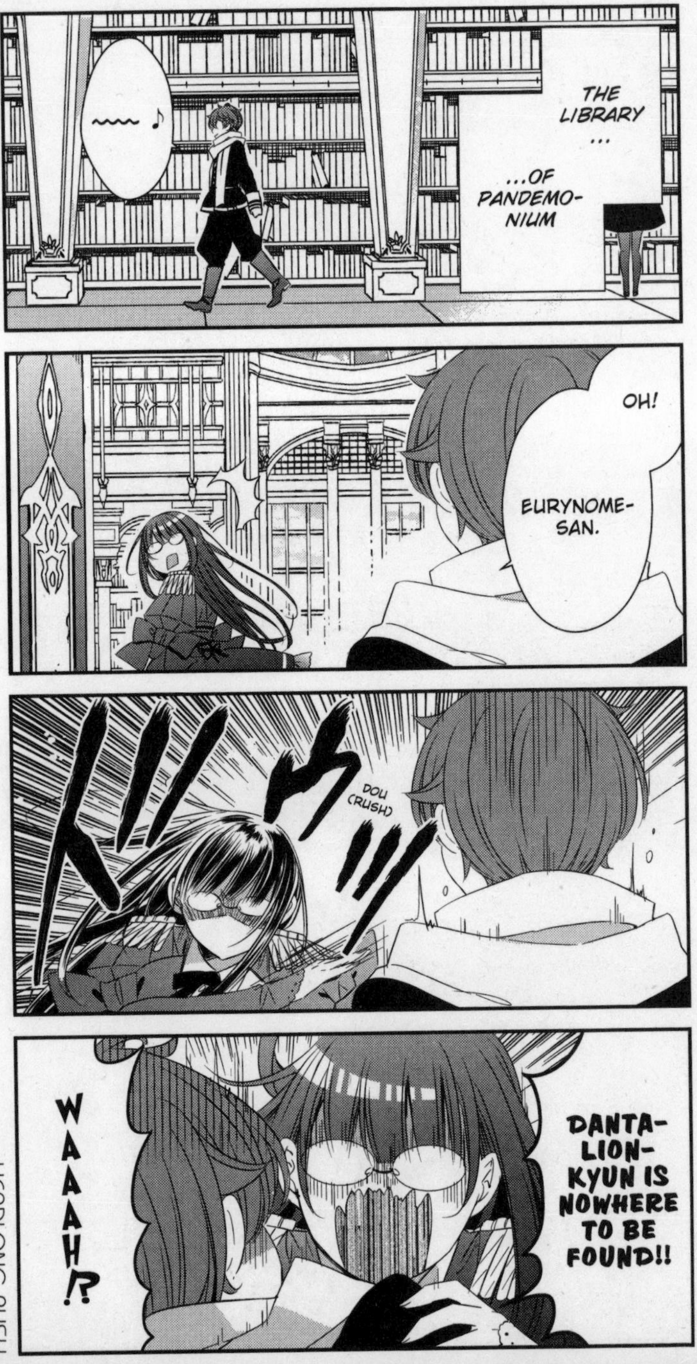
THE LIBRARY ...
...OF PANDEMONIUM
~~~ ♪
OH!
EURYNOME-SAN.
DOU (RUSH)
DANTALION-KYUN IS NOWHERE TO BE FOUND!!
WAAAAH!?
~~~

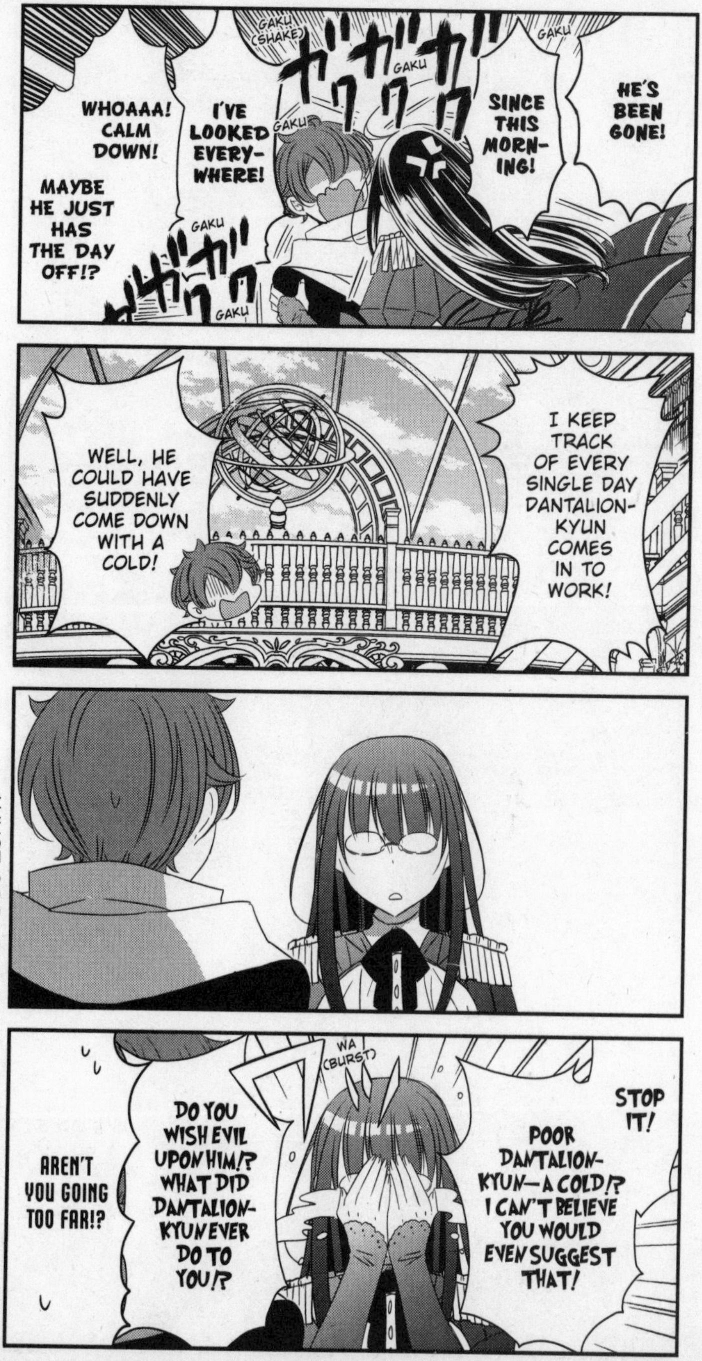
GAKU
HE'S BEEN GONE!
SINCE THIS MORNING!
GAKU
GAKU (SHAKE)
I'VE LOOKED EVERYWHERE!
GAKU
WHOAAA! CALM DOWN!
MAYBE HE JUST HAS THE DAY OFF!?
GAKU
GAKU
I KEEP TRACK OF EVERY SINGLE DAY DANTALION-KYUN COMES IN TO WORK!
WELL, HE COULD HAVE SUDDENLY COME DOWN WITH A COLD!
STOP IT!
POOR DANTALION-KYUN—A COLD!? I CAN'T BELIEVE YOU WOULD EVEN SUGGEST THAT!
WA (BURST)
DO YOU WISH EVIL UPON HIM!? WHAT DID DANTALION-KYUN EVER DO TO YOU!?
AREN'T YOU GOING TOO FAR!?

WHAT ABOUT YOUR OWN JOB, EURYNOME-SAN!?

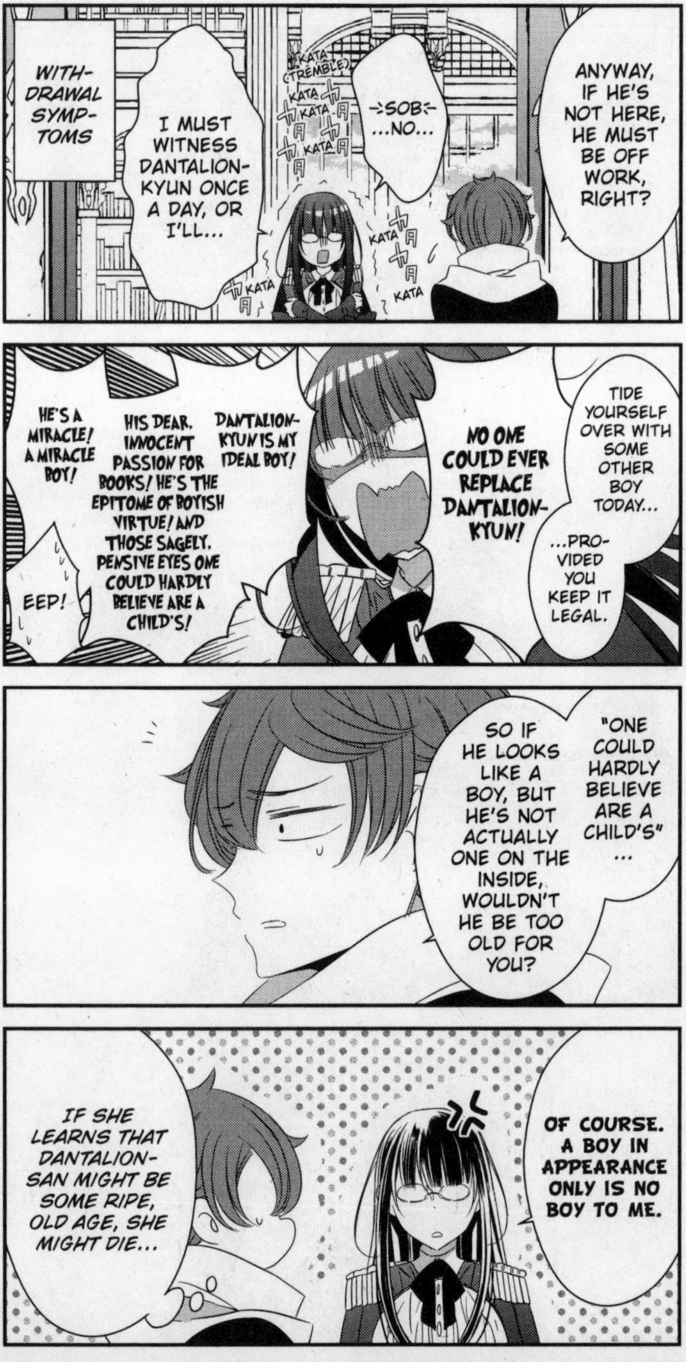
ANYWAY, IF HE'S NOT HERE, HE MUST BE OFF WORK, RIGHT?
-SOB- ...NO...
KATA (TREMBLE) KATA KATA KATA
KATA KATA KATA
I MUST WITNESS DANTALION-KYUN ONCE A DAY, OR I'LL...
WITH-DRAWAL SYMP-TOMS
TIDE YOURSELF OVER WITH SOME OTHER BOY TODAY...
...PRO-VIDED YOU KEEP IT LEGAL.
NO ONE COULD EVER REPLACE DANTALION-KYUN!
DANTALION-KYUN IS MY IDEAL BOY!
HIS DEAR, INNOCENT PASSION FOR BOOKS! HE'S THE EPITOME OF BOYISH VIRTUE! AND THOSE SAGELY, PENSIVE EYES ONE COULD HARDLY BELIEVE ARE A CHILD'S!
HE'S A MIRACLE! A MIRACLE BOY!
EEP!
"ONE COULD HARDLY BELIEVE ARE A CHILD'S"...
SO IF HE LOOKS LIKE A BOY, BUT HE'S NOT ACTUALLY ONE ON THE INSIDE, WOULDN'T HE BE TOO OLD FOR YOU?
OF COURSE. A BOY IN APPEARANCE ONLY IS NO BOY TO ME.
IF SHE LEARNS THAT DANTALION-SAN MIGHT BE SOME RIPE, OLD AGE, SHE MIGHT DIE...

WOBBLE, WOBBLE

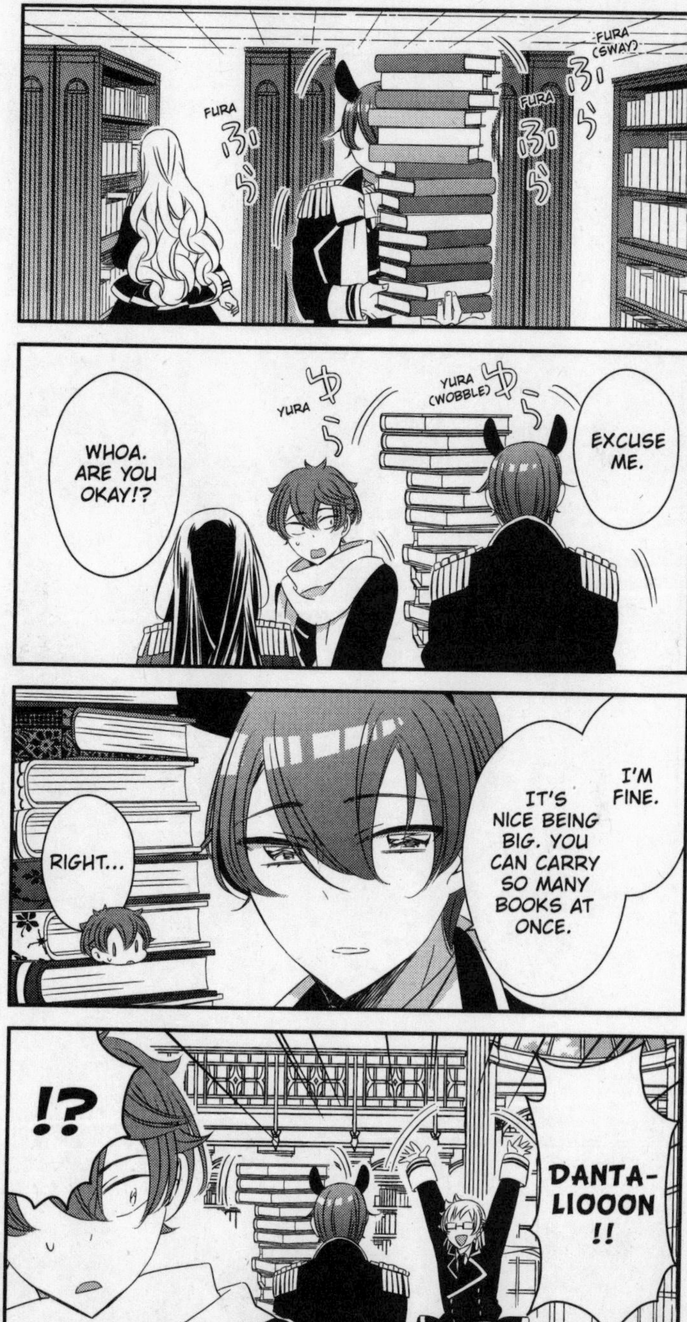
FURA (SWAY)
ふら
FURA
ふら
FURA
ふら
EXCUSE ME.
YURA (WOBBLE)
ゆら
YURA
ゆら
WHOA. ARE YOU OKAY!?
I'M FINE.
IT'S NICE BEING BIG. YOU CAN CARRY SO MANY BOOKS AT ONCE.
RIGHT...
DANTA-LIOOON!!
!?

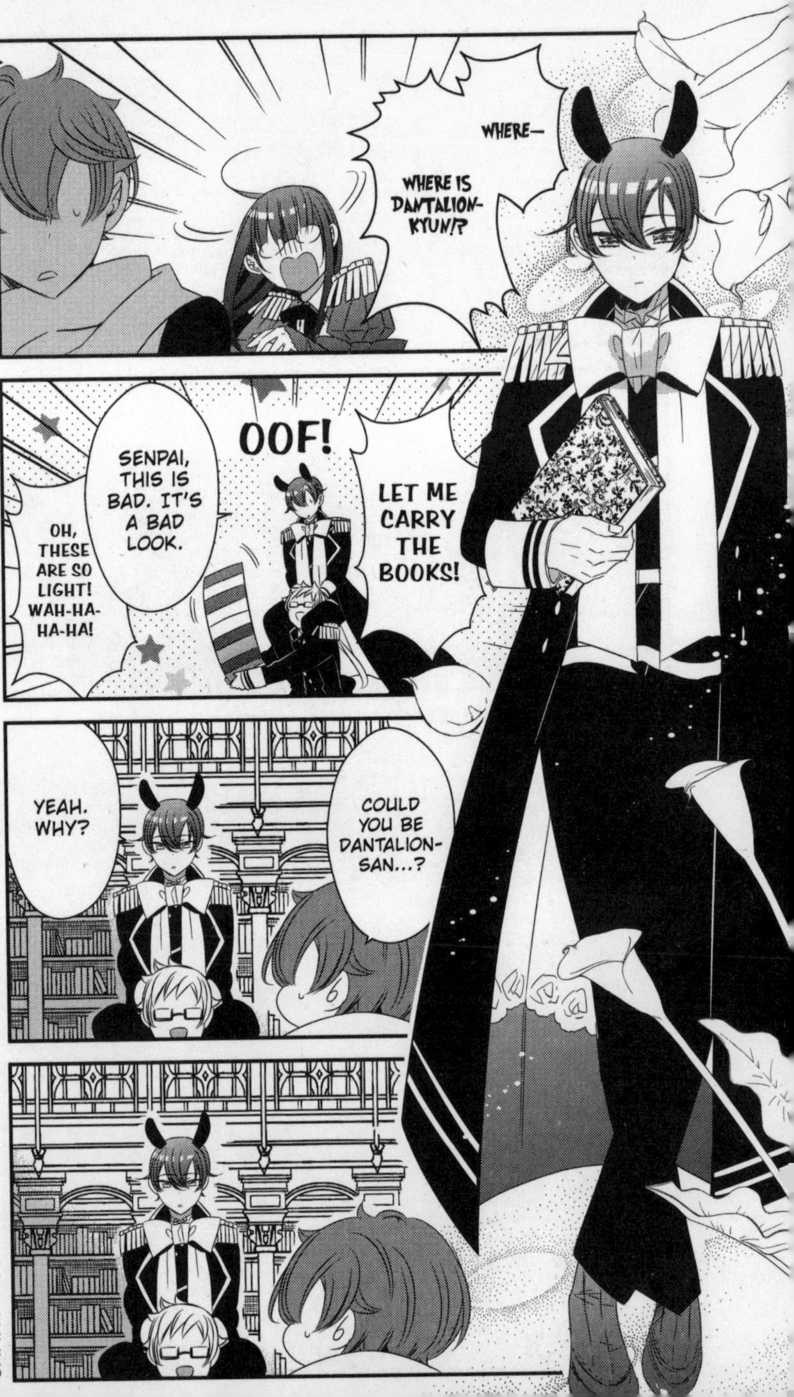
WHERE—
WHERE IS DANTALION-KYUN!?
OOF!
LET ME CARRY THE BOOKS!
SENPAI, THIS IS BAD. IT'S A BAD LOOK.
OH, THESE ARE SO LIGHT! WAH-HA-HA-HA!
COULD YOU BE DANTALION-SAN...?
YEAH. WHY?

YEAH. WHY?

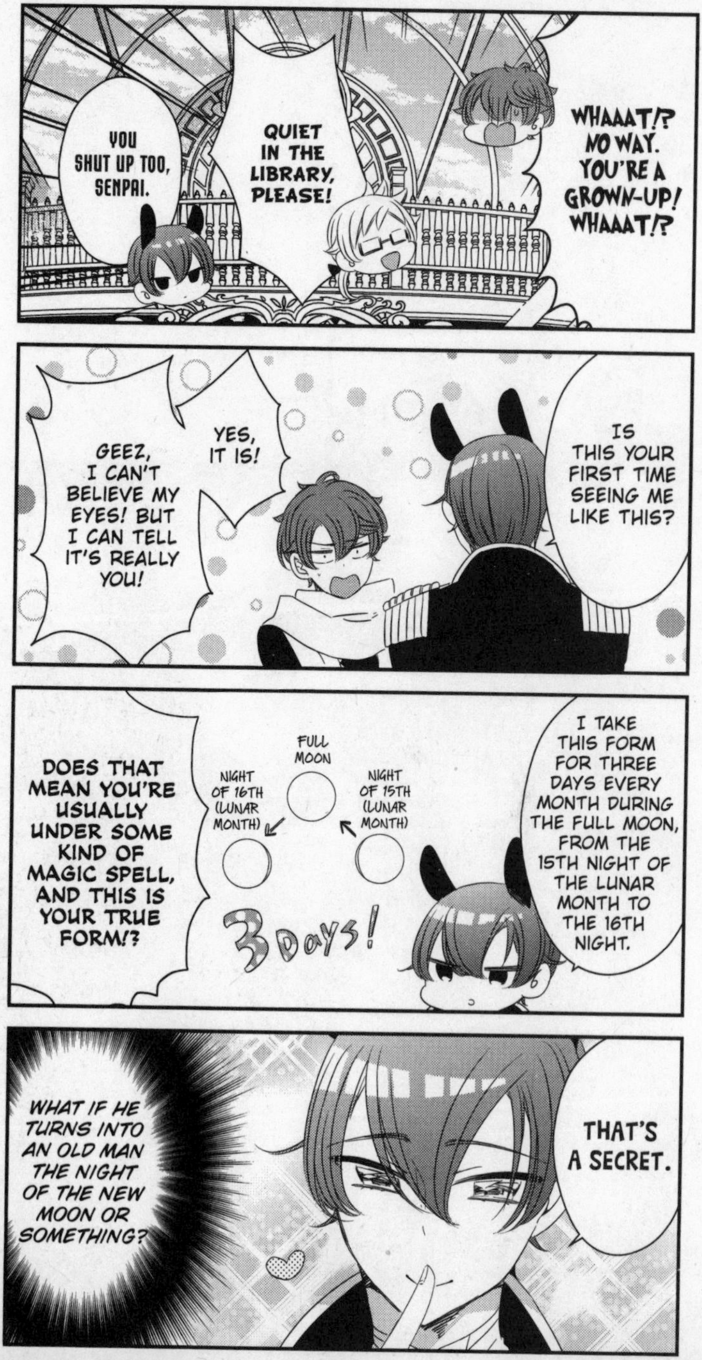
WHAAAT!? NO WAY. YOU'RE A GROWN-UP! WHAAAT!?
QUIET IN THE LIBRARY, PLEASE!
YOU SHUT UP TOO, SENPAI.
IS THIS YOUR FIRST TIME SEEING ME LIKE THIS?
YES, IT IS!
GEEZ, I CAN'T BELIEVE MY EYES! BUT I CAN TELL IT'S REALLY YOU!
I TAKE THIS FORM FOR THREE DAYS EVERY MONTH DURING THE FULL MOON, FROM THE 15TH NIGHT OF THE LUNAR MONTH TO THE 16TH NIGHT.
NIGHT OF 15TH (LUNAR MONTH)
FULL MOON
NIGHT OF 16TH (LUNAR MONTH)
3 DAYS!
DOES THAT MEAN YOU'RE USUALLY UNDER SOME KIND OF MAGIC SPELL, AND THIS IS YOUR TRUE FORM!?
THAT'S A SECRET.
WHAT IF HE TURNS INTO AN OLD MAN THE NIGHT OF THE NEW MOON OR SOMETHING?

OLD MAN SET UP AS A MIDDLE SCHOOLER

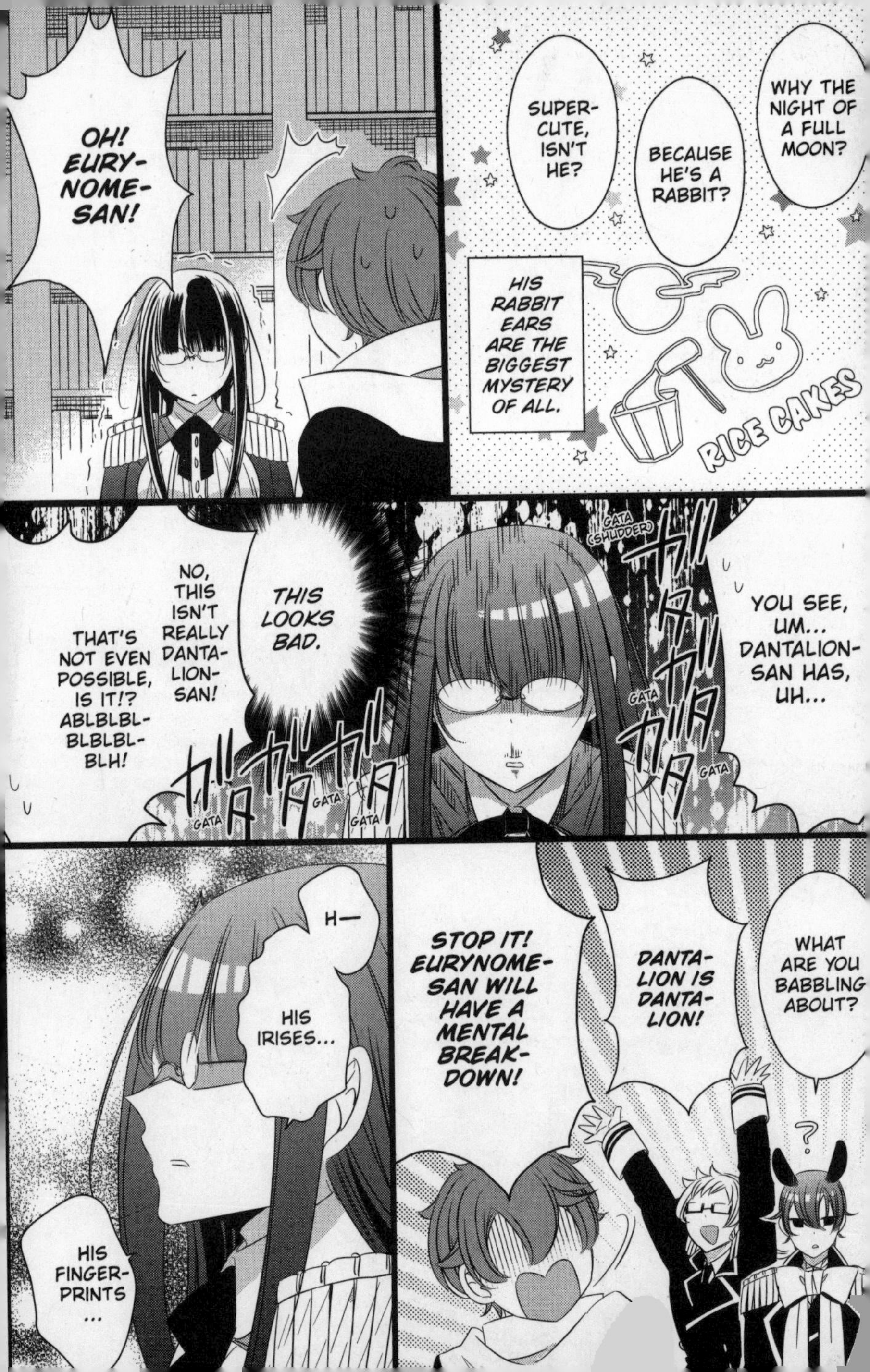
WHY THE NIGHT OF A FULL MOON?
BECAUSE HE'S A RABBIT?
SUPER-CUTE, ISN'T HE?
HIS RABBIT EARS ARE THE BIGGEST MYSTERY OF ALL.
RICE CAKES
OH! EURYNOME-SAN!
YOU SEE, UM... DANTALION-SAN HAS, UH...
GATA (SHUDDER)
GATA
GATA
THIS LOOKS BAD.
NO, THIS ISN'T REALLY DANTALION-SAN!
THAT'S NOT EVEN POSSIBLE, IS IT!? ABLBLBLBLBLBLBLH!
GATA
GATA
GATA
WHAT ARE YOU BABBLING ABOUT?
?
DANTALION IS DANTALION!
STOP IT! EURYNOME-SAN WILL HAVE A MENTAL BREAKDOWN!
H—
HIS IRISES...
HIS FINGERPRINTS...

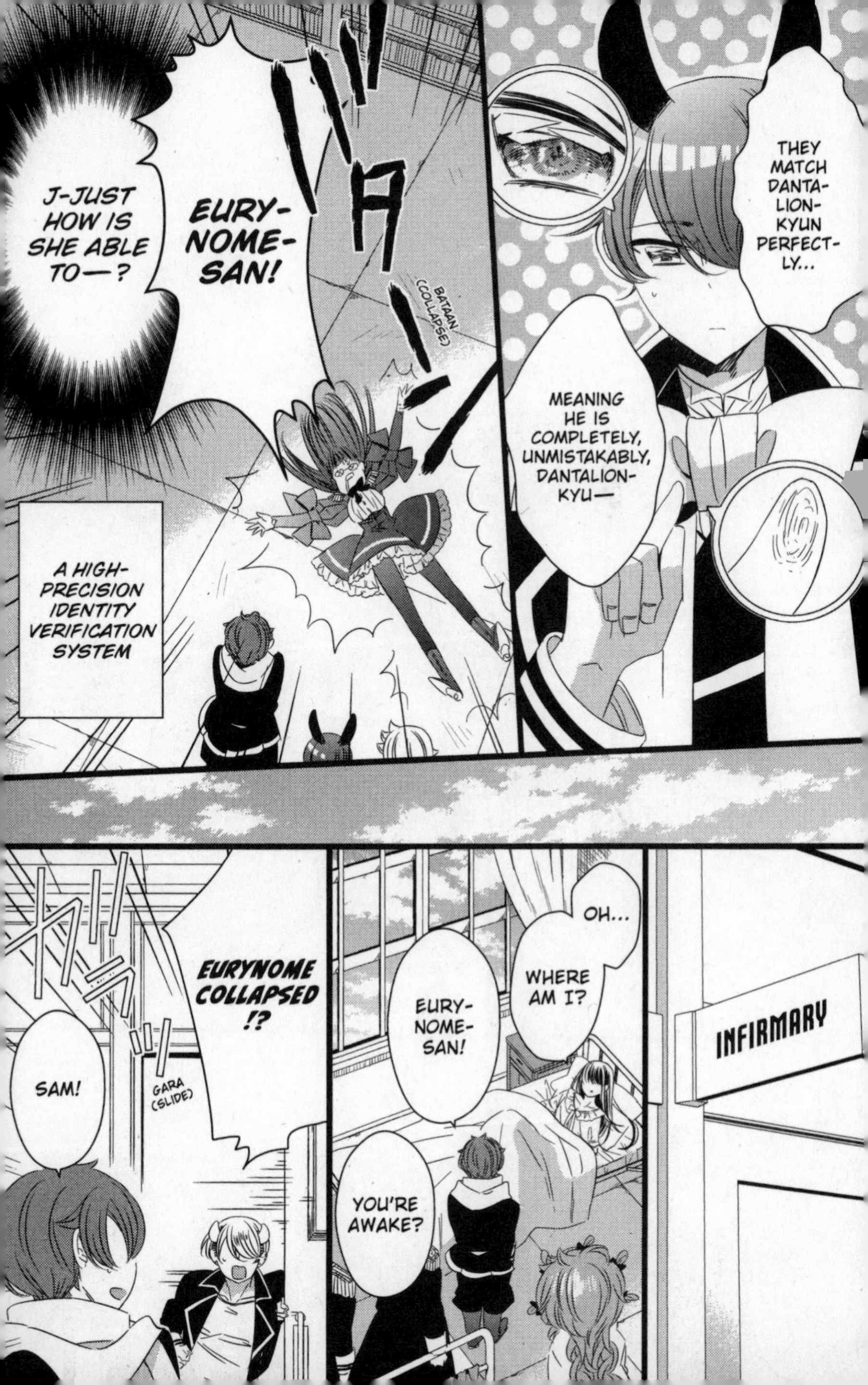
THEY MATCH DANTALION-KYUN PERFECTLY...
MEANING HE IS COMPLETELY, UNMISTAKABLY, DANTALION-KYU—
EURYNOME-SAN!
BATAAN (COLLAPSE)
J-JUST HOW IS SHE ABLE TO—?
A HIGH-PRECISION IDENTITY VERIFICATION SYSTEM
INFIRMARY
OH...
WHERE AM I?
EURYNOME-SAN!
YOU'RE AWAKE?
EURYNOME COLLAPSED!?
GARA (SLIDE)
SAM!

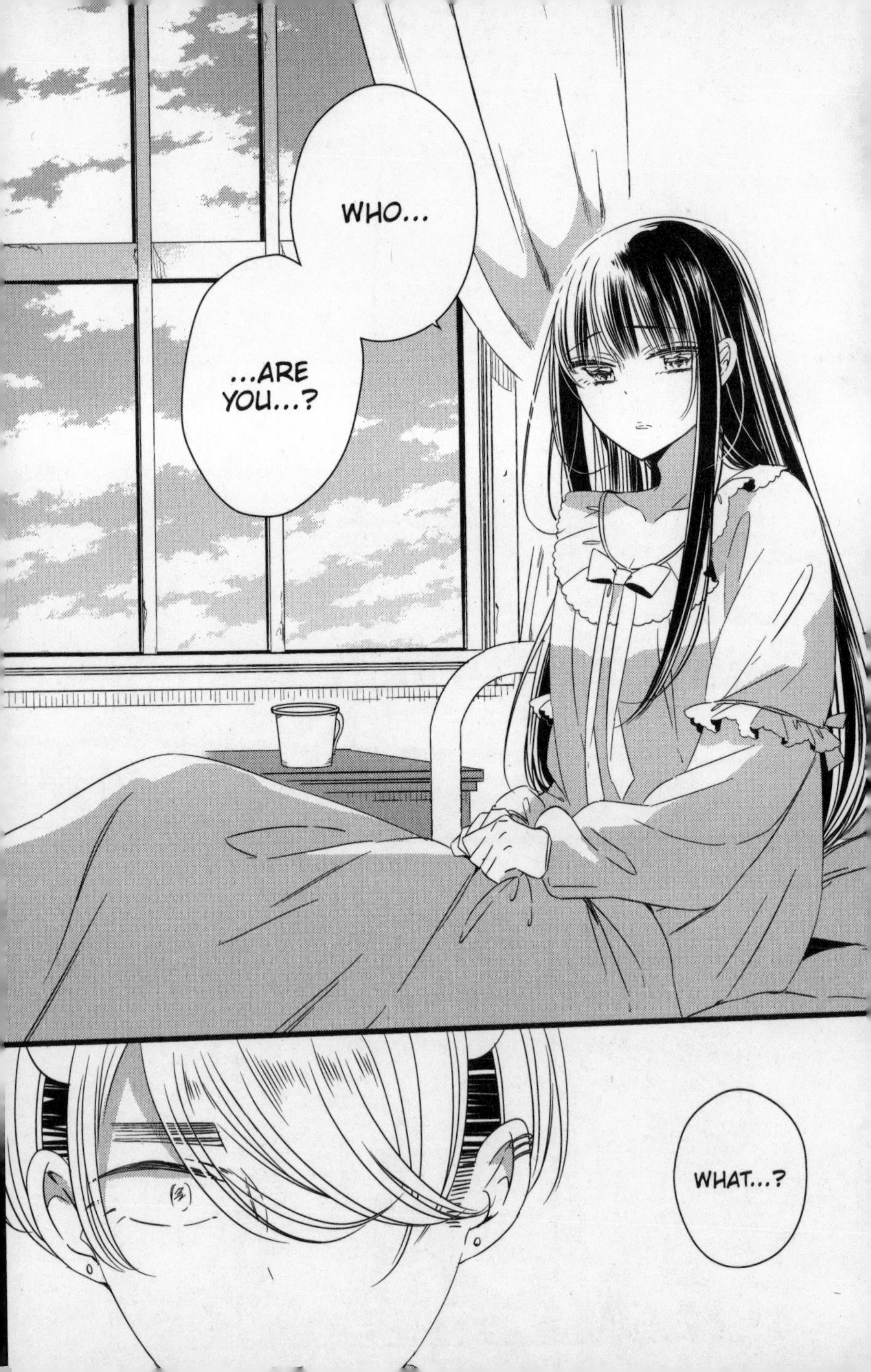
WHO...
...ARE YOU...?
WHAT...?

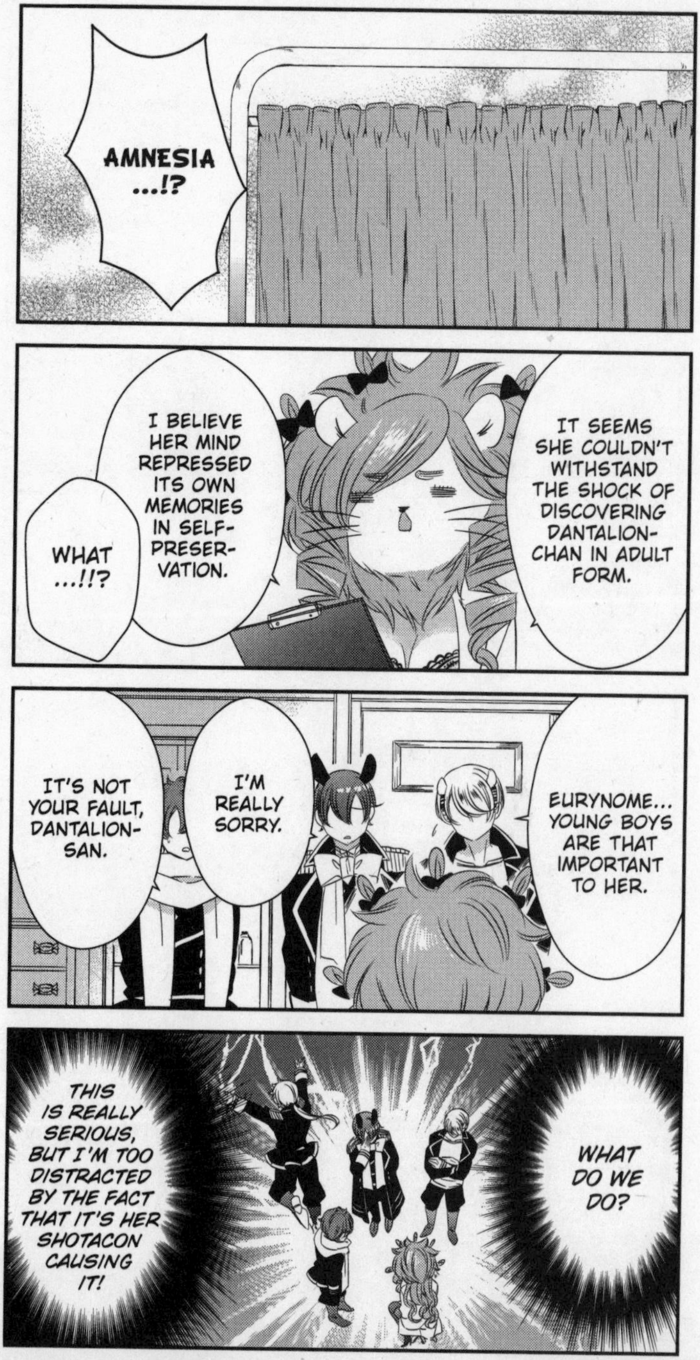
AMNESIA ...!?
IT SEEMS SHE COULDN'T WITHSTAND THE SHOCK OF DISCOVERING DANTALION-CHAN IN ADULT FORM.
I BELIEVE HER MIND REPRESSED ITS OWN MEMORIES IN SELF-PRESERVATION.
WHAT ...!!?
EURYNOME... YOUNG BOYS ARE THAT IMPORTANT TO HER.
I'M REALLY SORRY.
IT'S NOT YOUR FAULT, DANTALION-SAN.
WHAT DO WE DO?
THIS IS REALLY SERIOUS, BUT I'M TOO DISTRACTED BY THE FACT THAT IT'S HER SHOTACON CAUSING IT!

SERIOUSLY

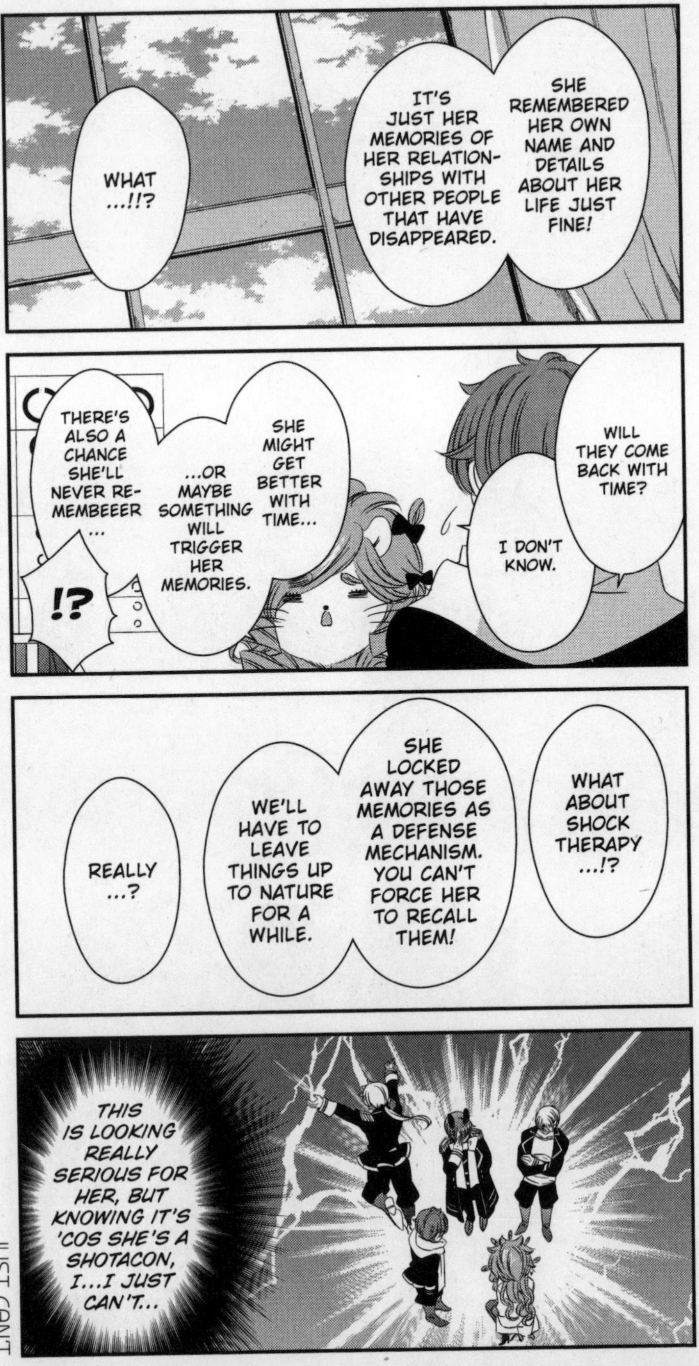
SHE REMEMBERED HER OWN NAME AND DETAILS ABOUT HER LIFE JUST FINE!
IT'S JUST HER MEMORIES OF HER RELATION-SHIPS WITH OTHER PEOPLE THAT HAVE DISAPPEARED.
WHAT ...!!?
WILL THEY COME BACK WITH TIME?
I DON'T KNOW.
SHE MIGHT GET BETTER WITH TIME...
...OR MAYBE SOMETHING WILL TRIGGER HER MEMORIES.
THERE'S ALSO A CHANCE SHE'LL NEVER RE-MEMBEEER...
!?
WHAT ABOUT SHOCK THERAPY ...!?
SHE LOCKED AWAY THOSE MEMORIES AS A DEFENSE MECHANISM. YOU CAN'T FORCE HER TO RECALL THEM!
WE'LL HAVE TO LEAVE THINGS UP TO NATURE FOR A WHILE.
REALLY ...?
THIS IS LOOKING REALLY SERIOUS FOR HER, BUT KNOWING IT'S 'COS SHE'S A SHOTACON, I...I JUST CAN'T...

JUST CAN'T

DON'T GIVE ME THAT LOOK

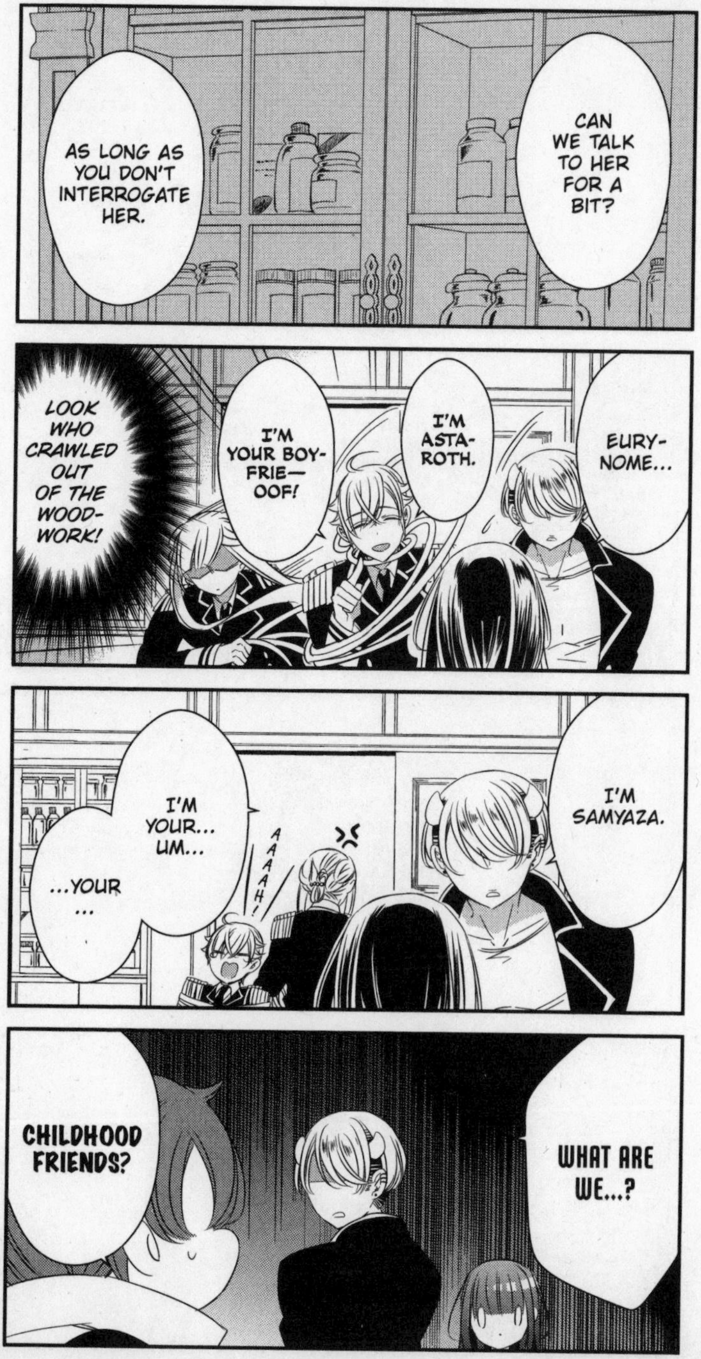
CAN WE TALK TO HER FOR A BIT?
AS LONG AS YOU DON'T INTERROGATE HER.
EURY-NOME...
I'M ASTA-ROTH.
I'M YOUR BOY-FRIE—OOF!
LOOK WHO CRAWLED OUT OF THE WOOD-WORK!
I'M SAMYAZA.
AAAAH!
I'M YOUR... UM...
...YOUR ...
WHAT ARE WE...?
CHILDHOOD FRIENDS?

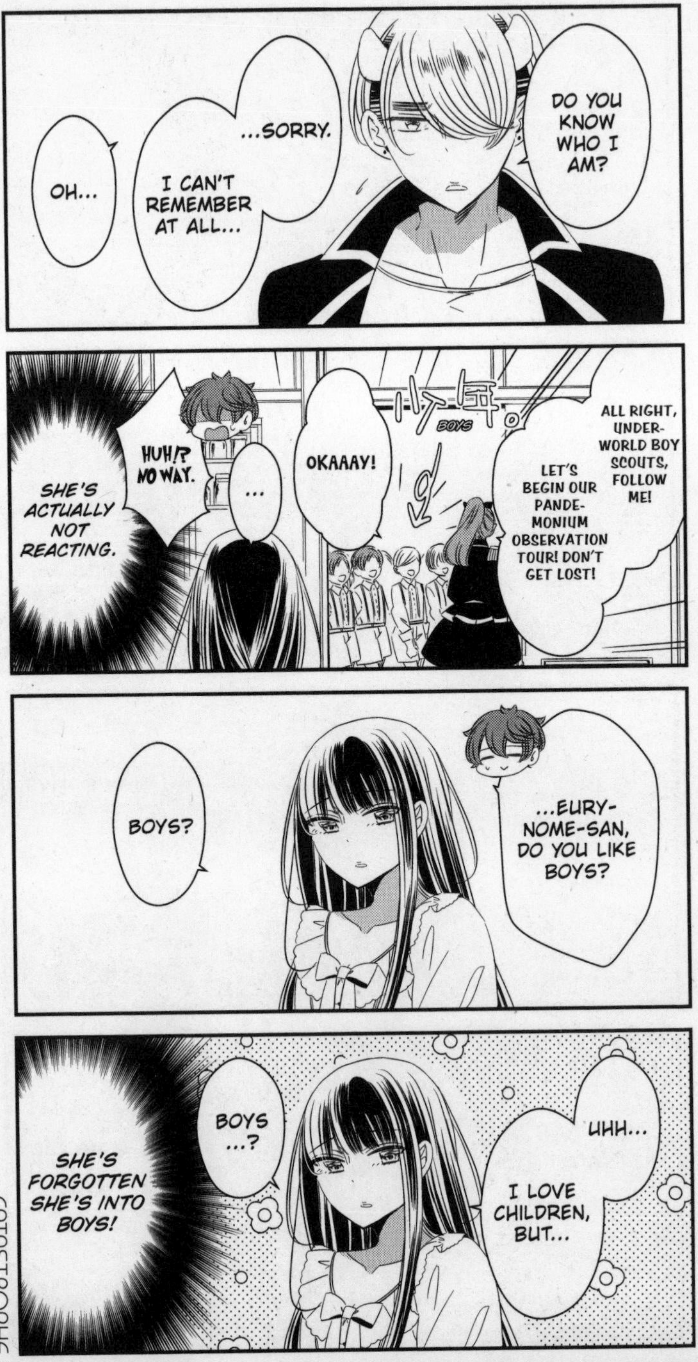
DO YOU KNOW WHO I AM?
...SORRY.
I CAN'T REMEMBER AT ALL...
OH...
ALL RIGHT, UNDER-WORLD BOY SCOUTS, FOLLOW ME!
LET'S BEGIN OUR PANDE-MONIUM OBSERVATION TOUR! DON'T GET LOST!
BOYS
OKAAAY!
...
HUH!? NO WAY.
SHE'S ACTUALLY NOT REACTING.
...EURY-NOME-SAN, DO YOU LIKE BOYS?
BOYS?
UHH...
I LOVE CHILDREN, BUT...
BOYS ...?
SHE'S FORGOTTEN SHE'S INTO BOYS!

CATASTROPHE

LOSS OF IDENTITY

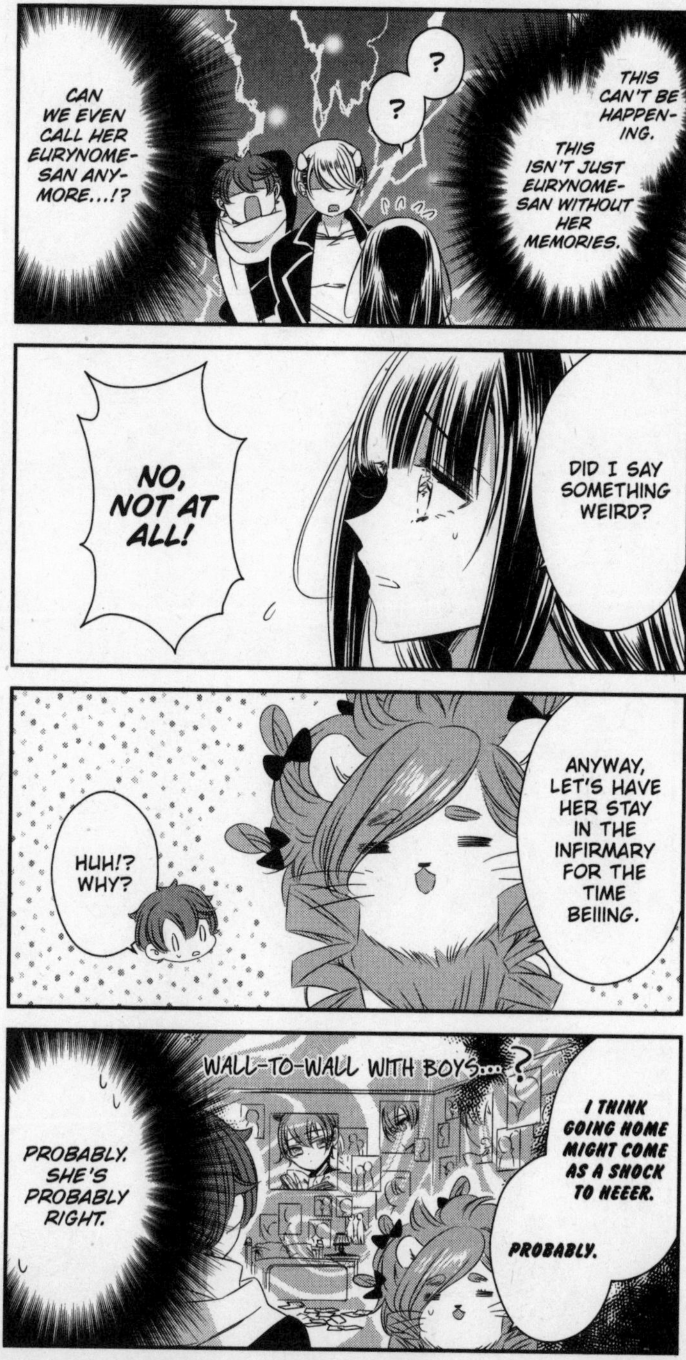
THIS CAN'T BE HAPPEN-ING.
THIS ISN'T JUST EURYNOME-SAN WITHOUT HER MEMORIES.
?
?
CAN WE EVEN CALL HER EURYNOME-SAN ANY-MORE...!?
DID I SAY SOMETHING WEIRD?
NO, NOT AT ALL!
ANYWAY, LET'S HAVE HER STAY IN THE INFIRMARY FOR THE TIME BEIIING.
HUH!? WHY?
WALL-TO-WALL WITH BOYS...?
I THINK GOING HOME MIGHT COME AS A SHOCK TO HEEER.
PROBABLY.
PROBABLY. SHE'S PROBABLY RIGHT.

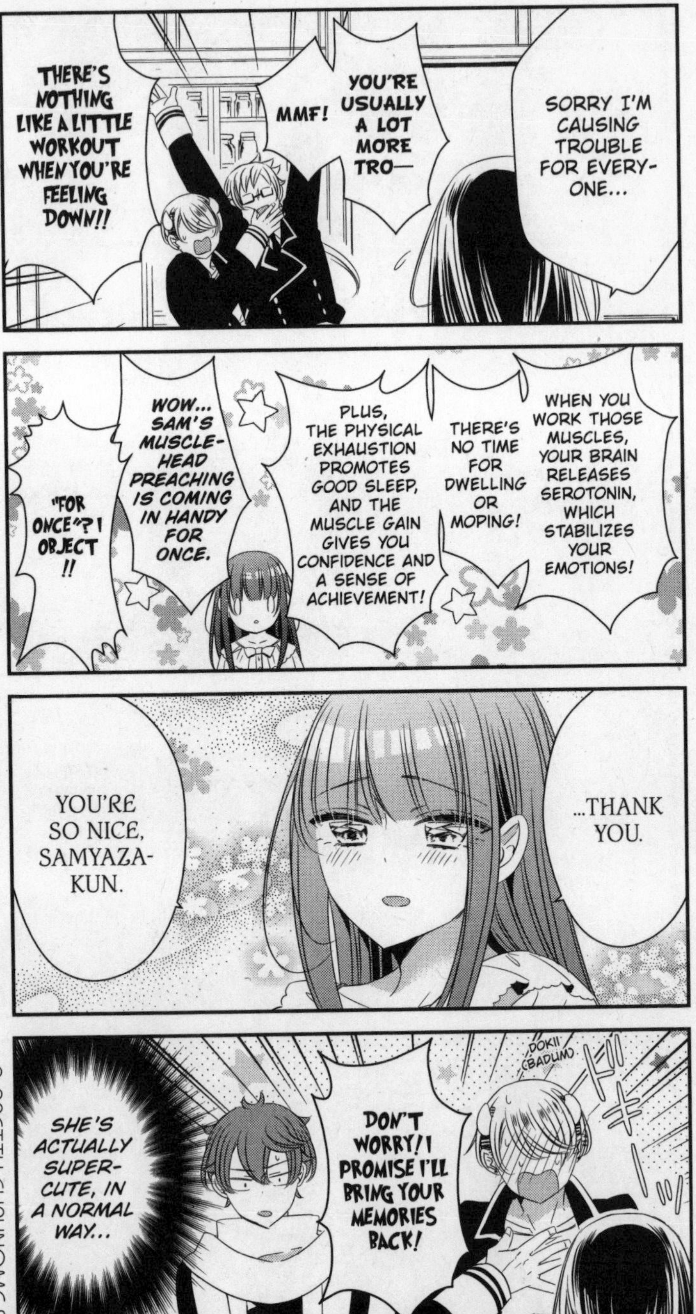
SORRY I'M CAUSING TROUBLE FOR EVERY-ONE...
YOU'RE USUALLY A LOT MORE TRO—
MMF!
THERE'S NOTHING LIKE A LITTLE WORKOUT WHEN YOU'RE FEELING DOWN!!
WHEN YOU WORK THOSE MUSCLES, YOUR BRAIN RELEASES SEROTONIN, WHICH STABILIZES YOUR EMOTIONS!
THERE'S NO TIME FOR DWELLING OR MOPING!
PLUS, THE PHYSICAL EXHAUSTION PROMOTES GOOD SLEEP, AND THE MUSCLE GAIN GIVES YOU CONFIDENCE AND A SENSE OF ACHIEVEMENT!
WOW... SAM'S MUSCLE-HEAD PREACHING IS COMING IN HANDY FOR ONCE.
"FOR ONCE"?! OBJECT!!
...THANK YOU.
YOU'RE SO NICE, SAMYAZA-KUN.
DOKI (BADUM)
DON'T WORRY! I PROMISE I'LL BRING YOUR MEMORIES BACK!
SHE'S ACTUALLY SUPER-CUTE, IN A NORMAL WAY...

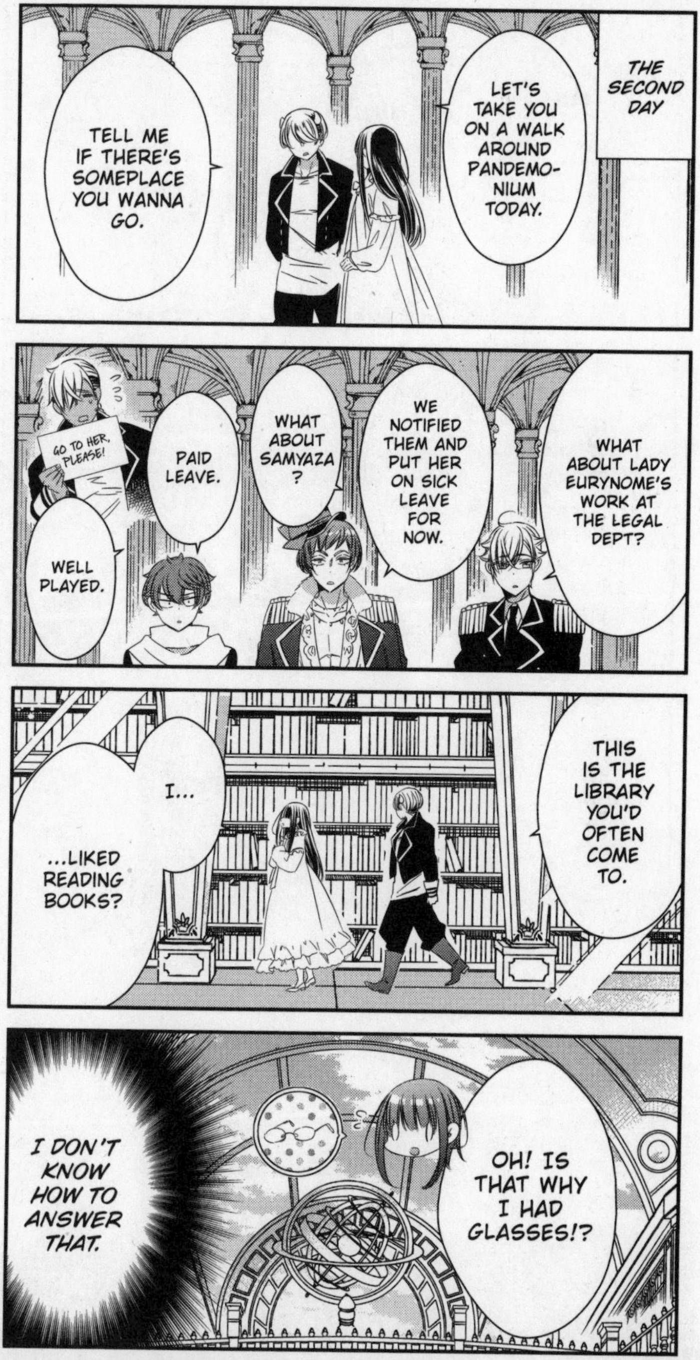
THE SECOND DAY
LET'S TAKE YOU ON A WALK AROUND PANDEMO-NIUM TODAY.
TELL ME IF THERE'S SOMEPLACE YOU WANNA GO.
WHAT ABOUT LADY EURYNOME'S WORK AT THE LEGAL DEPT?
WE NOTIFIED THEM AND PUT HER ON SICK LEAVE FOR NOW.
WHAT ABOUT SAMYAZA?
PAID LEAVE.
GO TO HER, PLEASE!
WELL PLAYED.
THIS IS THE LIBRARY YOU'D OFTEN COME TO.
I...
...LIKED READING BOOKS?
OH! IS THAT WHY I HAD GLASSES!?
I DON'T KNOW HOW TO ANSWER THAT.

TO PEEP

THEY'VE GOT A NICE MOOD GOING

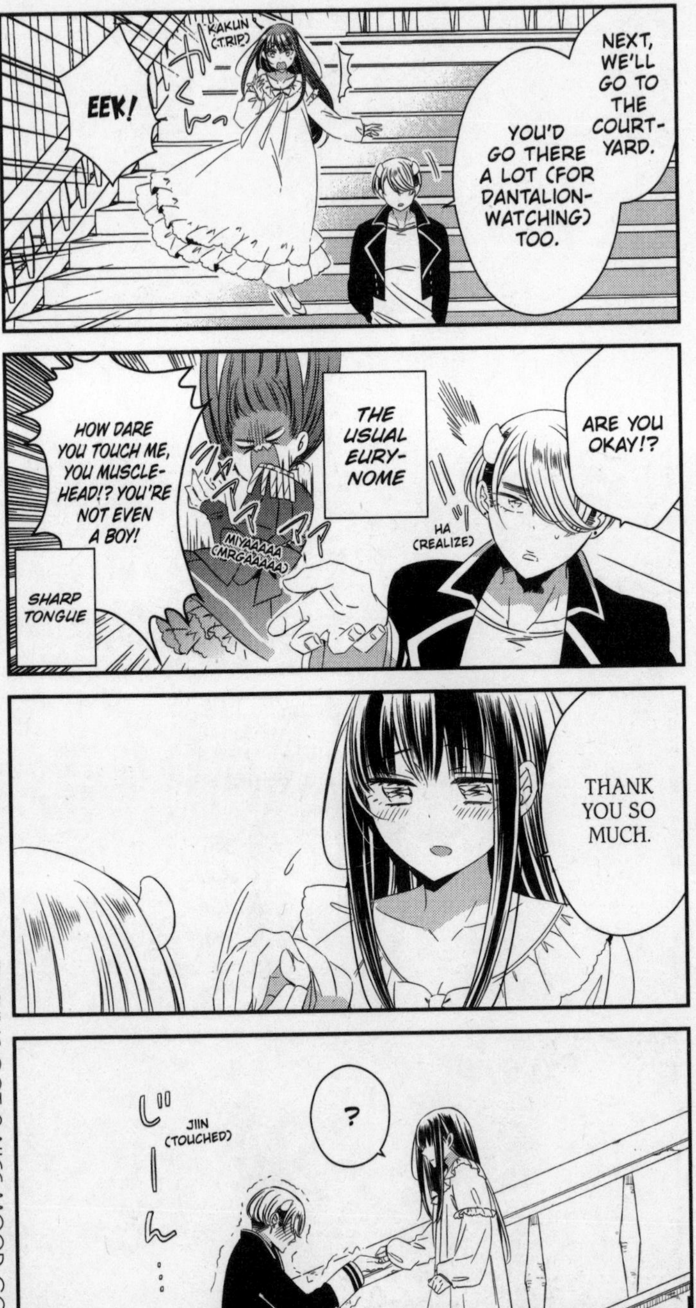
NEXT, WE'LL GO TO THE COURTYARD.
YOU'D GO THERE A LOT (FOR DANTALION-WATCHING) TOO.
KAKUN (TRIP)
EEK!
ARE YOU OKAY!?
HA (REALIZE)
THE USUAL EURYNOME
HOW DARE YOU TOUCH ME, YOU MUSCLE-HEAD!? YOU'RE NOT EVEN A BOY!
MIYAAAAA (MRGAAAAA)
SHARP TONGUE
THANK YOU SO MUCH.
?
JIIN (TOUCHED)

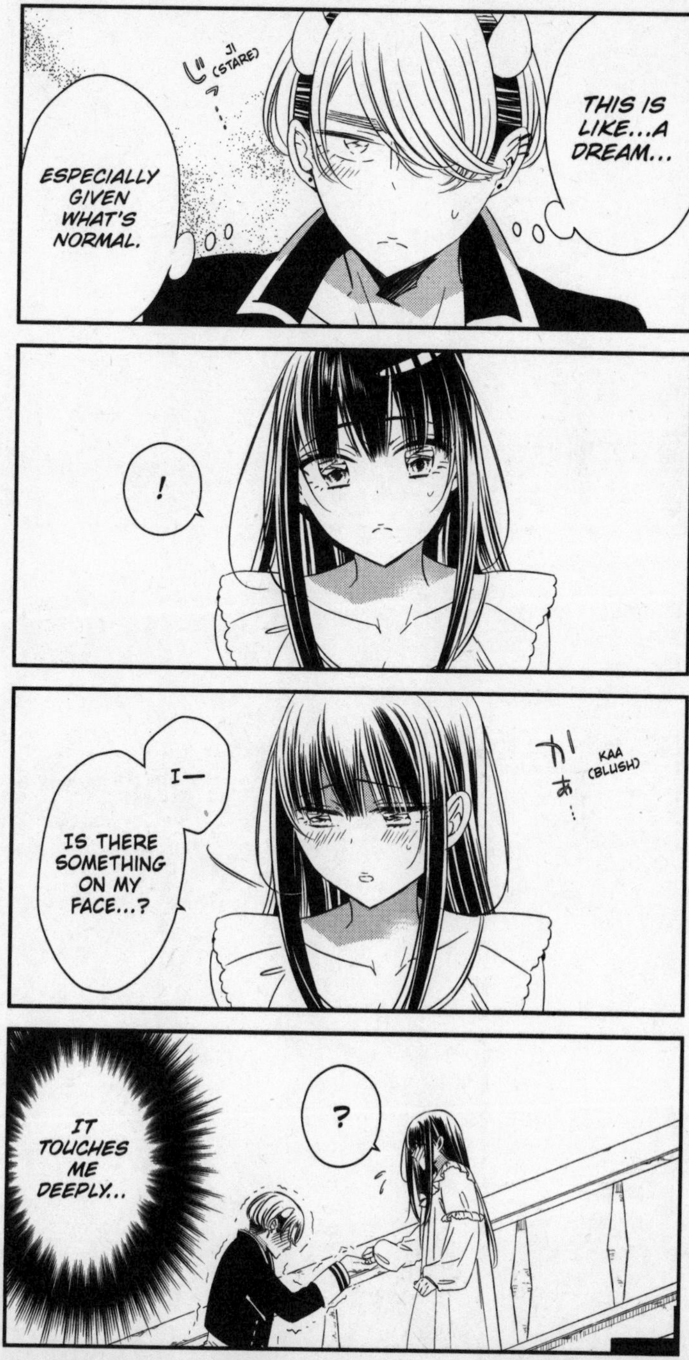
THIS IS LIKE...A DREAM...
JI (STARE)
ESPECIALLY GIVEN WHAT'S NORMAL.
!
KAA (BLUSH)
I—
IS THERE SOMETHING ON MY FACE...?
?
IT TOUCHES ME DEEPLY...

IN MY HEART

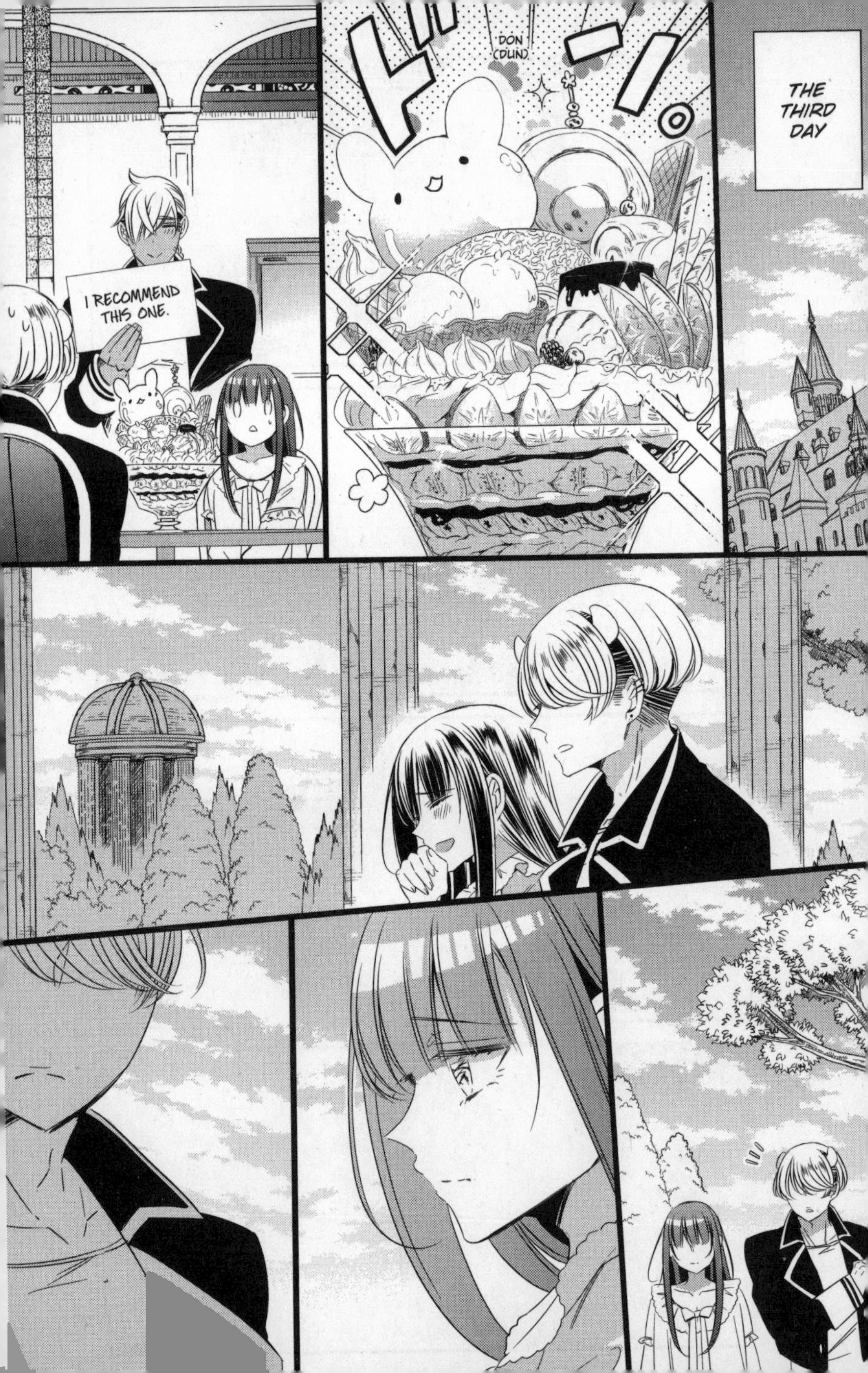
THE THIRD DAY
DON (DUN)
I RECOMMEND THIS ONE.

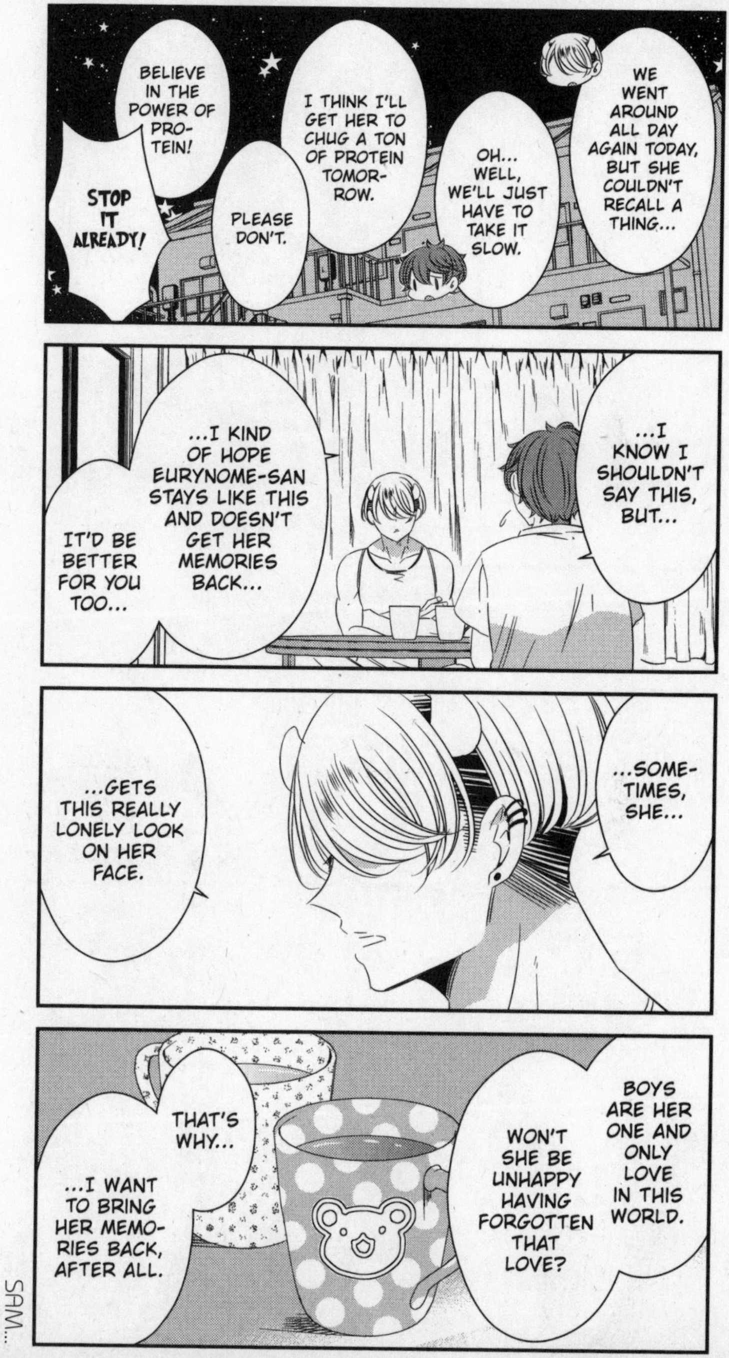
WE WENT AROUND ALL DAY AGAIN TODAY, BUT SHE COULDN'T RECALL A THING...
OH... WELL, WE'LL JUST HAVE TO TAKE IT SLOW.
I THINK I'LL GET HER TO CHUG A TON OF PROTEIN TOMOR-ROW.
PLEASE DON'T.
BELIEVE IN THE POWER OF PRO-TEIN!
STOP IT ALREADY!
...I KNOW I SHOULDN'T SAY THIS, BUT...
...I KIND OF HOPE EURYNOME-SAN STAYS LIKE THIS AND DOESN'T GET HER MEMORIES BACK...
IT'D BE BETTER FOR YOU TOO...
...SOME-TIMES, SHE...
...GETS THIS REALLY LONELY LOOK ON HER FACE.
BOYS ARE HER ONE AND ONLY LOVE IN THIS WORLD.
WON'T SHE BE UNHAPPY HAVING FORGOTTEN THAT LOVE?
THAT'S WHY...
...I WANT TO BRING HER MEMO-RIES BACK, AFTER ALL.
SAM...

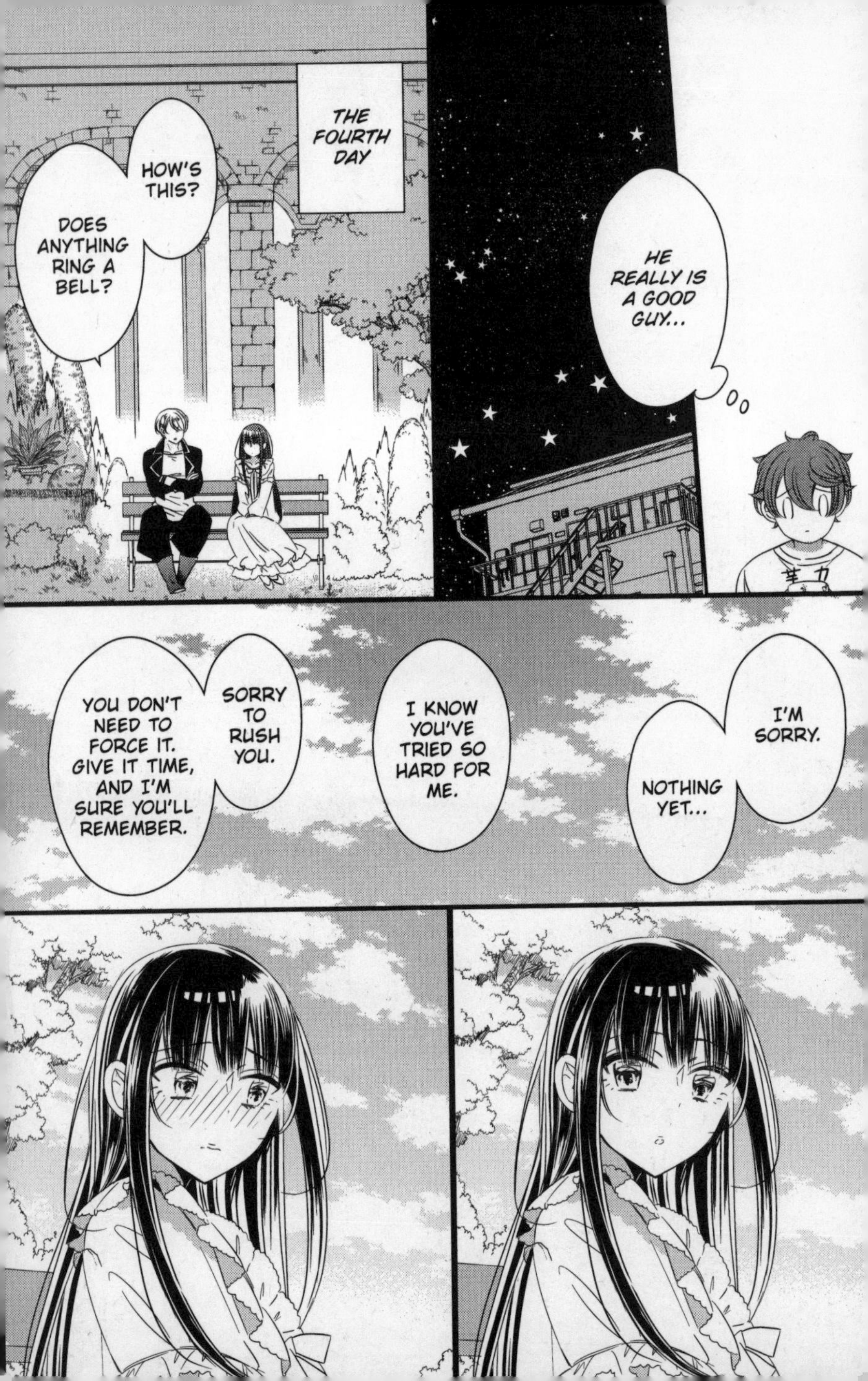
HE REALLY IS A GOOD GUY...
THE FOURTH DAY
HOW'S THIS?
DOES ANYTHING RING A BELL?
I'M SORRY.
NOTHING YET...
I KNOW YOU'VE TRIED SO HARD FOR ME.
SORRY TO RUSH YOU.
YOU DON'T NEED TO FORCE IT. GIVE IT TIME, AND I'M SURE YOU'LL REMEMBER.

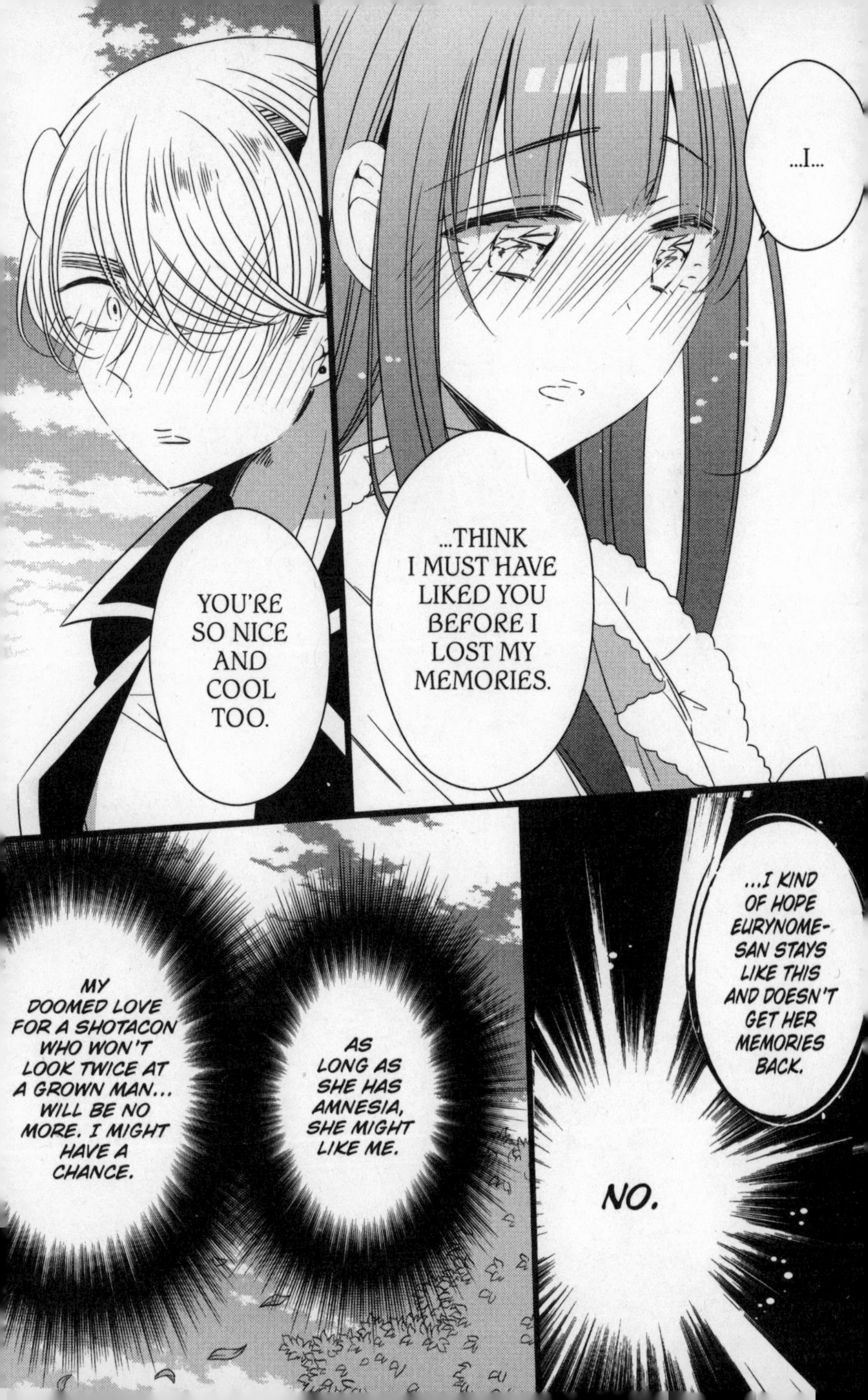
...I...
...THINK I MUST HAVE LIKED YOU BEFORE I LOST MY MEMORIES.
YOU'RE SO NICE AND COOL TOO.
...I KIND OF HOPE EURYNOME-SAN STAYS LIKE THIS AND DOESN'T GET HER MEMORIES BACK.
NO.
AS LONG AS SHE HAS AMNESIA, SHE MIGHT LIKE ME.
MY DOOMED LOVE FOR A SHOTACON WHO WON'T LOOK TWICE AT A GROWN MAN... WILL BE NO MORE. I MIGHT HAVE A CHANCE.

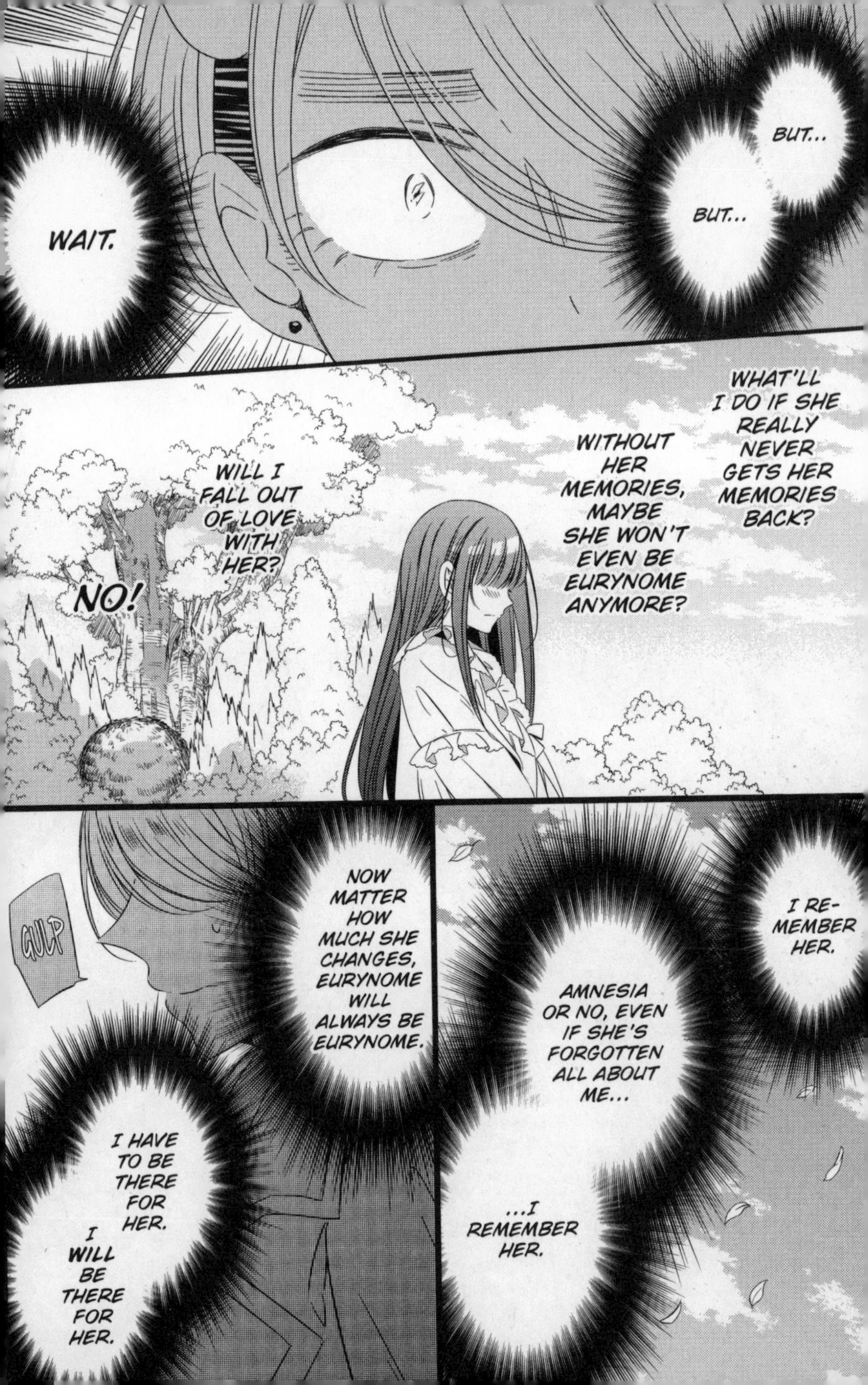
BUT...
BUT...
WAIT.
WHAT'LL I DO IF SHE REALLY NEVER GETS HER MEMORIES BACK?
WITHOUT HER MEMORIES, MAYBE SHE WON'T EVEN BE EURYNOME ANYMORE?
WILL I FALL OUT OF LOVE WITH HER?
NO!
I RE-MEMBER HER.
AMNESIA OR NO, EVEN IF SHE'S FORGOTTEN ALL ABOUT ME...
...I REMEMBER HER.
NOW MATTER HOW MUCH SHE CHANGES, EURYNOME WILL ALWAYS BE EURYNOME.
GULP
I HAVE TO BE THERE FOR HER.
I WILL BE THERE FOR HER.

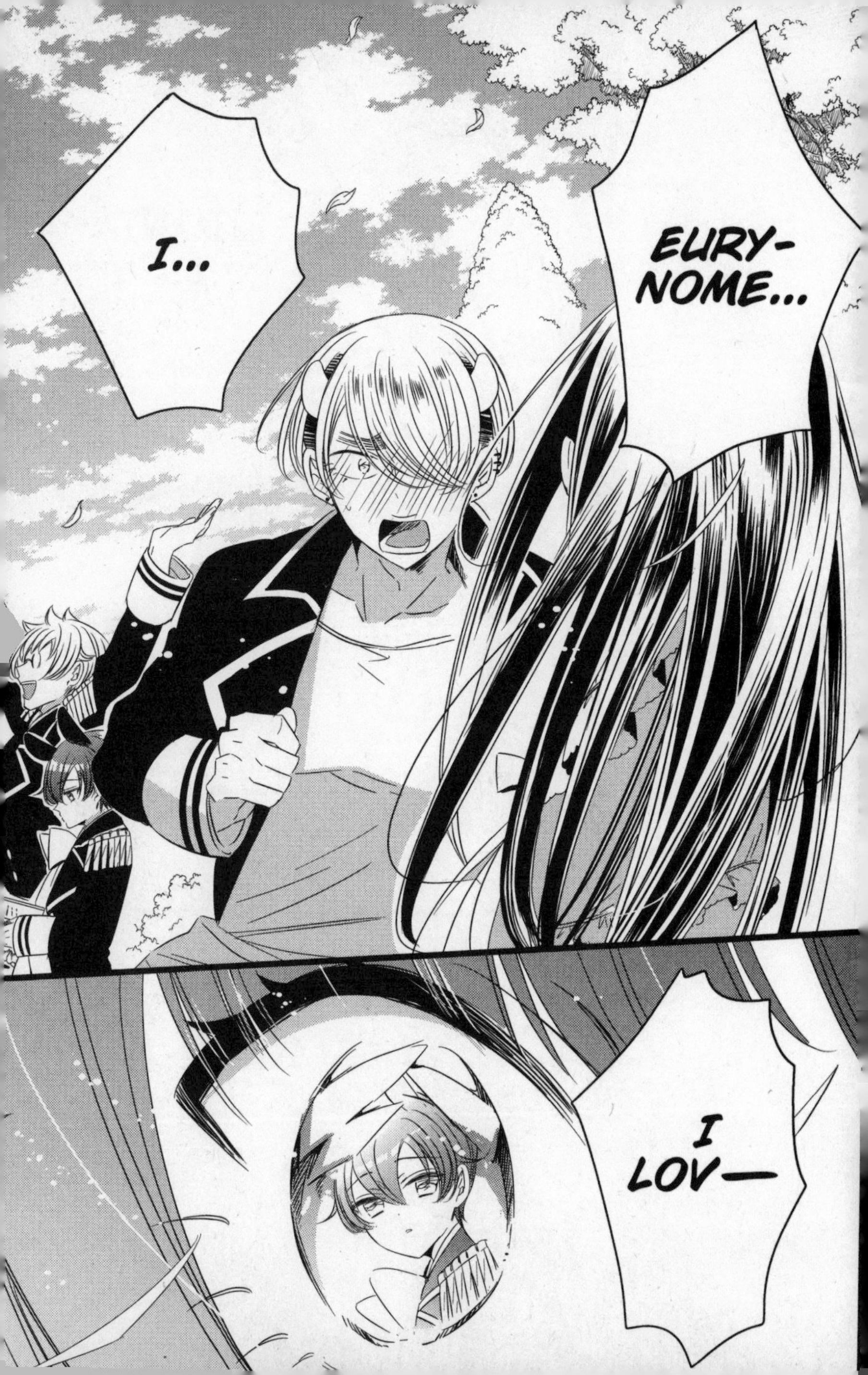
EURY-NOME...
I...
I LOV—

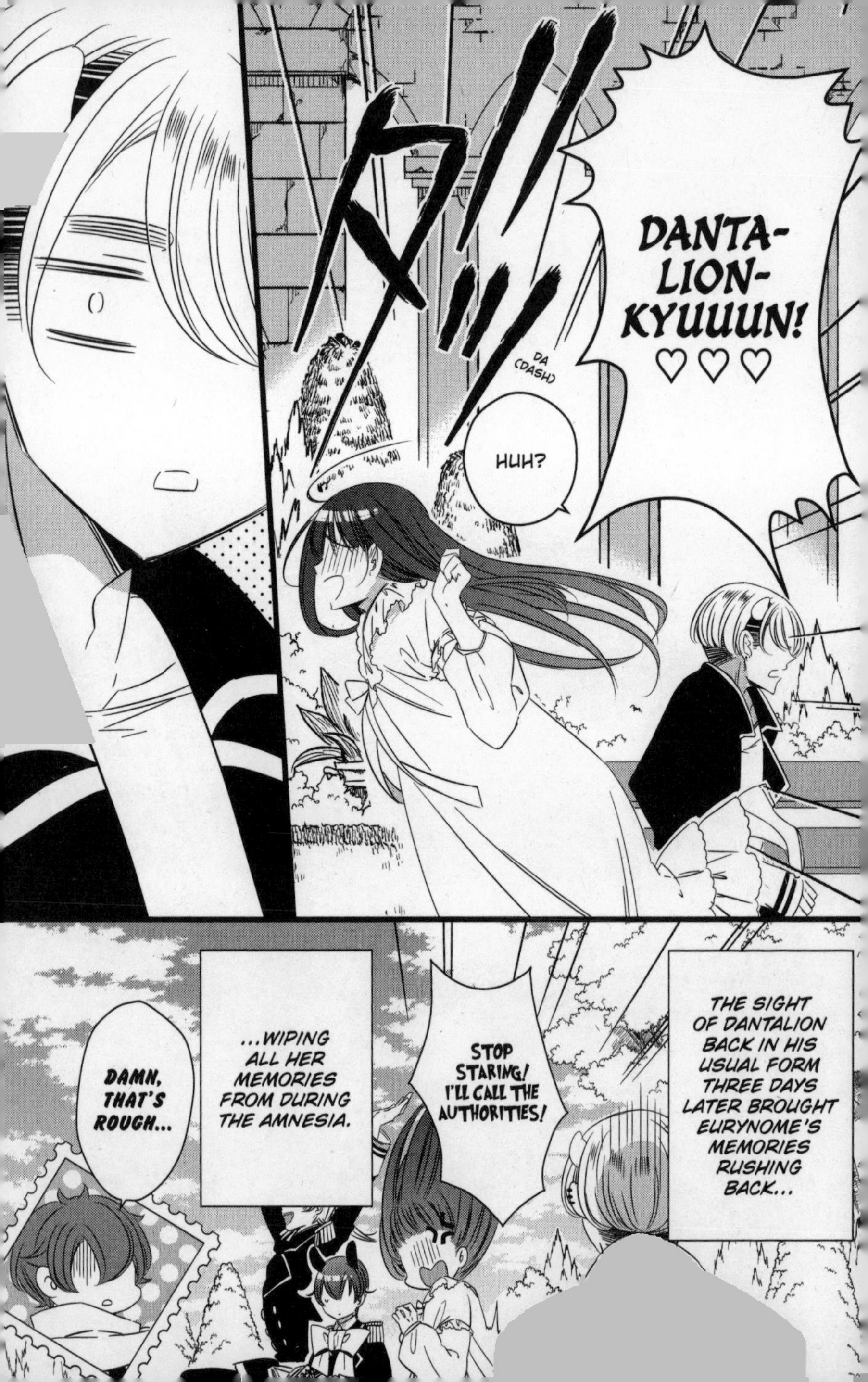
DANTA-LION-KYUUUN! ♡♡♡
DA (DASH)
HUH?
THE SIGHT OF DANTALION BACK IN HIS USUAL FORM THREE DAYS LATER BROUGHT EURYNOME'S MEMORIES RUSHING BACK...
STOP STARING! I'LL CALL THE AUTHORITIES!
...WIPING ALL HER MEMORIES FROM DURING THE AMNESIA.
DAMN, THAT'S ROUGH...

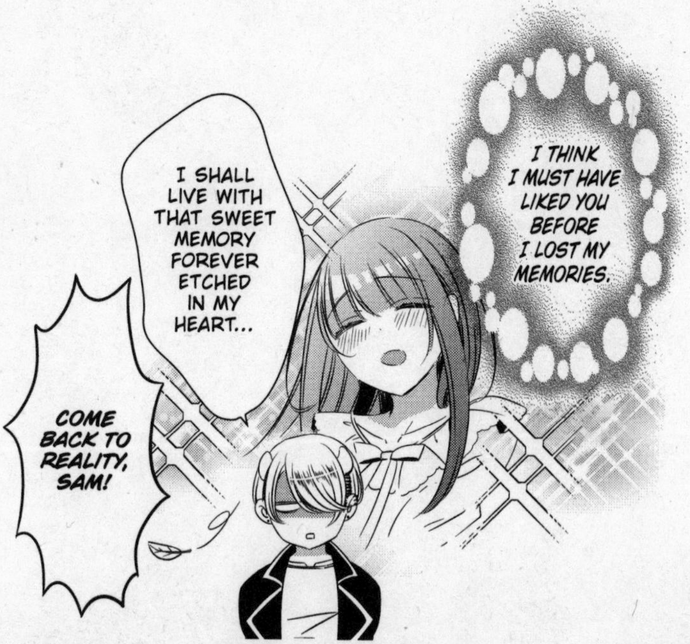
I THINK I MUST HAVE LIKED YOU BEFORE I LOST MY MEMORIES.
I SHALL LIVE WITH THAT SWEET MEMORY FOREVER ETCHED IN MY HEART...
COME BACK TO REALITY, SAM!

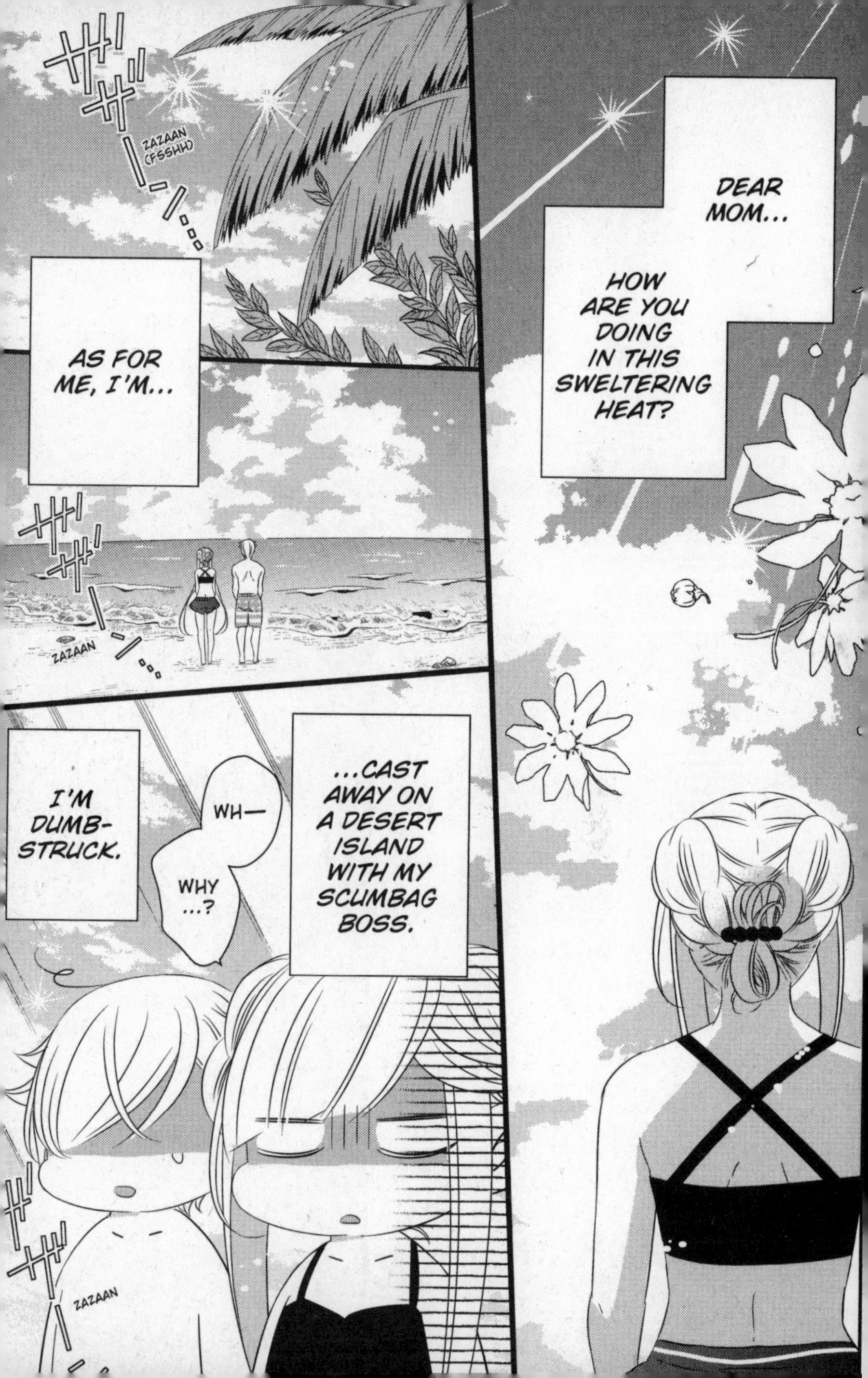
DEAR MOM...
HOW ARE YOU DOING IN THIS SWELTERING HEAT?
ZAZAAN (FSSHH)
AS FOR ME, I'M...
ZAZAAN
...CAST AWAY ON A DESERT ISLAND WITH MY SCUMBAG BOSS.
WH—
WHY ...?
I'M DUMB-STRUCK.
ZAZAAN

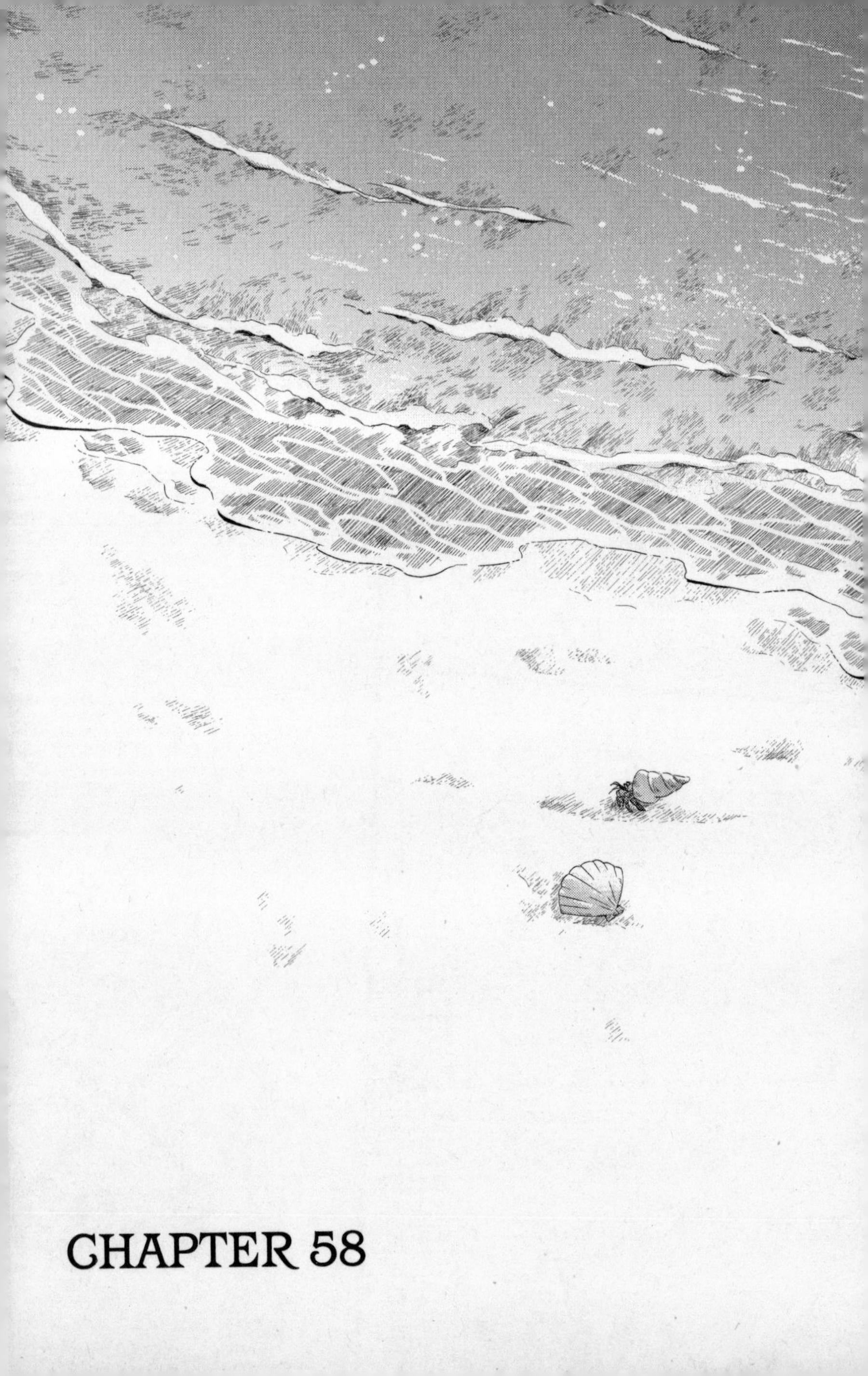

CHAPTER 58

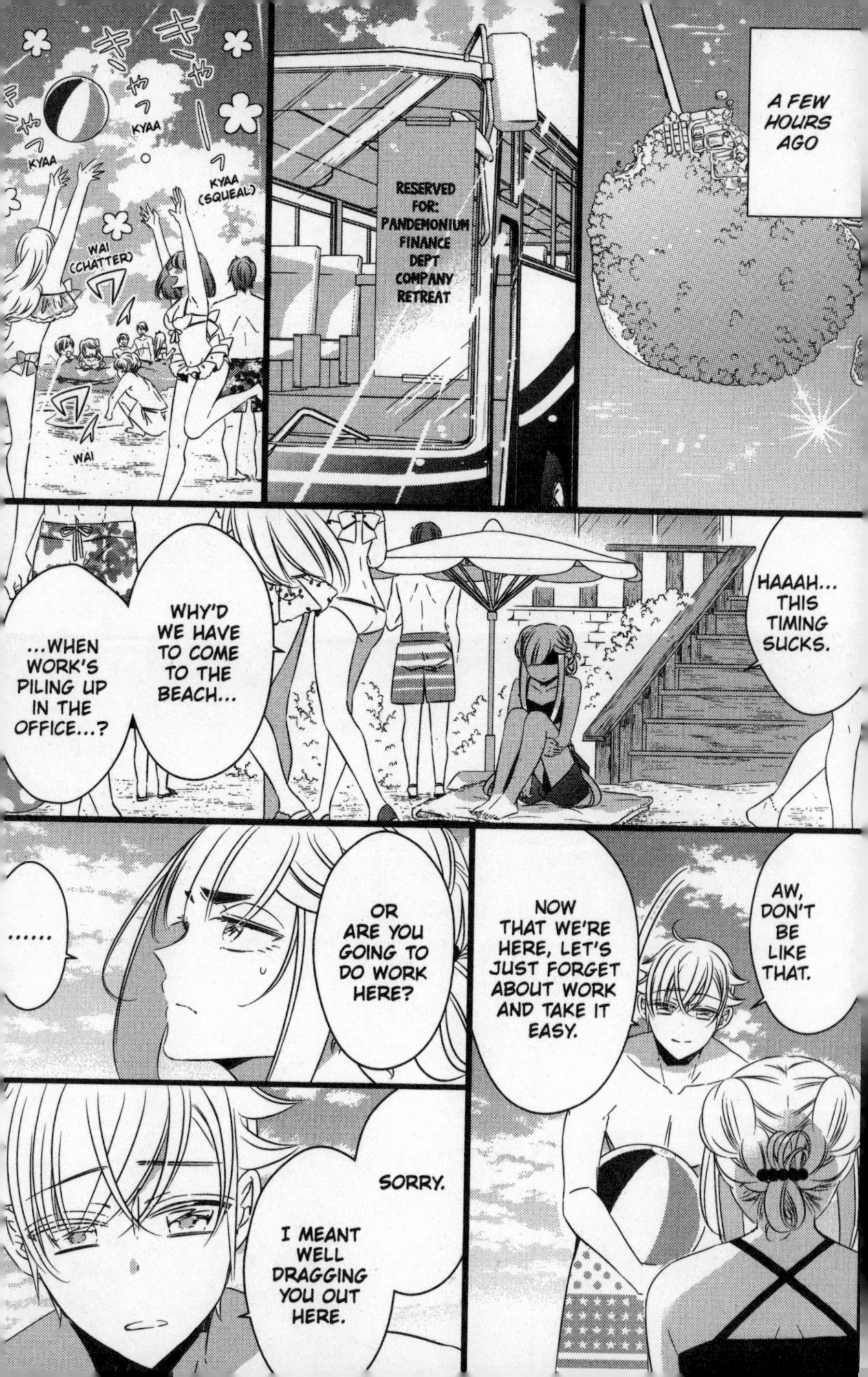
A FEW HOURS AGO
RESERVED FOR: PANDEMONIUM FINANCE DEPT COMPANY RETREAT
KYAA (SQUEAL)
KYAA
KYAA
WAI (CHATTER)
WAI
HAAAH... THIS TIMING SUCKS.
WHY'D WE HAVE TO COME TO THE BEACH...
...WHEN WORK'S PILING UP IN THE OFFICE...?
AW, DON'T BE LIKE THAT.
NOW THAT WE'RE HERE, LET'S JUST FORGET ABOUT WORK AND TAKE IT EASY.
OR ARE YOU GOING TO DO WORK HERE?
......
SORRY.
I MEANT WELL DRAGGING YOU OUT HERE.

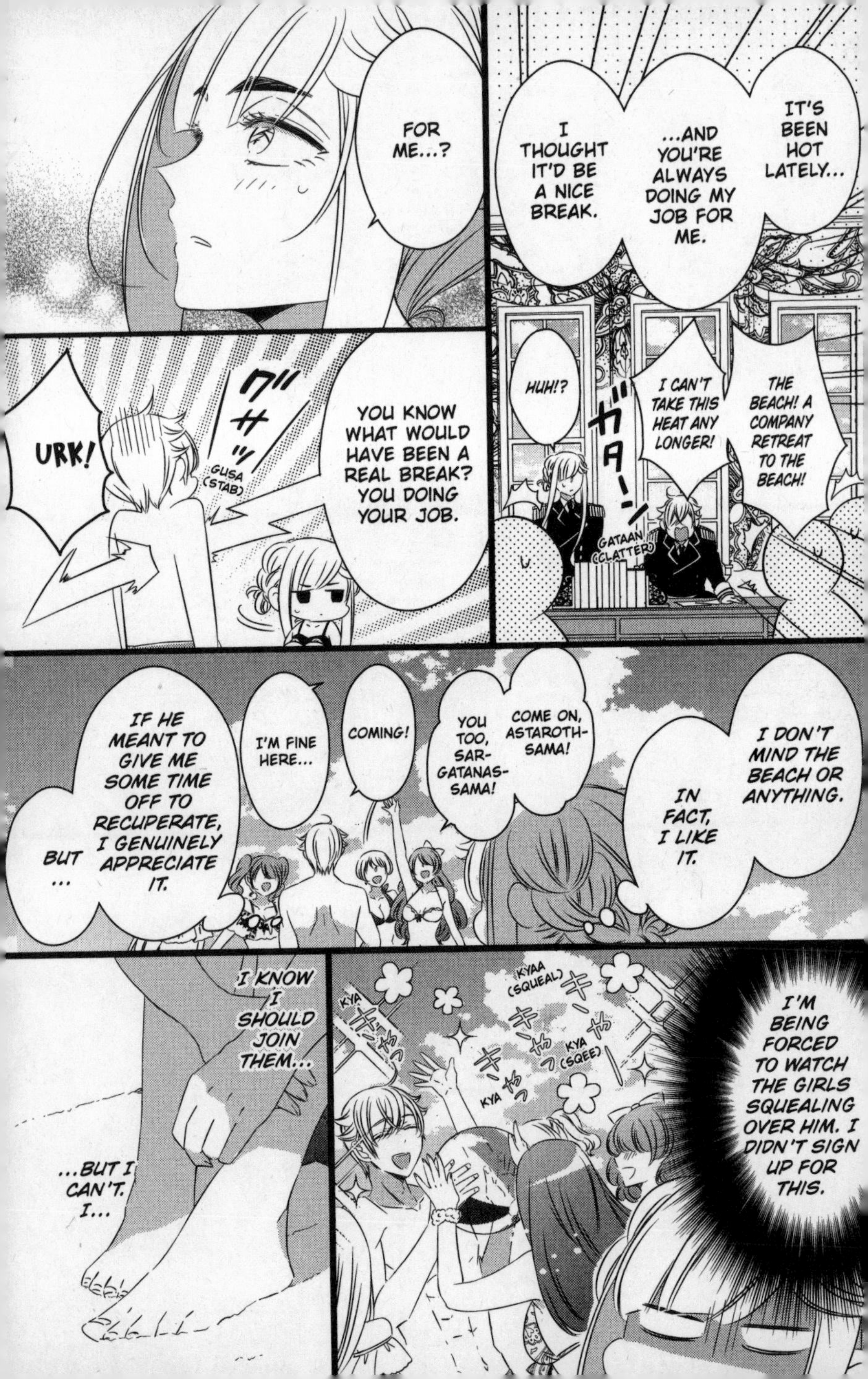
IT'S BEEN HOT LATELY...
...AND YOU'RE ALWAYS DOING MY JOB FOR ME.
I THOUGHT IT'D BE A NICE BREAK.
THE BEACH! A COMPANY RETREAT TO THE BEACH!
I CAN'T TAKE THIS HEAT ANY LONGER!
GATAAN (CLATTER)
HUH!?
FOR ME...?
YOU KNOW WHAT WOULD HAVE BEEN A REAL BREAK? YOU DOING YOUR JOB.
GUSA (STAB)
URK!
I DON'T MIND THE BEACH OR ANYTHING.
IN FACT, I LIKE IT.
COME ON, ASTAROTH-SAMA!
YOU TOO, SAR-GATANAS-SAMA!
COMING!
I'M FINE HERE...
IF HE MEANT TO GIVE ME SOME TIME OFF TO RECUPERATE, I GENUINELY APPRECIATE IT.
BUT ...
I'M BEING FORCED TO WATCH THE GIRLS SQUEALING OVER HIM. I DIDN'T SIGN UP FOR THIS.
KYAA (SQUEAL)
KYA (SQEE)
KYA
KYA
I KNOW I SHOULD JOIN THEM...
...BUT I CAN'T. I...

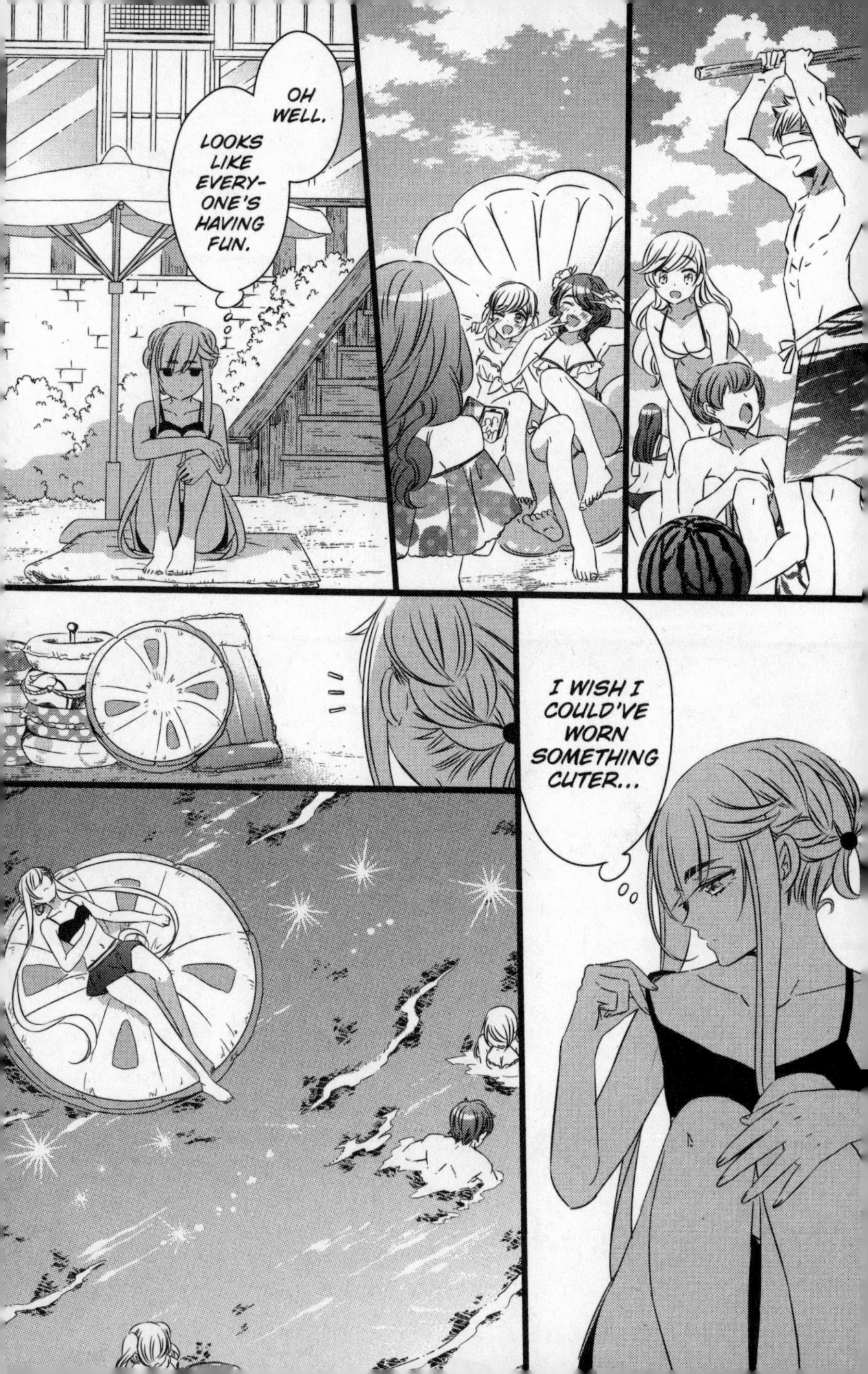
OH WELL.
LOOKS LIKE EVERYONE'S HAVING FUN.
I WISH I COULD'VE WORN SOMETHING CUTER...

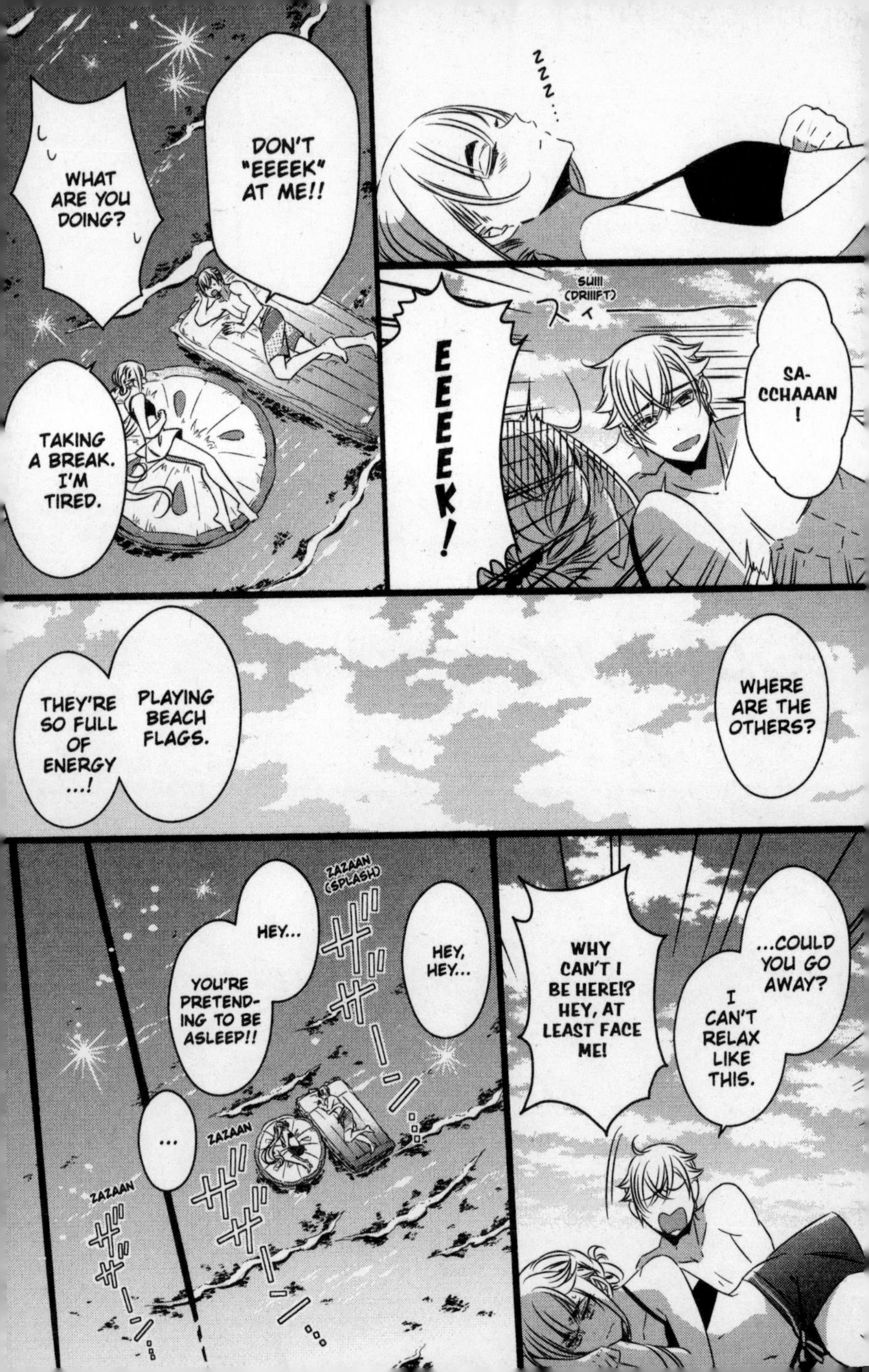

ZZZ...
SA-CCHAAAN!
SUIII (DRIIIFT)
EEEEK!
DON'T "EEEEK" AT ME!!
WHAT ARE YOU DOING?
TAKING A BREAK. I'M TIRED.
WHERE ARE THE OTHERS?
PLAYING BEACH FLAGS.
THEY'RE SO FULL OF ENERGY...!
...COULD YOU GO AWAY?
I CAN'T RELAX LIKE THIS.
WHY CAN'T I BE HERE!? HEY, AT LEAST FACE ME!
HEY, HEY...
ZAZAAN (SPLASH)
HEY...
YOU'RE PRETENDING TO BE ASLEEP!!
...
ZAZAAN
ZAZAAN

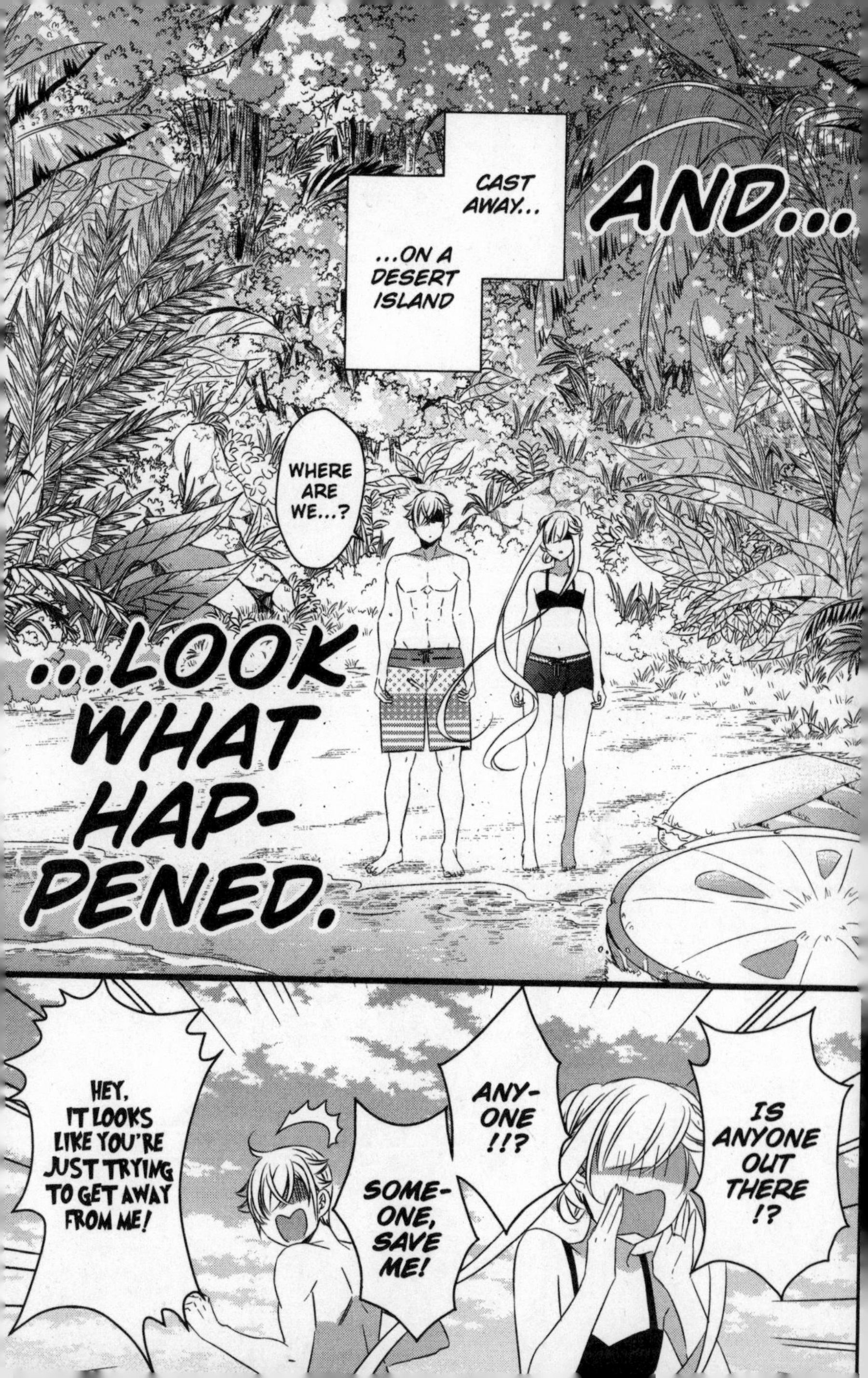
AND...
CAST AWAY...
...ON A DESERT ISLAND
WHERE ARE WE...?
...LOOK WHAT HAP-PENED.
IS ANYONE OUT THERE!?
ANY-ONE!!?
SOME-ONE, SAVE ME!
HEY, IT LOOKS LIKE YOU'RE JUST TRYING TO GET AWAY FROM ME!

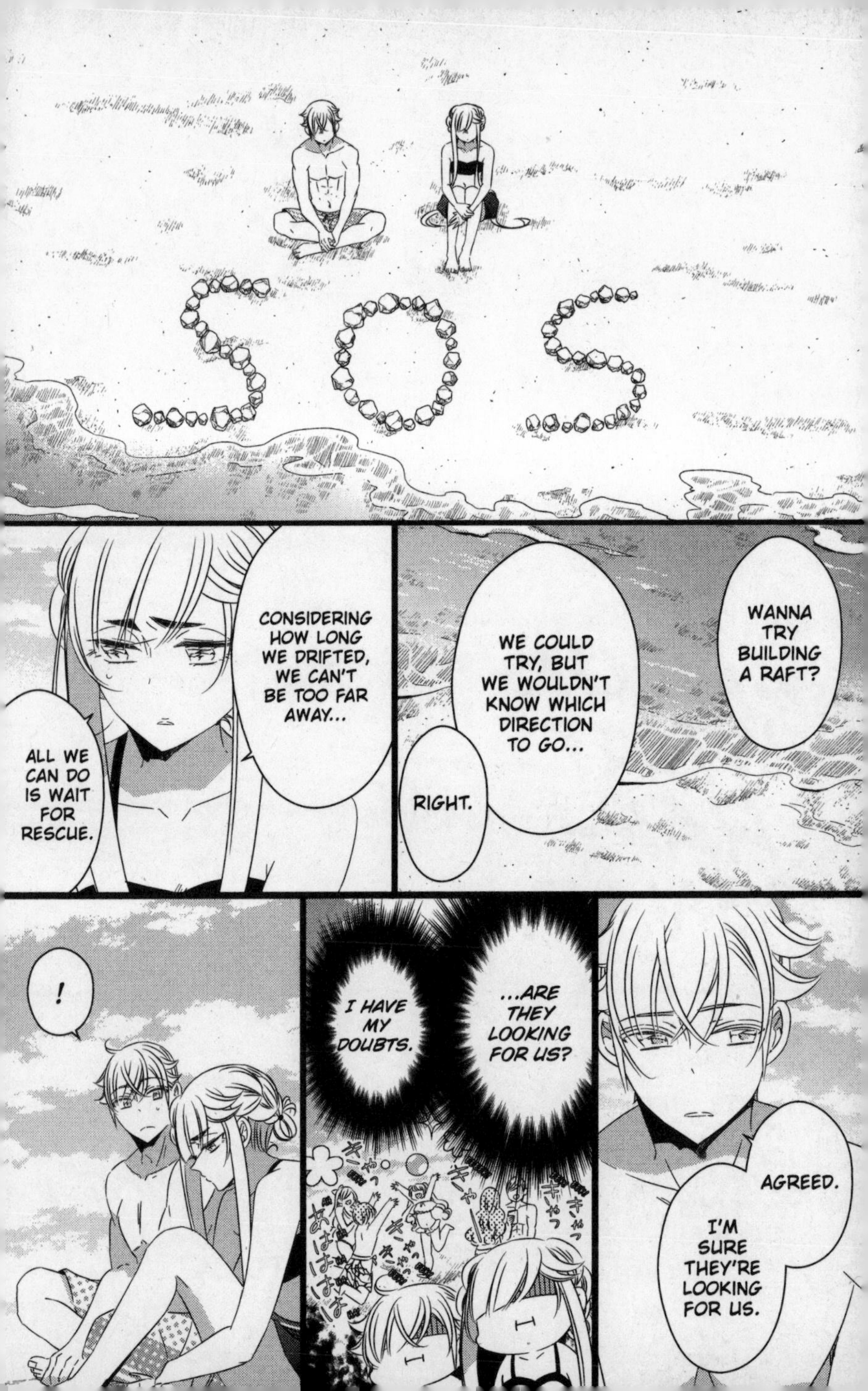
SOS
WANNA TRY BUILDING A RAFT?
WE COULD TRY, BUT WE WOULDN'T KNOW WHICH DIRECTION TO GO...
RIGHT.
CONSIDERING HOW LONG WE DRIFTED, WE CAN'T BE TOO FAR AWAY...
ALL WE CAN DO IS WAIT FOR RESCUE.
AGREED.
I'M SURE THEY'RE LOOKING FOR US.
...ARE THEY LOOKING FOR US?
I HAVE MY DOUBTS.
!

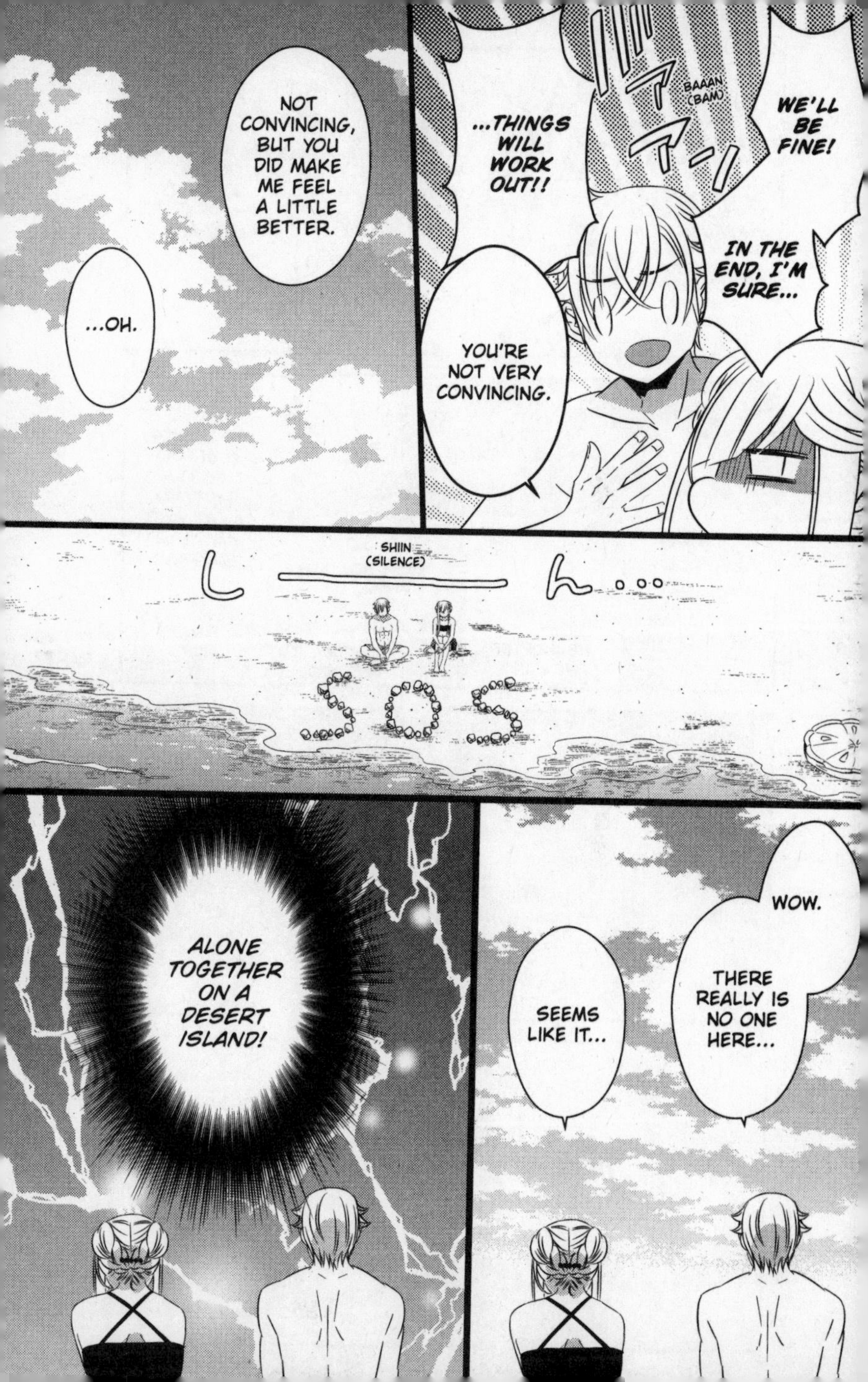
WE'LL BE FINE!
BAAAN (BAM)
IN THE END, I'M SURE...
...THINGS WILL WORK OUT!!
YOU'RE NOT VERY CONVINCING.
NOT CONVINCING, BUT YOU DID MAKE ME FEEL A LITTLE BETTER.
...OH.
SHIIN (SILENCE)
SOS
WOW.
THERE REALLY IS NO ONE HERE...
SEEMS LIKE IT...
ALONE TOGETHER ON A DESERT ISLAND!

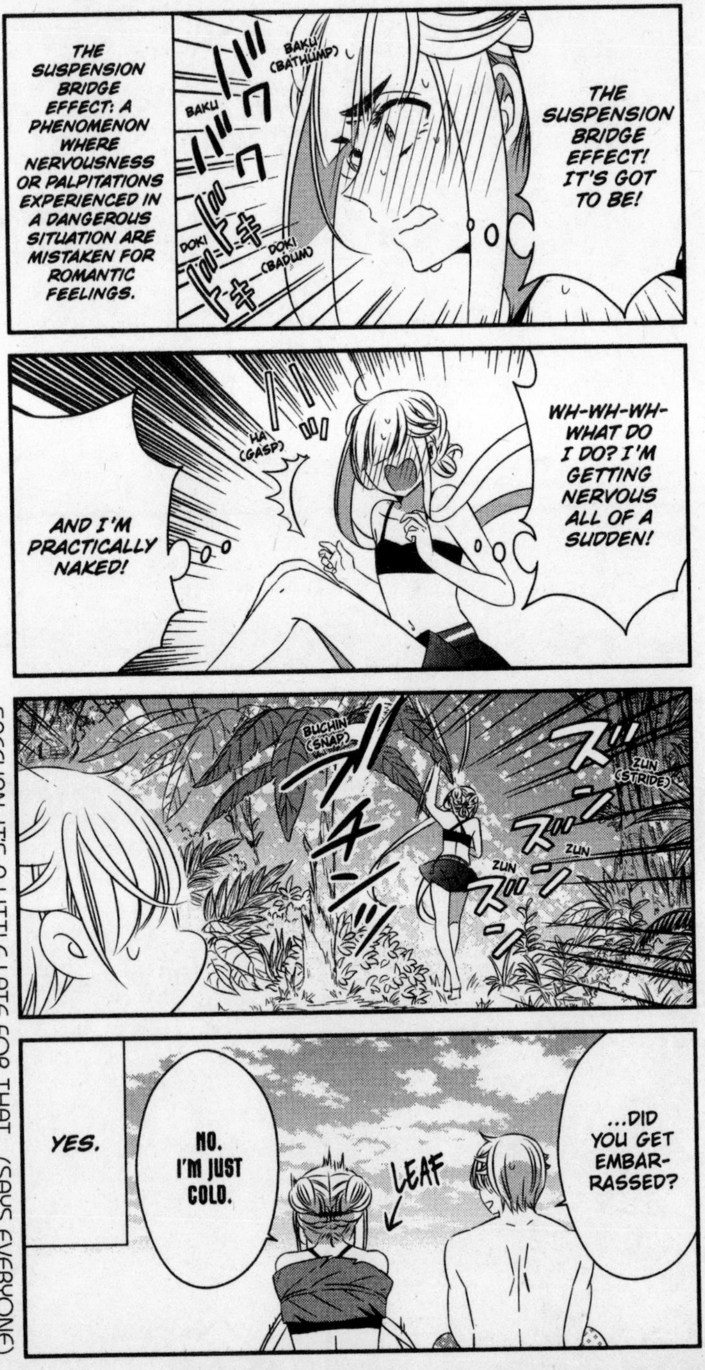
THE SUSPENSION BRIDGE EFFECT! IT'S GOT TO BE!
BAKU (BATHUMP)
BAKU
DOKI (BADUM)
DOKI
THE SUSPENSION BRIDGE EFFECT: A PHENOMENON WHERE NERVOUSNESS OR PALPITATIONS EXPERIENCED IN A DANGEROUS SITUATION ARE MISTAKEN FOR ROMANTIC FEELINGS.
WH-WH-WH-WHAT DO I DO? I'M GETTING NERVOUS ALL OF A SUDDEN!
HA (GASP)
AND I'M PRACTICALLY NAKED!
ZUN (STRIDE)
ZUN
ZUN
BUCHIN (SNAP)
...DID YOU GET EMBAR-RASSED?
LEAF
NO. I'M JUST COLD.
YES.

SACCHAN, IT'S A LITTLE LATE FOR THAT... (SAYS EVERYONE)

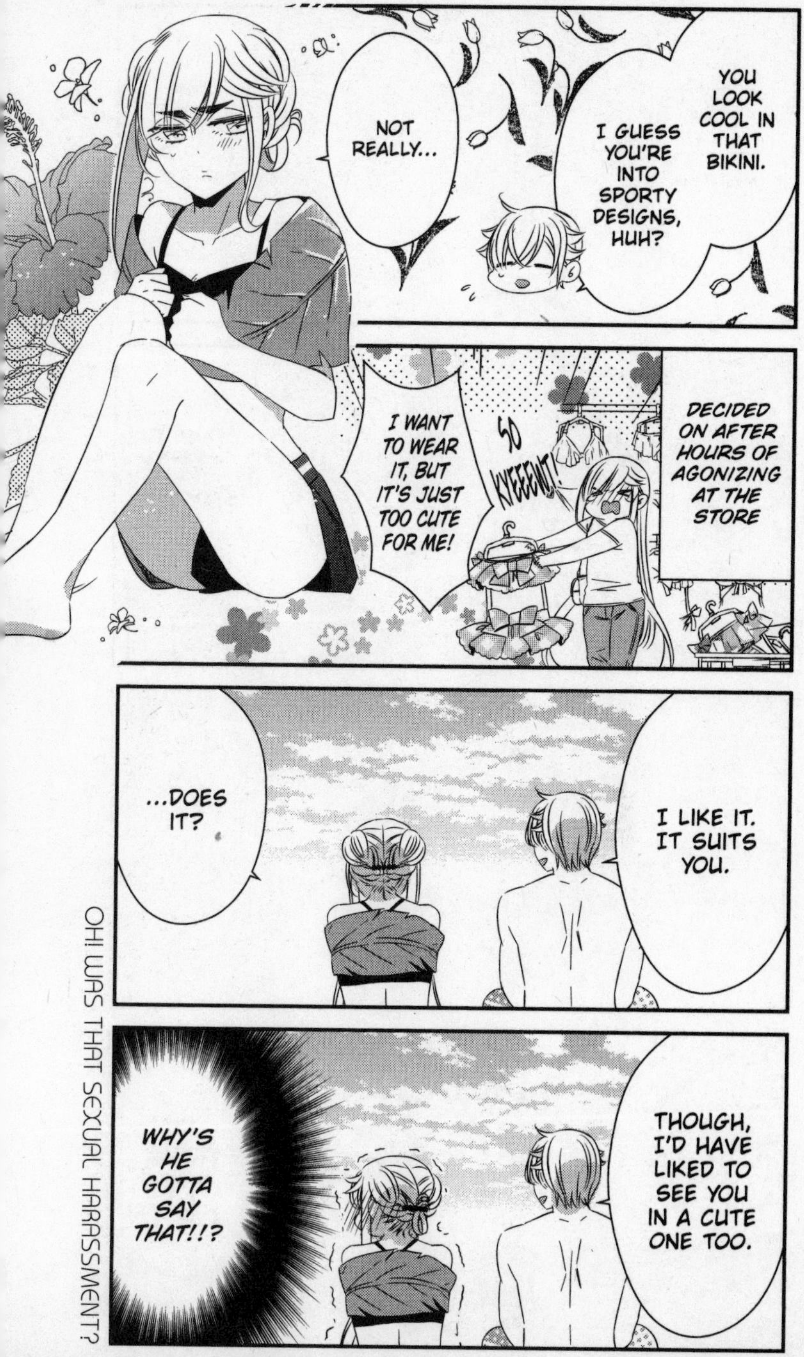
YOU LOOK COOL IN THAT BIKINI.
I GUESS YOU'RE INTO SPORTY DESIGNS, HUH?
NOT REALLY...
DECIDED ON AFTER HOURS OF AGONIZING AT THE STORE
SO KYEEEUT!
I WANT TO WEAR IT, BUT IT'S JUST TOO CUTE FOR ME!
I LIKE IT. IT SUITS YOU.
...DOES IT?
THOUGH, I'D HAVE LIKED TO SEE YOU IN A CUTE ONE TOO.
WHY'S HE GOTTA SAY THAT!!?

OH! WAS THAT SEXUAL HARASSMENT?

NOT MY PROBLEM

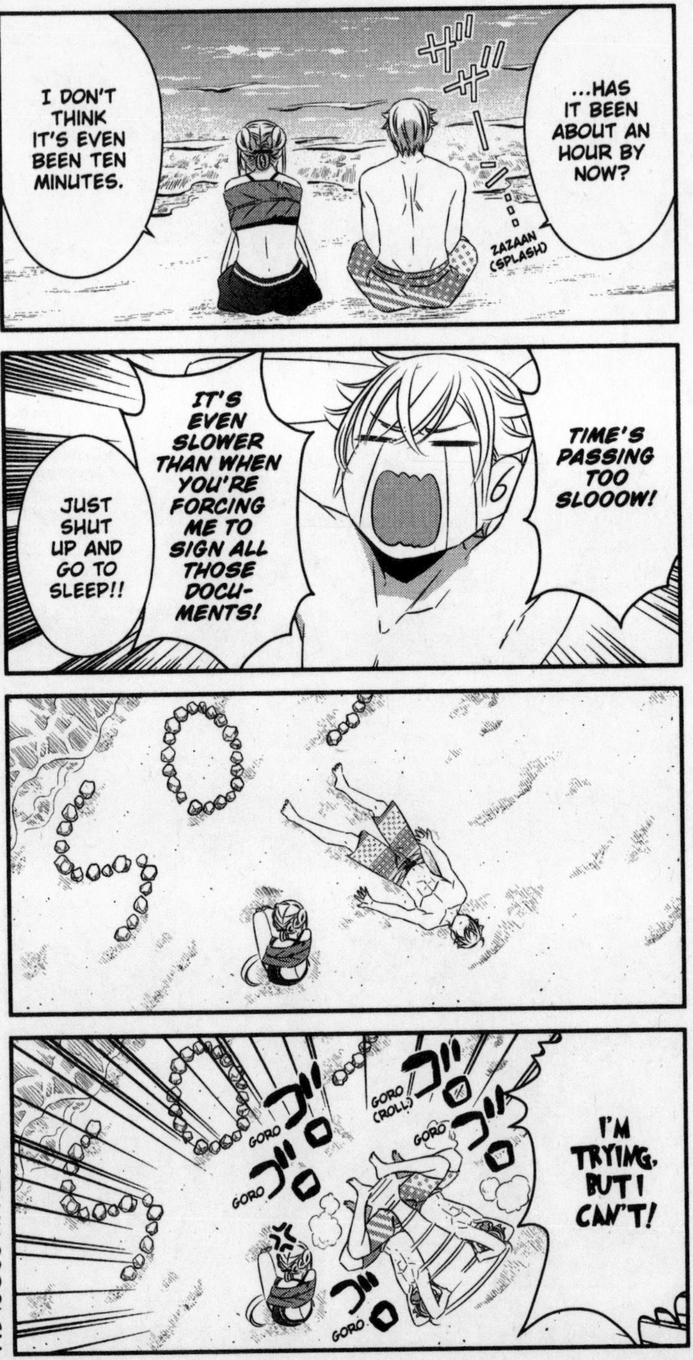

...HAS IT BEEN ABOUT AN HOUR BY NOW?
ZAZAAN (SPLASH)
I DON'T THINK IT'S EVEN BEEN TEN MINUTES.
TIME'S PASSING TOO SLOOOW!
IT'S EVEN SLOWER THAN WHEN YOU'RE FORCING ME TO SIGN ALL THOSE DOCU-MENTS!
JUST SHUT UP AND GO TO SLEEP!!
I'M TRYING, BUT I CAN'T!
GORO (ROLL)
GORO
GORO
GORO
GORO

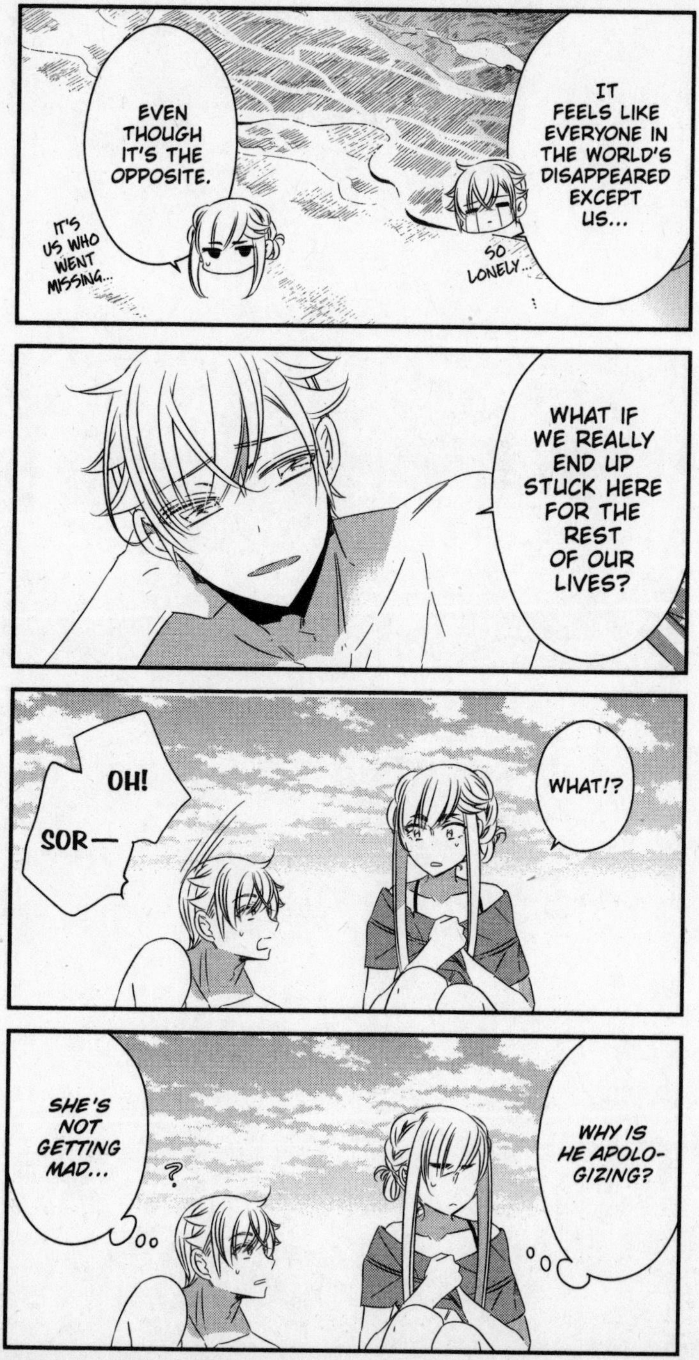
IT FEELS LIKE EVERYONE IN THE WORLD'S DISAPPEARED EXCEPT US...
SO LONELY...
EVEN THOUGH IT'S THE OPPOSITE.
IT'S US WHO WENT MISSING...
WHAT IF WE REALLY END UP STUCK HERE FOR THE REST OF OUR LIVES?
WHAT!?
OH!
SOR—
WHY IS HE APOLOGIZING?
SHE'S NOT GETTING MAD...
?

WHY?

WORRIES

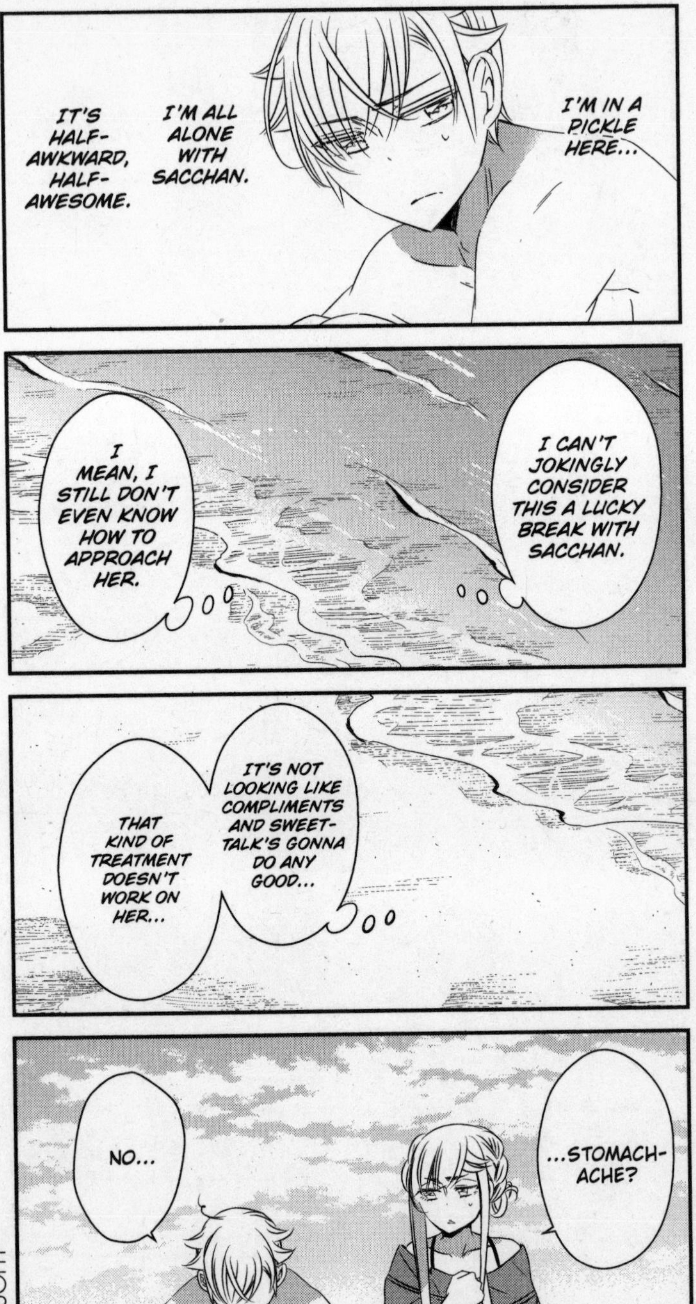
I'M IN A PICKLE HERE...
I'M ALL ALONE WITH SACCHAN.
IT'S HALF-AWKWARD, HALF-AWESOME.
I CAN'T JOKINGLY CONSIDER THIS A LUCKY BREAK WITH SACCHAN.
I MEAN, I STILL DON'T EVEN KNOW HOW TO APPROACH HER.
IT'S NOT LOOKING LIKE COMPLIMENTS AND SWEET-TALK'S GONNA DO ANY GOOD...
THAT KIND OF TREATMENT DOESN'T WORK ON HER...
...STOMACH-ACHE?
NO...

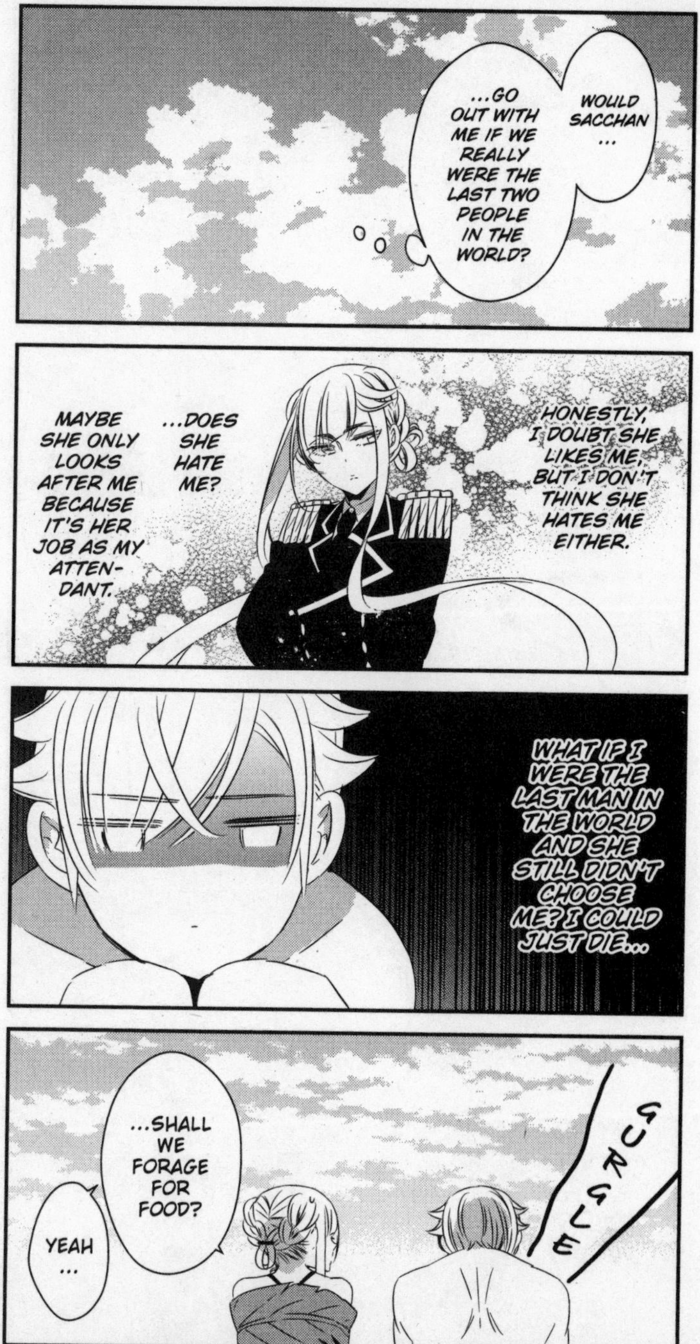
WOULD SACCHAN...
...GO OUT WITH ME IF WE REALLY WERE THE LAST TWO PEOPLE IN THE WORLD?
HONESTLY, I DOUBT SHE LIKES ME, BUT I DON'T THINK SHE HATES ME EITHER.
...DOES SHE HATE ME?
MAYBE SHE ONLY LOOKS AFTER ME BECAUSE IT'S HER JOB AS MY ATTEN-DANT.
WHAT IF I WERE THE LAST MAN IN THE WORLD AND SHE STILL DIDN'T CHOOSE ME? I COULD JUST DIE...
GURGLE
...SHALL WE FORAGE FOR FOOD?
YEAH...

ONE P.M.

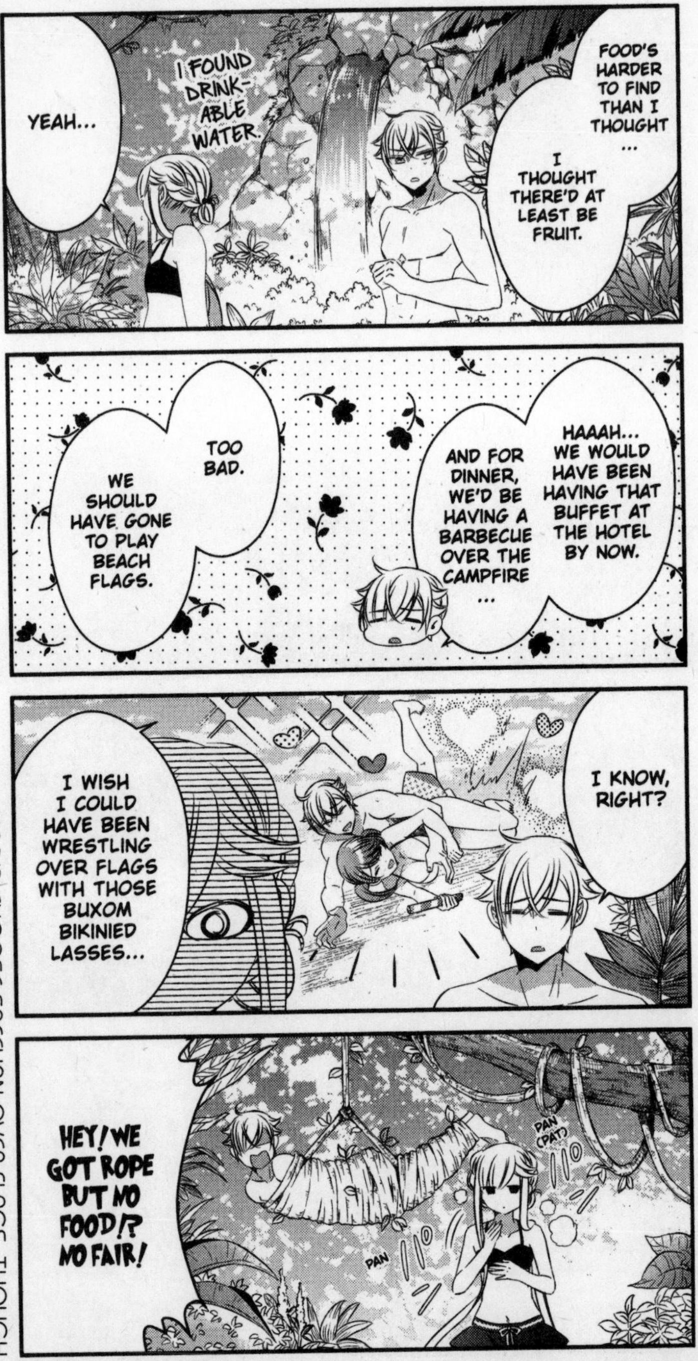
FOOD'S HARDER TO FIND THAN I THOUGHT ...
I THOUGHT THERE'D AT LEAST BE FRUIT.
I FOUND DRINK-ABLE WATER.
YEAH...
HAAAH... WE WOULD HAVE BEEN HAVING THAT BUFFET AT THE HOTEL BY NOW.
AND FOR DINNER, WE'D BE HAVING A BARBECUE OVER THE CAMPFIRE ...
TOO BAD.
WE SHOULD HAVE GONE TO PLAY BEACH FLAGS.
I KNOW, RIGHT?
I WISH I COULD HAVE BEEN WRESTLING OVER FLAGS WITH THOSE BUXOM BIKINIED LASSES...
PAN (PAT)
PAN
HEY! WE GOT ROPE BUT NO FOOD!? NO FAIR!

HE DID CHOOSE SACCHAN OVER FLAGS, THOUGH

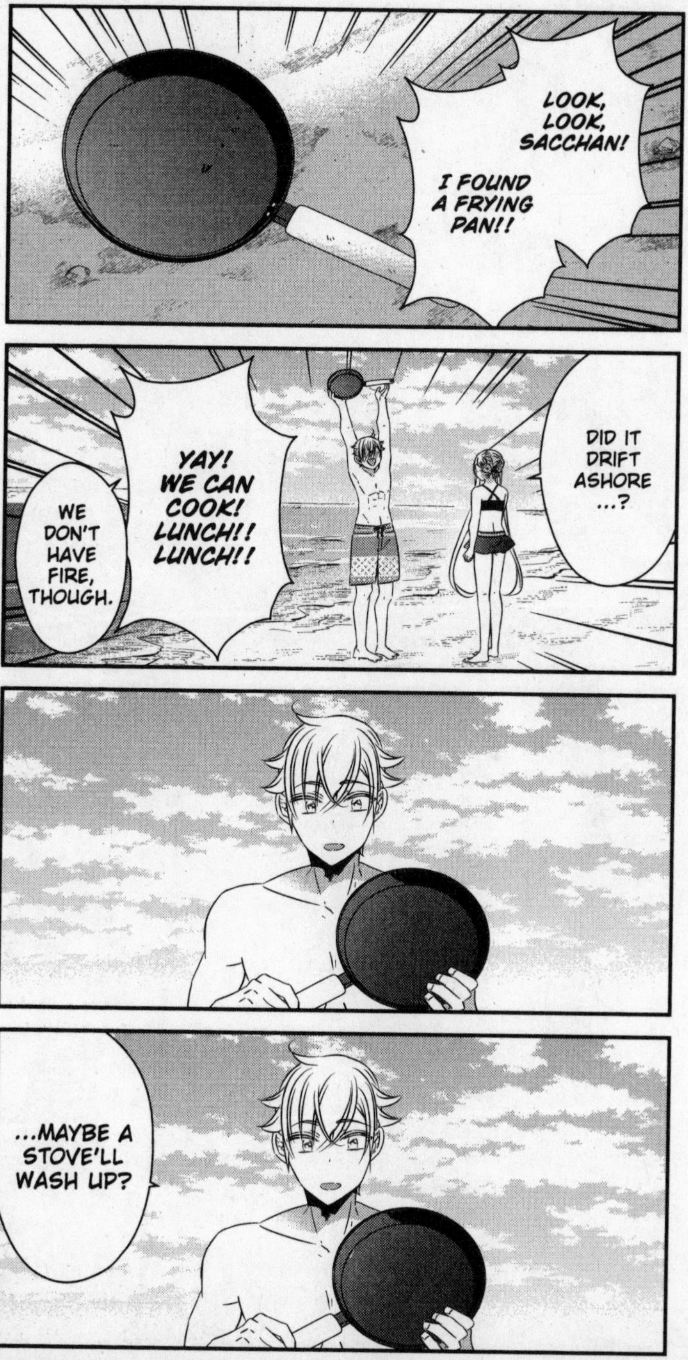
LOOK, LOOK, SACCHAN!
I FOUND A FRYING PAN!!
DID IT DRIFT ASHORE ...?
YAY! WE CAN COOK! LUNCH!! LUNCH!!
WE DON'T HAVE FIRE, THOUGH.
...MAYBE A STOVE'LL WASH UP?

THAT'D BE NICE

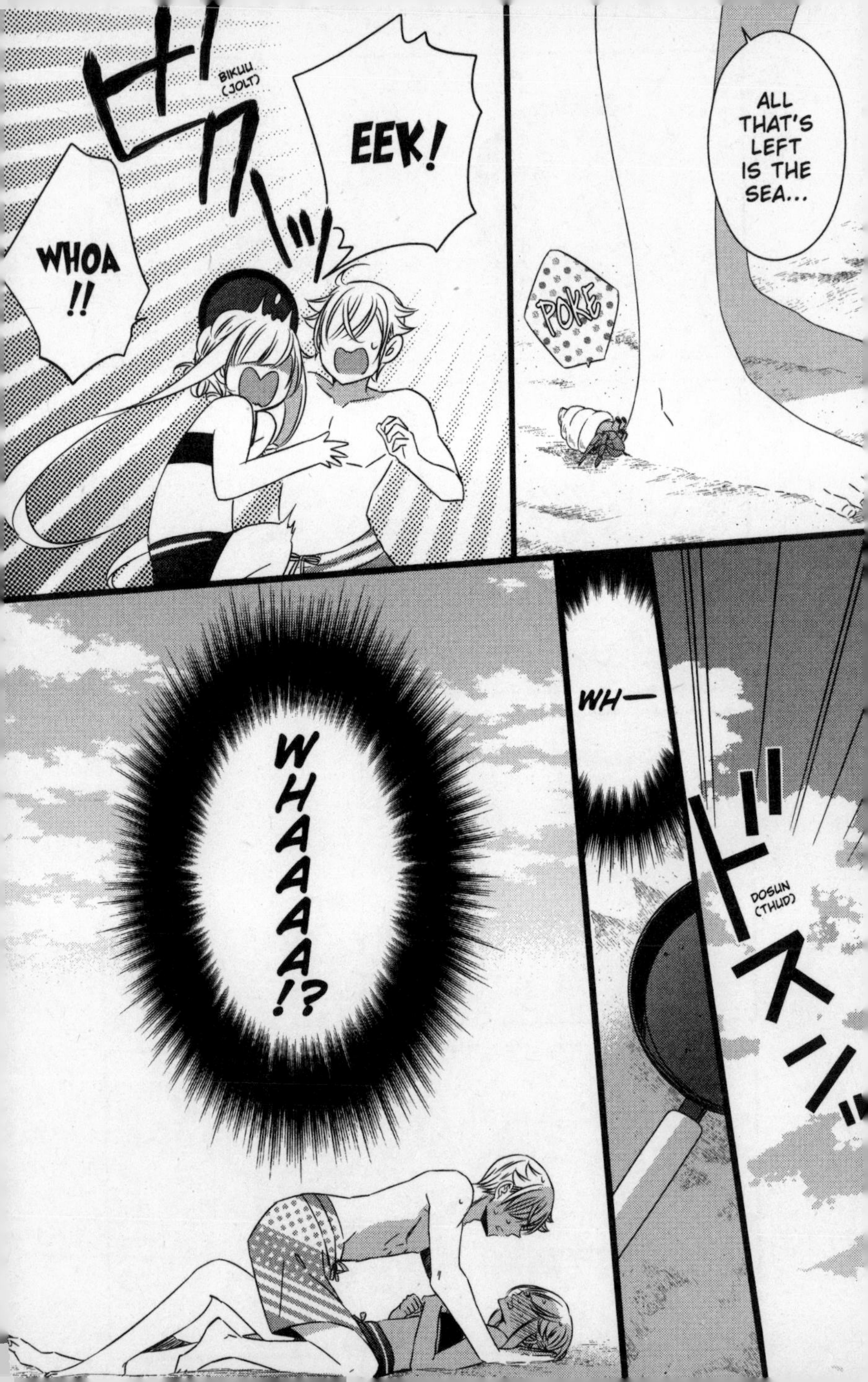
ALL THAT'S LEFT IS THE SEA...
POKE
EEK!
BIKUU (JOLT)
WHOA !!
WH—
DOSUN (THUD)
WHAAAAA!?

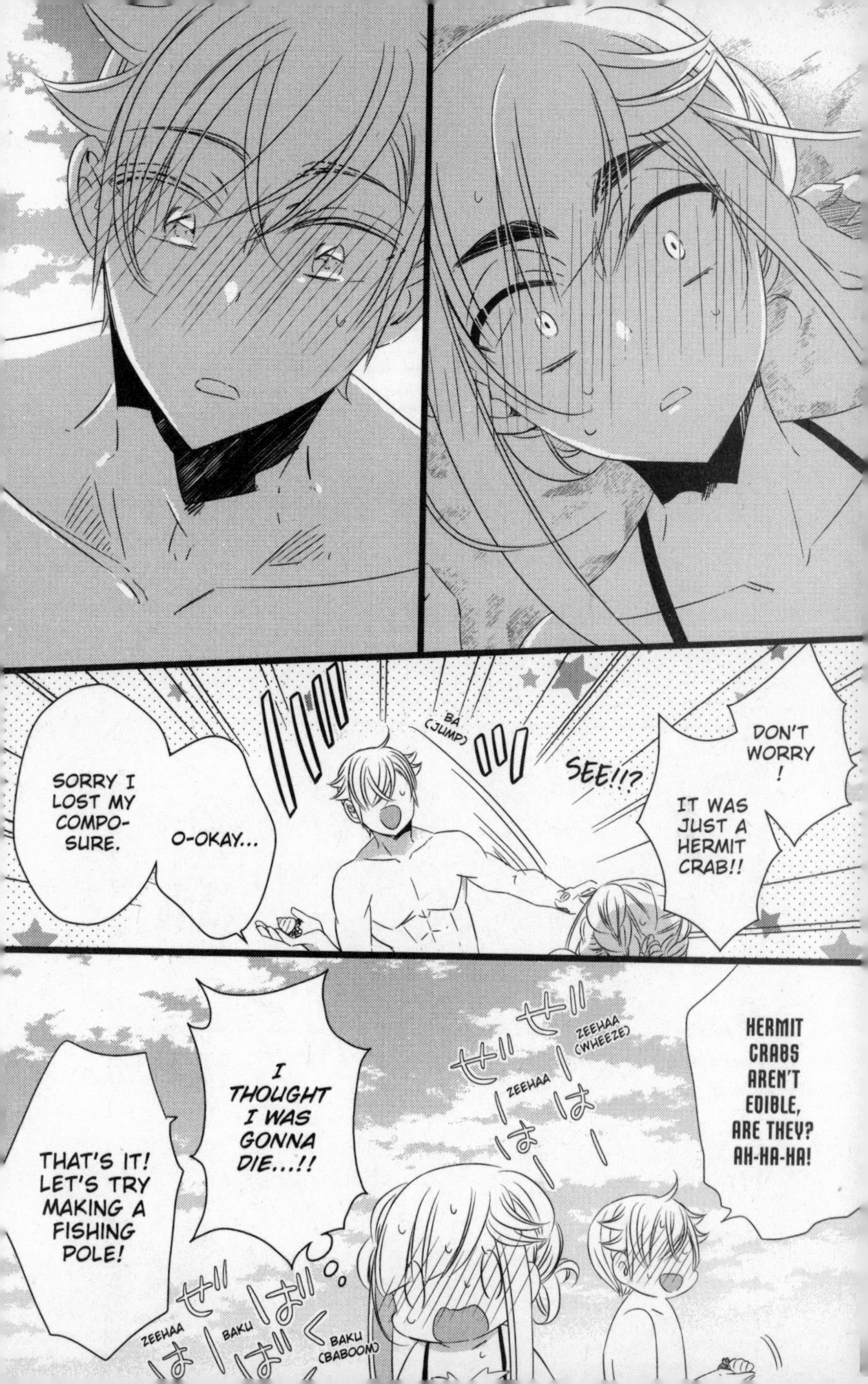
DON'T WORRY! IT WAS JUST A HERMIT CRAB!!
SEE!!?
BA (JUMP)
O-OKAY...
SORRY I LOST MY COMPOSURE.
HERMIT CRABS AREN'T EDIBLE, ARE THEY? AH-HA-HA!
ぜーはーぜーはー
ZEEHAA (WHEEZE)
ZEEHAA
I THOUGHT I WAS GONNA DIE...!!
THAT'S IT! LET'S TRY MAKING A FISHING POLE!
ぜーはー
ZEEHAA
ばくばく
BAKU
BAKU (BABOOM)

THE TYPE THAT NEVER GOT BREATHING TECHNIQUE DOWN

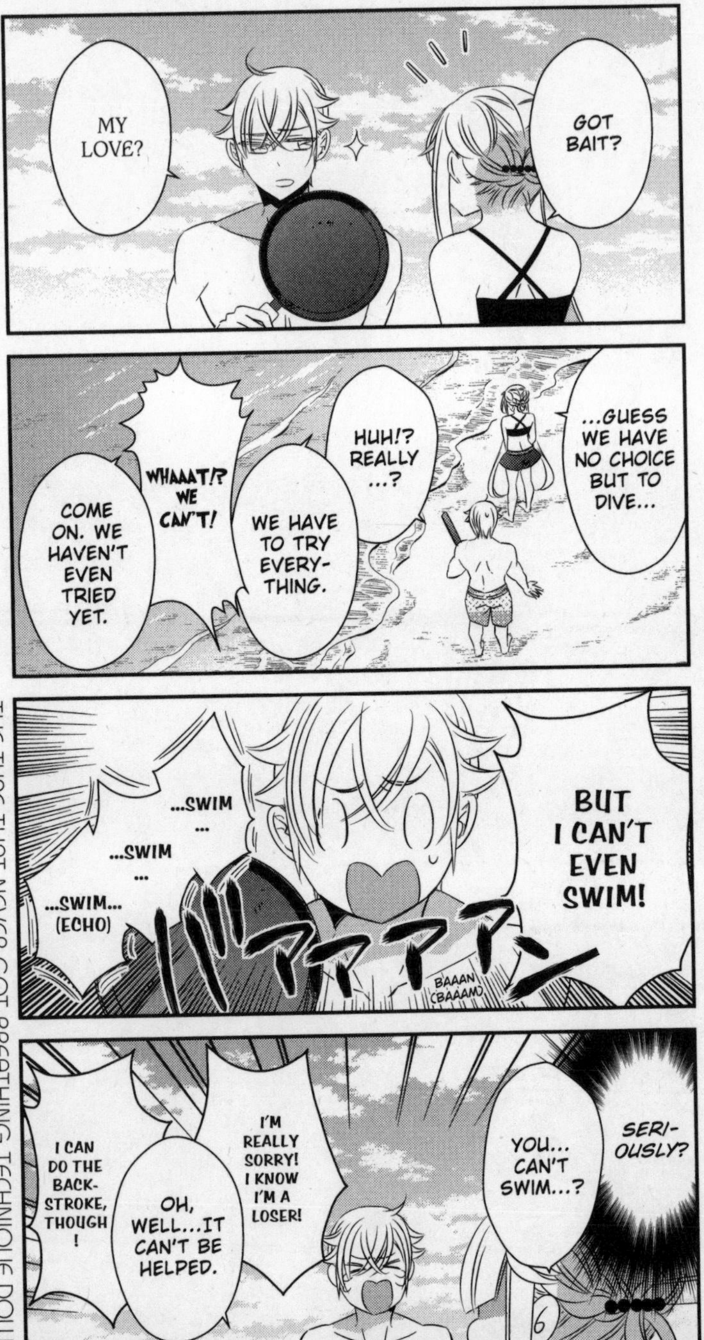

GOT BAIT?
MY LOVE?
...GUESS WE HAVE NO CHOICE BUT TO DIVE...
HUH!? REALLY ...?
WHAAAT!? WE CAN'T!
WE HAVE TO TRY EVERY-THING.
COME ON. WE HAVEN'T EVEN TRIED YET.
BUT I CAN'T EVEN SWIM!
...SWIM ...
...SWIM ...
...SWIM... (ECHO)
BAAAN (BAAAM)
SERI-OUSLY?
YOU... CAN'T SWIM...?
I'M REALLY SORRY! I KNOW I'M A LOSER!
OH, WELL...IT CAN'T BE HELPED.
I CAN DO THE BACK-STROKE, THOUGH!

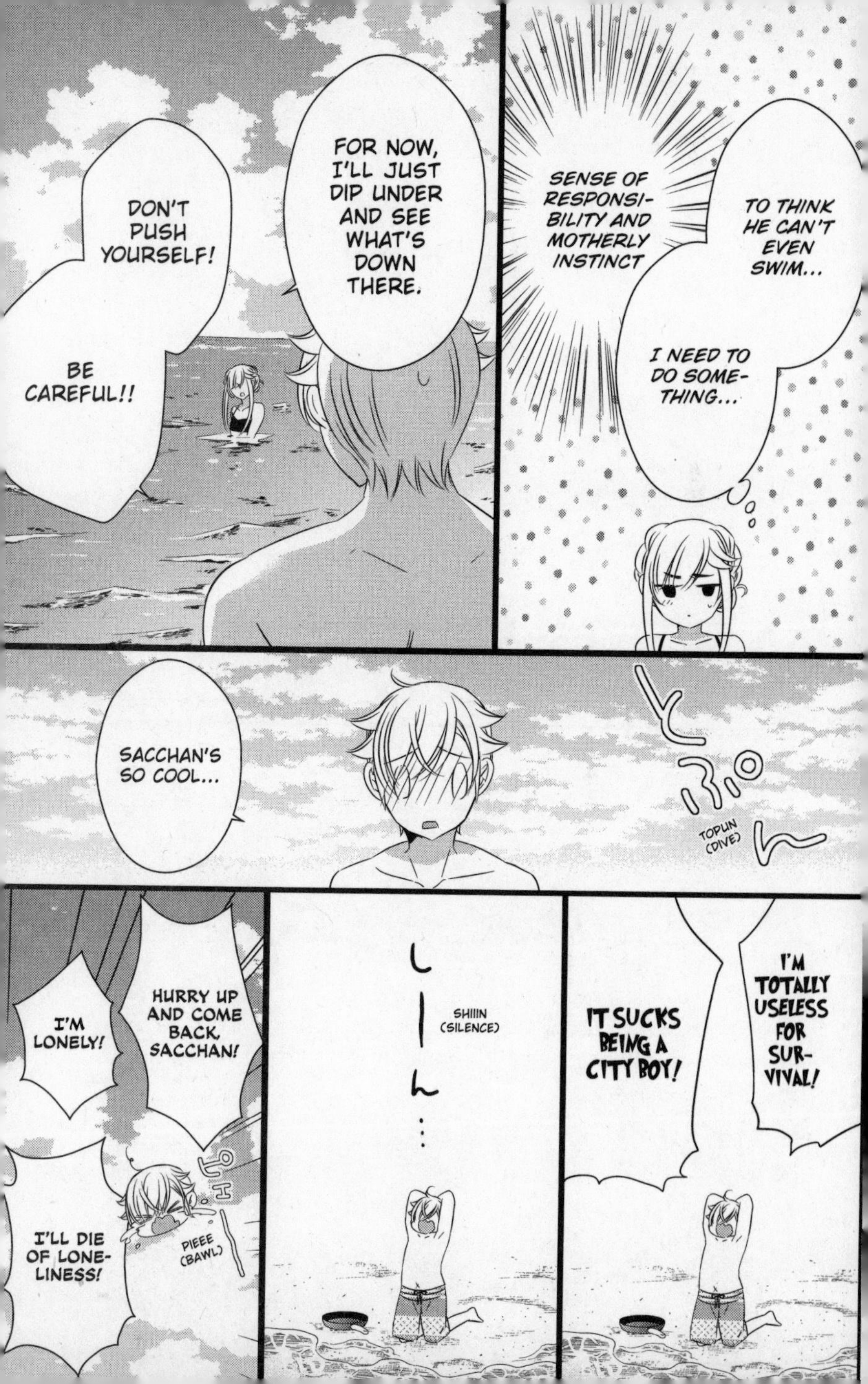
TO THINK HE CAN'T EVEN SWIM...
SENSE OF RESPONSI-BILITY AND MOTHERLY INSTINCT
I NEED TO DO SOME-THING...
FOR NOW, I'LL JUST DIP UNDER AND SEE WHAT'S DOWN THERE.
DON'T PUSH YOURSELF!
BE CAREFUL!!
とぷん
TOPUN (DIVE)
SACCHAN'S SO COOL...
I'M TOTALLY USELESS FOR SUR-VIVAL!
IT SUCKS BEING A CITY BOY!
しーん…
SHIIIN (SILENCE)
HURRY UP AND COME BACK, SACCHAN!
I'M LONELY!
PIEEE (BAWL)
I'LL DIE OF LONE-LINESS!

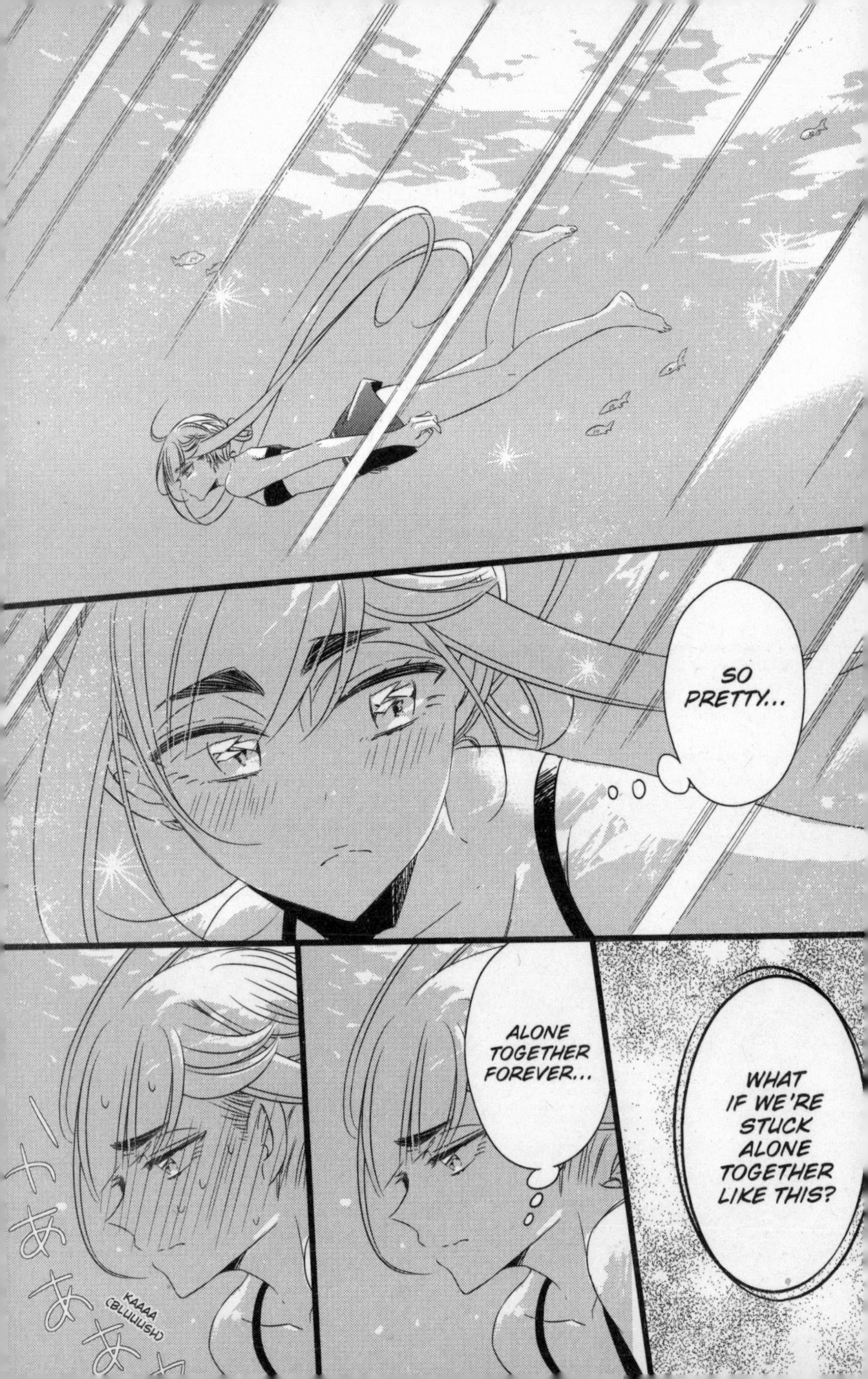
SO PRETTY...
WHAT IF WE'RE STUCK ALONE TOGETHER LIKE THIS?
ALONE TOGETHER FOREVER...
かああああ
KAAAA (BLUUUSH)

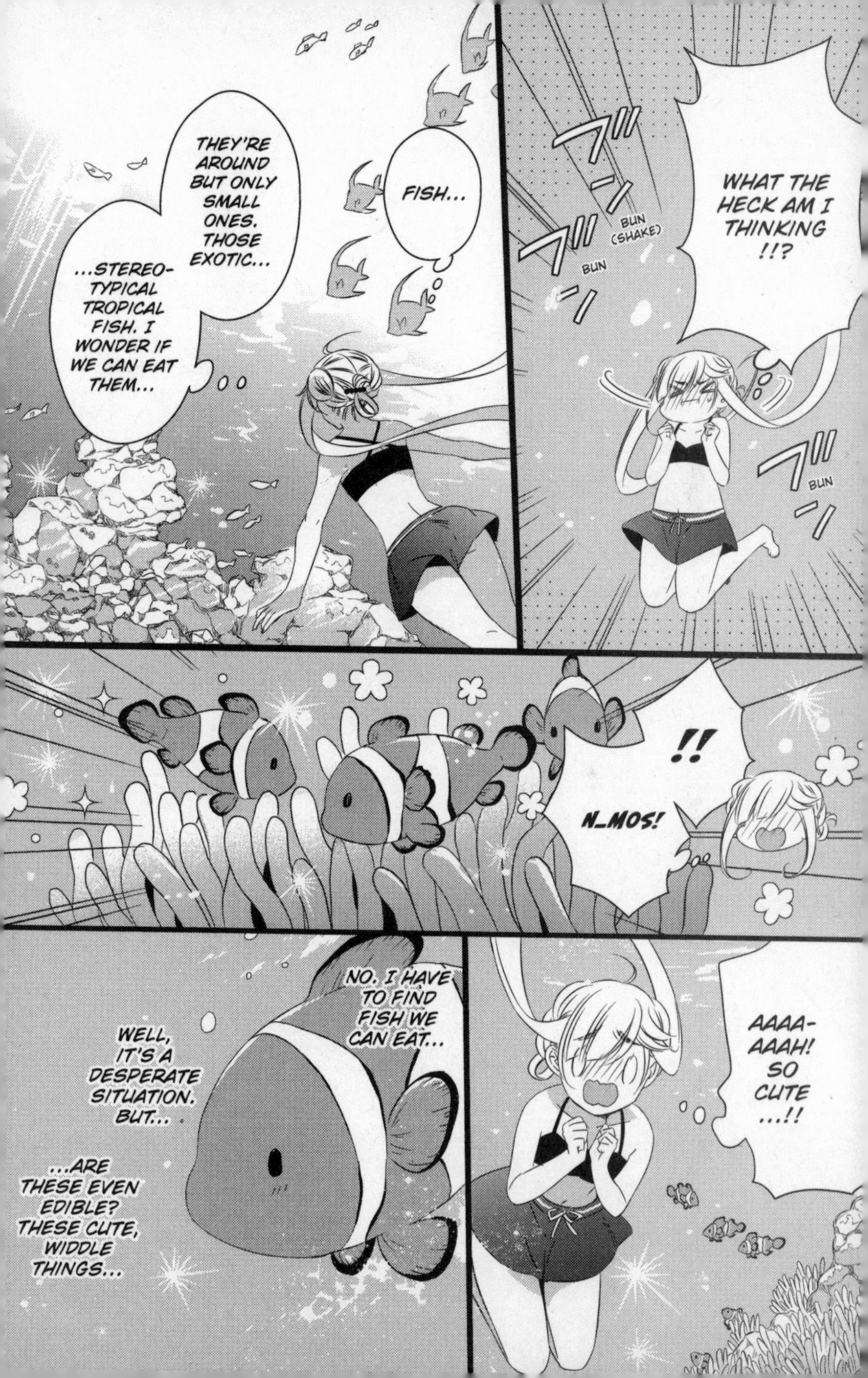
WHAT THE HECK AM I THINKING !!?
BUN (SHAKE)
BUN
BUN
FISH...
THEY'RE AROUND BUT ONLY SMALL ONES. THOSE EXOTIC...
...STEREO-TYPICAL TROPICAL FISH. I WONDER IF WE CAN EAT THEM...
!!
N_MOS!
AAAA-AAAH! SO CUTE ...!!
NO. I HAVE TO FIND FISH WE CAN EAT...
WELL, IT'S A DESPERATE SITUATION. BUT...
...ARE THESE EVEN EDIBLE? THESE CUTE, WIDDLE THINGS...

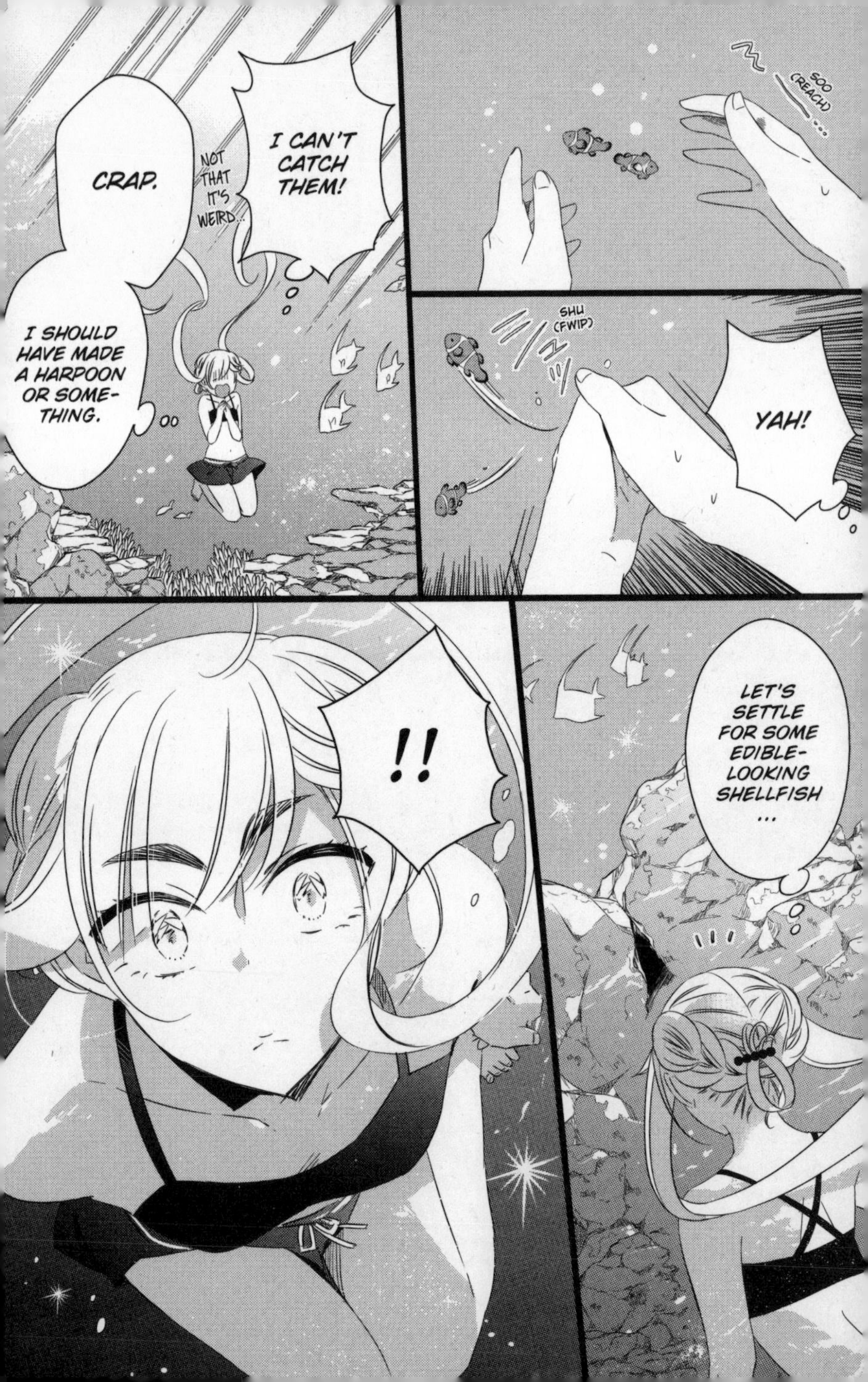
SOO (REACH) ...
SHU (FWIP)
YAH!
I CAN'T CATCH THEM!
NOT THAT IT'S WEIRD...
CRAP.
I SHOULD HAVE MADE A HARPOON OR SOME-THING.
LET'S SETTLE FOR SOME EDIBLE-LOOKING SHELLFISH ...
!!

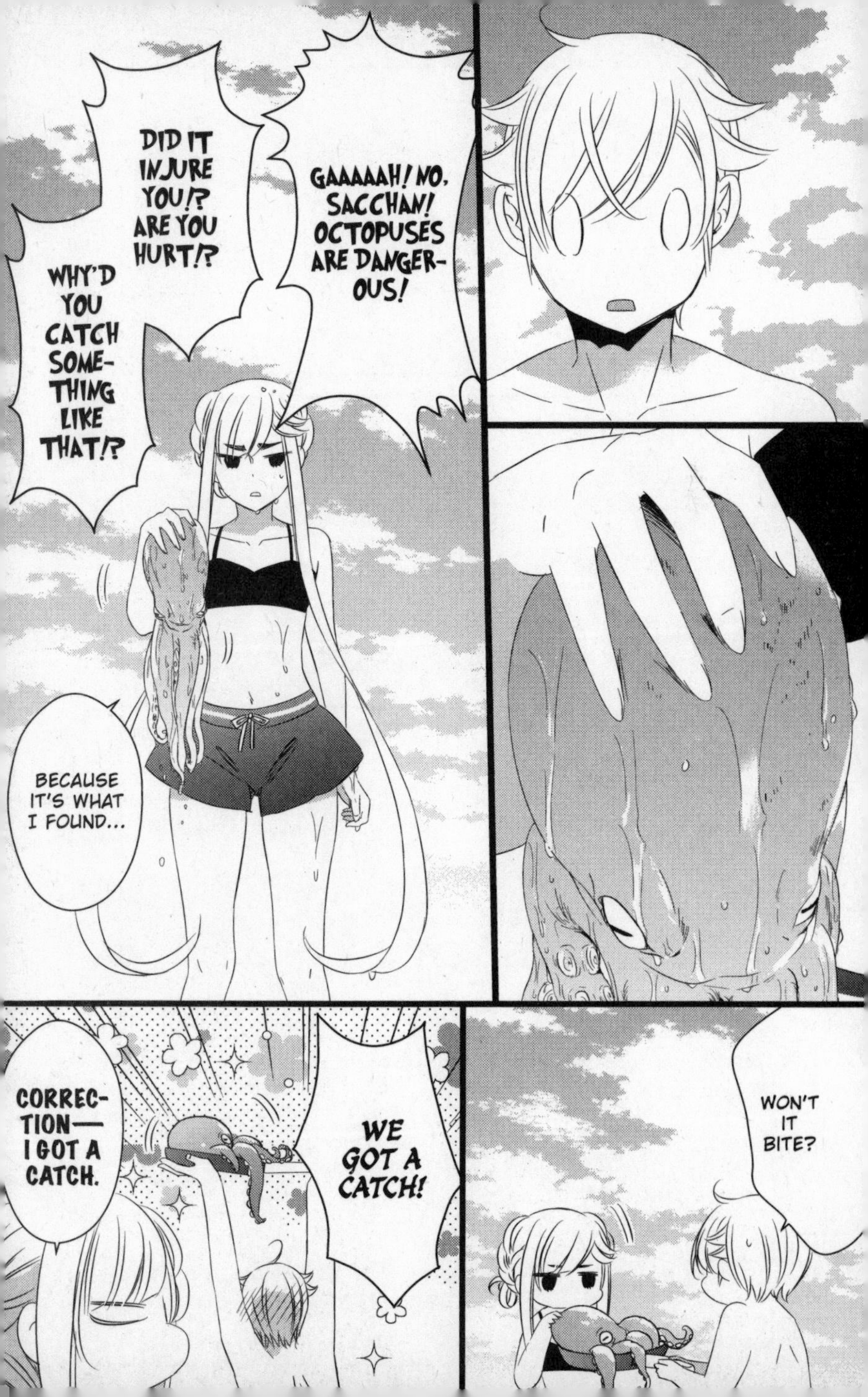
GAAAAAH! NO, SACCHAN! OCTOPUSES ARE DANGER-OUS!
DID IT INJURE YOU!? ARE YOU HURT!?
WHY'D YOU CATCH SOME-THING LIKE THAT!?
BECAUSE IT'S WHAT I FOUND...
WON'T IT BITE?
WE GOT A CATCH!
CORREC-TION— I GOT A CATCH.

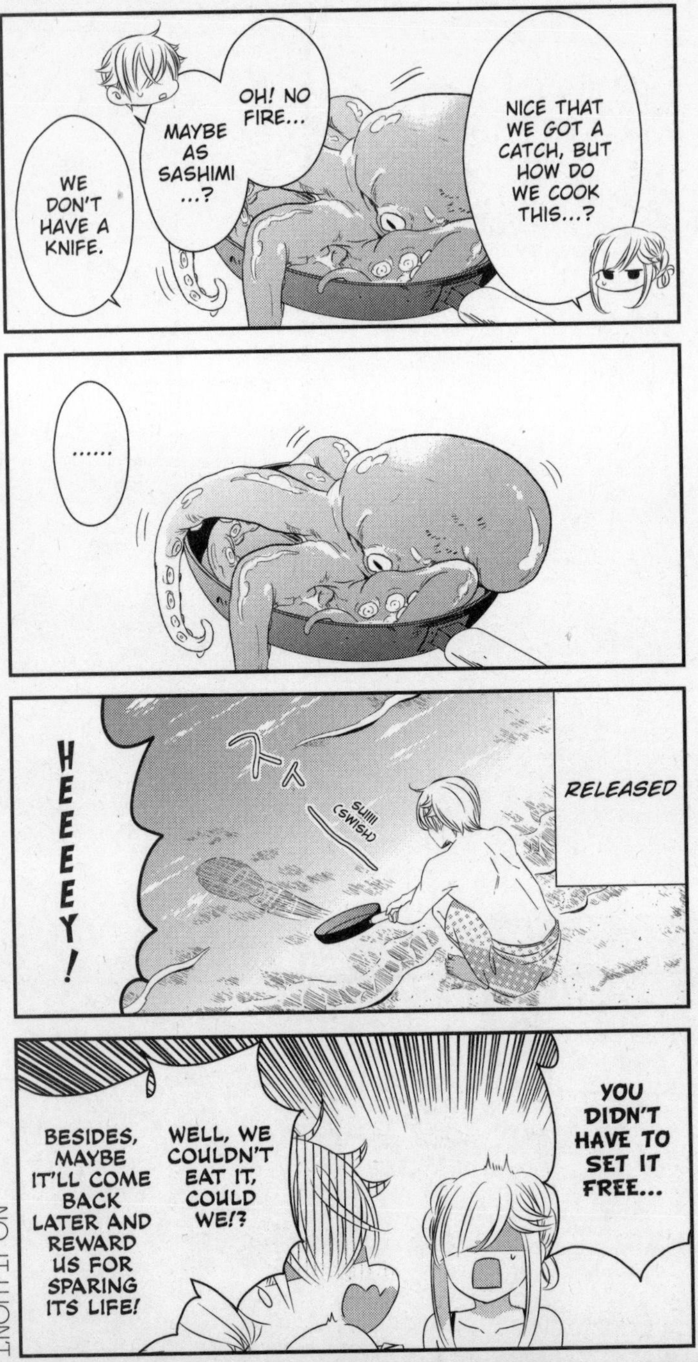
NICE THAT WE GOT A CATCH, BUT HOW DO WE COOK THIS...?
OH! NO FIRE...
MAYBE AS SASHIMI ...?
WE DON'T HAVE A KNIFE.
......
RELEASED
スイ
SUIIII (SWISH)
HEEEEEY!
YOU DIDN'T HAVE TO SET IT FREE...
WELL, WE COULDN'T EAT IT, COULD WE!?
BESIDES, MAYBE IT'LL COME BACK LATER AND REWARD US FOR SPARING ITS LIFE!

NO, IT WON'T

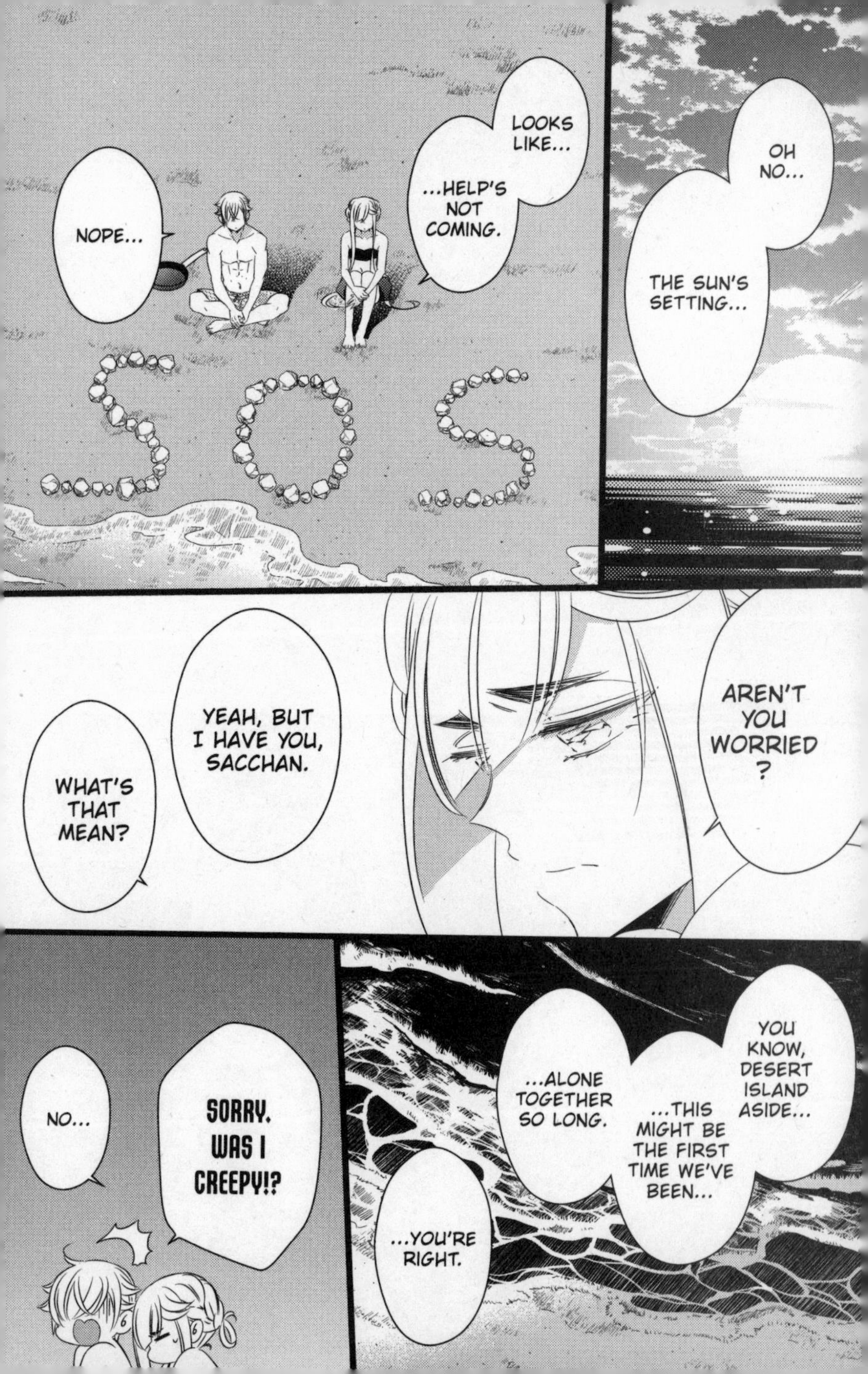
OH NO...
THE SUN'S SETTING...
LOOKS LIKE...
...HELP'S NOT COMING.
NOPE...
AREN'T YOU WORRIED?
YEAH, BUT I HAVE YOU, SACCHAN.
WHAT'S THAT MEAN?
YOU KNOW, DESERT ISLAND ASIDE...
...THIS MIGHT BE THE FIRST TIME WE'VE BEEN...
...ALONE TOGETHER SO LONG.
...YOU'RE RIGHT.
SORRY. WAS I CREEPY!?
NO...

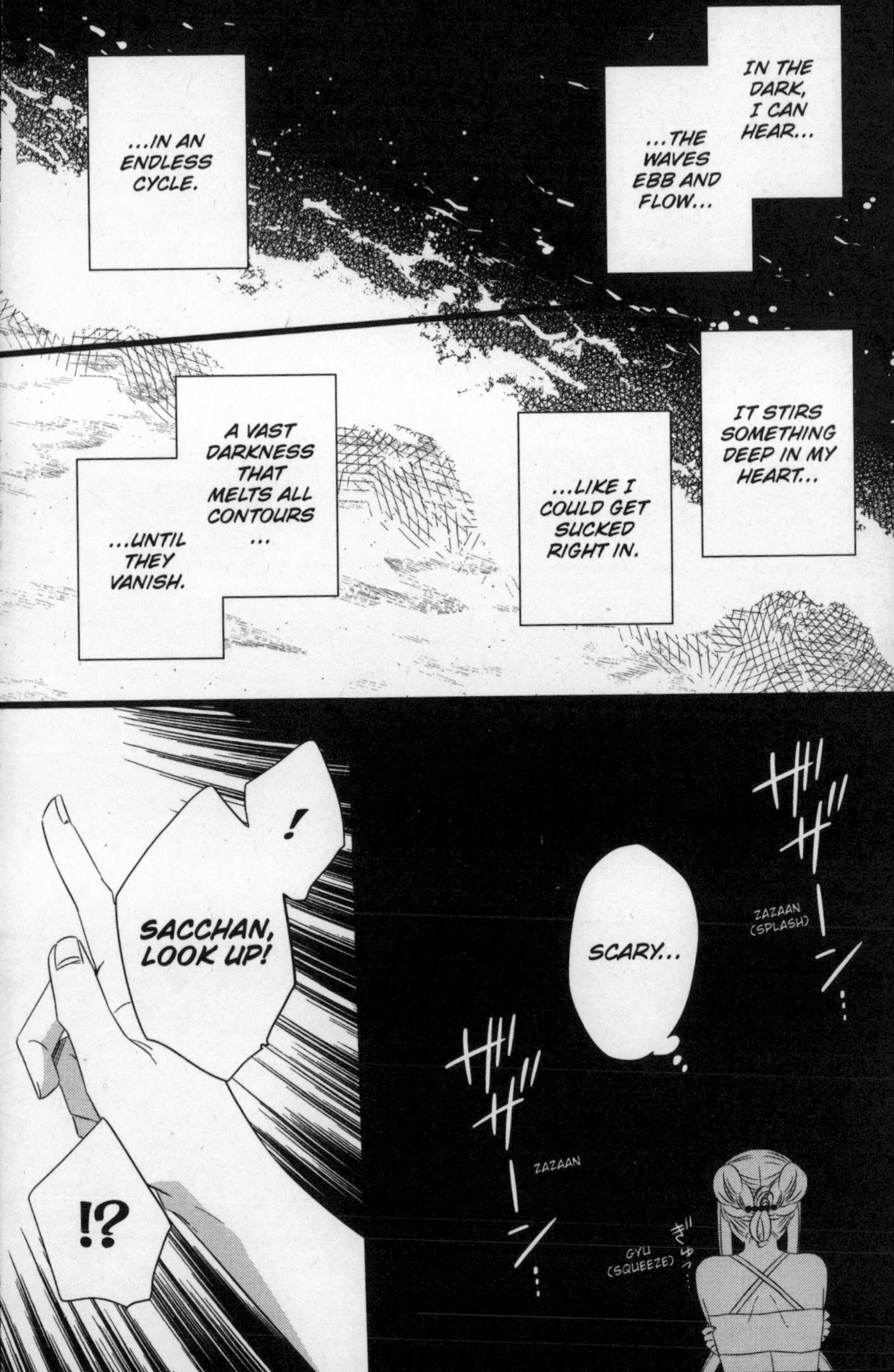

IN THE DARK, I CAN HEAR...
...THE WAVES EBB AND FLOW...
...IN AN ENDLESS CYCLE.
IT STIRS SOMETHING DEEP IN MY HEART...
...LIKE I COULD GET SUCKED RIGHT IN.
A VAST DARKNESS THAT MELTS ALL CONTOURS ...
...UNTIL THEY VANISH.
ZAZAAN (SPLASH)
SCARY...
ZAZAAN
ぎゅっ
GYU (SQUEEZE)
!
SACCHAN, LOOK UP!
!?

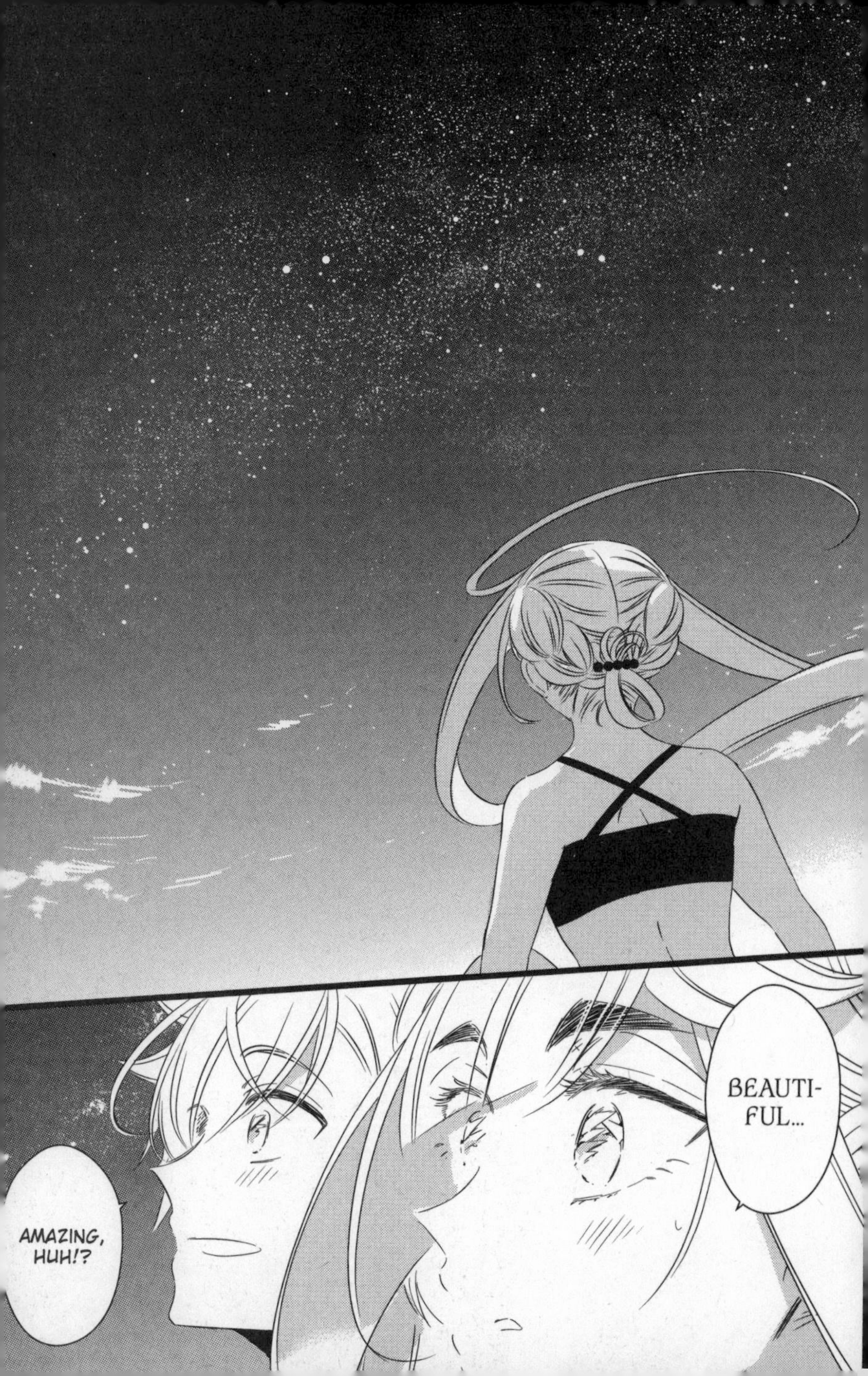
BEAUTI-FUL...
AMAZING, HUH!?

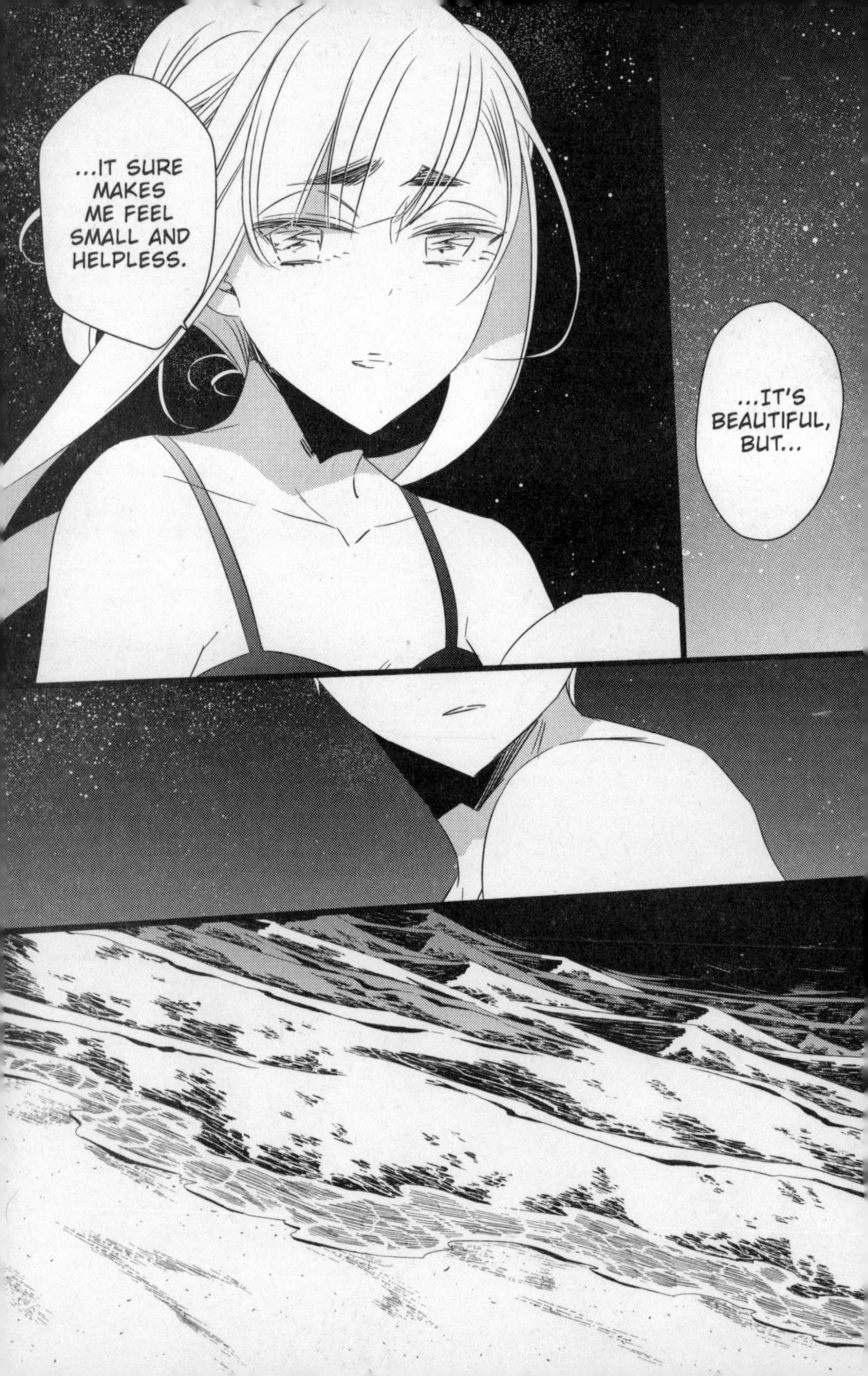
...IT'S BEAUTIFUL, BUT...
...IT SURE MAKES ME FEEL SMALL AND HELPLESS.

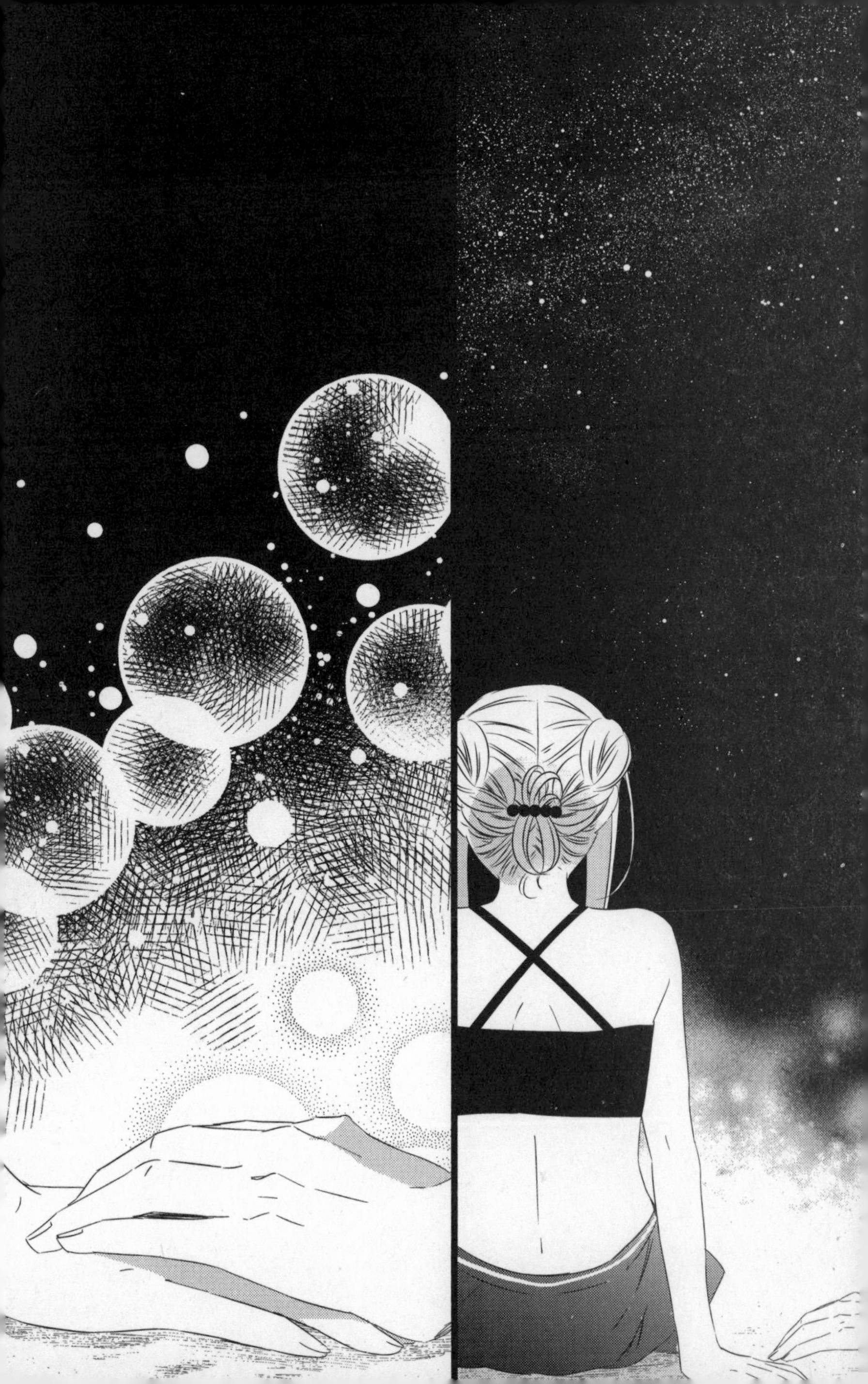

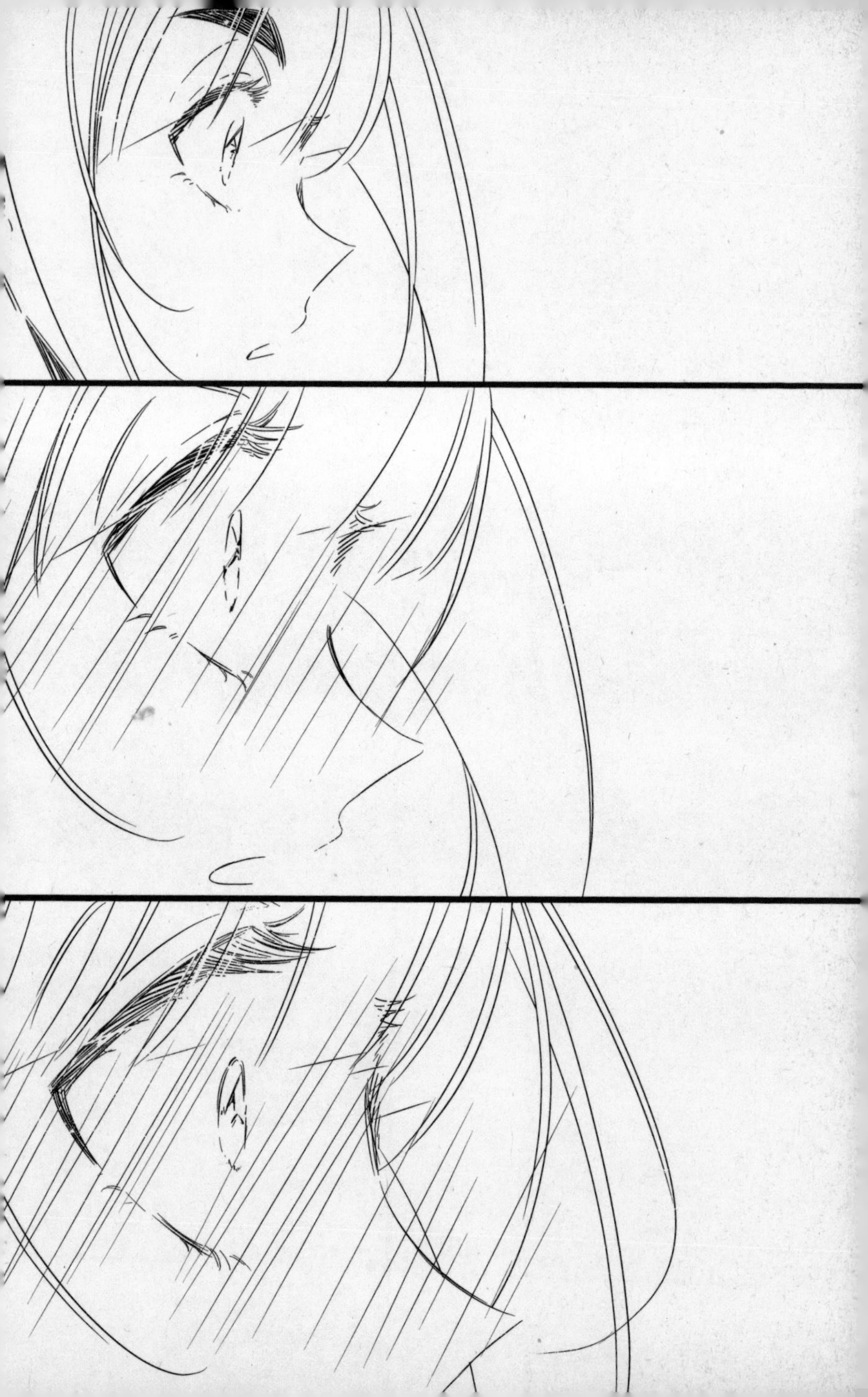

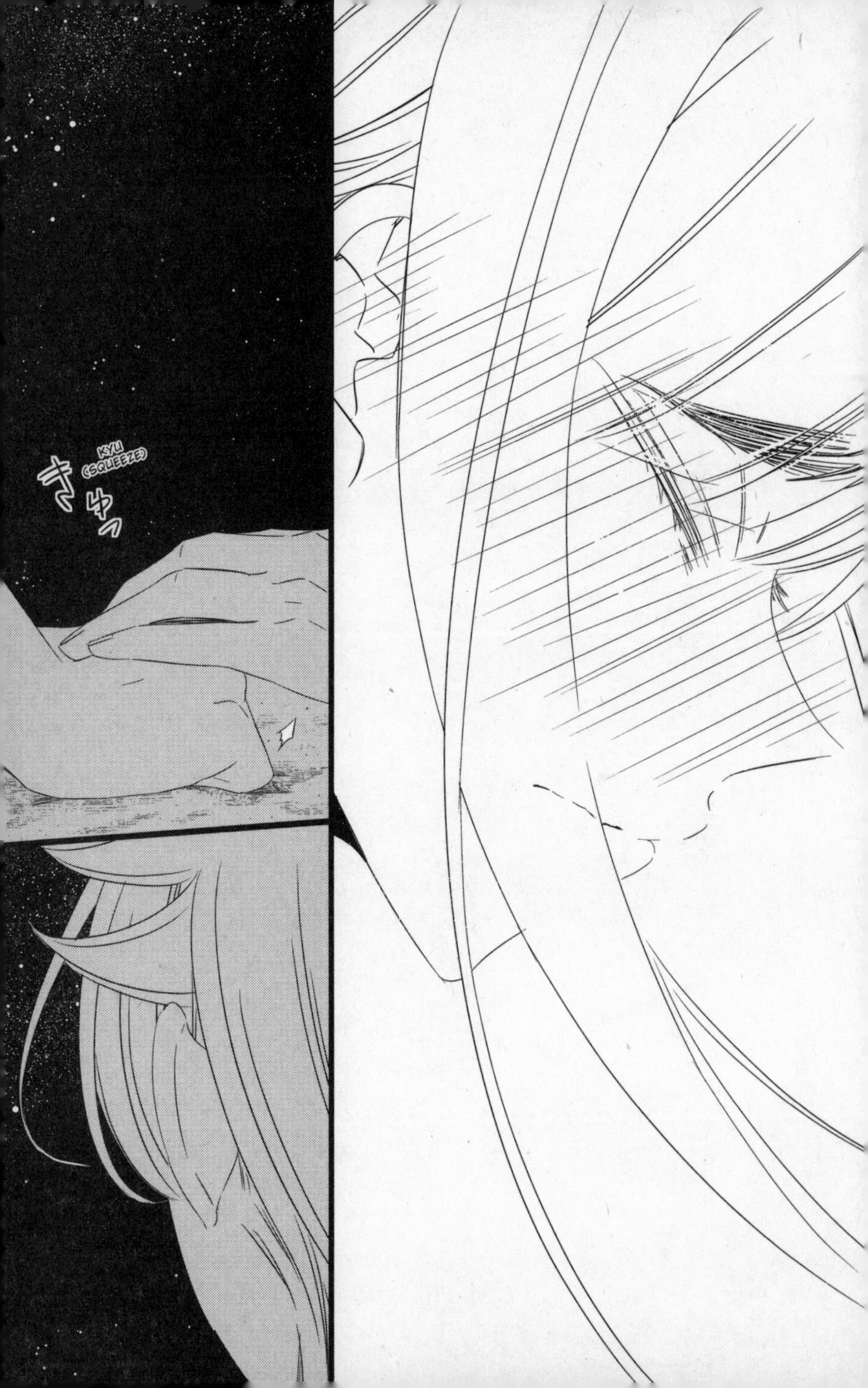
きゅっ
KYU (SQUEEZE)

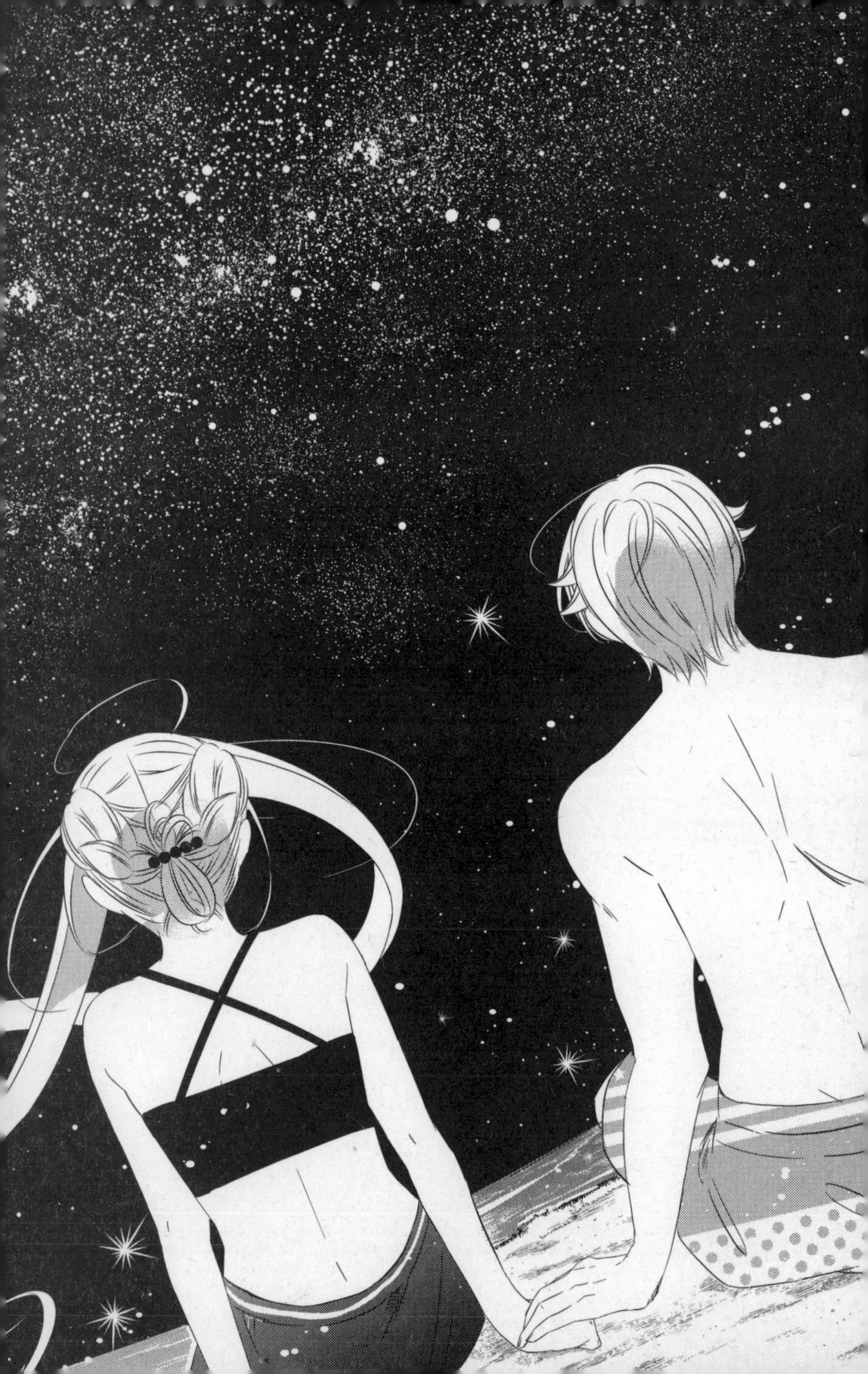

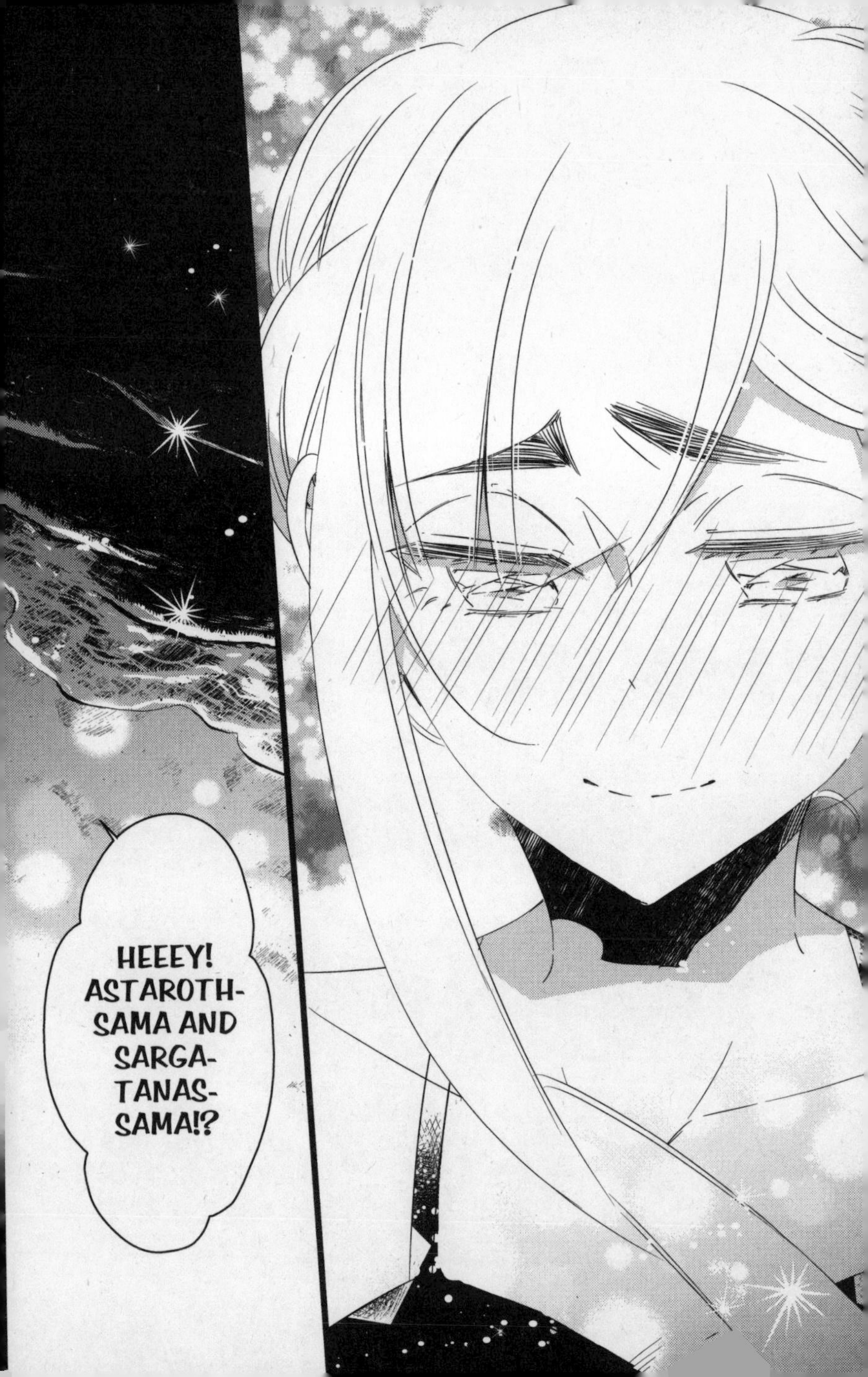
HEEEY! ASTAROTH-SAMA AND SARGA-TANAS-SAMA!?

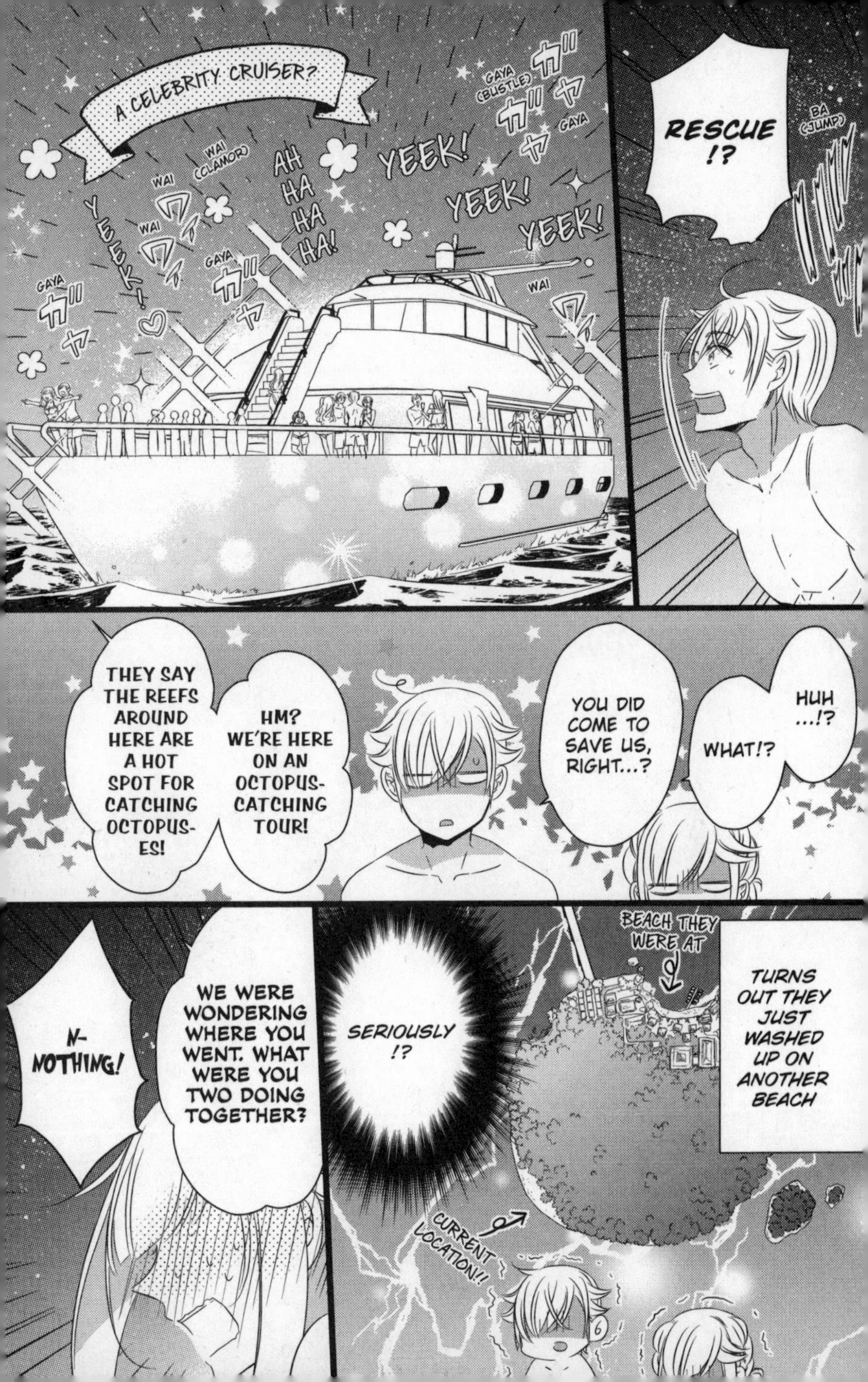

RESCUE !?
BA (JUMP)
A CELEBRITY CRUISER?
GAYA (BUSTLE)
GAYA
YEEK!
YEEK!
YEEK!
AH HA HA HA HA!
WAI (CLAMOR)
WAI
WAI
YEEEK! ♡
GAYA
GAYA
WAI
HUH ...!?
WHAT!?
YOU DID COME TO SAVE US, RIGHT...?
HM? WE'RE HERE ON AN OCTOPUS-CATCHING TOUR!
THEY SAY THE REEFS AROUND HERE ARE A HOT SPOT FOR CATCHING OCTOPUSES!
TURNS OUT THEY JUST WASHED UP ON ANOTHER BEACH
BEACH THEY WERE AT
SERIOUSLY !?
CURRENT LOCATION!!
WE WERE WONDERING WHERE YOU WENT. WHAT WERE YOU TWO DOING TOGETHER?
N-NOTHING!

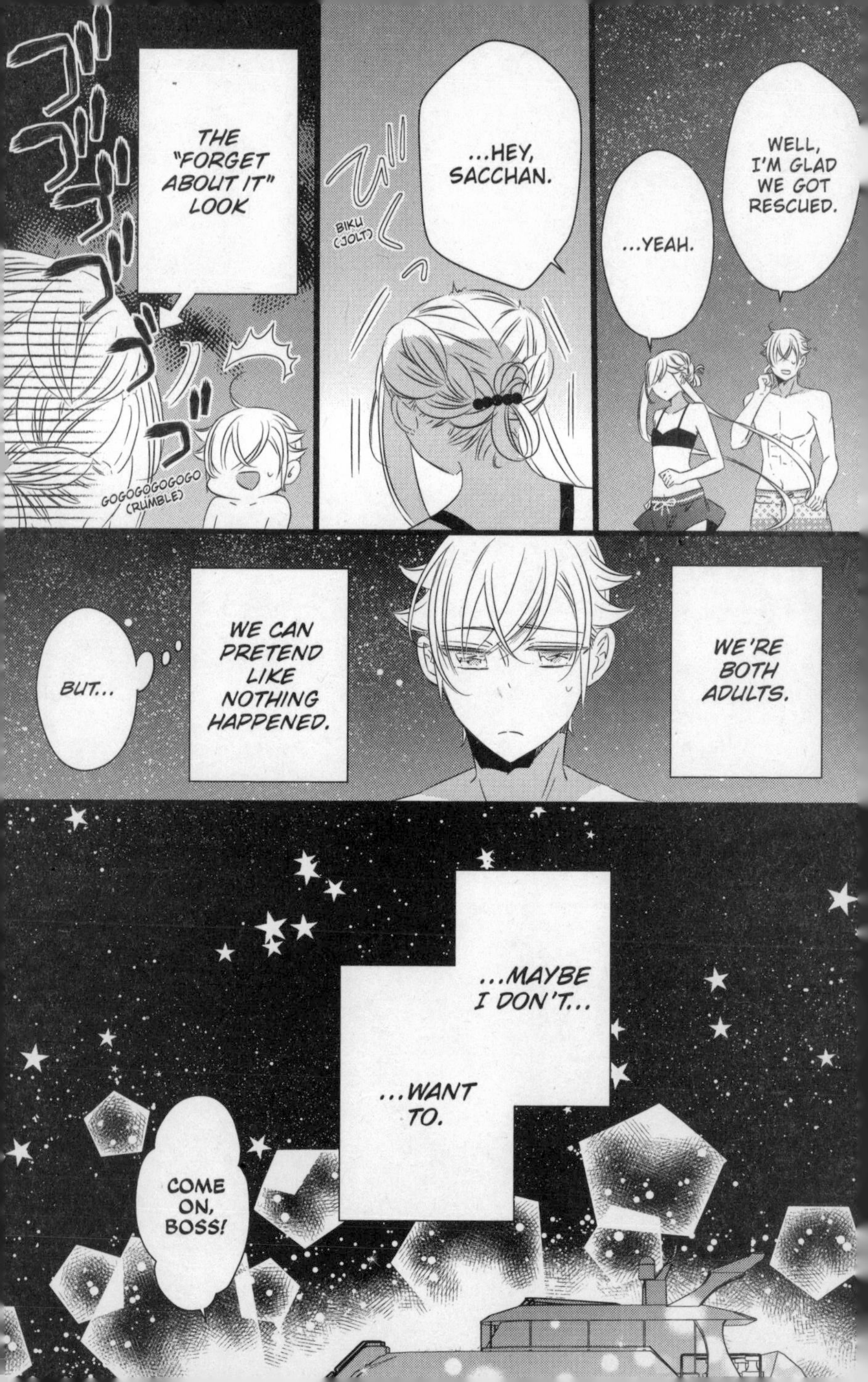
WELL, I'M GLAD WE GOT RESCUED.
...YEAH.
...HEY, SACCHAN.
BIKU (JOLT)
THE "FORGET ABOUT IT" LOOK
GOGOGOGOGOGO (RUMBLE)
WE'RE BOTH ADULTS.
WE CAN PRETEND LIKE NOTHING HAPPENED.
BUT...
...MAYBE I DON'T...
...WANT TO.
COME ON, BOSS!

FOR A WHILE AFTER THAT, EVERY TIME SHE SAW HER SUNBURN...

...HER FACE BURNED RED.

FAINT...

THE MEMO- RIES...

As Miss Beelzebub Likes

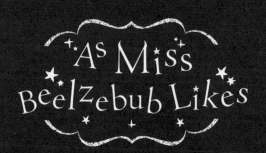

CHAPTER 59

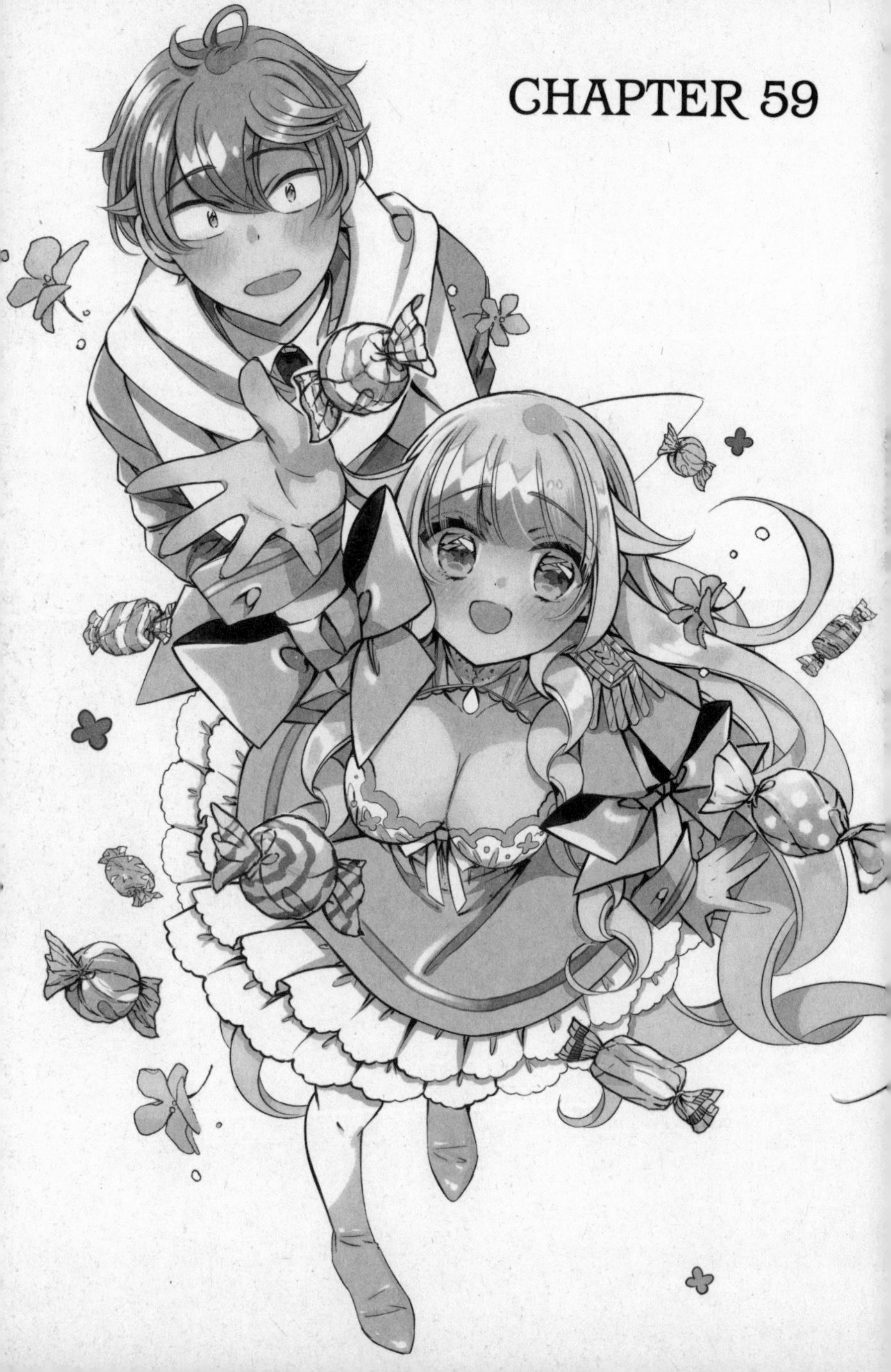

As Miss Beelzebub Likes

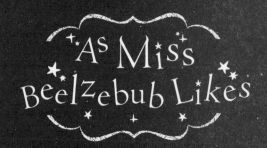

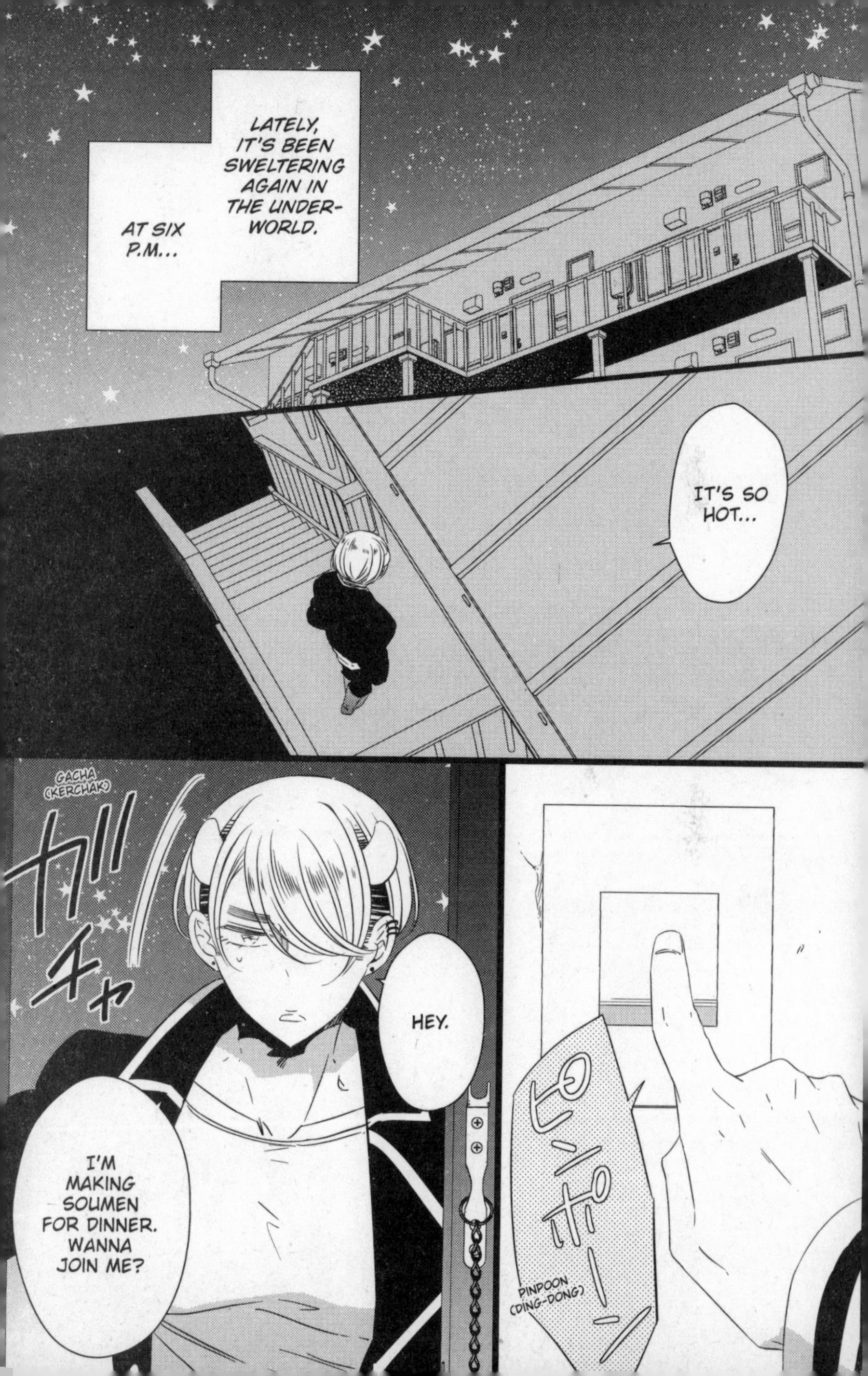
LATELY, IT'S BEEN SWELTERING AGAIN IN THE UNDER-WORLD.
AT SIX P.M...
IT'S SO HOT...
PINPOON (DING-DONG)
GACHA (KERCHAK)
HEY.
I'M MAKING SOUMEN FOR DINNER. WANNA JOIN ME?

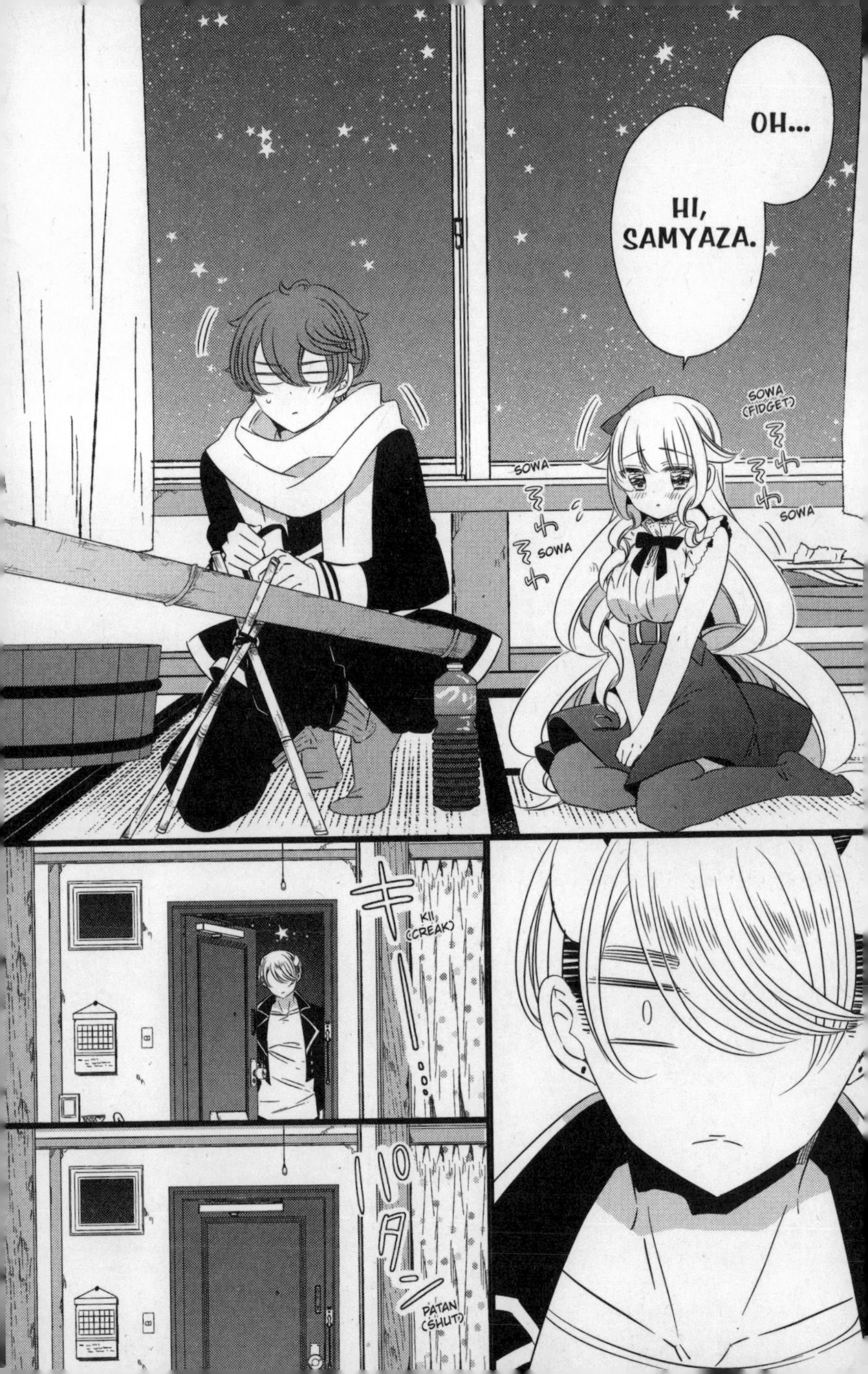
OH...
HI, SAMYAZA.
SOWA (FIDGET)
SOWA
SOWA
SOWA
KII (CREAK)
PATAN (SHUT)

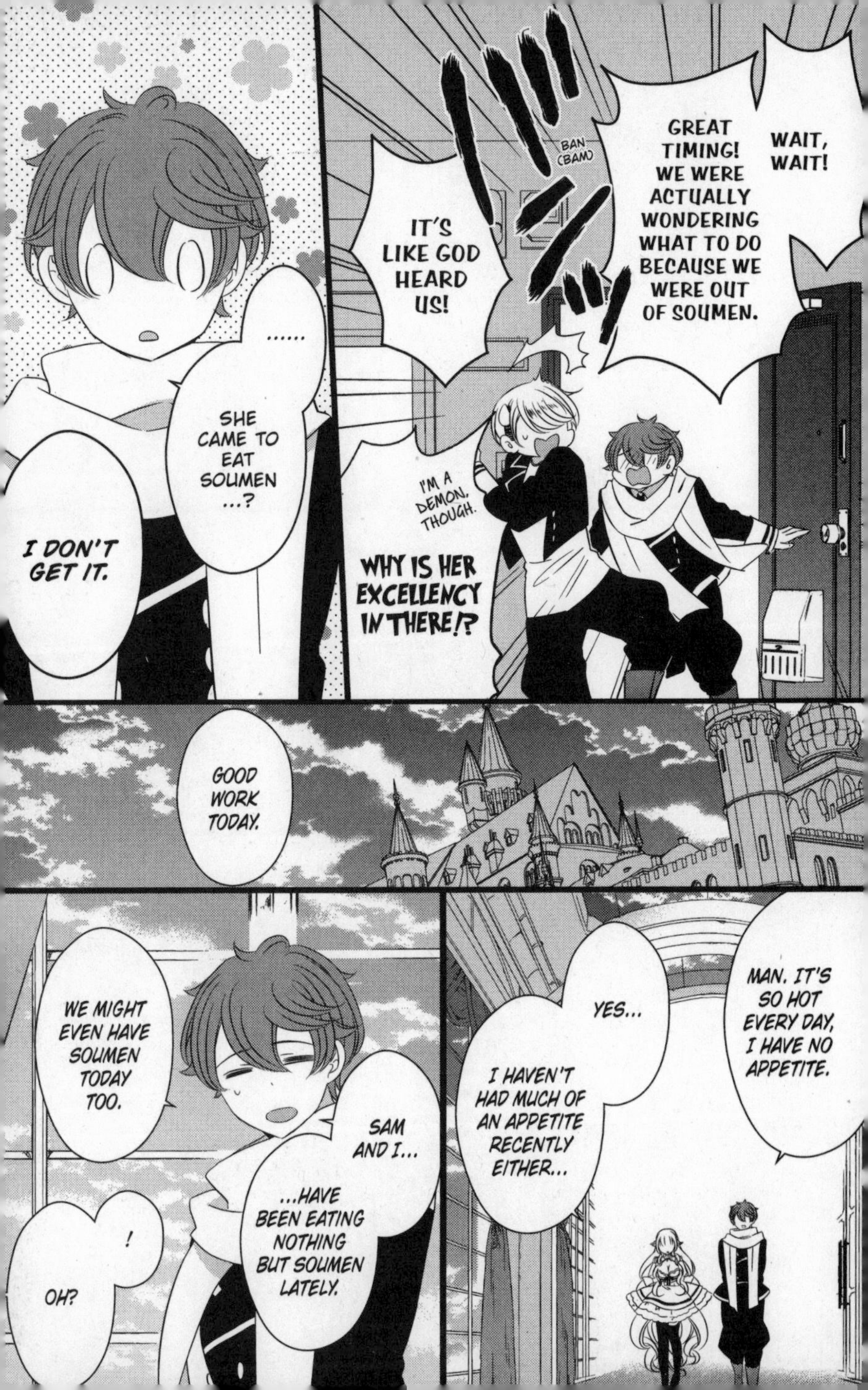
WAIT, WAIT!
GREAT TIMING! WE WERE ACTUALLY WONDERING WHAT TO DO BECAUSE WE WERE OUT OF SOUMEN.
BAN (BAM)
IT'S LIKE GOD HEARD US!
I'M A DEMON, THOUGH.
WHY IS HER EXCELLENCY IN THERE!?
......
SHE CAME TO EAT SOUMEN ...?
I DON'T GET IT.
GOOD WORK TODAY.
MAN. IT'S SO HOT EVERY DAY, I HAVE NO APPETITE.
YES...
I HAVEN'T HAD MUCH OF AN APPETITE RECENTLY EITHER...
SAM AND I...
...HAVE BEEN EATING NOTHING BUT SOUMEN LATELY.
WE MIGHT EVEN HAVE SOUMEN TODAY TOO.
!
OH?

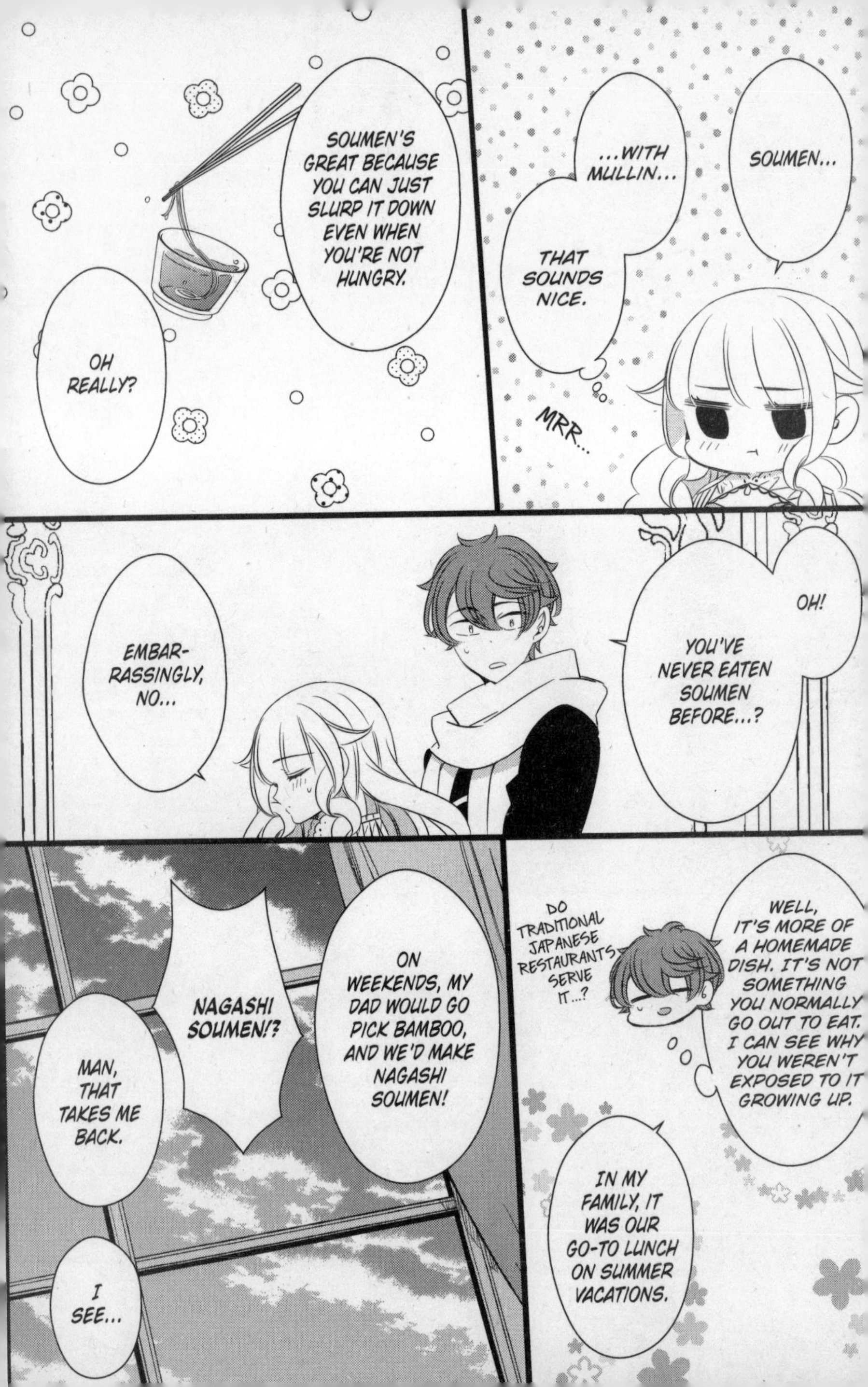
SOUMEN...
...WITH MULLIN... THAT SOUNDS NICE.
MRR...
SOUMEN'S GREAT BECAUSE YOU CAN JUST SLURP IT DOWN EVEN WHEN YOU'RE NOT HUNGRY.
OH REALLY?
OH! YOU'VE NEVER EATEN SOUMEN BEFORE...?
EMBAR-RASSINGLY, NO...
WELL, IT'S MORE OF A HOMEMADE DISH. IT'S NOT SOMETHING YOU NORMALLY GO OUT TO EAT. I CAN SEE WHY YOU WEREN'T EXPOSED TO IT GROWING UP.
DO TRADITIONAL JAPANESE RESTAURANTS SERVE IT...?
IN MY FAMILY, IT WAS OUR GO-TO LUNCH ON SUMMER VACATIONS.
ON WEEKENDS, MY DAD WOULD GO PICK BAMBOO, AND WE'D MAKE NAGASHI SOUMEN!
NAGASHI SOUMEN!?
MAN, THAT TAKES ME BACK.
I SEE...

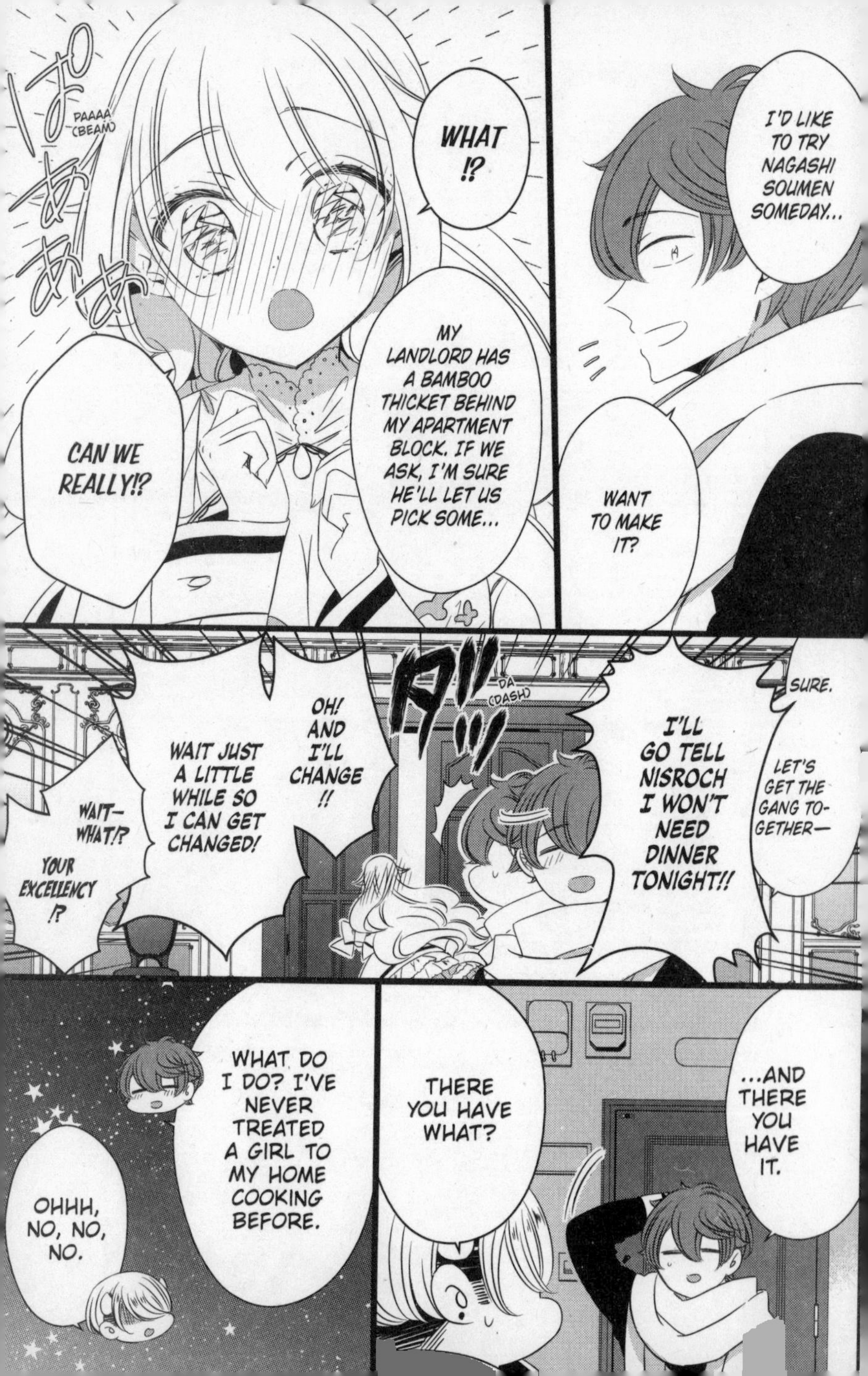
I'D LIKE TO TRY NAGASHI SOUMEN SOMEDAY...
WANT TO MAKE IT?
WHAT!?
MY LANDLORD HAS A BAMBOO THICKET BEHIND MY APARTMENT BLOCK. IF WE ASK, I'M SURE HE'LL LET US PICK SOME...
PAAAA (BEAM)
CAN WE REALLY!?
SURE.
LET'S GET THE GANG TO-GETHER—
I'LL GO TELL NISROCH I WON'T NEED DINNER TONIGHT!!
DA (DASH)
OH! AND I'LL CHANGE!!
WAIT JUST A LITTLE WHILE SO I CAN GET CHANGED!
WAIT—WHAT!?
YOUR EXCELLENCY!?
...AND THERE YOU HAVE IT.
THERE YOU HAVE WHAT?
WHAT DO I DO? I'VE NEVER TREATED A GIRL TO MY HOME COOKING BEFORE.
OHHH, NO, NO, NO.

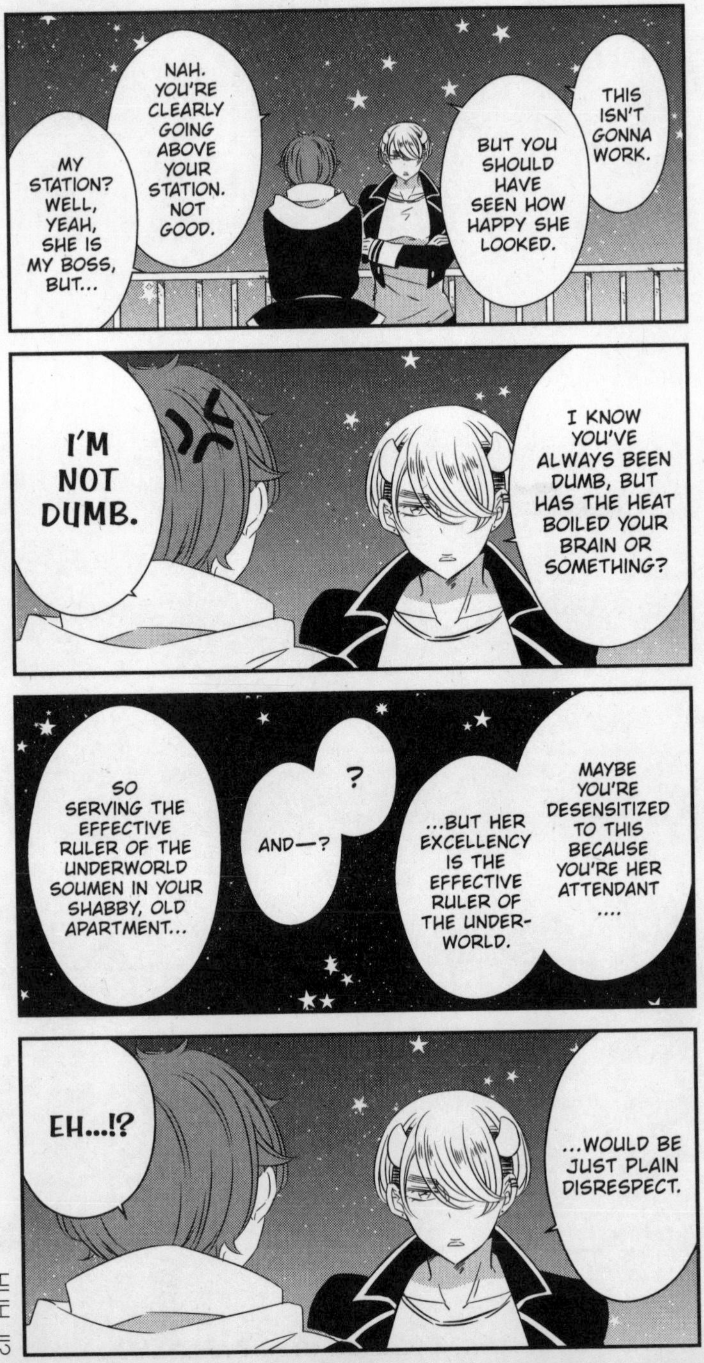
THIS ISN'T GONNA WORK.
BUT YOU SHOULD HAVE SEEN HOW HAPPY SHE LOOKED.
NAH. YOU'RE CLEARLY GOING ABOVE YOUR STATION. NOT GOOD.
MY STATION? WELL, YEAH, SHE IS MY BOSS, BUT...
I KNOW YOU'VE ALWAYS BEEN DUMB, BUT HAS THE HEAT BOILED YOUR BRAIN OR SOMETHING?
I'M NOT DUMB.
MAYBE YOU'RE DESENSITIZED TO THIS BECAUSE YOU'RE HER ATTENDANT....
...BUT HER EXCELLENCY IS THE EFFECTIVE RULER OF THE UNDER-WORLD.
?
AND—?
SO SERVING THE EFFECTIVE RULER OF THE UNDERWORLD SOUMEN IN YOUR SHABBY, OLD APARTMENT...
...WOULD BE JUST PLAIN DISRESPECT.
EH...!?
HUH...!?

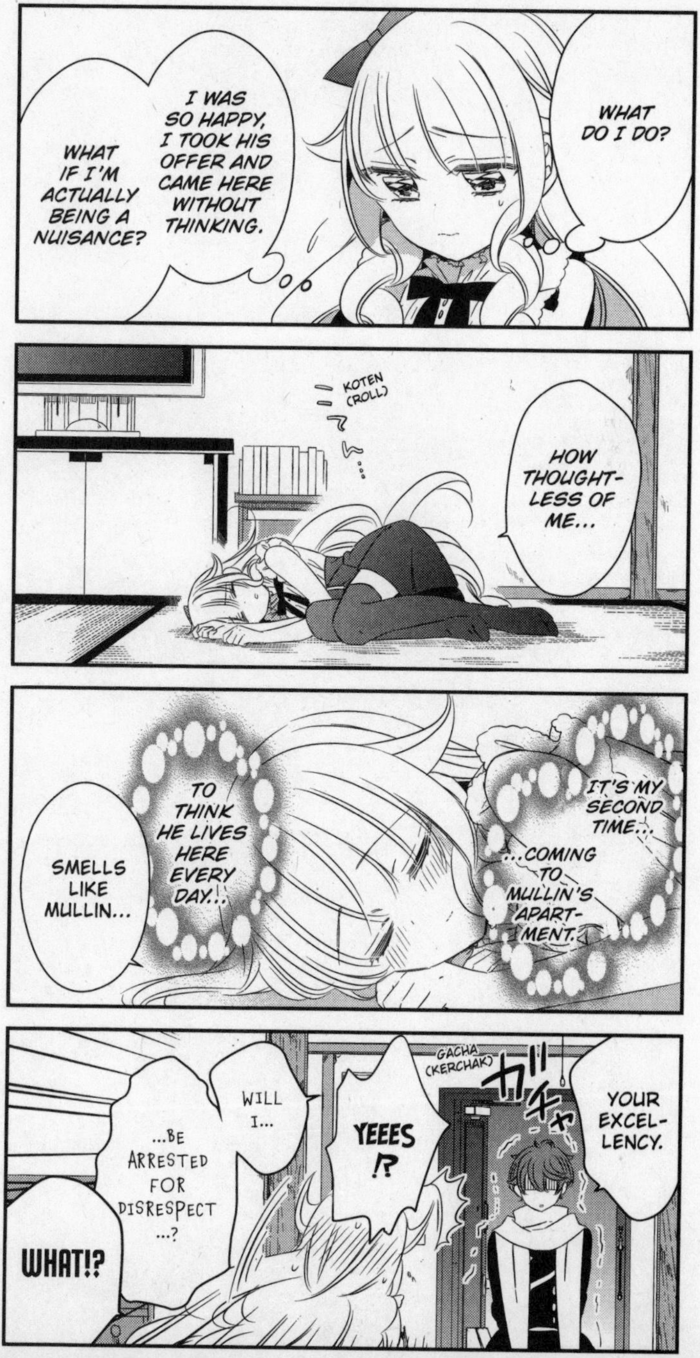
WHAT DO I DO?
I WAS SO HAPPY, I TOOK HIS OFFER AND CAME HERE WITHOUT THINKING.
WHAT IF I'M ACTUALLY BEING A NUISANCE?
HOW THOUGHT-LESS OF ME...
KOTEN (ROLL)
IT'S MY SECOND TIME...
...COMING TO MULLIN'S APART-MENT.
TO THINK HE LIVES HERE EVERY DAY...
SMELLS LIKE MULLIN...
YOUR EXCEL-LENCY.
GACHA (KERCHAK)
YEEES!?
WILL I...
...BE ARRESTED FOR DISRESPECT...?
WHAT!?

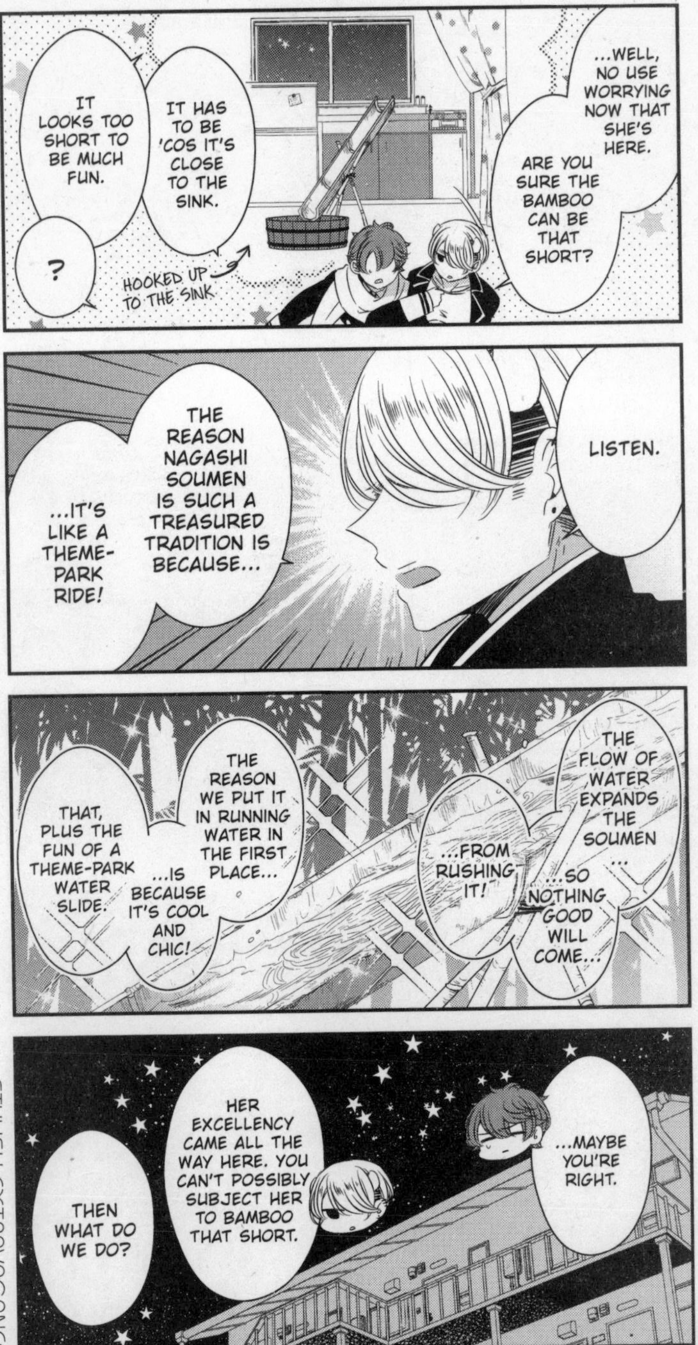

...WELL, NO USE WORRYING NOW THAT SHE'S HERE.
ARE YOU SURE THE BAMBOO CAN BE THAT SHORT?
IT HAS TO BE 'COS IT'S CLOSE TO THE SINK.
HOOKED UP TO THE SINK
IT LOOKS TOO SHORT TO BE MUCH FUN.
?
LISTEN.
THE REASON NAGASHI SOUMEN IS SUCH A TREASURED TRADITION IS BECAUSE...
...IT'S LIKE A THEME-PARK RIDE!
THE FLOW OF WATER EXPANDS THE SOUMEN...
...SO NOTHING GOOD WILL COME...
...FROM RUSHING IT!
THE REASON WE PUT IT IN RUNNING WATER IN THE FIRST PLACE...
...IS BECAUSE IT'S COOL AND CHIC!
THAT, PLUS THE FUN OF A THEME-PARK WATER SLIDE.
...MAYBE YOU'RE RIGHT.
HER EXCELLENCY CAME ALL THE WAY HERE. YOU CAN'T POSSIBLY SUBJECT HER TO BAMBOO THAT SHORT.
THEN WHAT DO WE DO?

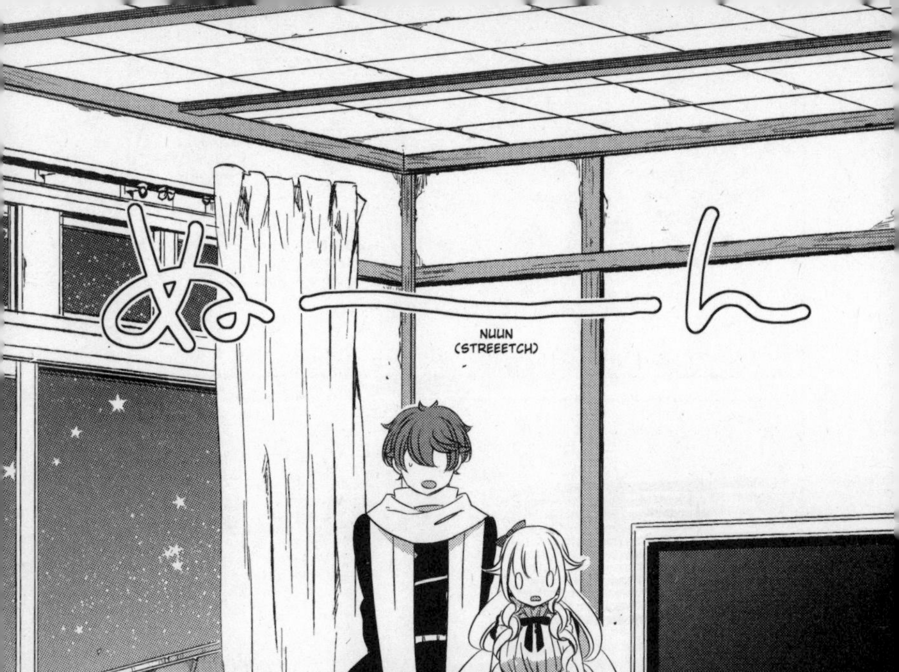
ぬーん
NUUN
(STREEETCH)

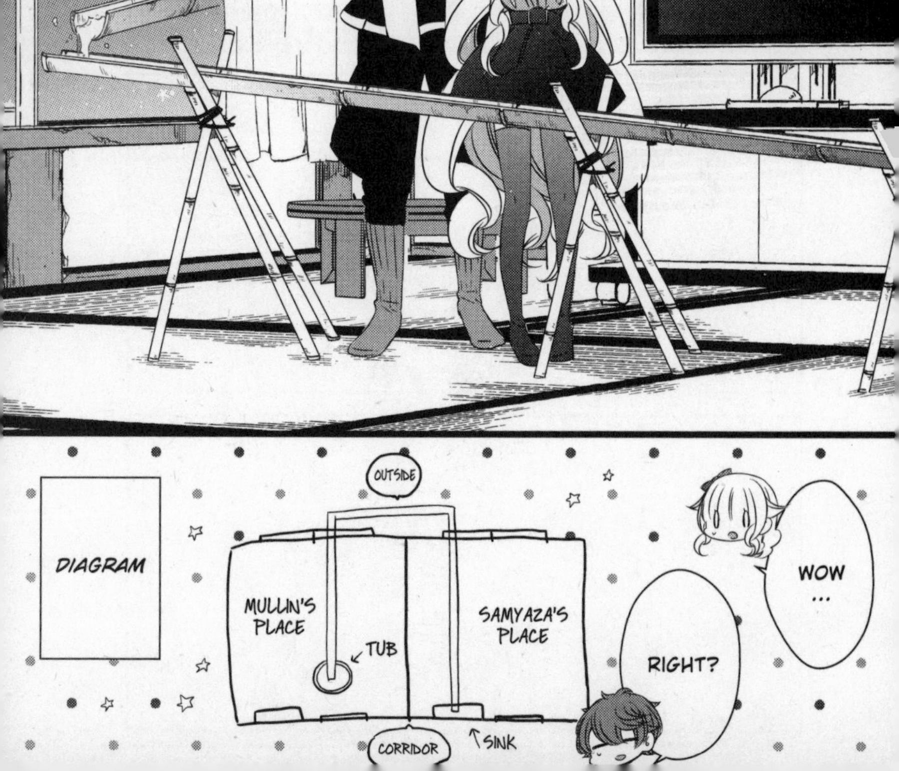
WOW...
RIGHT?
OUTSIDE
DIAGRAM
SAMYAZA'S PLACE
MULLIN'S PLACE
TUB
SINK
CORRIDOR

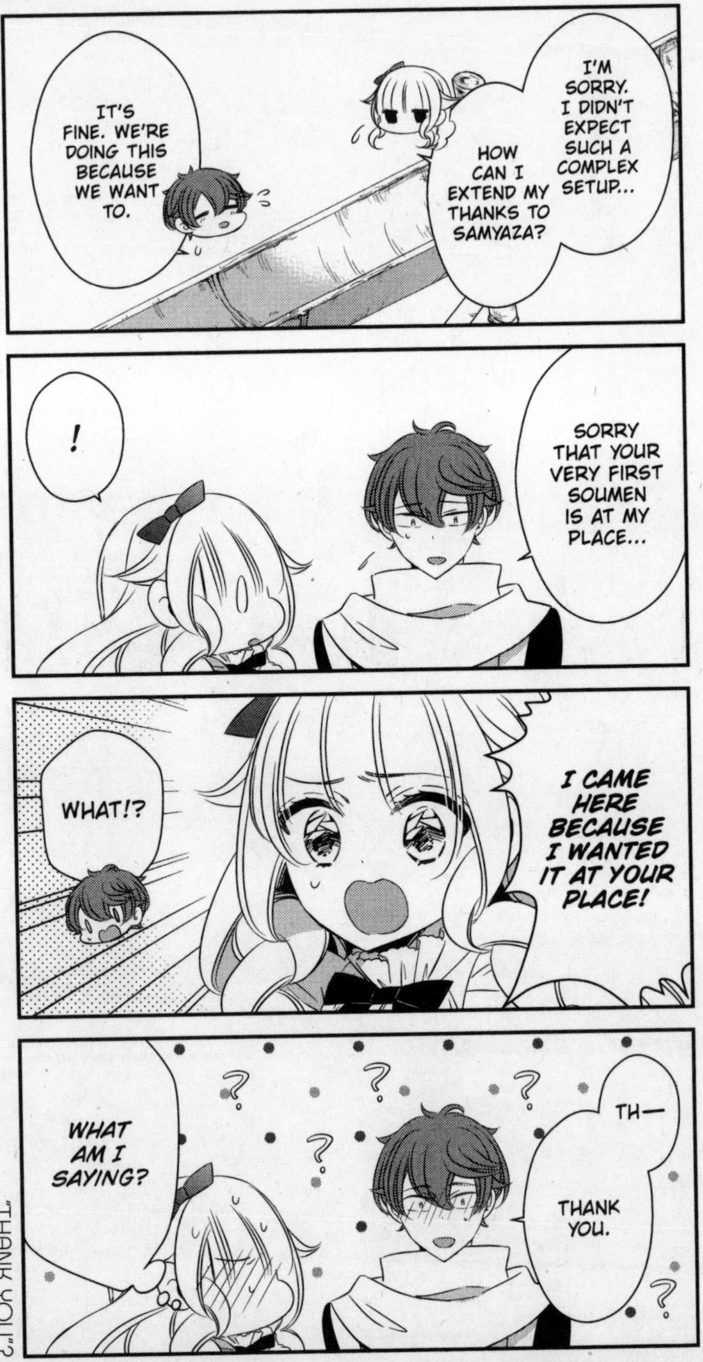
I'M SORRY. I DIDN'T EXPECT SUCH A COMPLEX SETUP...
HOW CAN I EXTEND MY THANKS TO SAMYAZA?
IT'S FINE. WE'RE DOING THIS BECAUSE WE WANT TO.
SORRY THAT YOUR VERY FIRST SOUMEN IS AT MY PLACE...
!
I CAME HERE BECAUSE I WANTED IT AT YOUR PLACE!
WHAT!?
TH—
THANK YOU.
?
WHAT AM I SAYING?

"THANK YOU"?

THIN WALLS

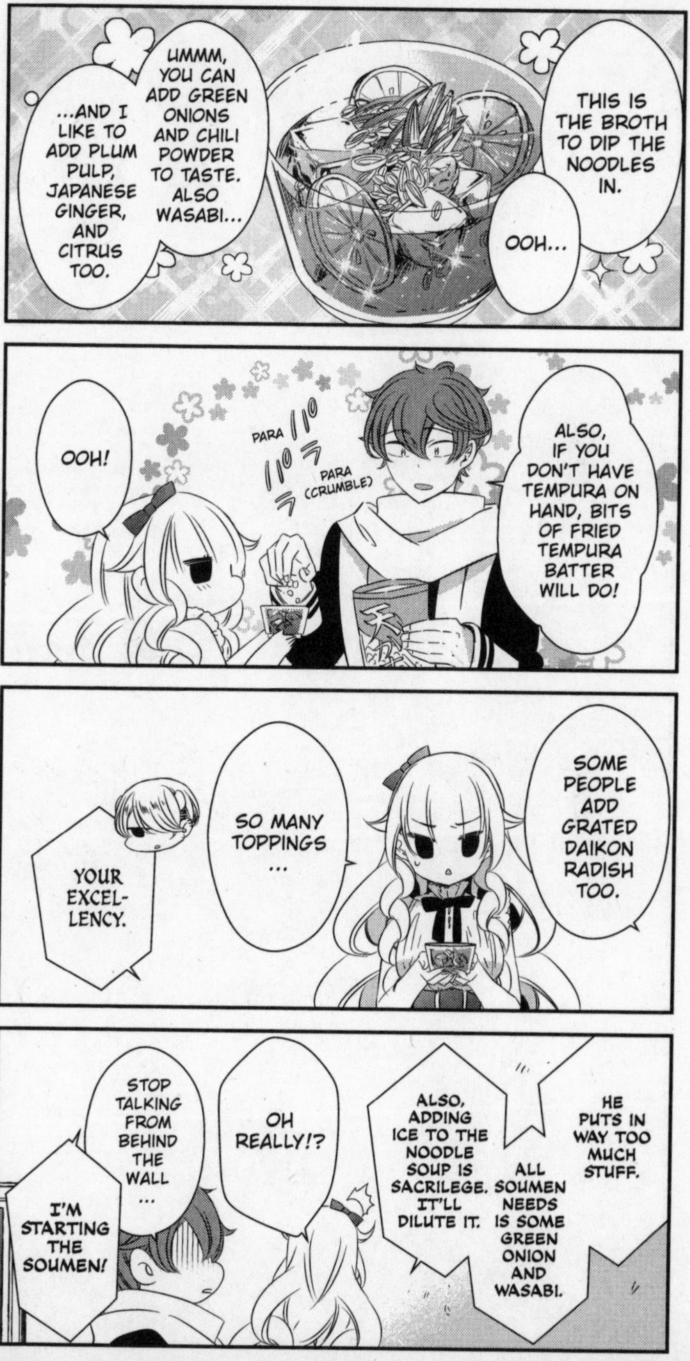
THIS IS THE BROTH TO DIP THE NOODLES IN.
OOH...
UMMM, YOU CAN ADD GREEN ONIONS AND CHILI POWDER TO TASTE. ALSO WASABI...
...AND I LIKE TO ADD PLUM PULP, JAPANESE GINGER, AND CITRUS TOO.
ALSO, IF YOU DON'T HAVE TEMPURA ON HAND, BITS OF FRIED TEMPURA BATTER WILL DO!
パラ
PARA
パラ
PARA (CRUMBLE)
OOH!
SOME PEOPLE ADD GRATED DAIKON RADISH TOO.
SO MANY TOPPINGS ...
YOUR EXCEL-LENCY.
HE PUTS IN WAY TOO MUCH STUFF.
ALSO, ADDING ICE TO THE NOODLE SOUP IS SACRILEGE. IT'LL DILUTE IT.
ALL SOUMEN NEEDS IS SOME GREEN ONION AND WASABI.
OH REALLY!?
STOP TALKING FROM BEHIND THE WALL ...
I'M STARTING THE SOUMEN!

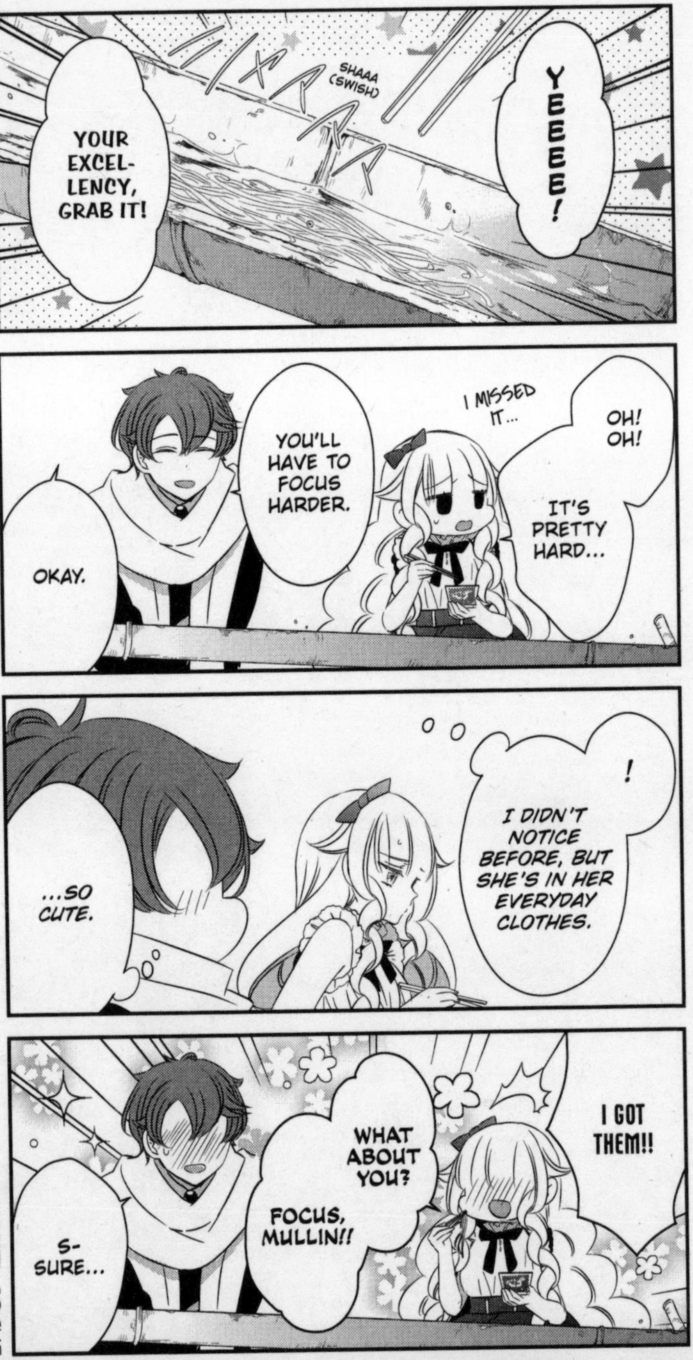
YEEEE!
SHAAA (SWISH)
YOUR EXCEL-LENCY, GRAB IT!
OH! OH!
IT'S PRETTY HARD...
I MISSED IT...
YOU'LL HAVE TO FOCUS HARDER.
OKAY.
!
I DIDN'T NOTICE BEFORE, BUT SHE'S IN HER EVERYDAY CLOTHES.
...SO CUTE.
I GOT THEM!!
WHAT ABOUT YOU?
FOCUS, MULLIN!!
S-SURE...

(CAN'T) FOCUS

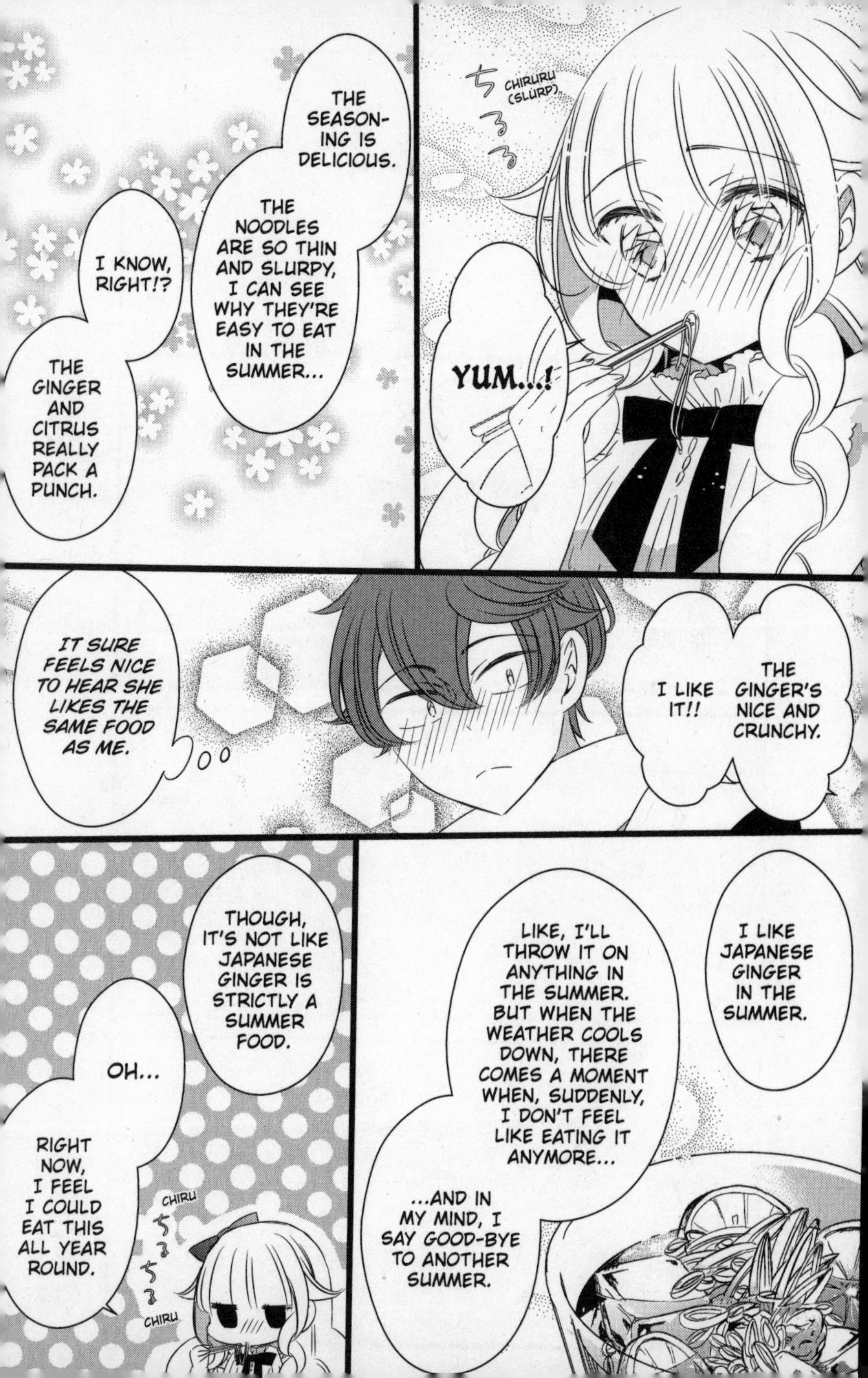
CHIRURU (SLURP)
YUM...!
THE SEASON-ING IS DELICIOUS.
THE NOODLES ARE SO THIN AND SLURPY, I CAN SEE WHY THEY'RE EASY TO EAT IN THE SUMMER...
I KNOW, RIGHT!?
THE GINGER AND CITRUS REALLY PACK A PUNCH.
THE GINGER'S NICE AND CRUNCHY.
I LIKE IT!!
IT SURE FEELS NICE TO HEAR SHE LIKES THE SAME FOOD AS ME.
I LIKE JAPANESE GINGER IN THE SUMMER.
LIKE, I'LL THROW IT ON ANYTHING IN THE SUMMER. BUT WHEN THE WEATHER COOLS DOWN, THERE COMES A MOMENT WHEN, SUDDENLY, I DON'T FEEL LIKE EATING IT ANYMORE...
...AND IN MY MIND, I SAY GOOD-BYE TO ANOTHER SUMMER.
THOUGH, IT'S NOT LIKE JAPANESE GINGER IS STRICTLY A SUMMER FOOD.
OH...
RIGHT NOW, I FEEL I COULD EAT THIS ALL YEAR ROUND.
CHIRU
CHIRU

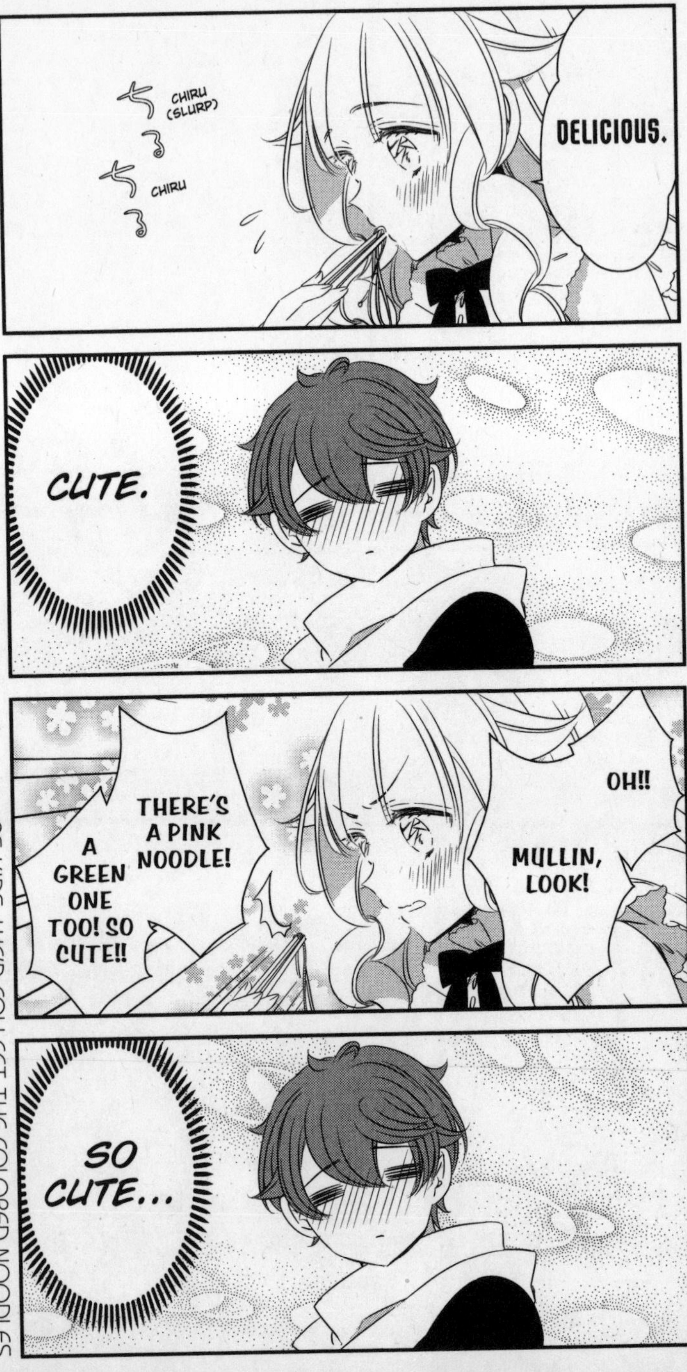
DELICIOUS.
ち CHIRU (SLURP)
る
ち CHIRU
る
CUTE.
OH!!
MULLIN, LOOK!
THERE'S A PINK NOODLE!
A GREEN ONE TOO! SO CUTE!!
SO CUTE...

AS KIDS, WE'D COLLECT THE COLORED NOODLES

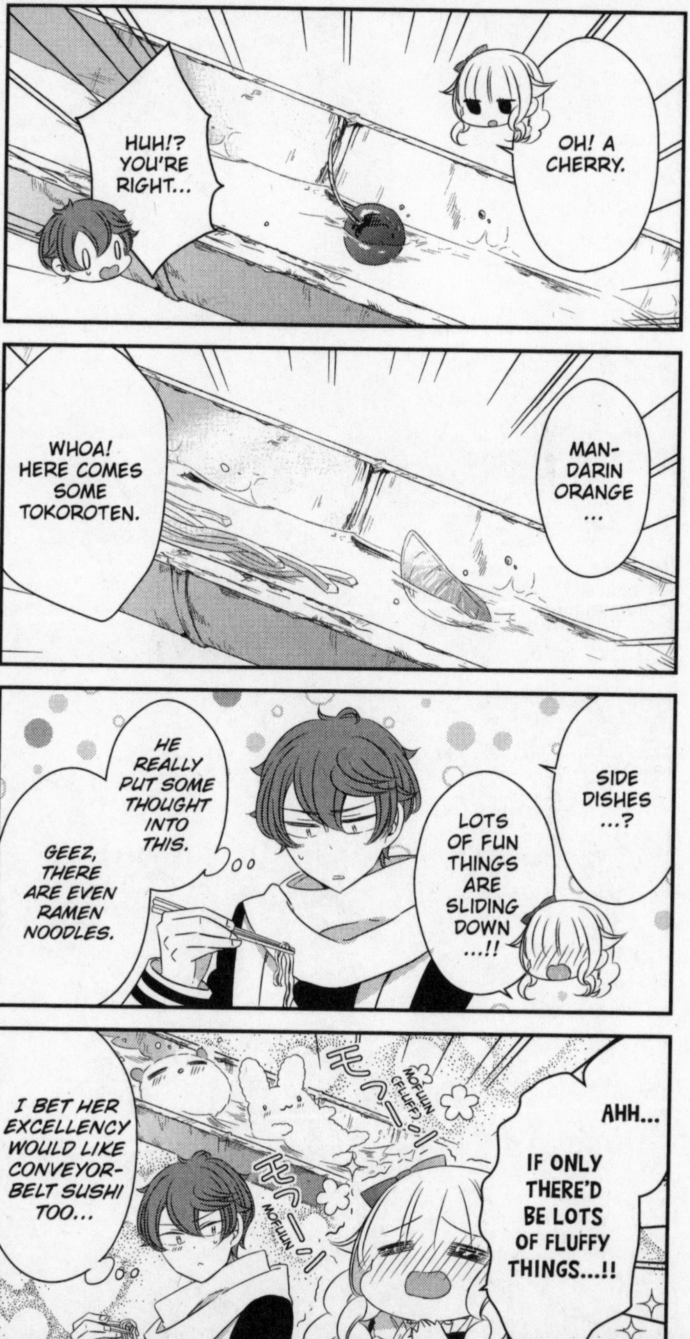
OH! A CHERRY.
HUH!? YOU'RE RIGHT...
MAN-DARIN ORANGE...
WHOA! HERE COMES SOME TOKOROTEN.
SIDE DISHES...?
LOTS OF FUN THINGS ARE SLIDING DOWN...!!
HE REALLY PUT SOME THOUGHT INTO THIS.
GEEZ, THERE ARE EVEN RAMEN NOODLES.
AHH...
IF ONLY THERE'D BE LOTS OF FLUFFY THINGS...!!
MOFUUN (FLUFF)
MOFUUN
I BET HER EXCELLENCY WOULD LIKE CONVEYOR-BELT SUSHI TOO...

EATING WITH SOMEONE SPECIAL

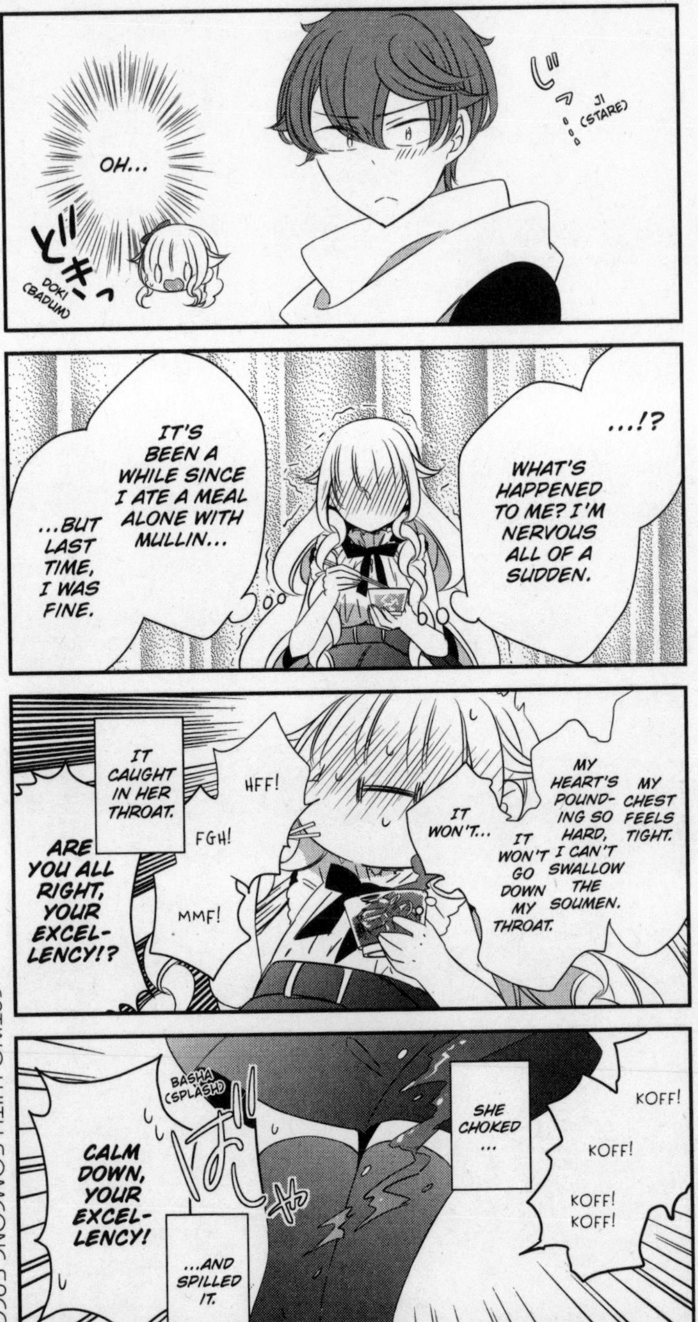

JI (STARE)
OH...
DOKI (BADUM)
...!? WHAT'S HAPPENED TO ME? I'M NERVOUS ALL OF A SUDDEN.
IT'S BEEN A WHILE SINCE I ATE A MEAL ALONE WITH MULLIN...
...BUT LAST TIME, I WAS FINE.
MY CHEST FEELS TIGHT.
MY HEART'S POUNDING SO HARD, I CAN'T SWALLOW THE SOUMEN.
IT WON'T GO DOWN MY THROAT.
IT WON'T...
HFF!
FGH!
MMF!
IT CAUGHT IN HER THROAT.
ARE YOU ALL RIGHT, YOUR EXCELLENCY!?
KOFF!
KOFF!
KOFF! KOFF!
SHE CHOKED...
BASHA (SPLASH)
...AND SPILLED IT.
CALM DOWN, YOUR EXCELLENCY!

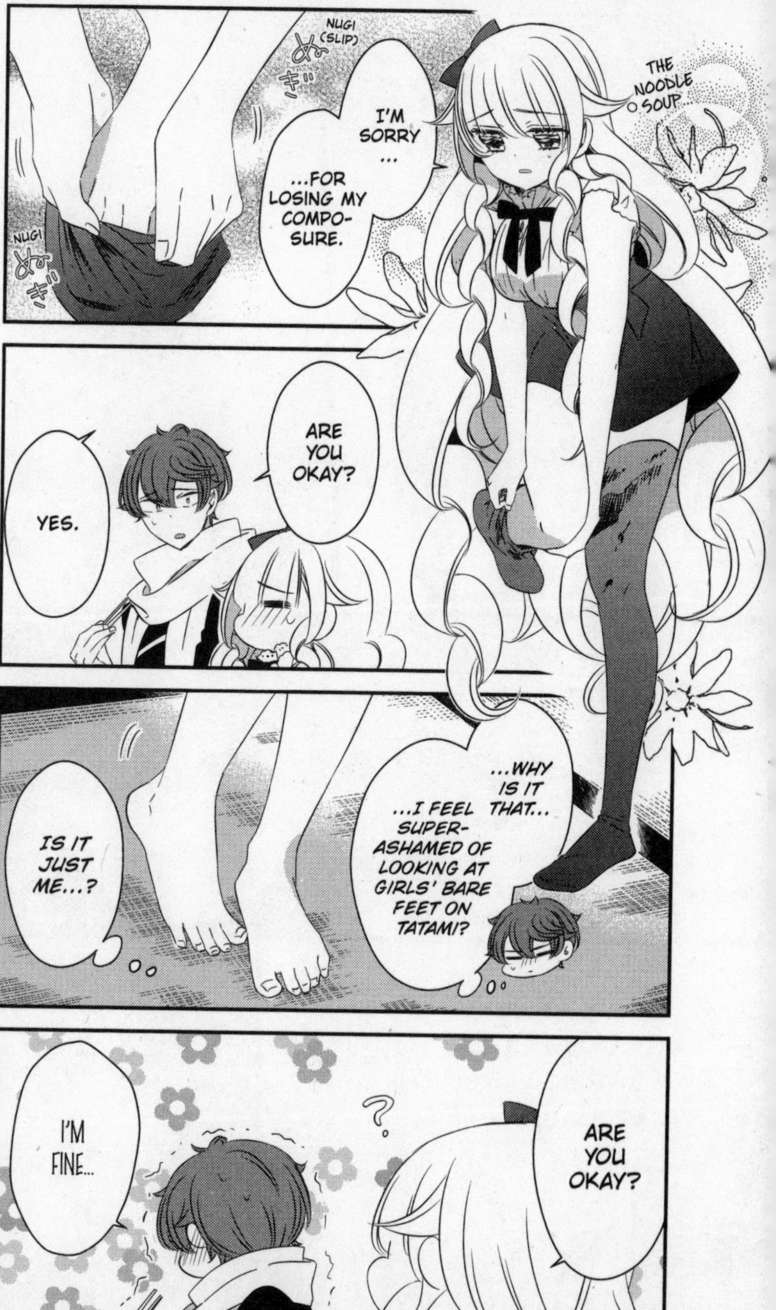
THE NOODLE SOUP
I'M SORRY...
...FOR LOSING MY COMPOSURE.
NUGI (SLIP)
NUGI
ARE YOU OKAY?
YES.
...WHY IS IT THAT...
...I FEEL SUPER-ASHAMED OF LOOKING AT GIRLS' BARE FEET ON TATAMI?
IS IT JUST ME...?
ARE YOU OKAY?
I'M FINE...

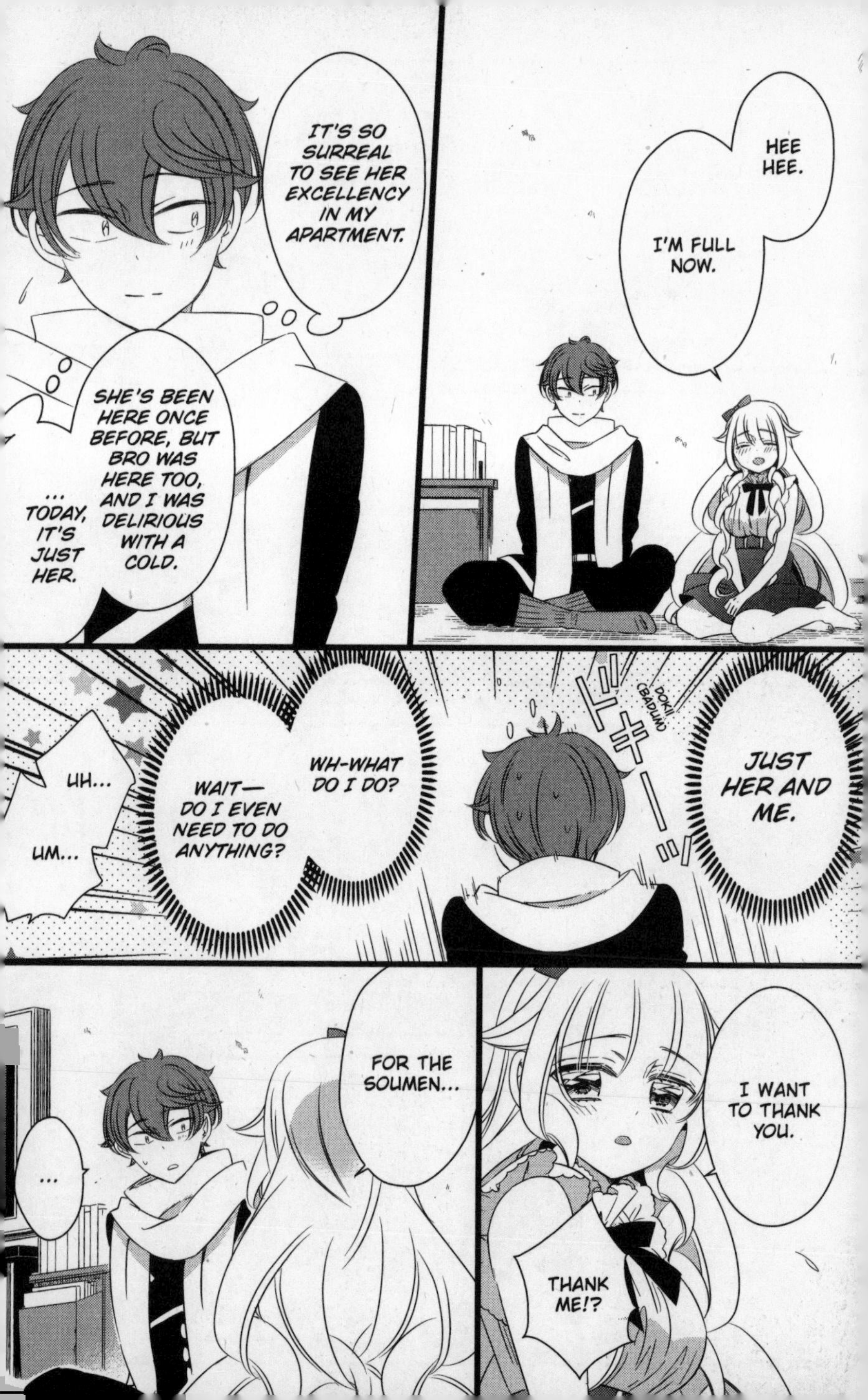
HEE HEE.
I'M FULL NOW.
IT'S SO SURREAL TO SEE HER EXCELLENCY IN MY APARTMENT.
SHE'S BEEN HERE ONCE BEFORE, BUT BRO WAS HERE TOO, AND I WAS DELIRIOUS WITH A COLD.
... TODAY, IT'S JUST HER.
JUST HER AND ME.
DOKI! (BADUM)
WH-WHAT DO I DO?
WAIT— DO I EVEN NEED TO DO ANYTHING?
UH...
UM...
I WANT TO THANK YOU.
THANK ME!?
FOR THE SOUMEN...
...

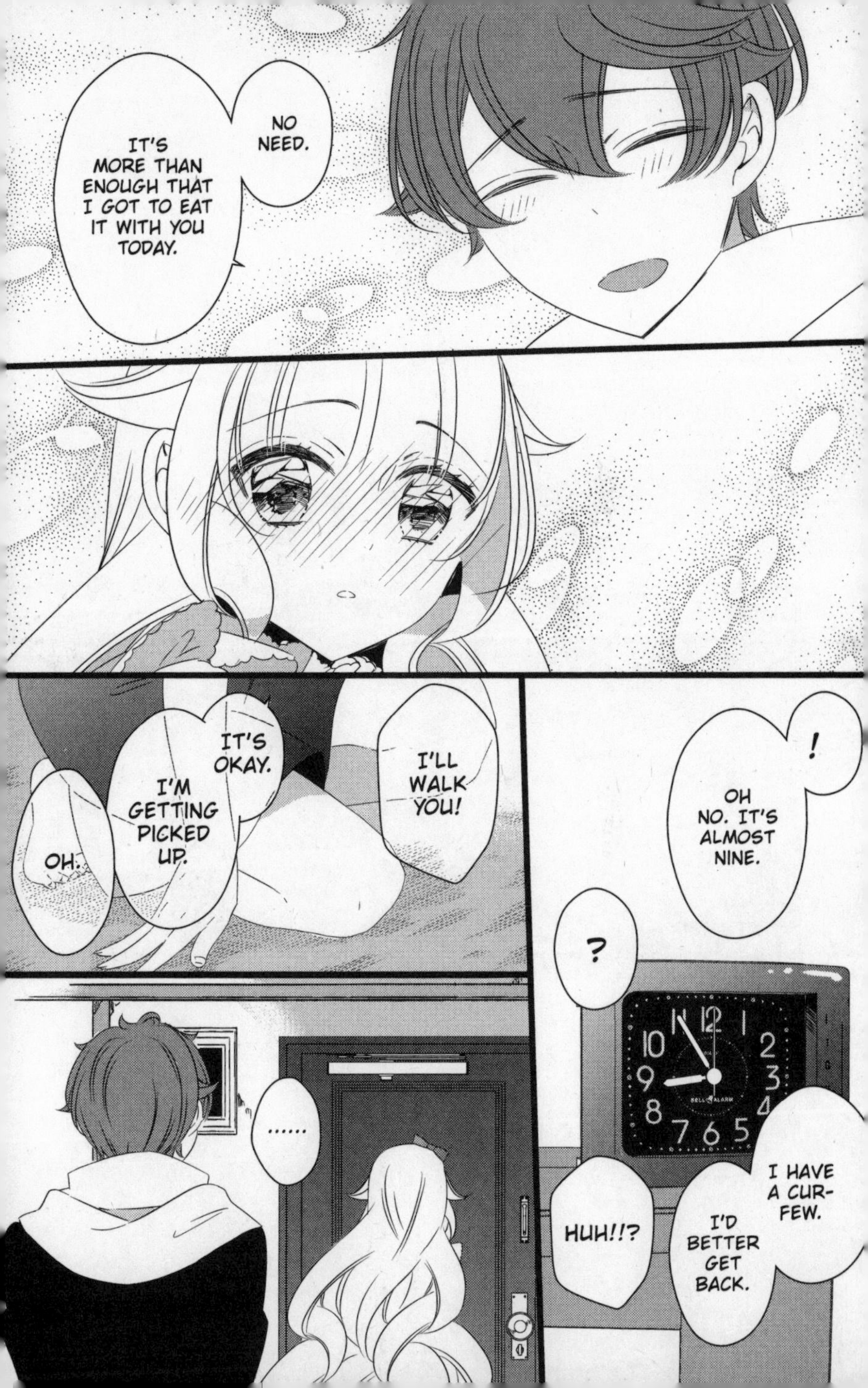
NO NEED.
IT'S MORE THAN ENOUGH THAT I GOT TO EAT IT WITH YOU TODAY.
!
OH NO. IT'S ALMOST NINE.
?
I HAVE A CUR-FEW.
I'D BETTER GET BACK.
HUH!!?
......
I'LL WALK YOU!
IT'S OKAY.
I'M GETTING PICKED UP.
OH...

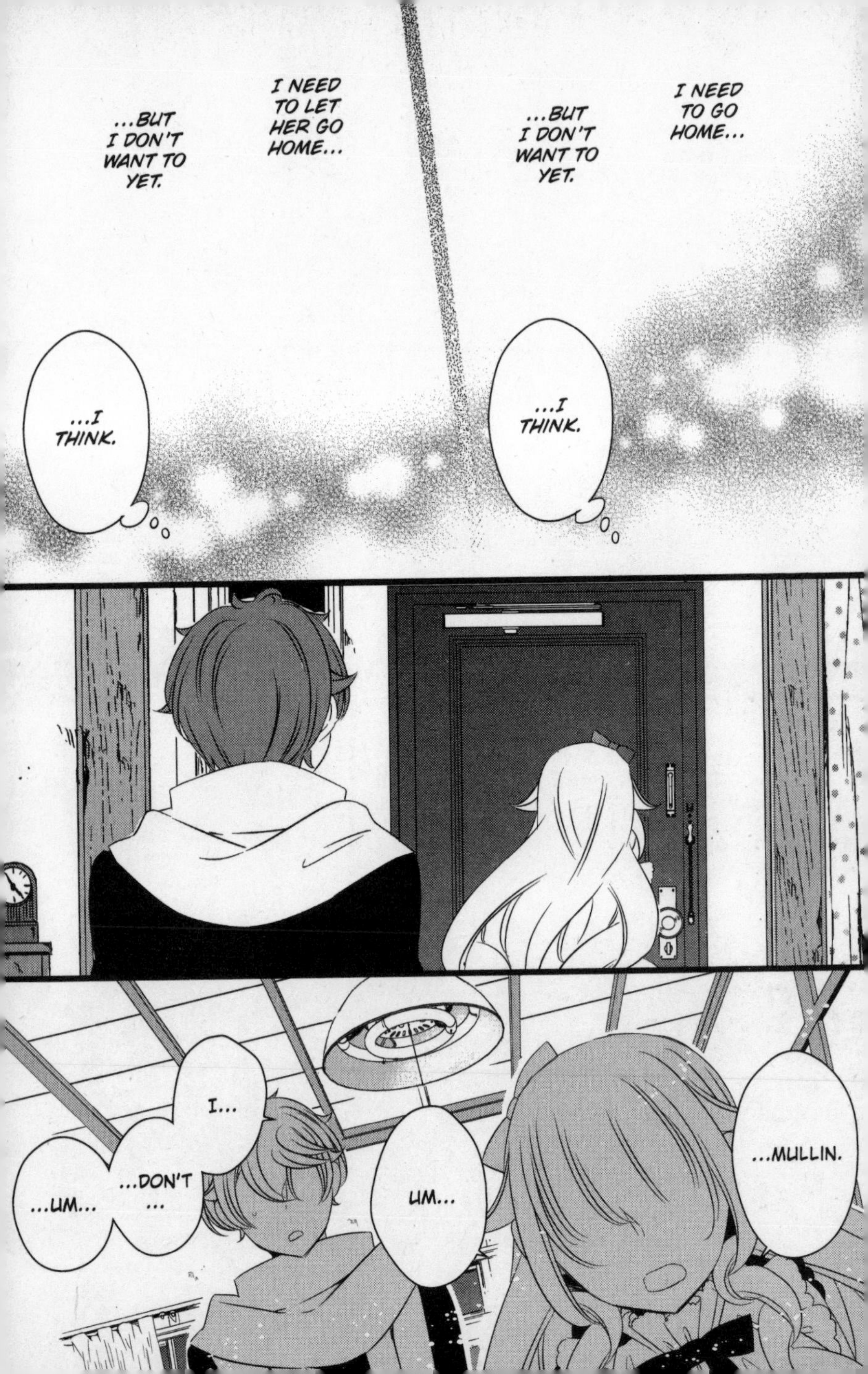
I NEED TO GO HOME...
...BUT I DON'T WANT TO YET.
...I THINK.
I NEED TO LET HER GO HOME...
...BUT I DON'T WANT TO YET.
...I THINK.
...MULLIN.
UM...
I...
...DON'T ...
...UM...

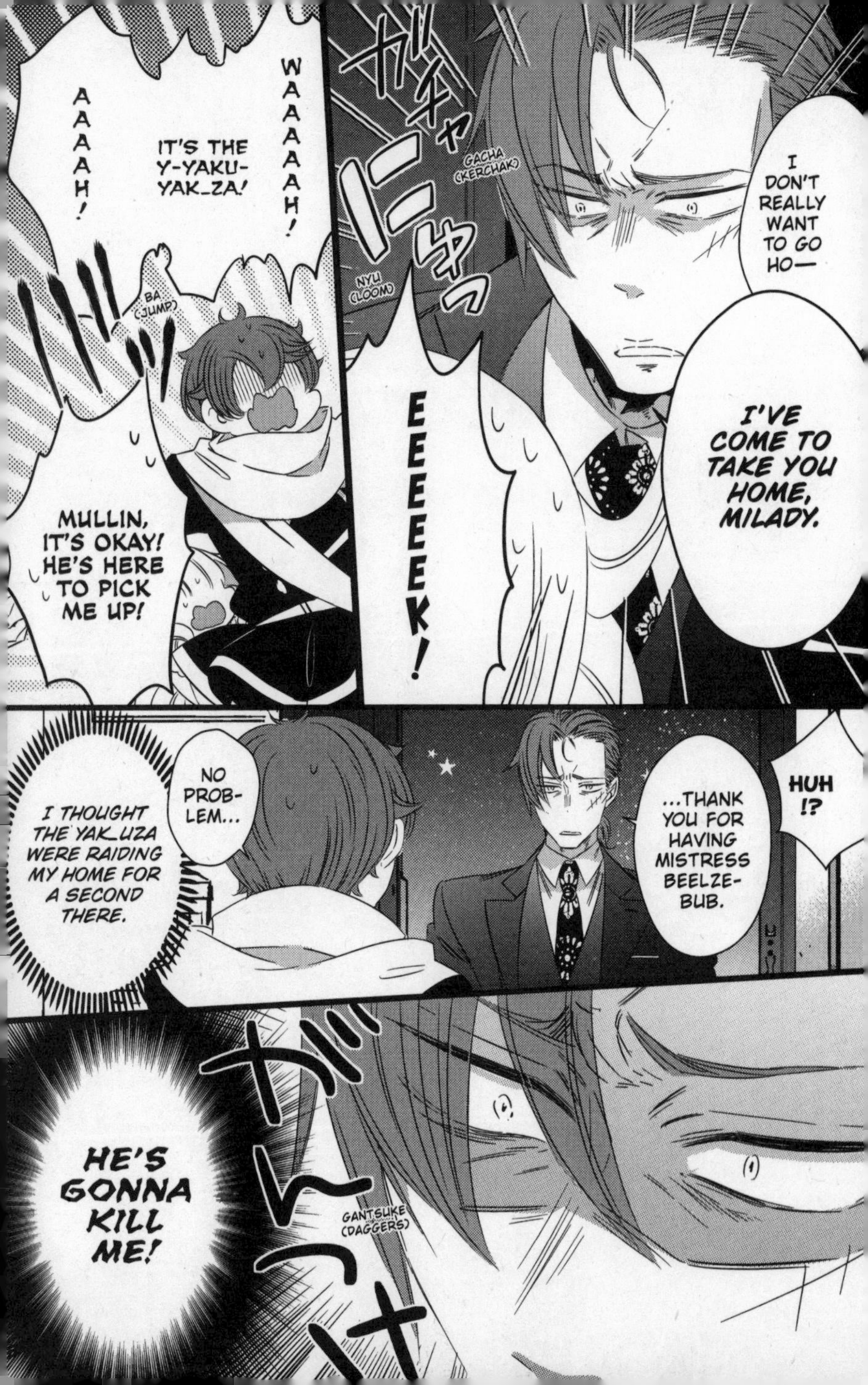

I DON'T REALLY WANT TO GO HO—
GACHA (KERCHAK)
I'VE COME TO TAKE YOU HOME, MILADY.
NYU (LOOM)
EEEEEEEK!
WAAAAAAAH!
IT'S THE Y-YAKU-YAK_ZA!
AAAAAH!
BA (JUMP)
MULLIN, IT'S OKAY! HE'S HERE TO PICK ME UP!
HUH!?
...THANK YOU FOR HAVING MISTRESS BEELZE-BUB.
NO PROB-LEM...
I THOUGHT THE YAK_UZA WERE RAIDING MY HOME FOR A SECOND THERE.
GANTSUKE (DAGGERS)
HE'S GONNA KILL ME!

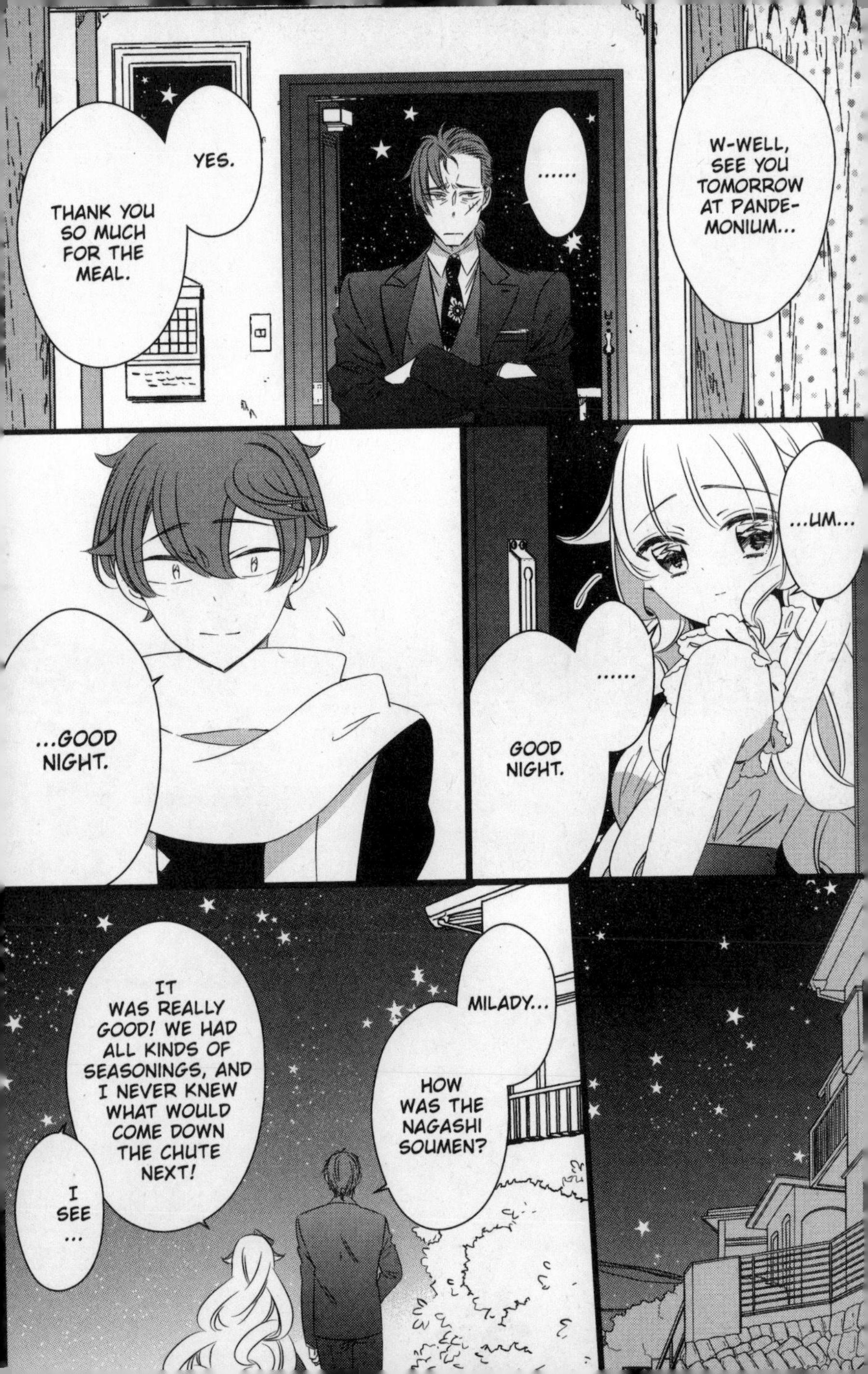
W-WELL, SEE YOU TOMORROW AT PANDE-MONIUM...
......
YES.
THANK YOU SO MUCH FOR THE MEAL.
...UM...
......
GOOD NIGHT.
...GOOD NIGHT.
MILADY...
HOW WAS THE NAGASHI SOUMEN?
IT WAS REALLY GOOD! WE HAD ALL KINDS OF SEASONINGS, AND I NEVER KNEW WHAT WOULD COME DOWN THE CHUTE NEXT!
I SEE ...

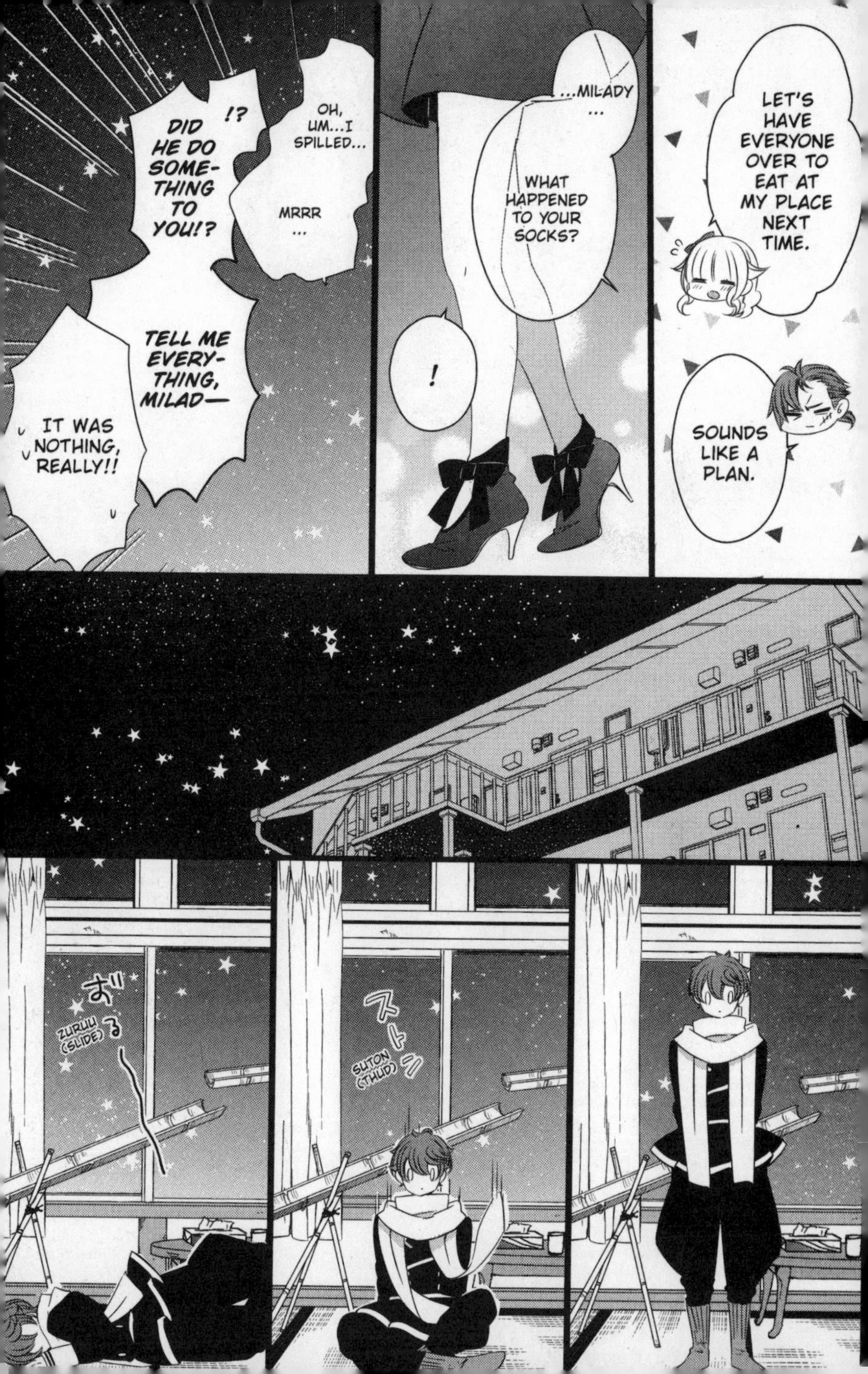
LET'S HAVE EVERYONE OVER TO EAT AT MY PLACE NEXT TIME.
SOUNDS LIKE A PLAN.
...MILADY...
WHAT HAPPENED TO YOUR SOCKS?
!
OH, UM...I SPILLED...
MRRR...
!?
DID HE DO SOME-THING TO YOU!?
TELL ME EVERY-THING, MILAD—
IT WAS NOTHING, REALLY!!
ストン
SUTON (THUD)
ずる
ZURUU (SLIDE)

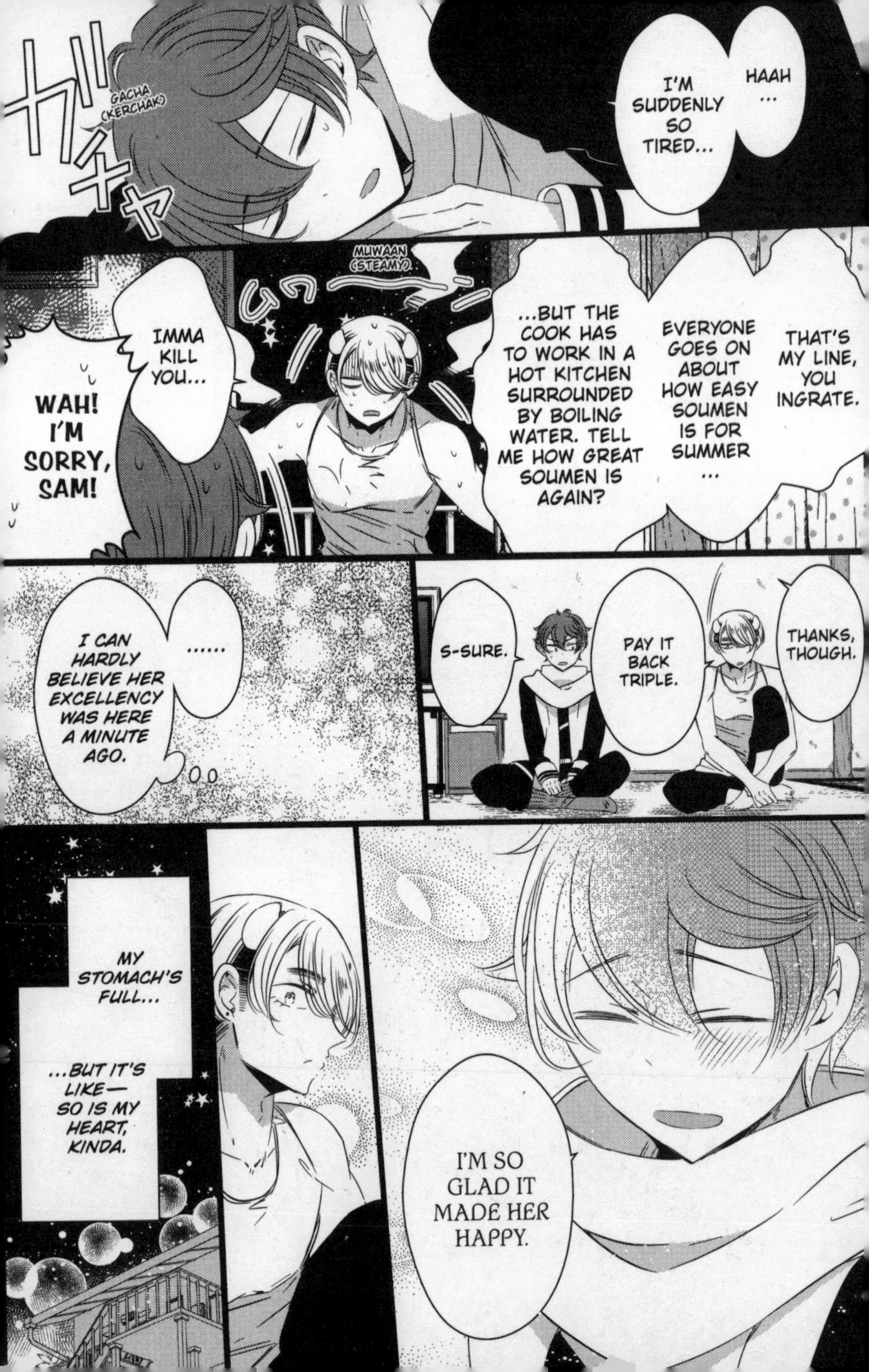
HAAH ...
I'M SUDDENLY SO TIRED...
GACHA (KERCHAK)
THAT'S MY LINE, YOU INGRATE.
EVERYONE GOES ON ABOUT HOW EASY SOUMEN IS FOR SUMMER ...
...BUT THE COOK HAS TO WORK IN A HOT KITCHEN SURROUNDED BY BOILING WATER. TELL ME HOW GREAT SOUMEN IS AGAIN?
MUWAAN (STEAMY)
IMMA KILL YOU...
WAH! I'M SORRY, SAM!
THANKS, THOUGH.
PAY IT BACK TRIPLE.
S-SURE.
......
I CAN HARDLY BELIEVE HER EXCELLENCY WAS HERE A MINUTE AGO.
I'M SO GLAD IT MADE HER HAPPY.
MY STOMACH'S FULL...
...BUT IT'S LIKE— SO IS MY HEART, KINDA.

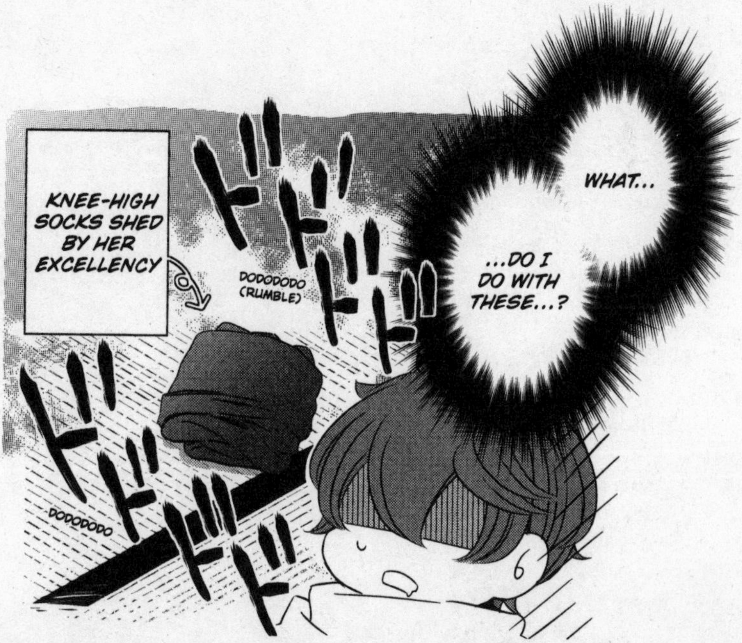
WHAT...
...DO I DO WITH THESE...?
DODODODO (RUMBLE)
KNEE-HIGH SOCKS SHED BY HER EXCELLENCY
DODODODO

As Miss Beelzebub Likes

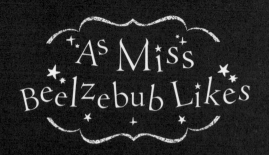

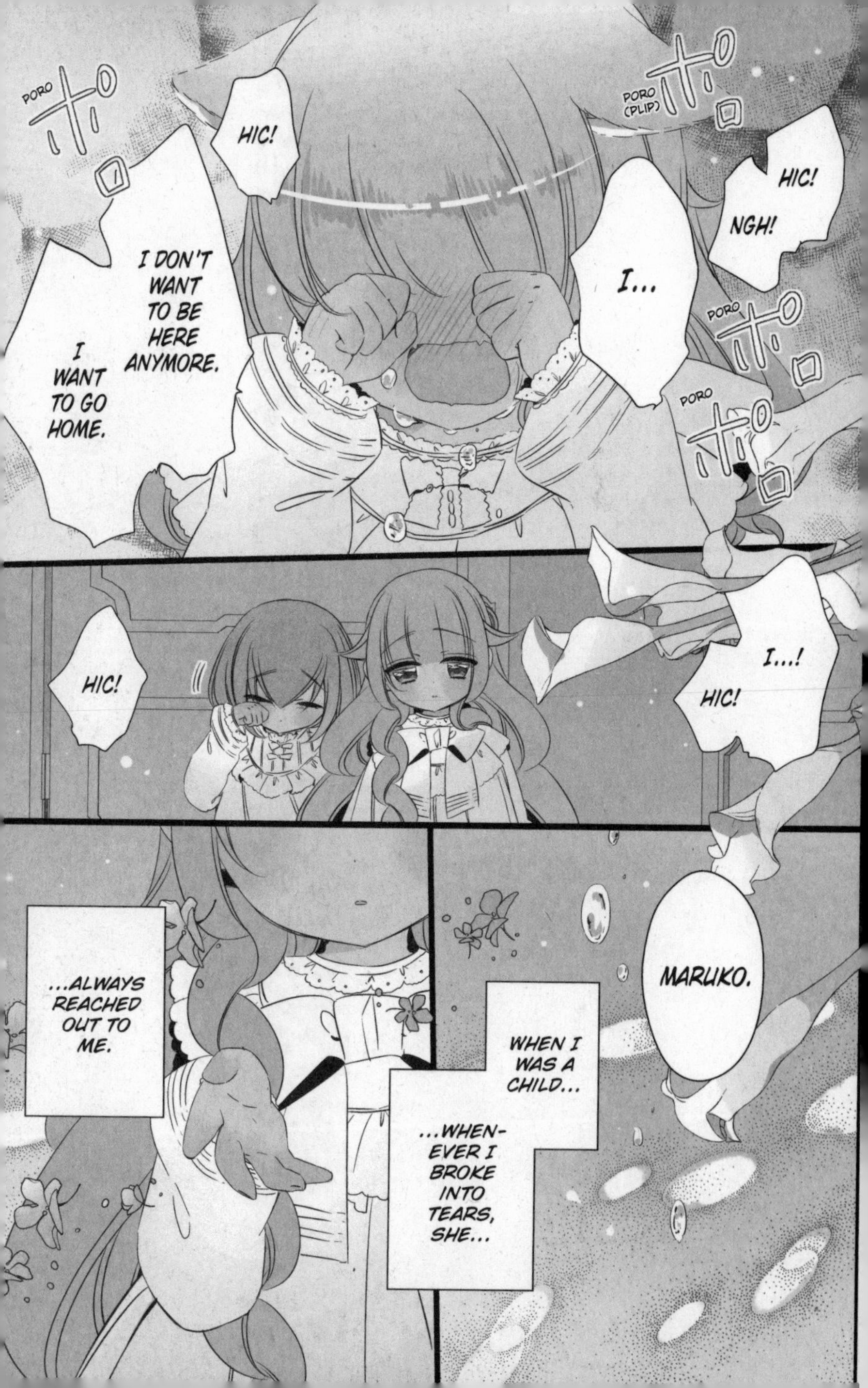
PORO (PLIP)
ポロ
HIC!
NGH!
I...
PORO
ポロ
PORO
ポロ
HIC!
PORO
ポロ
I DON'T WANT TO BE HERE ANYMORE.
I WANT TO GO HOME.
I...!
HIC!
HIC!
MARUKO.
WHEN I WAS A CHILD...
...WHENEVER I BROKE INTO TEARS, SHE...
...ALWAYS REACHED OUT TO ME.

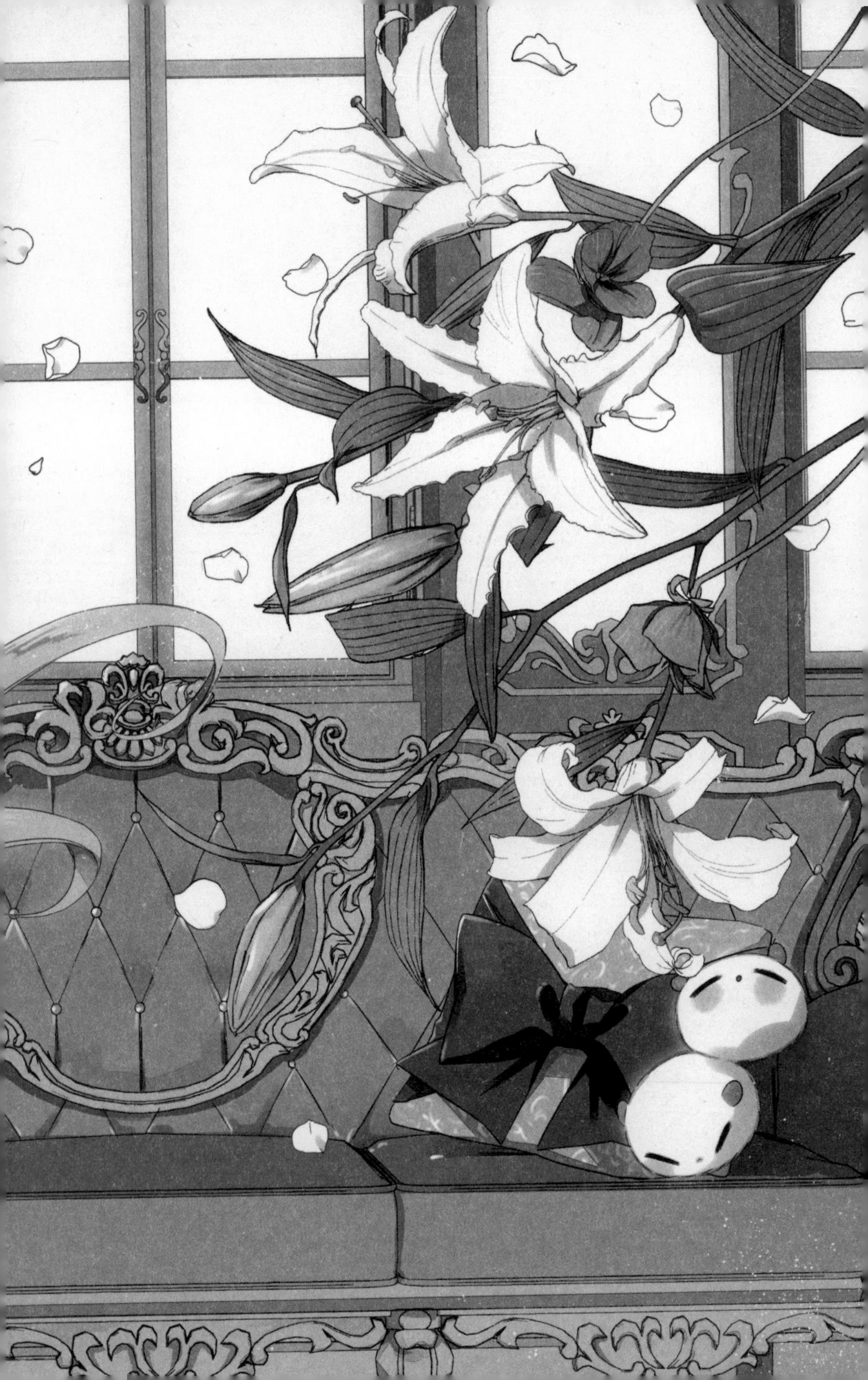

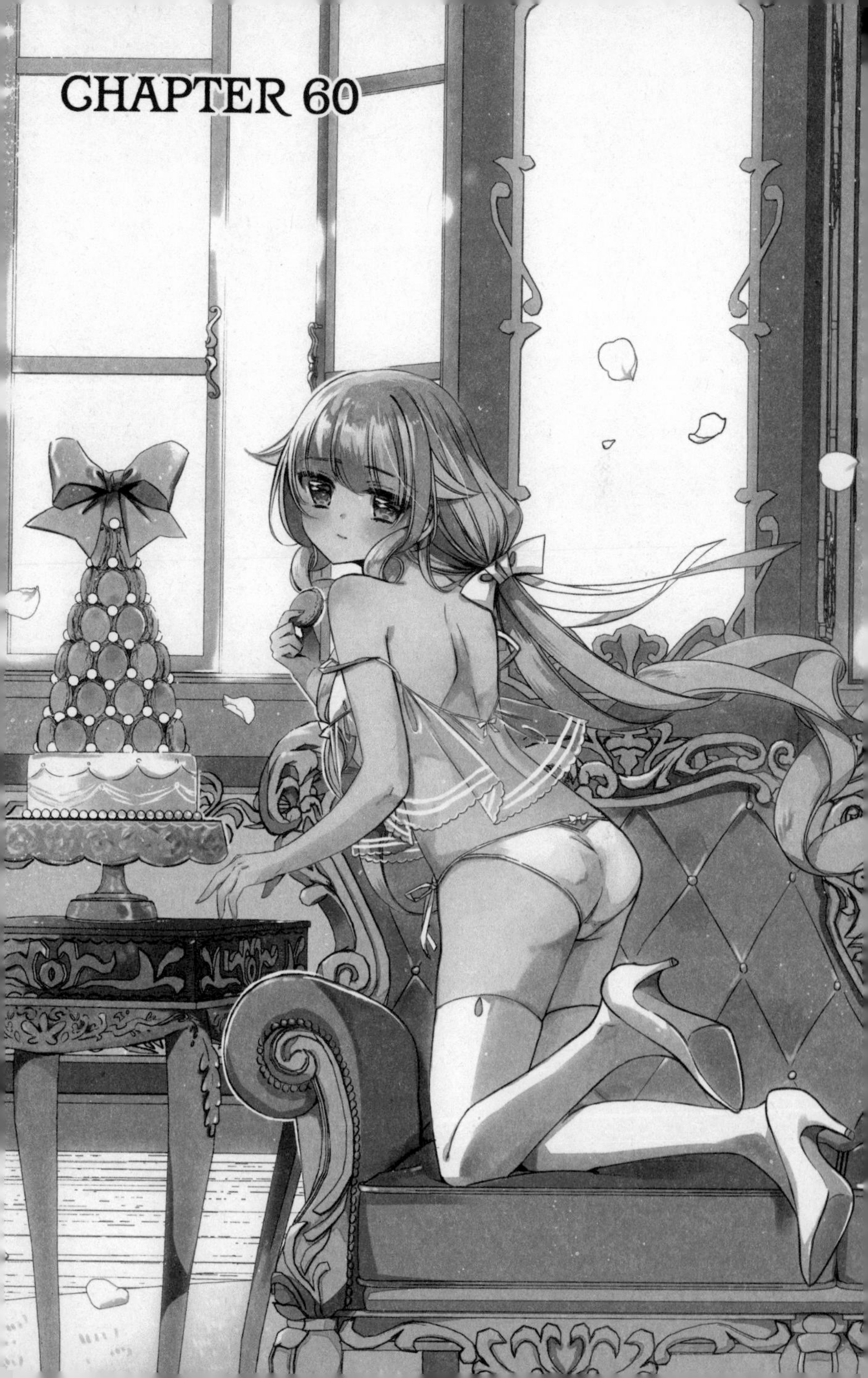
CHAPTER 60

As Miss Beelzebub Likes

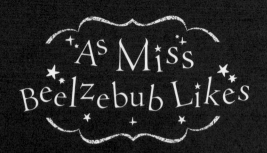

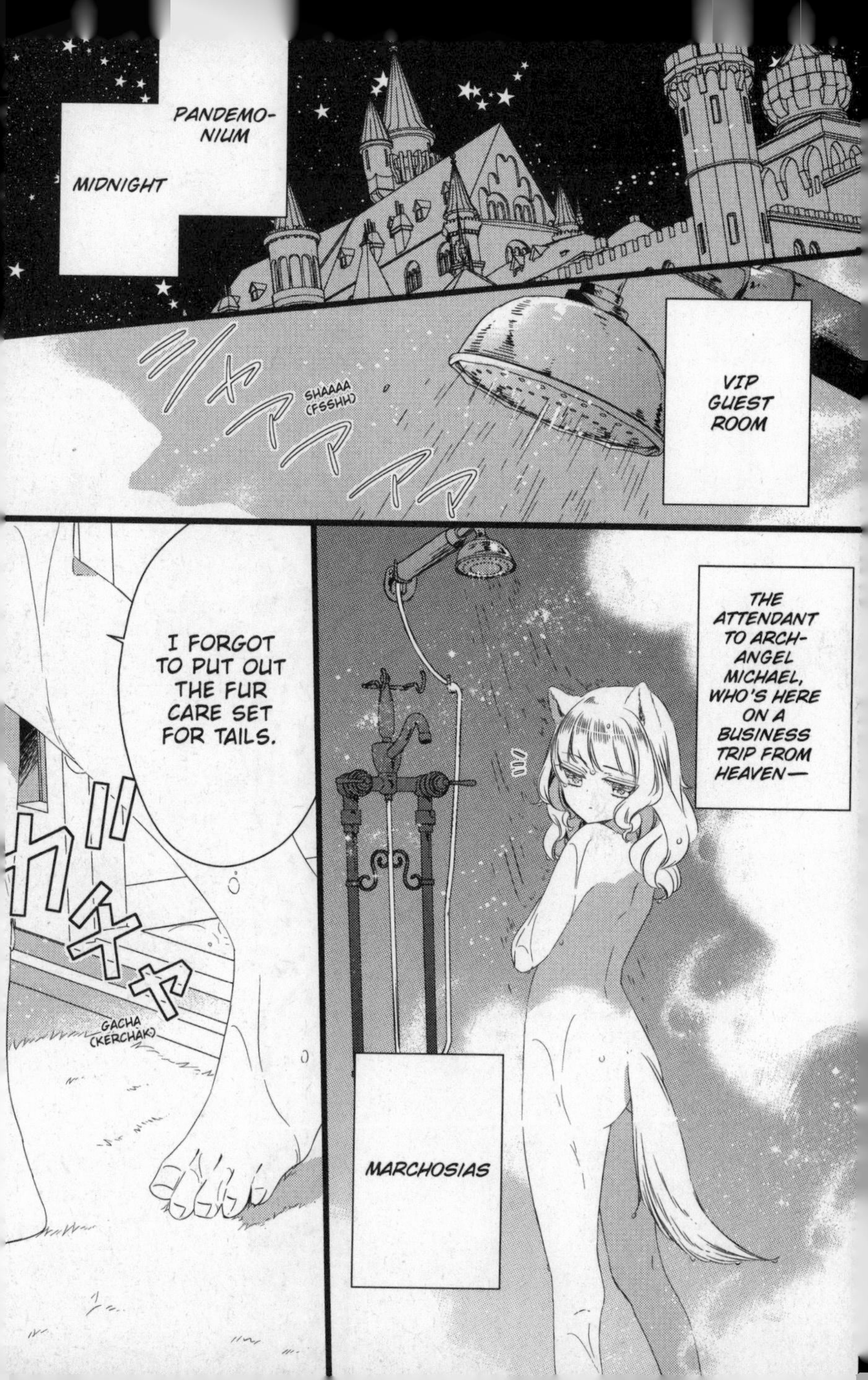
PANDEMONIUM
MIDNIGHT
VIP GUEST ROOM
SHAAAA (FSSHH)
THE ATTENDANT TO ARCHANGEL MICHAEL, WHO'S HERE ON A BUSINESS TRIP FROM HEAVEN—
MARCHOSIAS
I FORGOT TO PUT OUT THE FUR CARE SET FOR TAILS.
GACHA (KERCHAK)

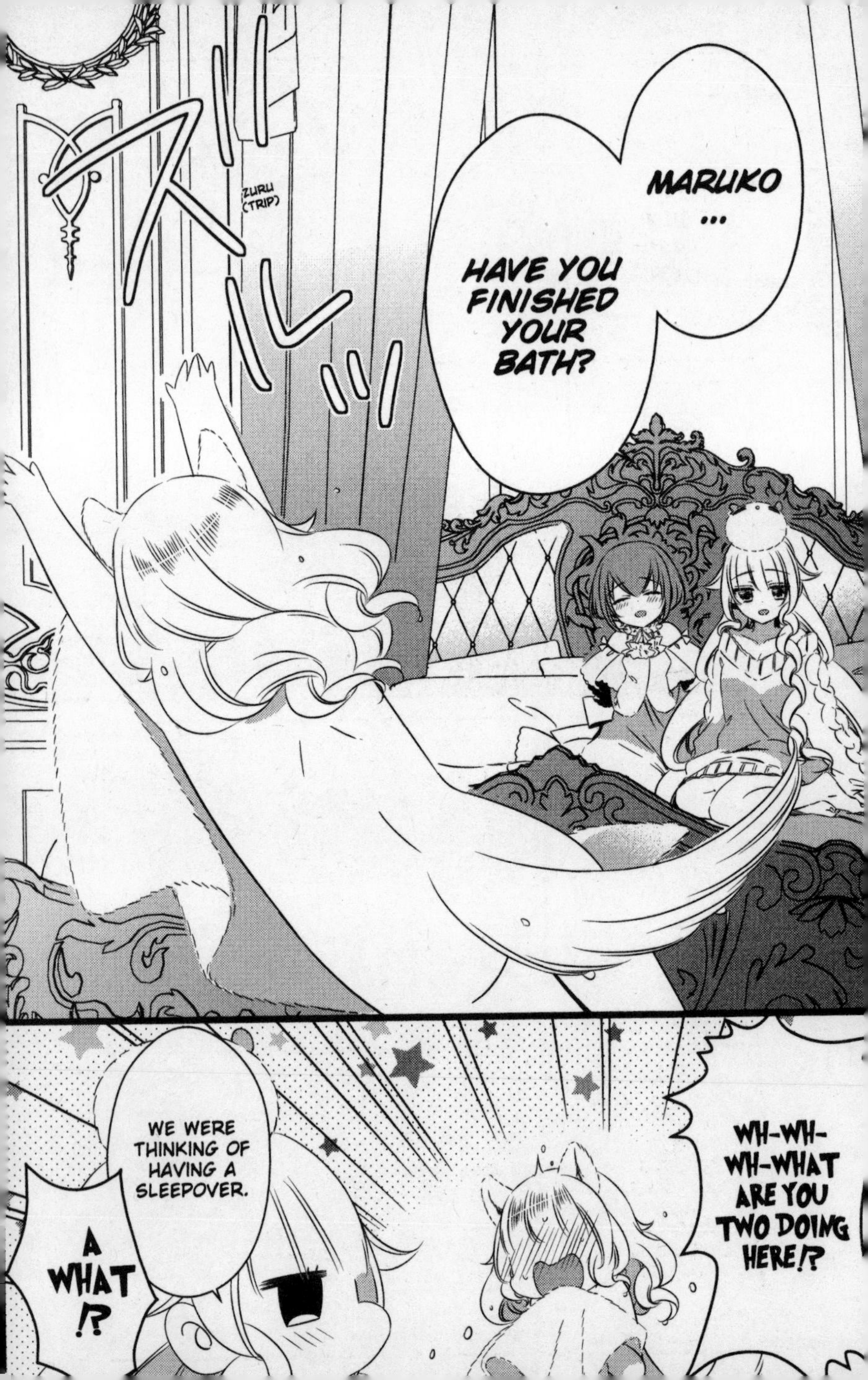
MARUKO ...
HAVE YOU FINISHED YOUR BATH?
ZURU (TRIP)
WH-WH-WH-WHAT ARE YOU TWO DOING HERE!?
WE WERE THINKING OF HAVING A SLEEPOVER.
A WHAT!?

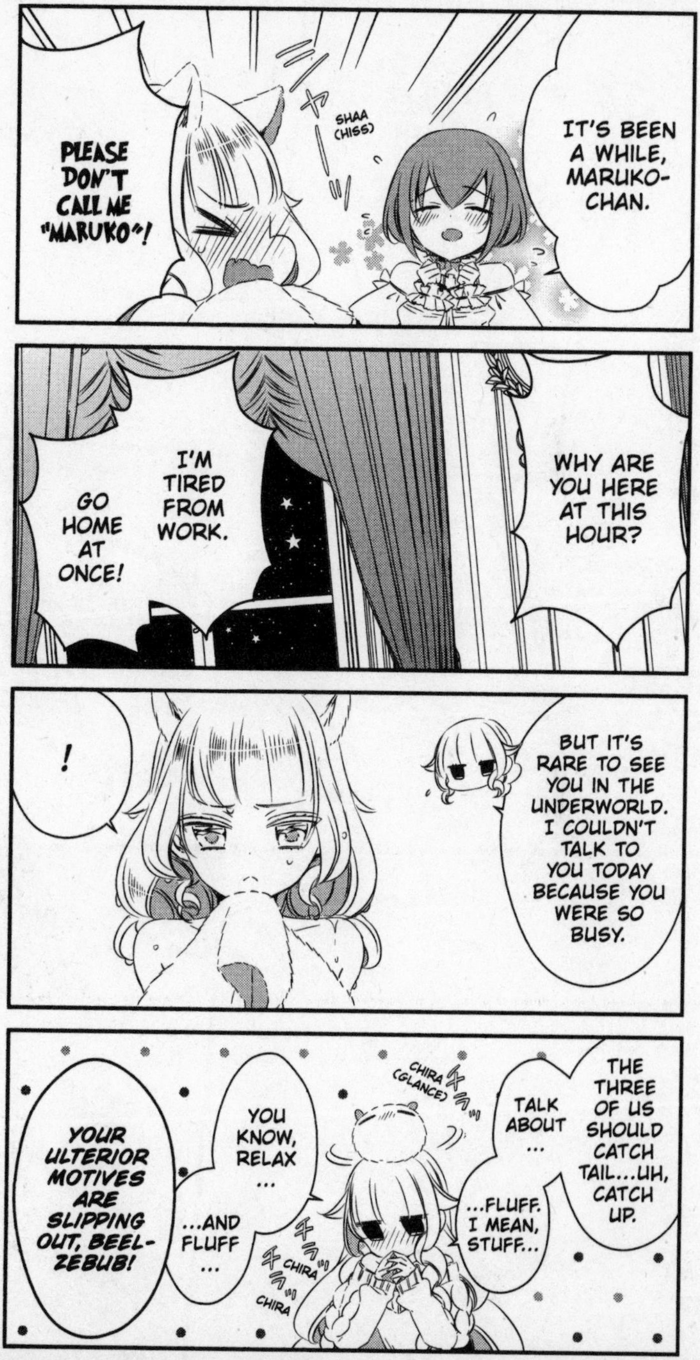
IT'S BEEN A WHILE, MARUKO-CHAN.
SHAA (HISS)
PLEASE DON'T CALL ME "MARUKO"!
WHY ARE YOU HERE AT THIS HOUR?
I'M TIRED FROM WORK.
GO HOME AT ONCE!
BUT IT'S RARE TO SEE YOU IN THE UNDERWORLD. I COULDN'T TALK TO YOU TODAY BECAUSE YOU WERE SO BUSY.
!
THE THREE OF US SHOULD CATCH TAIL...UH, CATCH UP.
TALK ABOUT ...
...FLUFF. I MEAN, STUFF...
CHIRA (GLANCE)
YOU KNOW, RELAX ...
...AND FLUFF ...
CHIRA
CHIRA
YOUR ULTERIOR MOTIVES ARE SLIPPING OUT, BEEL-ZEBUB!

TAIL

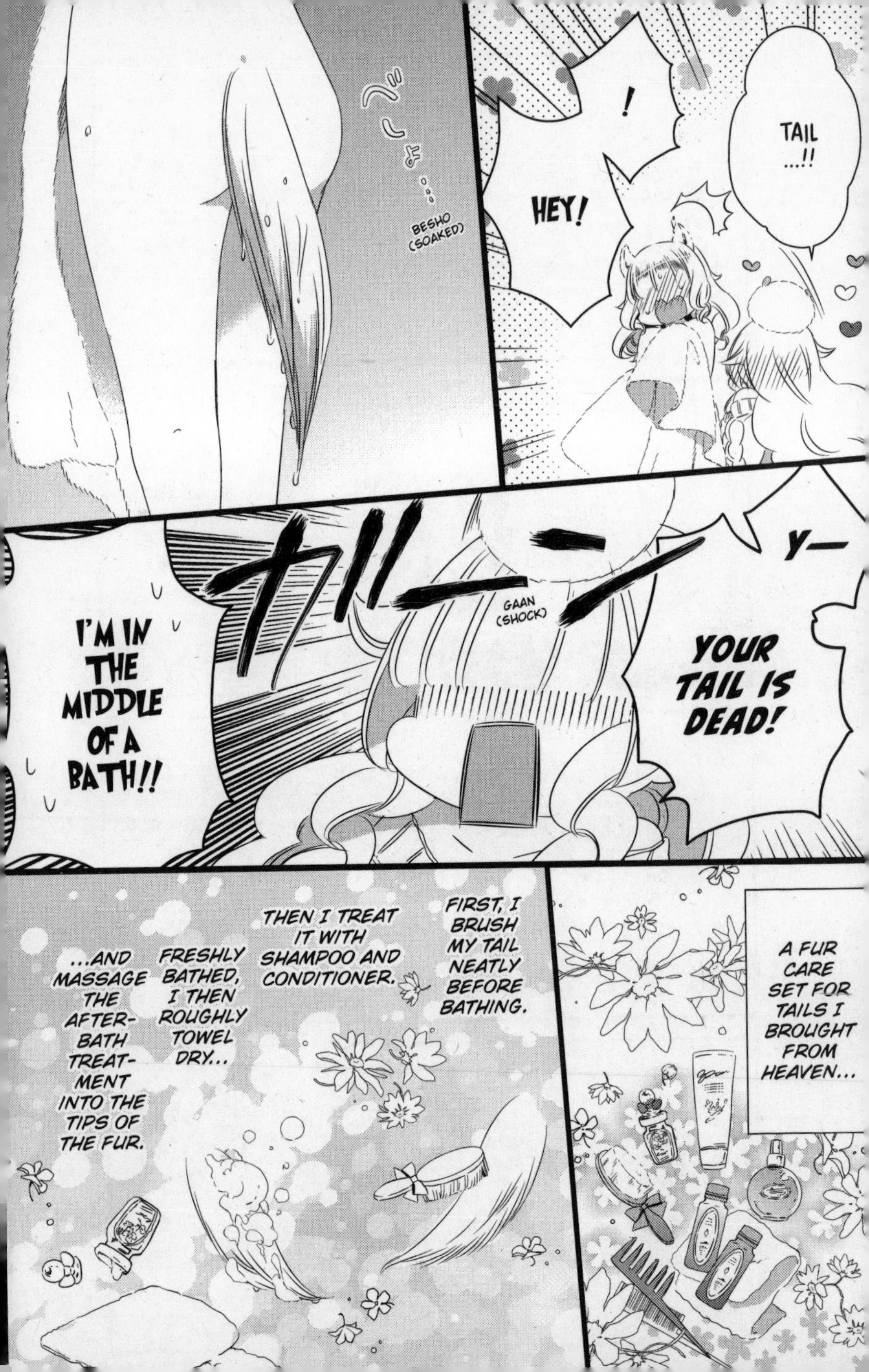
TAIL ...!!
!
HEY!
べしょ…
BESHO (SOAKED)
Y—
YOUR TAIL IS DEAD!
GAAN (SHOCK)
I'M IN THE MIDDLE OF A BATH!!
A FUR CARE SET FOR TAILS I BROUGHT FROM HEAVEN...
FIRST, I BRUSH MY TAIL NEATLY BEFORE BATHING.
THEN I TREAT IT WITH SHAMPOO AND CONDITIONER.
FRESHLY BATHED, I THEN ROUGHLY TOWEL DRY...
...AND MASSAGE THE AFTER-BATH TREAT-MENT INTO THE TIPS OF THE FUR.

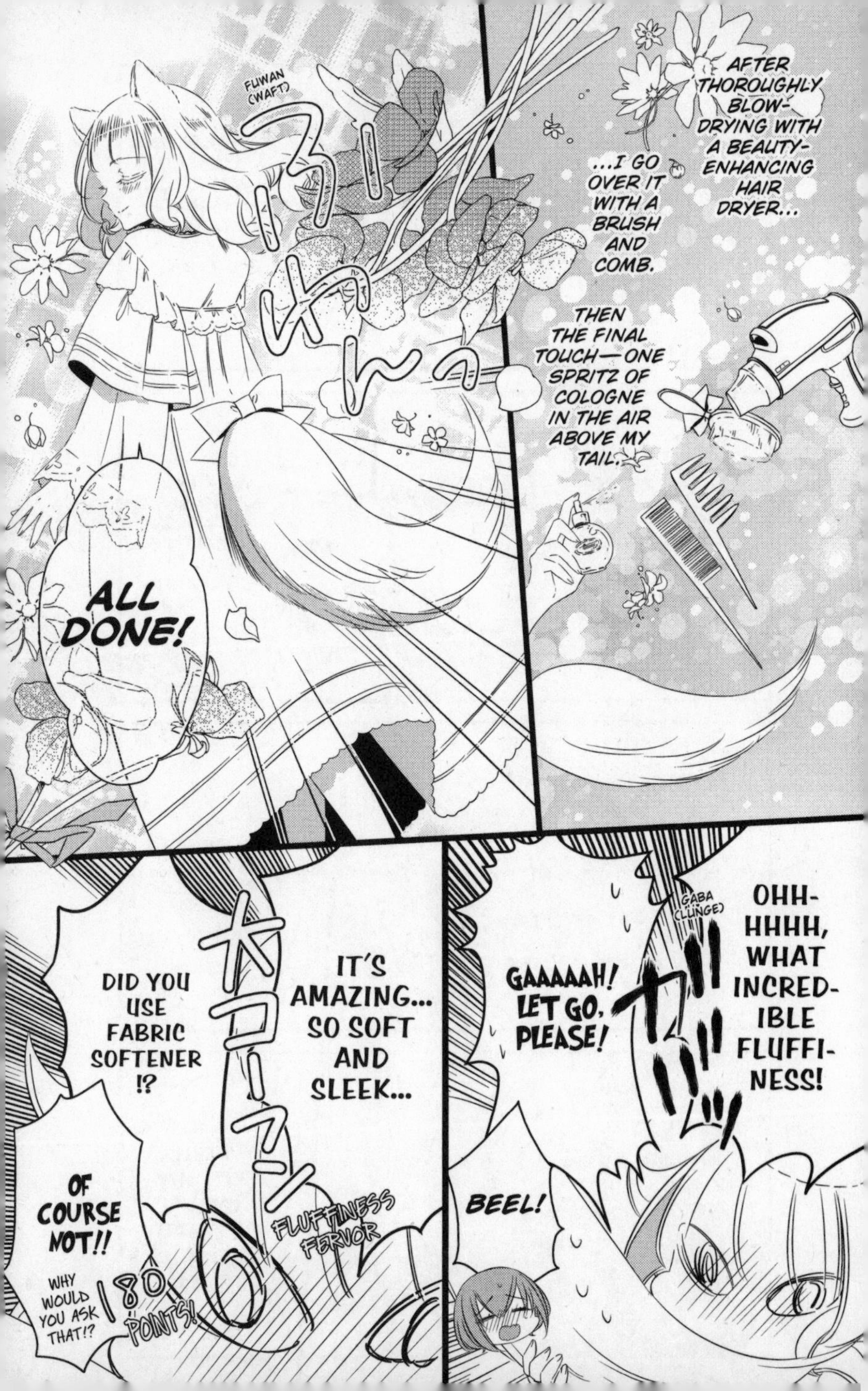

AFTER THOROUGHLY BLOW-DRYING WITH A BEAUTY-ENHANCING HAIR DRYER...
...I GO OVER IT WITH A BRUSH AND COMB.
THEN THE FINAL TOUCH—ONE SPRITZ OF COLOGNE IN THE AIR ABOVE MY TAIL.
FUWAN (WAFT)
ALL DONE!
GABA (LUNGE)
OHHHHHH, WHAT INCREDIBLE FLUFFINESS!
GAAAAAH! LET GO, PLEASE!
BEEL!
IT'S AMAZING... SO SOFT AND SLEEK...
DID YOU USE FABRIC SOFTENER!?
FLUFFINESS FERVOR
OF COURSE NOT!!
WHY WOULD YOU ASK THAT!?
180 POINTS!

HER REAL THOUGHTS!!

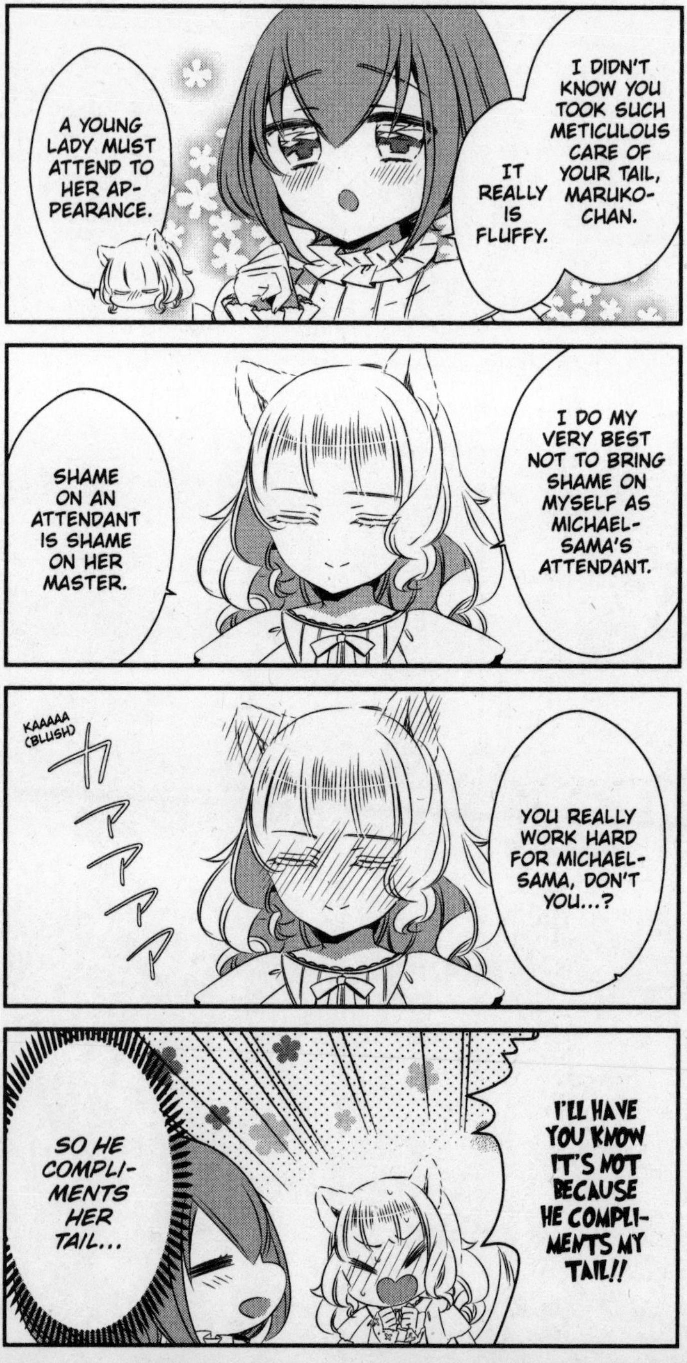
I DIDN'T KNOW YOU TOOK SUCH METICULOUS CARE OF YOUR TAIL, MARUKO-CHAN.
IT REALLY IS FLUFFY.
A YOUNG LADY MUST ATTEND TO HER AP-PEARANCE.
I DO MY VERY BEST NOT TO BRING SHAME ON MYSELF AS MICHAEL-SAMA'S ATTENDANT.
SHAME ON AN ATTENDANT IS SHAME ON HER MASTER.
YOU REALLY WORK HARD FOR MICHAEL-SAMA, DON'T YOU...?
KAAAAA (BLUSH)
I'LL HAVE YOU KNOW IT'S NOT BECAUSE HE COMPLI-MENTS MY TAIL!!
SO HE COMPLI-MENTS HER TAIL...

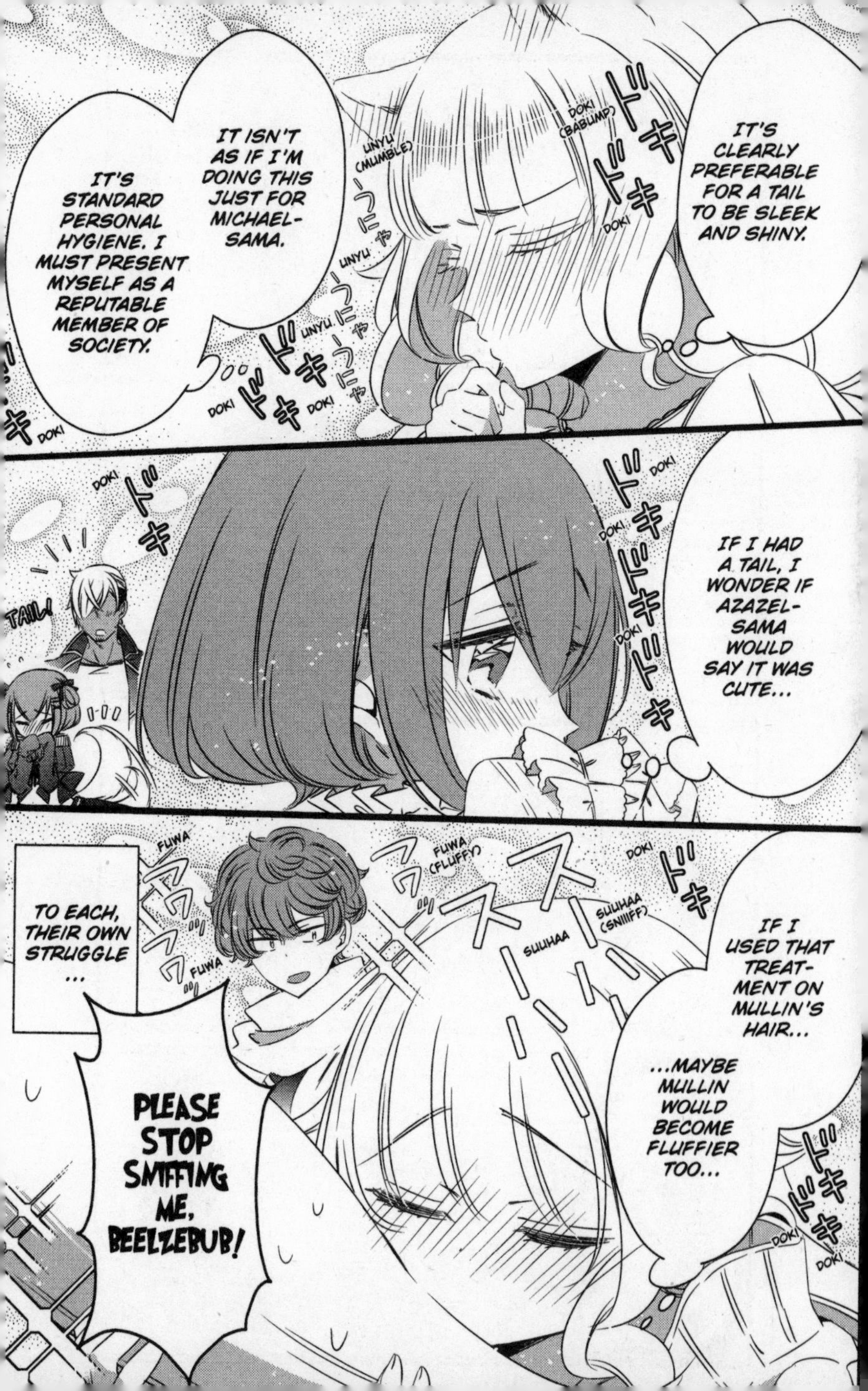
IT'S CLEARLY PREFERABLE FOR A TAIL TO BE SLEEK AND SHINY.
DOKI (BABUMP)
ドキドキ
DOKI
UNYU (MUMBLE)
UNYU
UNYU
IT ISN'T AS IF I'M DOING THIS JUST FOR MICHAEL-SAMA.
IT'S STANDARD PERSONAL HYGIENE. I MUST PRESENT MYSELF AS A REPUTABLE MEMBER OF SOCIETY.
ドキドキ
DOKI
DOKI
DOKI
IF I HAD A TAIL, I WONDER IF AZAZEL-SAMA WOULD SAY IT WAS CUTE...
DOKI
DOKI
DOKI
DOKI
TAIL!
IF I USED THAT TREATMENT ON MULLIN'S HAIR...
...MAYBE MULLIN WOULD BECOME FLUFFIER TOO...
DOKI
DOKI
DOKI
SUUHAA (SNIIIFF)
SUUHAA
FUWA (FLUFFY)
FUWA
FUWA
PLEASE STOP SNIFFING ME, BEELZEBUB!
TO EACH, THEIR OWN STRUGGLE...

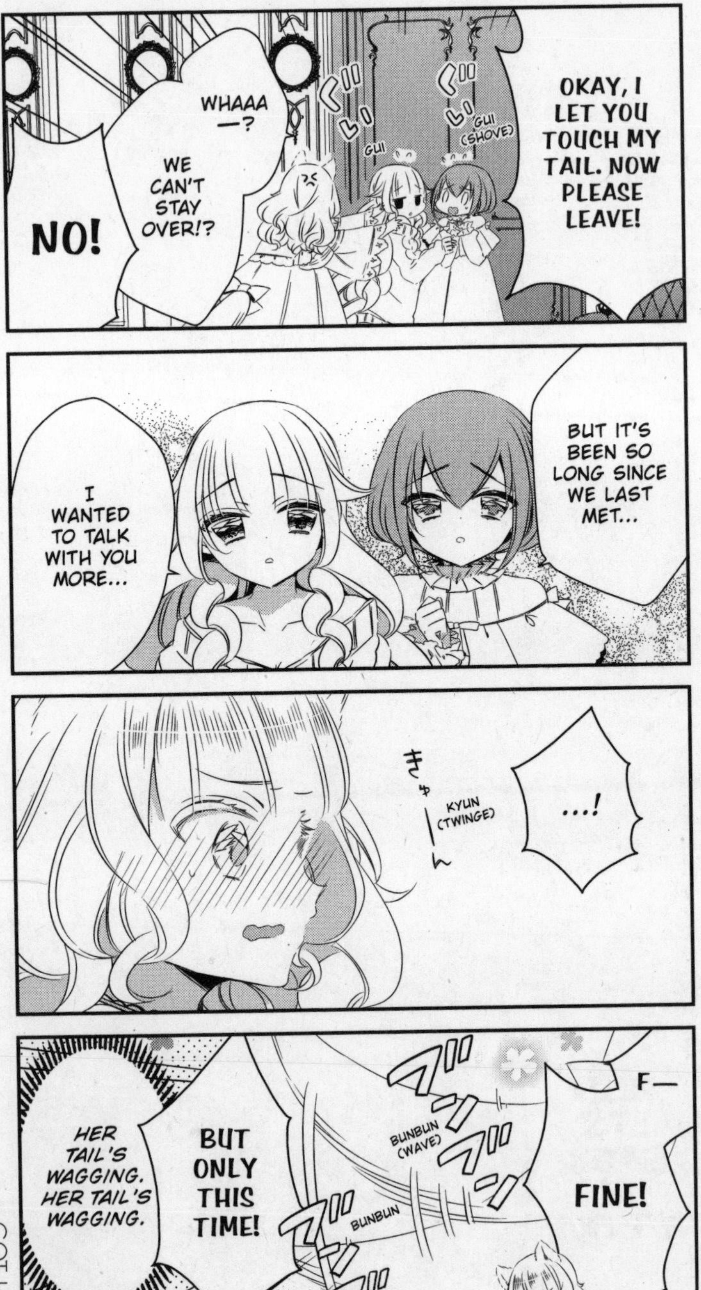
OKAY, I LET YOU TOUCH MY TAIL. NOW PLEASE LEAVE!
ぐい
GUI (SHOVE)
ぐい
GUI
WHAAA—?
WE CAN'T STAY OVER!?
NO!
BUT IT'S BEEN SO LONG SINCE WE LAST MET...
I WANTED TO TALK WITH YOU MORE...
...!
きゅーん
KYUN (TWINGE)
F—
FINE!
ブンブン
BUNBUN (WAVE)
ブンブン
BUNBUN
BUT ONLY THIS TIME!
HER TAIL'S WAGGING. HER TAIL'S WAGGING.

GOT HAPPY

SLEEPOVERS MEAN LOVE TALK

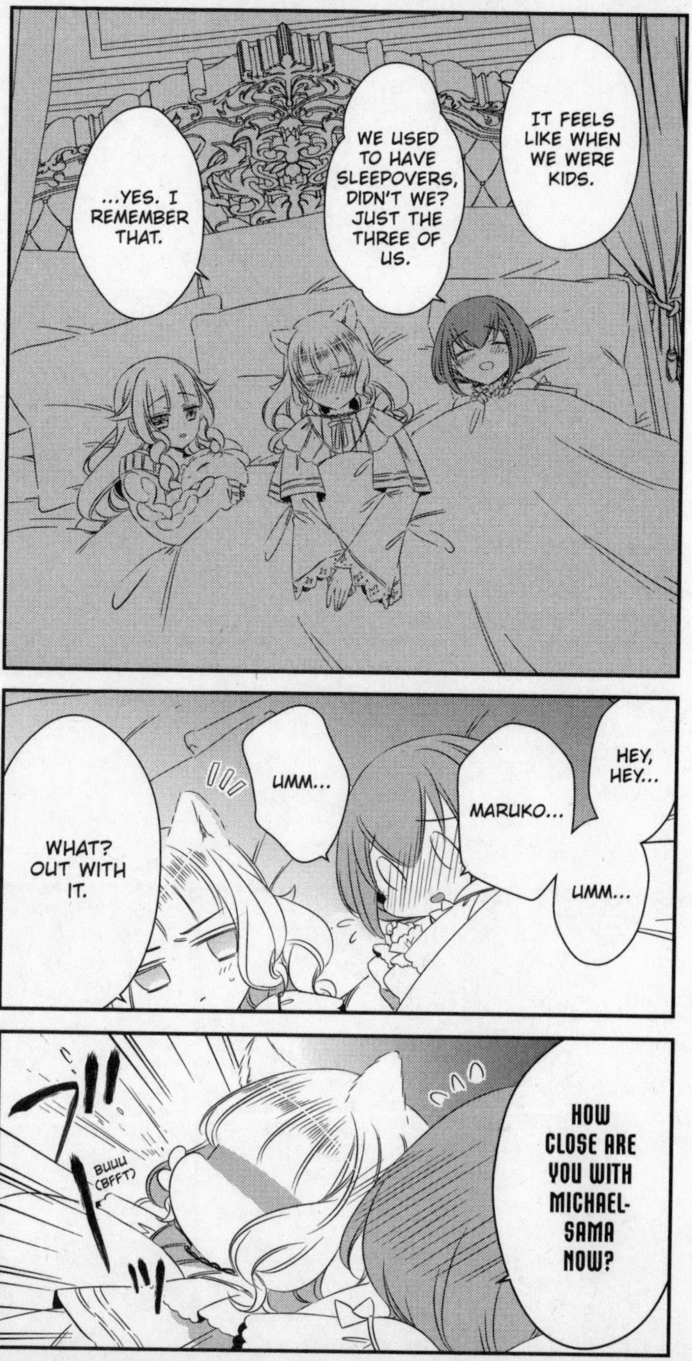
IT FEELS LIKE WHEN WE WERE KIDS.
WE USED TO HAVE SLEEPOVERS, DIDN'T WE? JUST THE THREE OF US.
...YES. I REMEMBER THAT.
HEY, HEY... MARUKO... UMM...
UMM...
WHAT? OUT WITH IT.
HOW CLOSE ARE YOU WITH MICHAEL-SAMA NOW?
BUUU (BFFT)

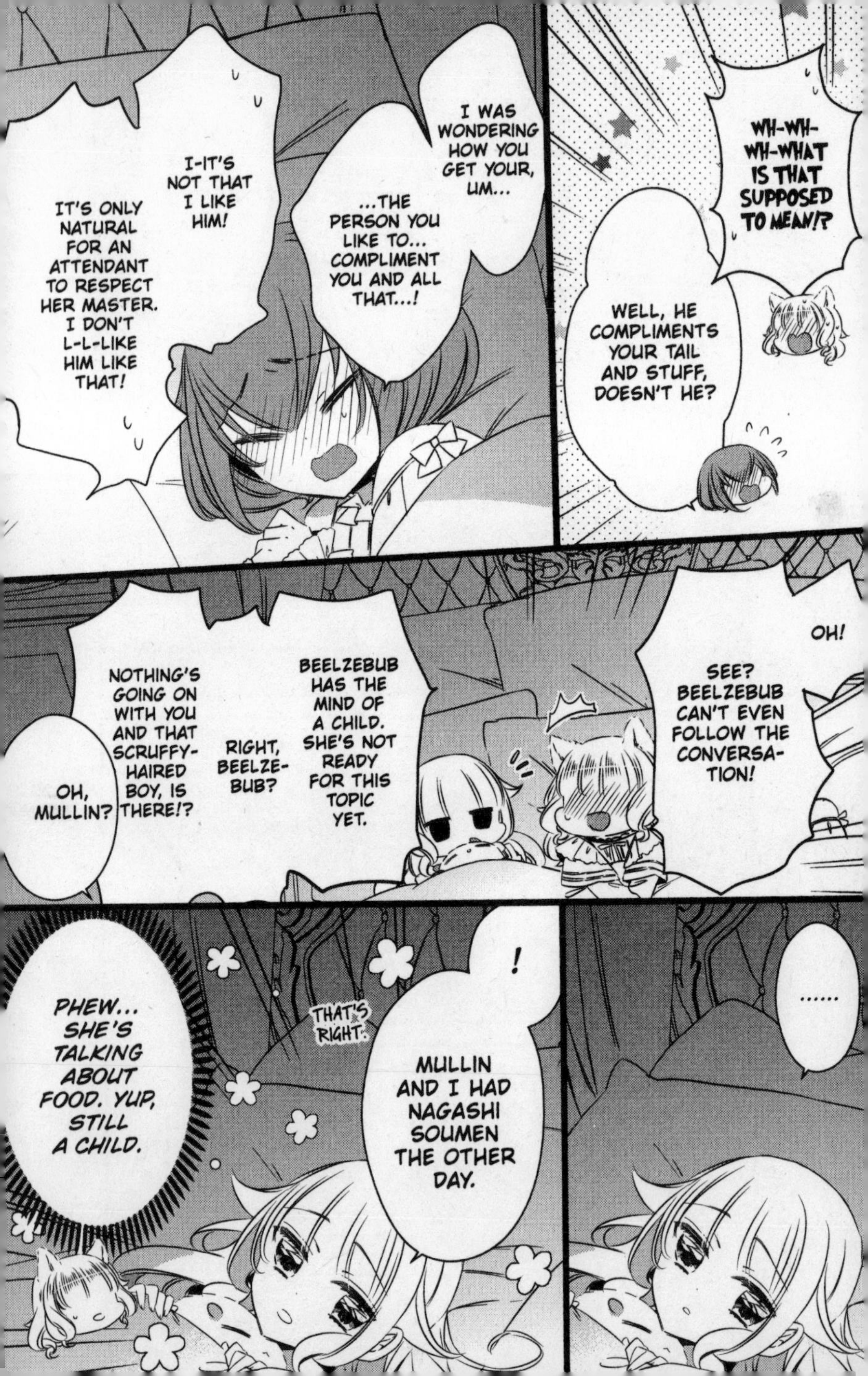
WH-WH-WH-WHAT IS THAT SUPPOSED TO MEAN!?
WELL, HE COMPLIMENTS YOUR TAIL AND STUFF, DOESN'T HE?
I WAS WONDERING HOW YOU GET YOUR, UM...
...THE PERSON YOU LIKE TO... COMPLIMENT YOU AND ALL THAT...!
I-IT'S NOT THAT I LIKE HIM!
IT'S ONLY NATURAL FOR AN ATTENDANT TO RESPECT HER MASTER. I DON'T L-L-LIKE HIM LIKE THAT!
OH!
SEE? BEELZEBUB CAN'T EVEN FOLLOW THE CONVERSA-TION!
BEELZEBUB HAS THE MIND OF A CHILD. SHE'S NOT READY FOR THIS TOPIC YET.
RIGHT, BEELZE-BUB?
NOTHING'S GOING ON WITH YOU AND THAT SCRUFFY-HAIRED BOY, IS THERE!?
OH, MULLIN?
......
!
MULLIN AND I HAD NAGASHI SOUMEN THE OTHER DAY.
THAT'S RIGHT.
PHEW... SHE'S TALKING ABOUT FOOD. YUP, STILL A CHILD.

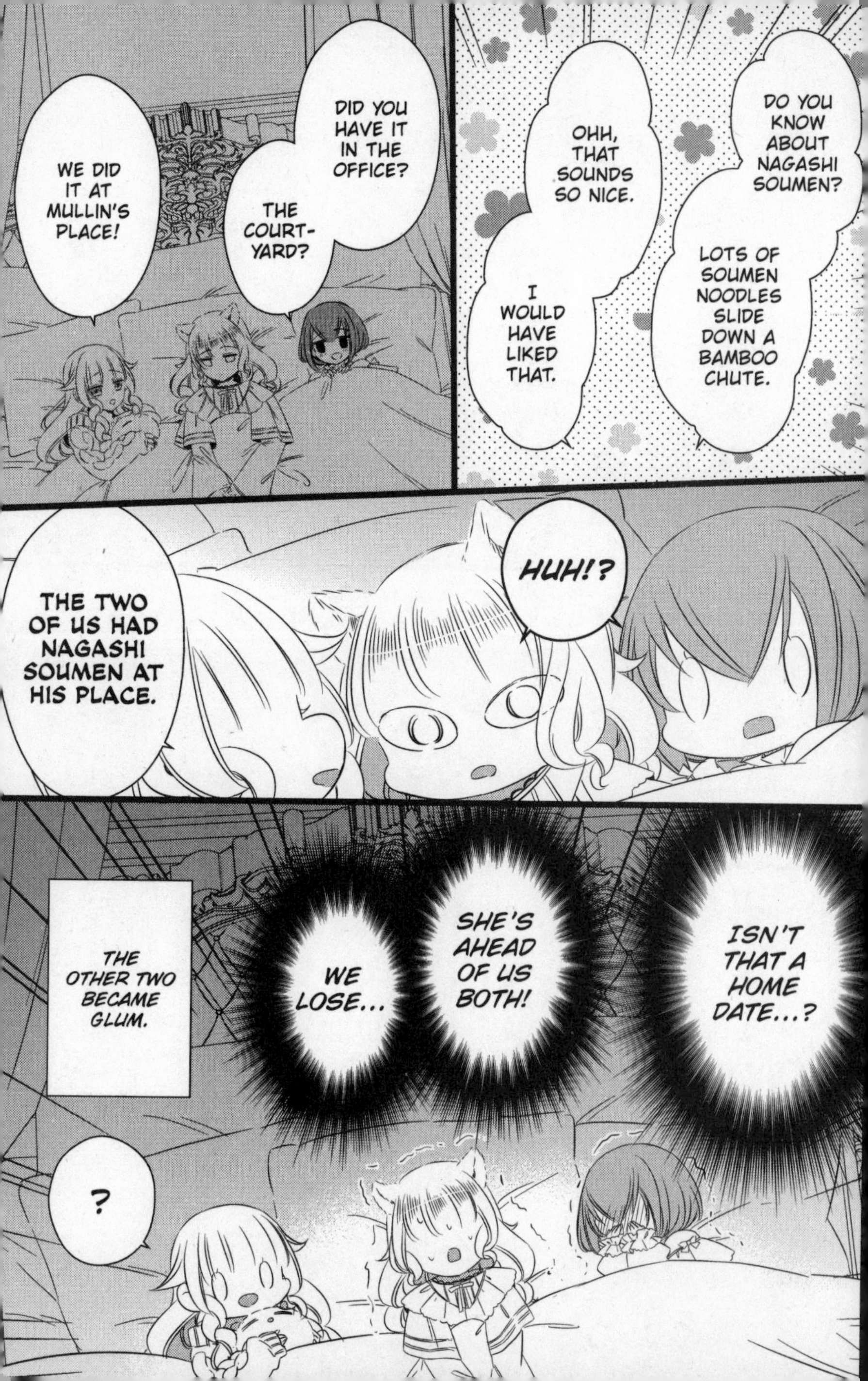
DO YOU KNOW ABOUT NAGASHI SOUMEN?
LOTS OF SOUMEN NOODLES SLIDE DOWN A BAMBOO CHUTE.
OHH, THAT SOUNDS SO NICE.
I WOULD HAVE LIKED THAT.
DID YOU HAVE IT IN THE OFFICE?
THE COURT-YARD?
WE DID IT AT MULLIN'S PLACE!
HUH!?
THE TWO OF US HAD NAGASHI SOUMEN AT HIS PLACE.
ISN'T THAT A HOME DATE...?
SHE'S AHEAD OF US BOTH!
WE LOSE...
THE OTHER TWO BECAME GLUM.
?

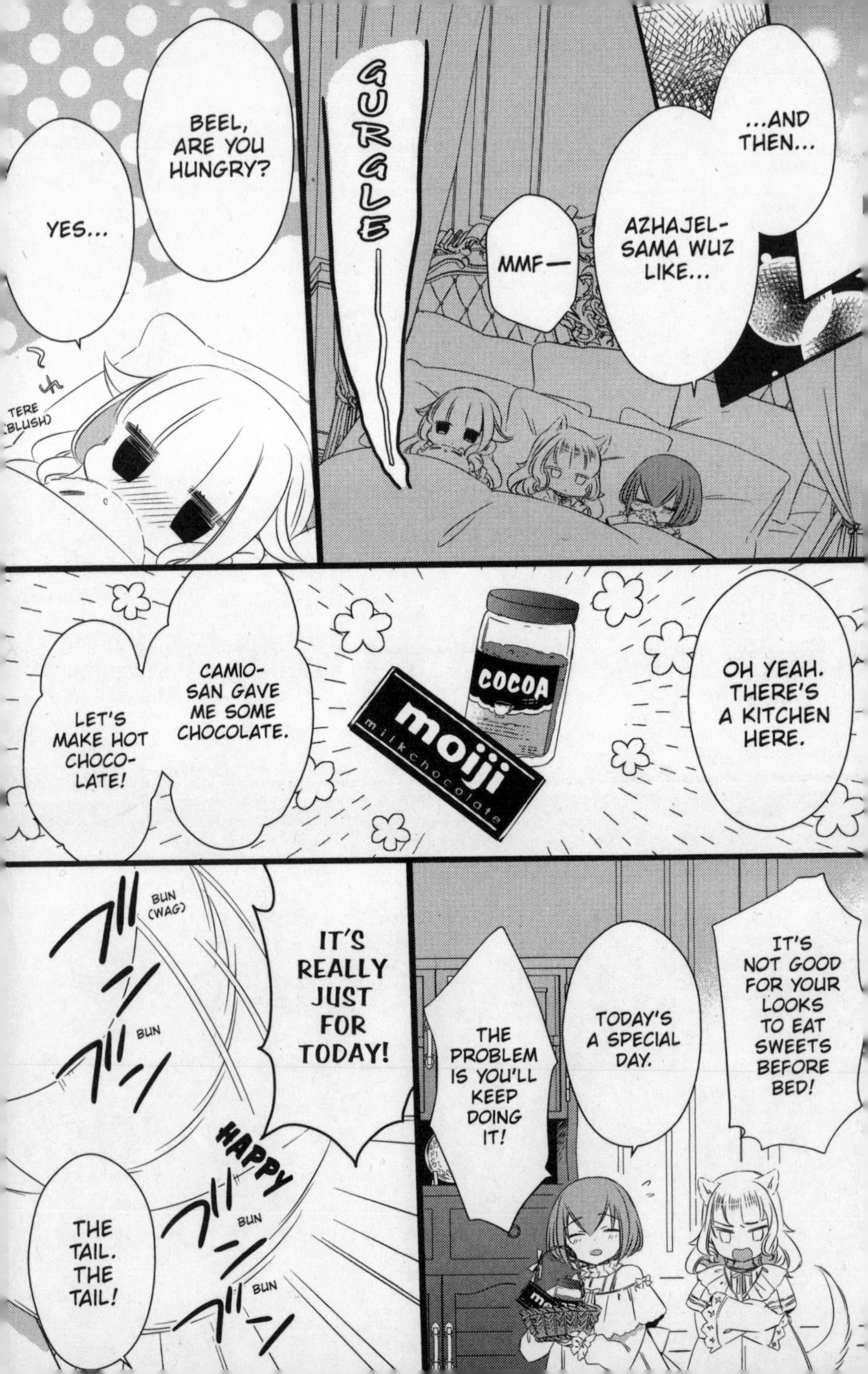
...AND THEN...
AZHAJEL-SAMA WUZ LIKE...
MMF—
GURGLE
BEEL, ARE YOU HUNGRY?
YES...
TERE (BLUSH)
OH YEAH. THERE'S A KITCHEN HERE.
COCOA
moiji
milkchocolate
CAMIO-SAN GAVE ME SOME CHOCOLATE.
LET'S MAKE HOT CHOCO-LATE!
IT'S NOT GOOD FOR YOUR LOOKS TO EAT SWEETS BEFORE BED!
TODAY'S A SPECIAL DAY.
THE PROBLEM IS YOU'LL KEEP DOING IT!
IT'S REALLY JUST FOR TODAY!
BUN (WAG)
BUN
HAPPY
BUN
BUN
THE TAIL. THE TAIL!

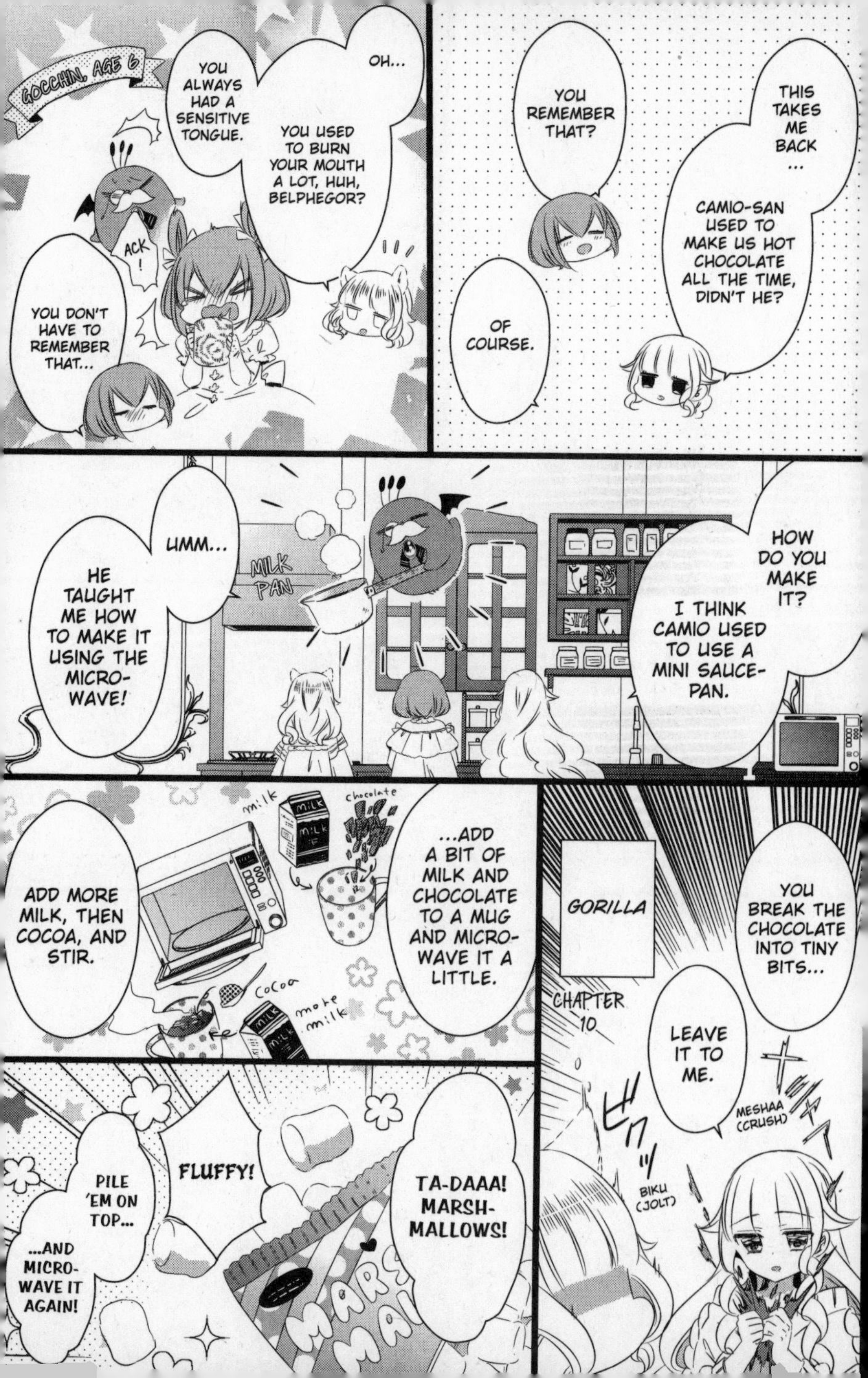
THIS TAKES ME BACK ...
CAMIO-SAN USED TO MAKE US HOT CHOCOLATE ALL THE TIME, DIDN'T HE?
YOU REMEMBER THAT?
OF COURSE.
OH...
YOU USED TO BURN YOUR MOUTH A LOT, HUH, BELPHEGOR?
YOU ALWAYS HAD A SENSITIVE TONGUE.
GOCCHIN, AGE 6
ACK!
YOU DON'T HAVE TO REMEMBER THAT...
HOW DO YOU MAKE IT?
I THINK CAMIO USED TO USE A MINI SAUCE-PAN.
MILK PAN
UMM...
HE TAUGHT ME HOW TO MAKE IT USING THE MICRO-WAVE!
CHAPTER 10
GORILLA
YOU BREAK THE CHOCOLATE INTO TINY BITS...
LEAVE IT TO ME.
MESHAA (CRUSH)
BIKU (JOLT)
...ADD A BIT OF MILK AND CHOCOLATE TO A MUG AND MICRO-WAVE IT A LITTLE.
milk
chocolate
ADD MORE MILK, THEN COCOA, AND STIR.
cocoa
more milk
TA-DAAA! MARSH-MALLOWS!
FLUFFY!
PILE 'EM ON TOP...
...AND MICRO-WAVE IT AGAIN!

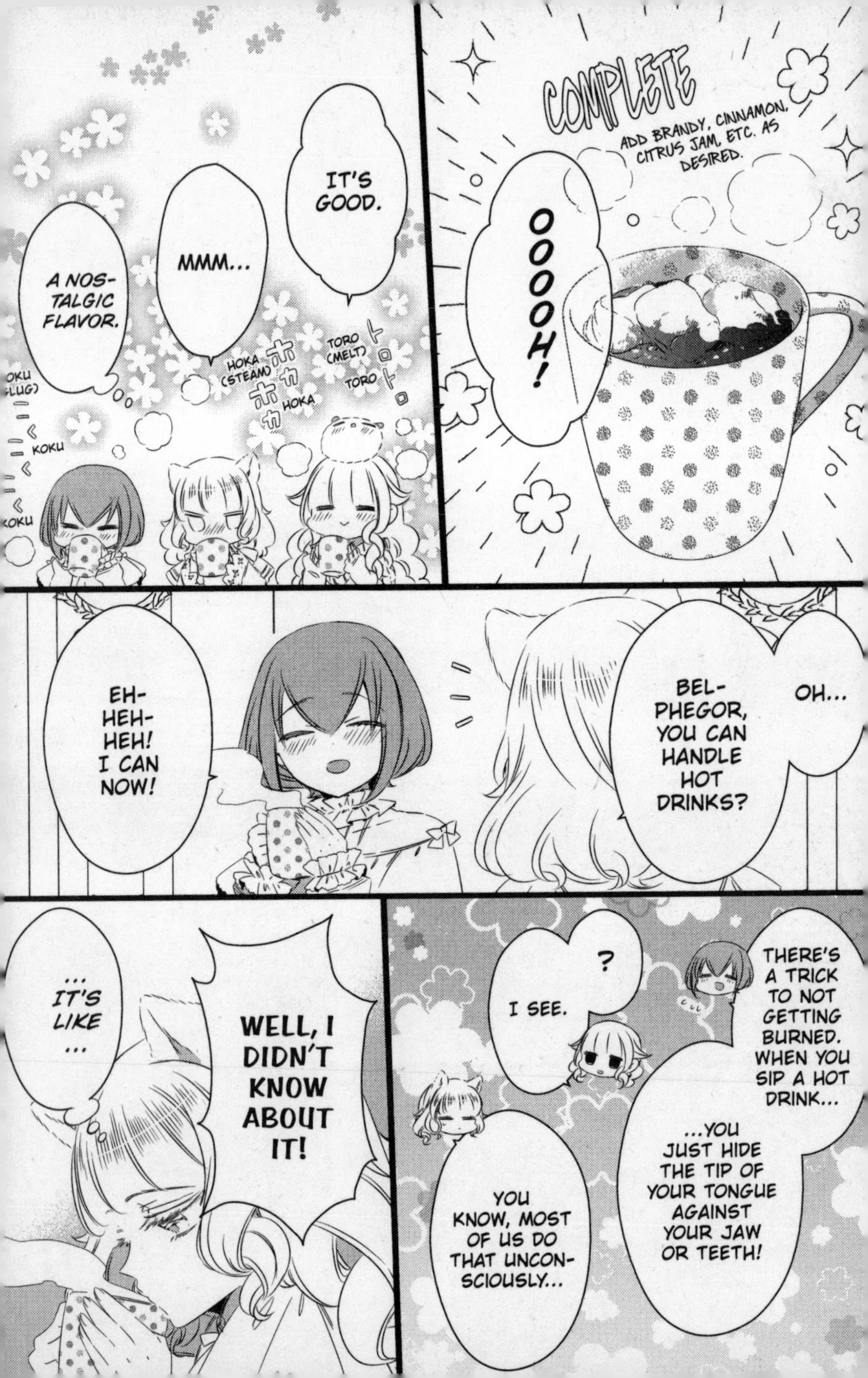
COMPLETE
ADD BRANDY, CINNAMON, CITRUS JAM, ETC. AS DESIRED.
OOOOOH!
IT'S GOOD.
MMM...
A NOS-TALGIC FLAVOR.
TORO (MELT) TORO
HOKA (STEAM) HOKA
KOKU (GLUG) KOKU KOKU
OH...
BEL-PHEGOR, YOU CAN HANDLE HOT DRINKS?
EH-HEH-HEH! I CAN NOW!
THERE'S A TRICK TO NOT GETTING BURNED. WHEN YOU SIP A HOT DRINK...
...YOU JUST HIDE THE TIP OF YOUR TONGUE AGAINST YOUR JAW OR TEETH!
?
I SEE.
YOU KNOW, MOST OF US DO THAT UNCONSCIOUSLY...
WELL, I DIDN'T KNOW ABOUT IT!
...IT'S LIKE...

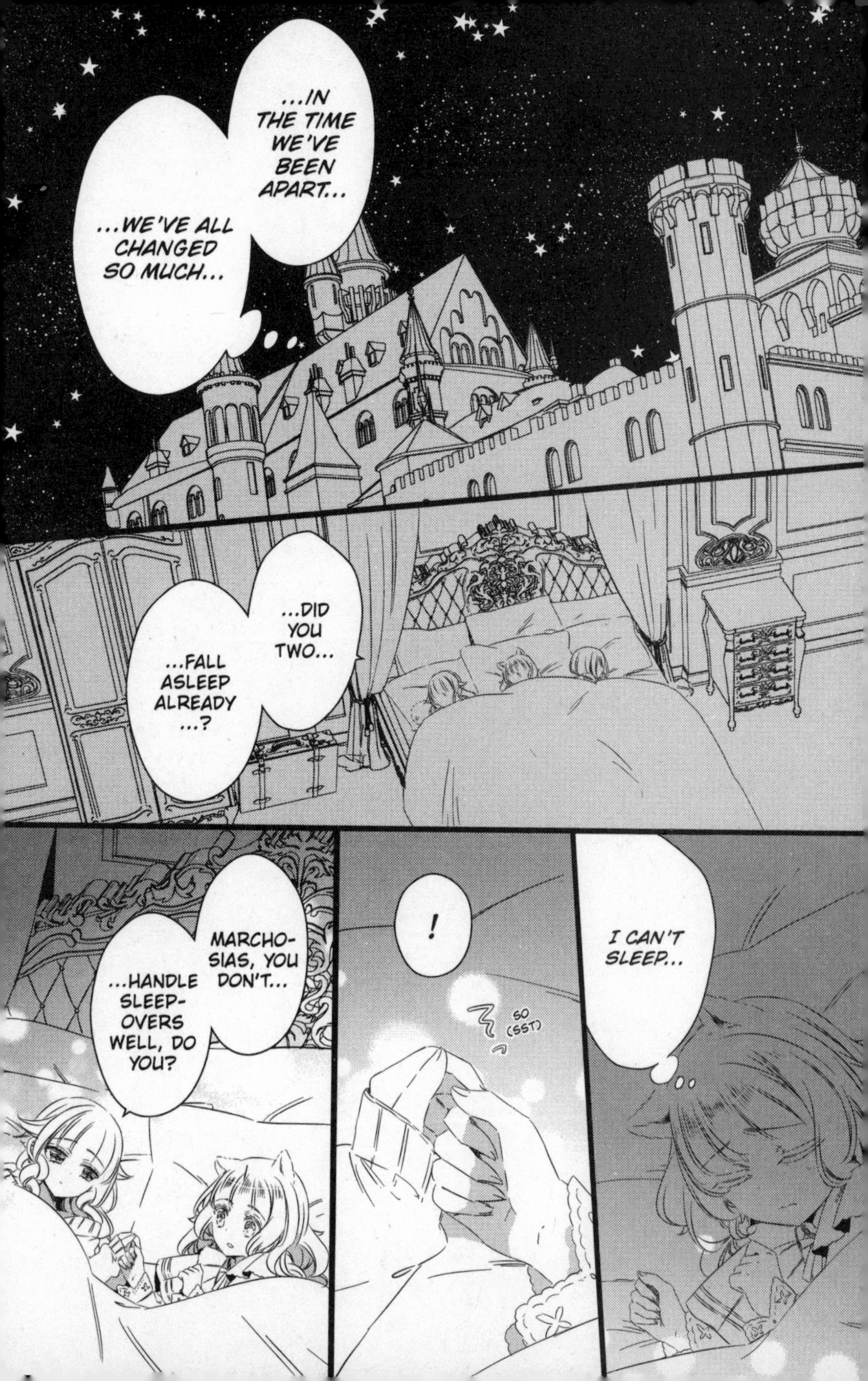
...IN THE TIME WE'VE BEEN APART...
...WE'VE ALL CHANGED SO MUCH...
...DID YOU TWO...
...FALL ASLEEP ALREADY...?
I CAN'T SLEEP...
!
SO (SST)
MARCHOSIAS, YOU DON'T...
...HANDLE SLEEPOVERS WELL, DO YOU?

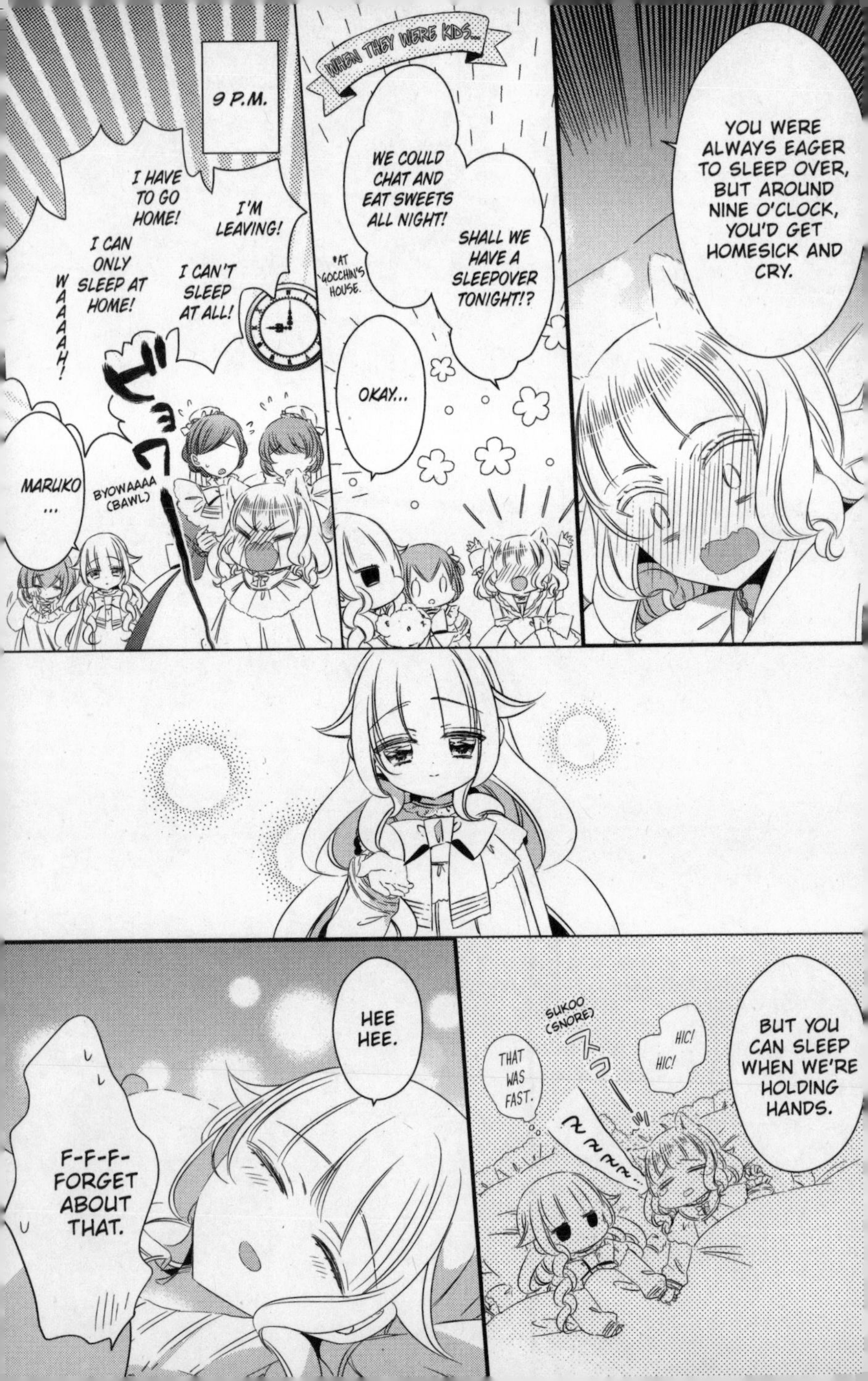
YOU WERE ALWAYS EAGER TO SLEEP OVER, BUT AROUND NINE O'CLOCK, YOU'D GET HOMESICK AND CRY.
WHEN THEY WERE KIDS...
SHALL WE HAVE A SLEEPOVER TONIGHT!?
WE COULD CHAT AND EAT SWEETS ALL NIGHT!
*AT GOCCHIN'S HOUSE.
OKAY...
9 P.M.
I'M LEAVING!
I HAVE TO GO HOME!
I CAN'T SLEEP AT ALL!
I CAN ONLY SLEEP AT HOME!
WAAAAAH!
BYOWAAAA (BAWL)
MARUKO ...
BUT YOU CAN SLEEP WHEN WE'RE HOLDING HANDS.
HIC!
HIC!
SUKOO (SNORE)
THAT WAS FAST.
HEE HEE.
F-F-F-FORGET ABOUT THAT.

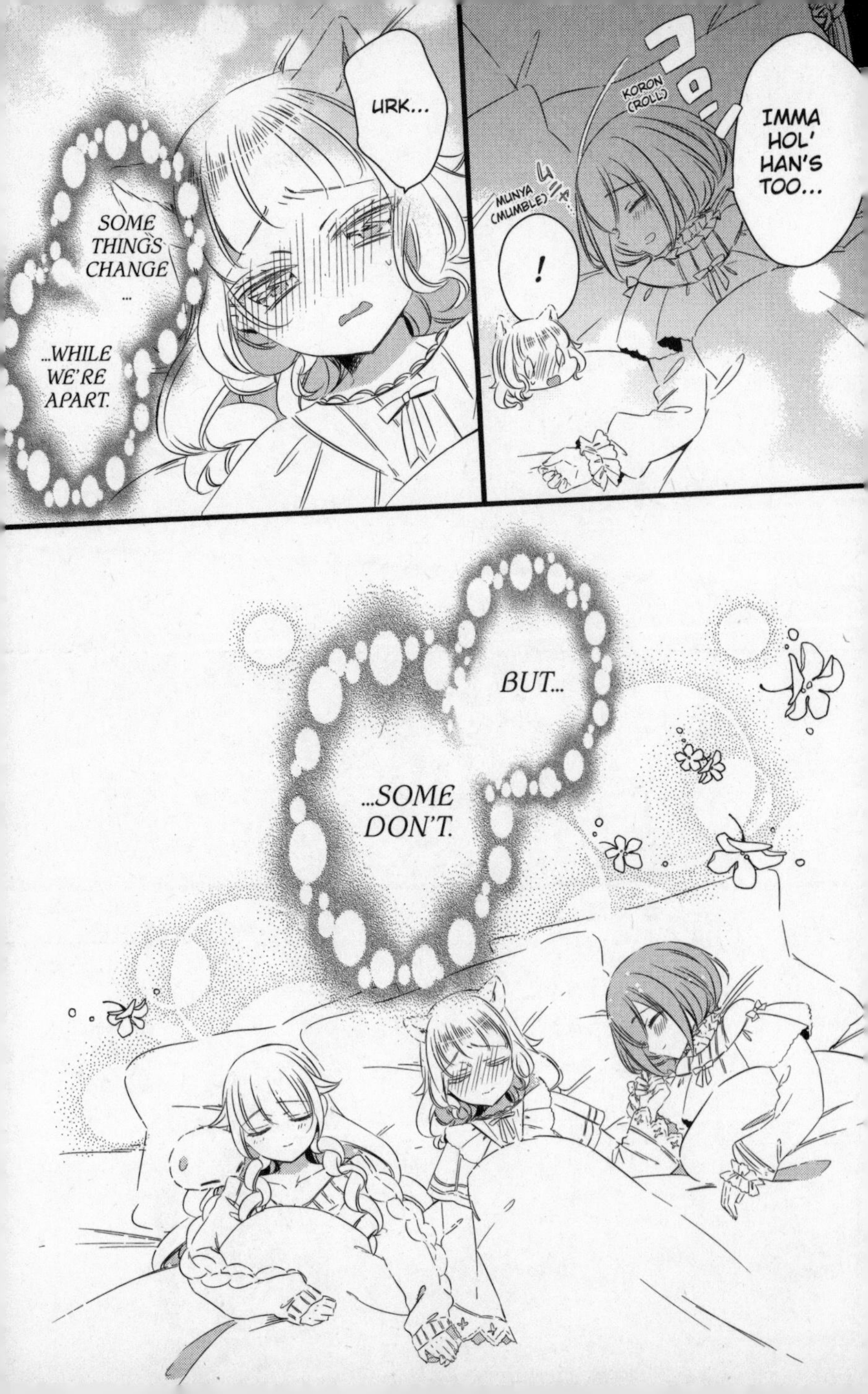
KORON (ROLL)
IMMA HOL' HAN'S TOO...
MUNYA (MUMBLE)
!
URK...
SOME THINGS CHANGE ...
...WHILE WE'RE APART.
BUT...
...SOME DON'T.

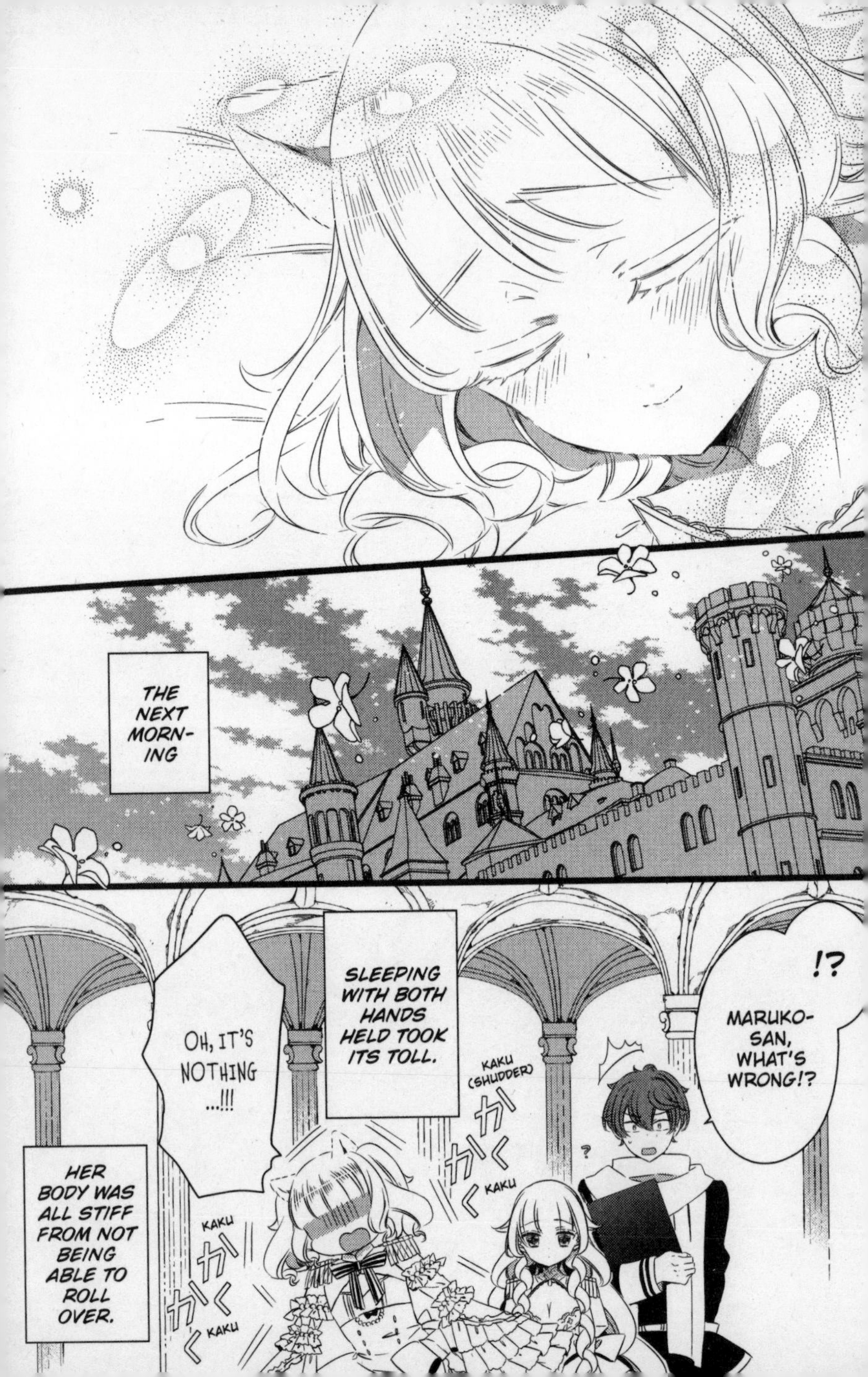
THE NEXT MORNING-
!?
MARUKO-SAN, WHAT'S WRONG!?
SLEEPING WITH BOTH HANDS HELD TOOK ITS TOLL.
KAKU (SHUDDER)
OH, IT'S NOTHING ...!!!
KAKU
KAKU
KAKU
HER BODY WAS ALL STIFF FROM NOT BEING ABLE TO ROLL OVER.

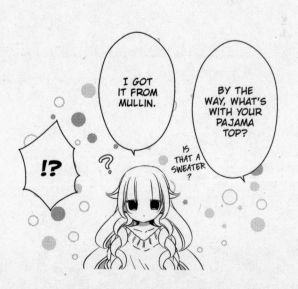

BY THE WAY, WHAT'S WITH YOUR PAJAMA TOP?
IS THAT A SWEATER?
I GOT IT FROM MULLIN.
!?

As Miss Beelzebub Likes

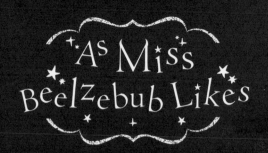

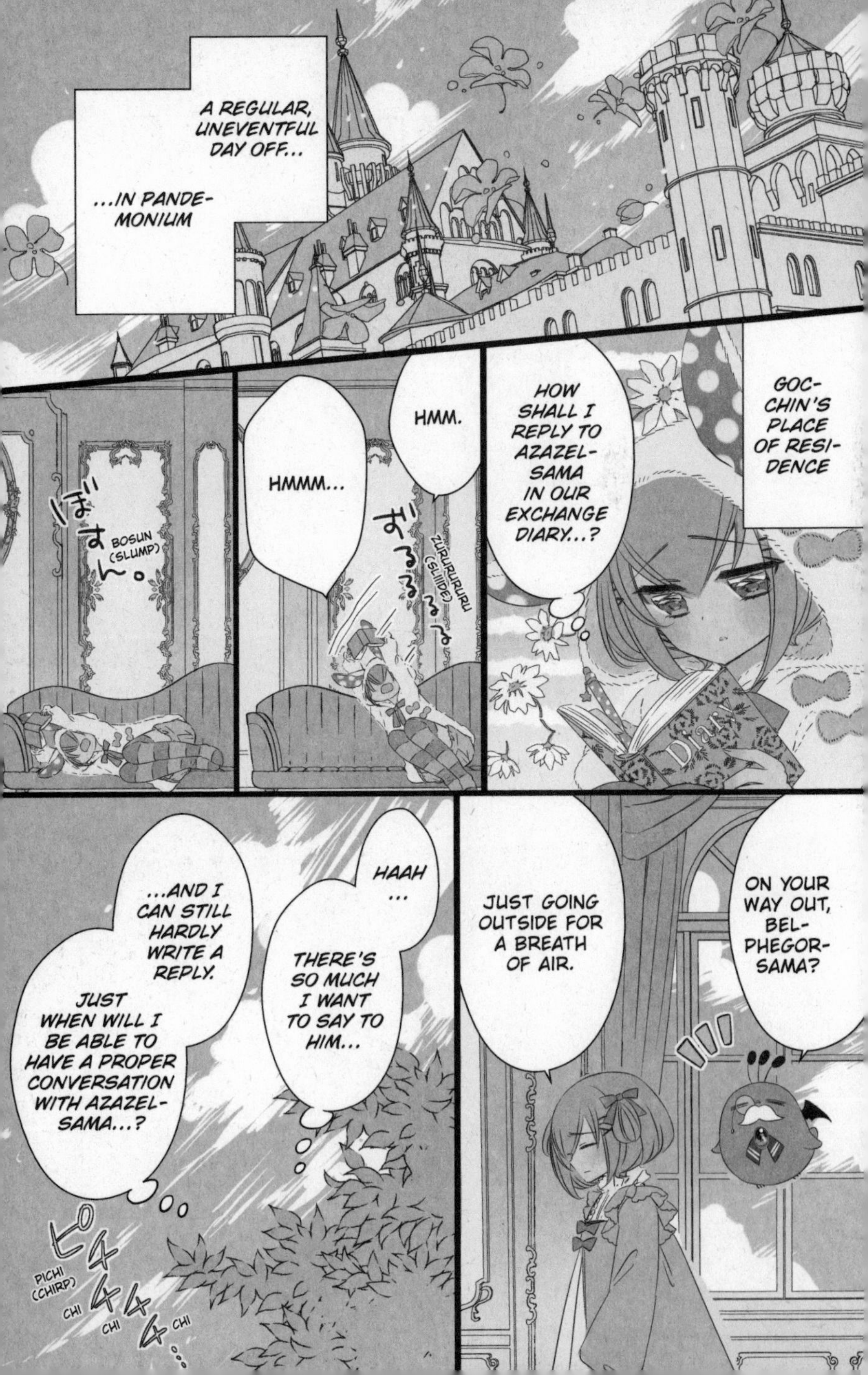
A REGULAR, UNEVENTFUL DAY OFF...
...IN PANDE-MONIUM
GOC-CHIN'S PLACE OF RESI-DENCE
HOW SHALL I REPLY TO AZAZEL-SAMA IN OUR EXCHANGE DIARY...?
Diary
HMM.
HMMM...
ずるるるるっ
ZURURURURU (SLIIIDE)
ぼすん。
BOSUN (SLUMP)
ON YOUR WAY OUT, BEL-PHEGOR-SAMA?
JUST GOING OUTSIDE FOR A BREATH OF AIR.
HAAH...
THERE'S SO MUCH I WANT TO SAY TO HIM...
...AND I CAN STILL HARDLY WRITE A REPLY.
JUST WHEN WILL I BE ABLE TO HAVE A PROPER CONVERSATION WITH AZAZEL-SAMA...?
ピチチチ...
PICHI (CHIRP)
CHI
CHI
CHI

CHAPTER 61

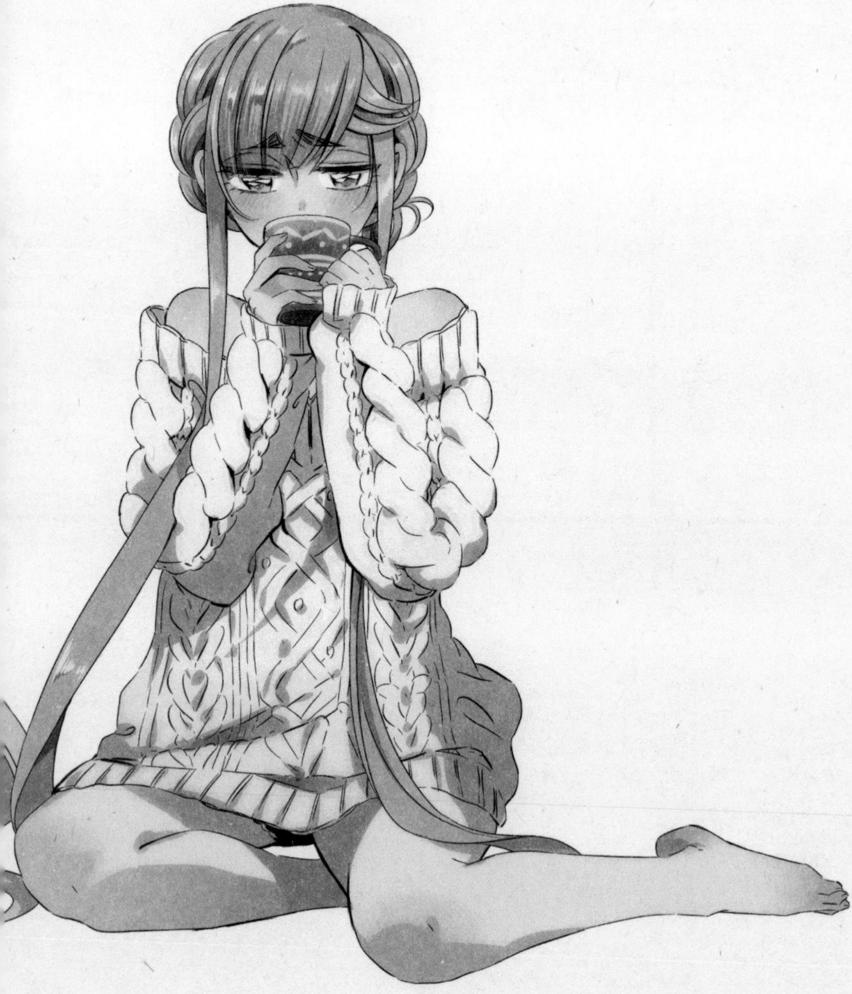

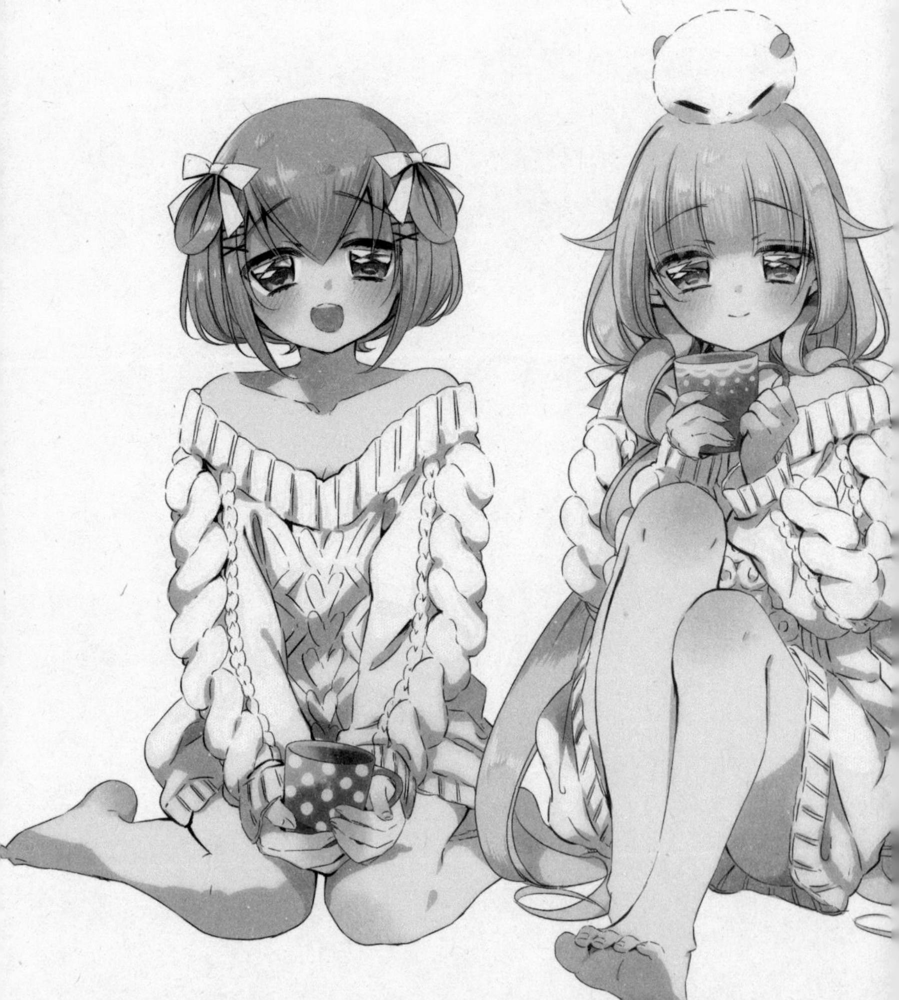

As Miss Beelzebub Likes

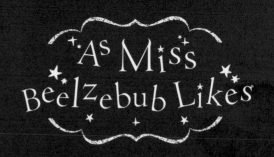

A SECRET GARDEN?

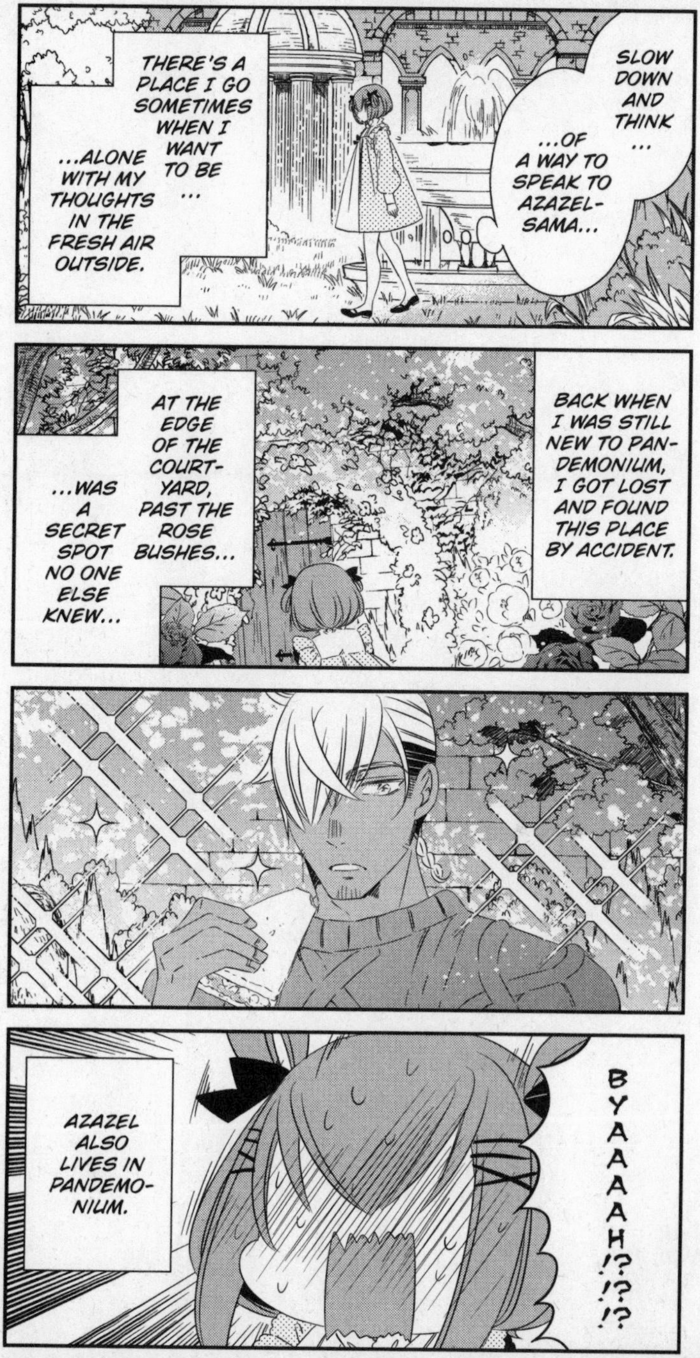
SLOW DOWN AND THINK...
...OF A WAY TO SPEAK TO AZAZEL-SAMA...
THERE'S A PLACE I GO SOMETIMES WHEN I WANT TO BE...
...ALONE WITH MY THOUGHTS IN THE FRESH AIR OUTSIDE.
BACK WHEN I WAS STILL NEW TO PANDEMONIUM, I GOT LOST AND FOUND THIS PLACE BY ACCIDENT.
AT THE EDGE OF THE COURTYARD, PAST THE ROSE BUSHES...
...WAS A SECRET SPOT NO ONE ELSE KNEW...
BYAAAAAH!?!?!?
AZAZEL ALSO LIVES IN PANDEMONIUM.

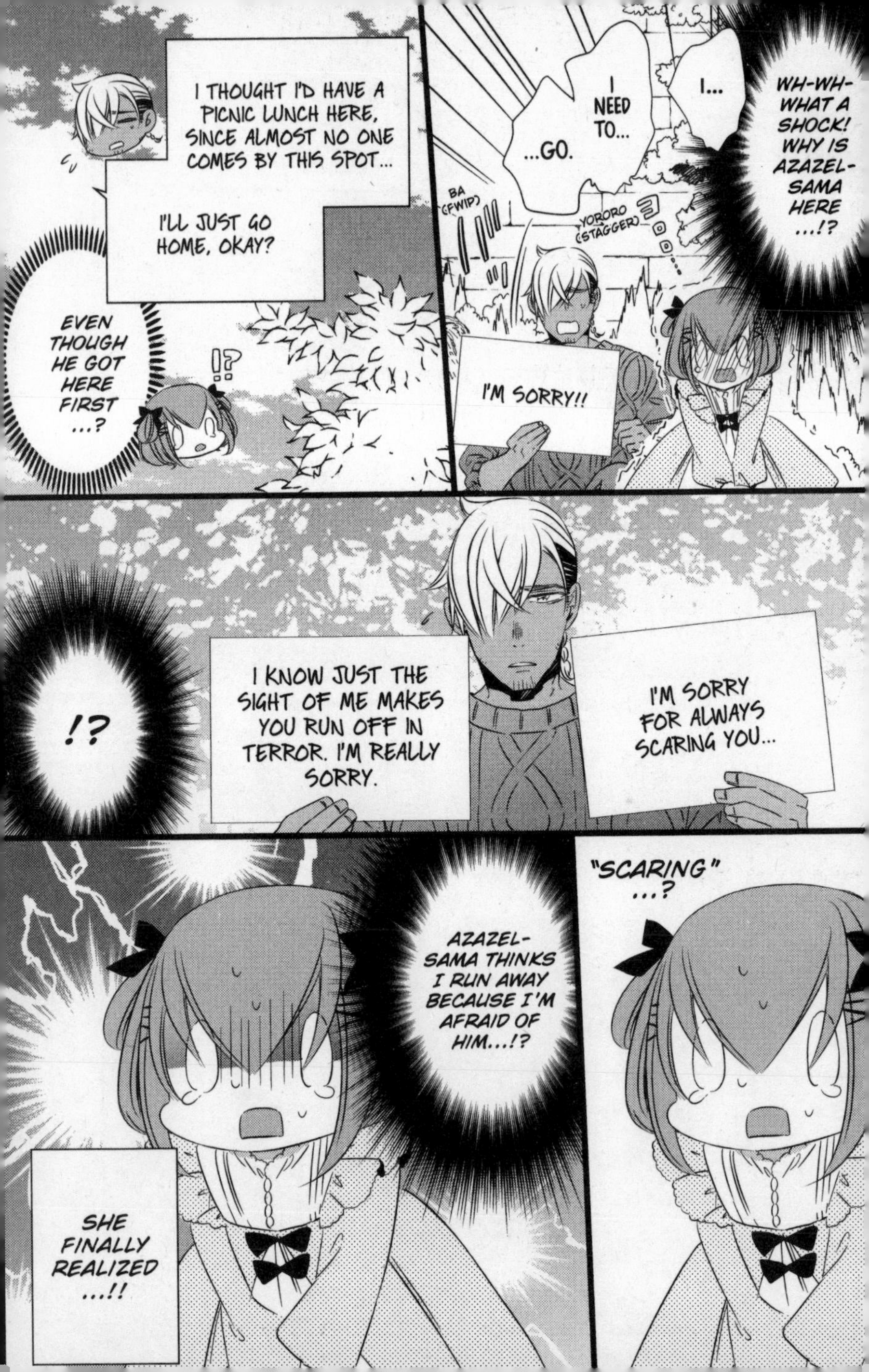
WH-WH-WHAT A SHOCK! WHY IS AZAZEL-SAMA HERE ...!?
I...
I NEED TO...
...GO.
BA (FWIP)
YORORO (STAGGER)
I'M SORRY!!
I THOUGHT I'D HAVE A PICNIC LUNCH HERE, SINCE ALMOST NO ONE COMES BY THIS SPOT...
I'LL JUST GO HOME, OKAY?
EVEN THOUGH HE GOT HERE FIRST ...?
!?
I'M SORRY FOR ALWAYS SCARING YOU...
I KNOW JUST THE SIGHT OF ME MAKES YOU RUN OFF IN TERROR. I'M REALLY SORRY.
!?
"SCARING" ...?
AZAZEL-SAMA THINKS I RUN AWAY BECAUSE I'M AFRAID OF HIM...!?
SHE FINALLY REALIZED ...!!

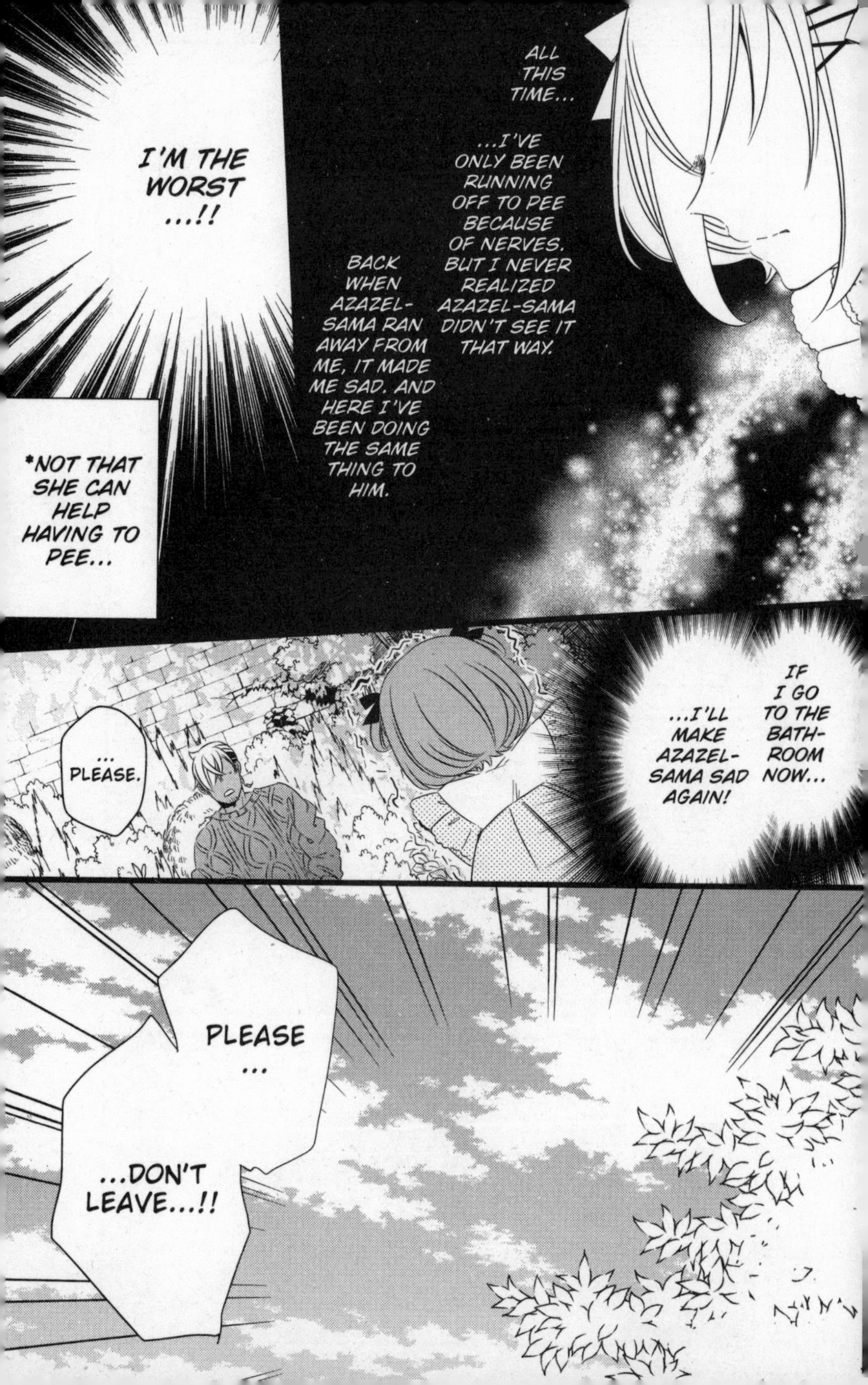
ALL THIS TIME...
...I'VE ONLY BEEN RUNNING OFF TO PEE BECAUSE OF NERVES. BUT I NEVER REALIZED AZAZEL-SAMA DIDN'T SEE IT THAT WAY.
BACK WHEN AZAZEL-SAMA RAN AWAY FROM ME, IT MADE ME SAD. AND HERE I'VE BEEN DOING THE SAME THING TO HIM.
I'M THE WORST ...!!
*NOT THAT SHE CAN HELP HAVING TO PEE...
IF I GO TO THE BATH-ROOM NOW...
...I'LL MAKE AZAZEL-SAMA SAD AGAIN!
...PLEASE.
PLEASE ...
...DON'T LEAVE...!!

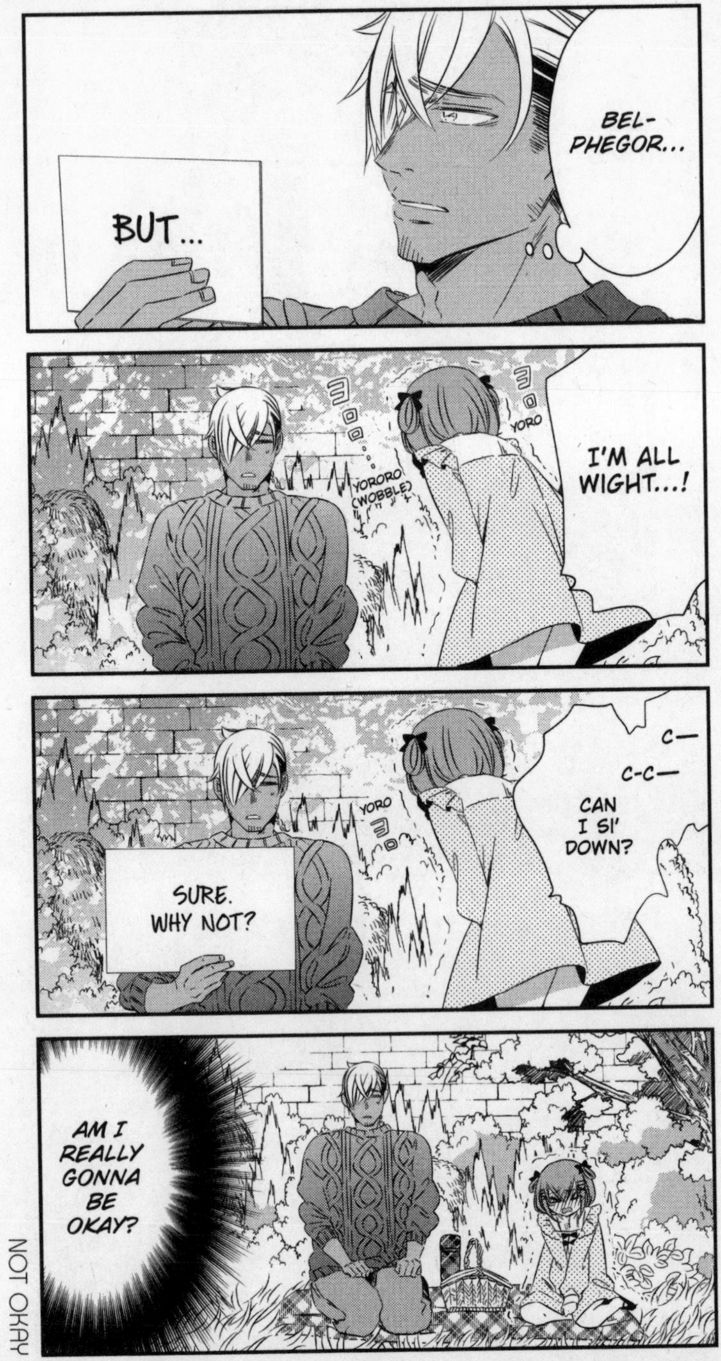
BEL-PHEGOR...
BUT...
YORO
I'M ALL WIGHT...!
YORORO (WOBBLE)
C—
C-C—
CAN I SI' DOWN?
YORO
SURE. WHY NOT?
AM I REALLY GONNA BE OKAY?
NOT OKAY

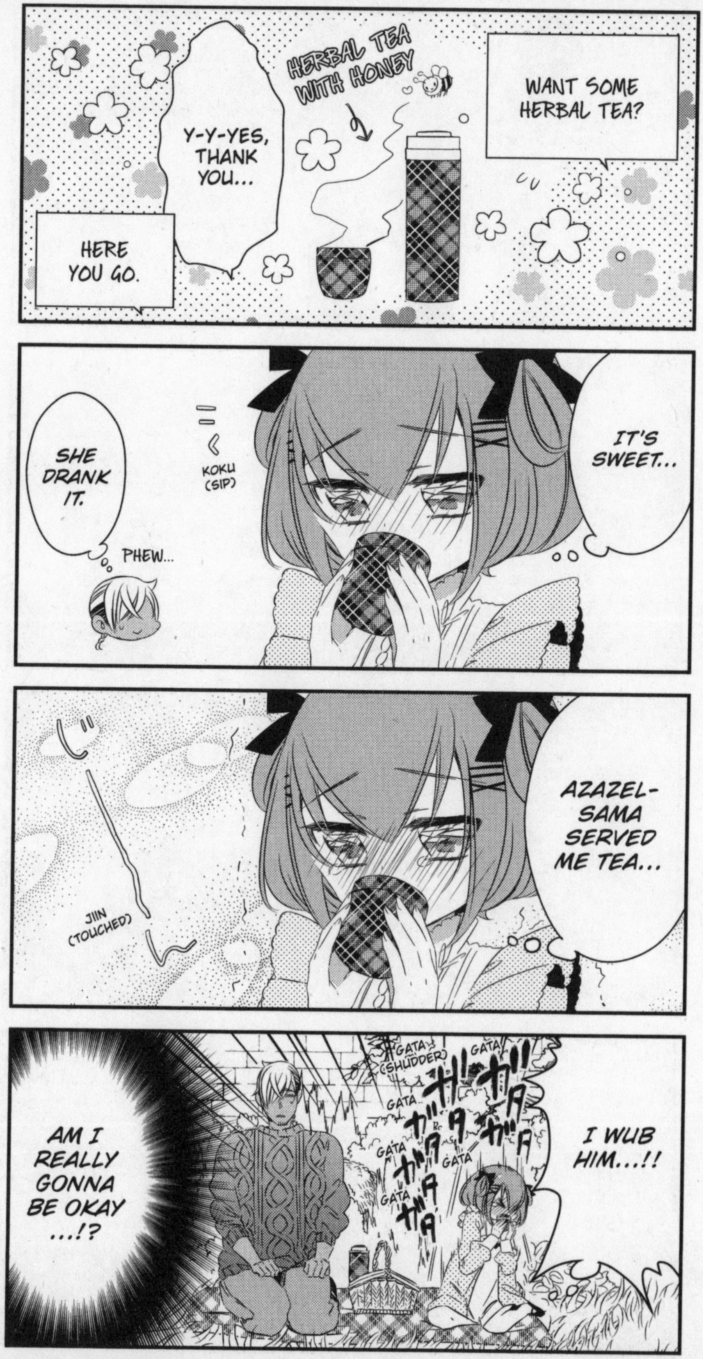
WANT SOME HERBAL TEA?
HERBAL TEA WITH HONEY
Y-Y-YES, THANK YOU...
HERE YOU GO.
IT'S SWEET...
KOKU (SIP)
SHE DRANK IT.
PHEW...
AZAZEL-SAMA SERVED ME TEA...
JIIN (TOUCHED)
I WUB HIM...!!
GATA
GATA (SHUDDER)
GATA
GATA
GATA
GATA
AM I REALLY GONNA BE OKAY ...!?

VERY NOT OKAY

YES, BUT NO

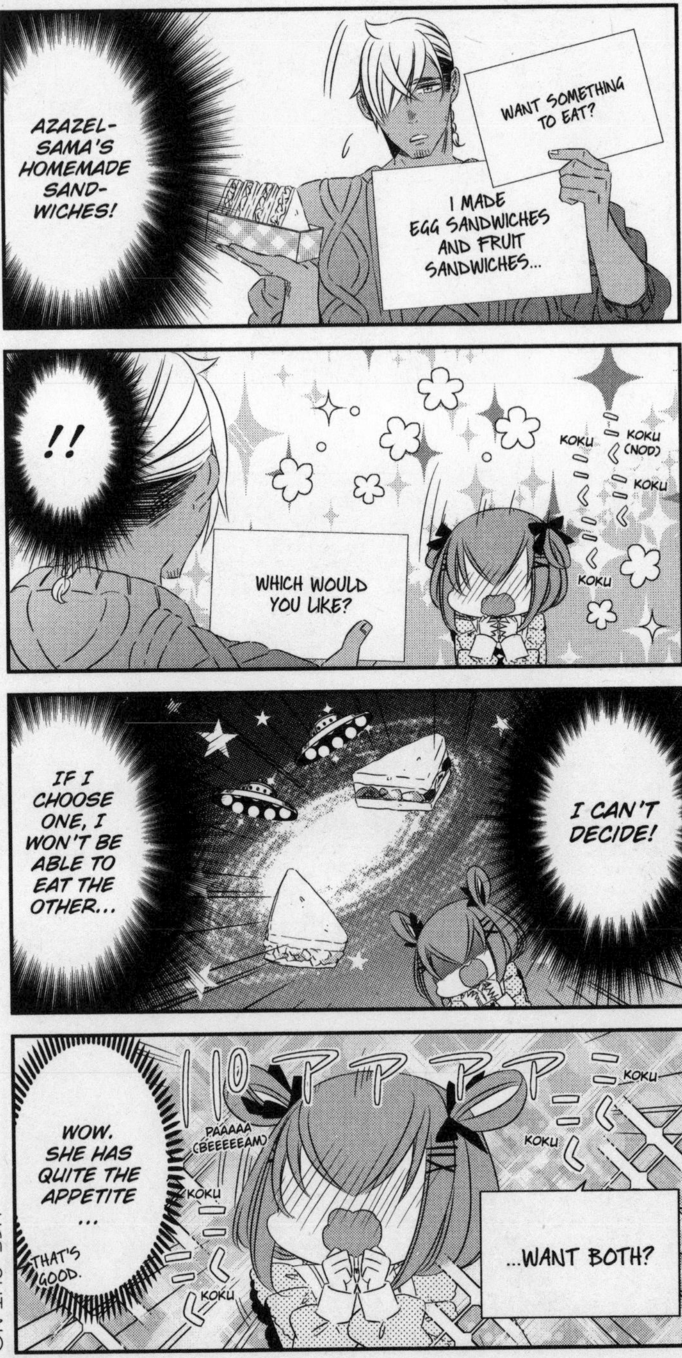
WANT SOMETHING TO EAT?
I MADE EGG SANDWICHES AND FRUIT SANDWICHES...
AZAZEL-SAMA'S HOMEMADE SANDWICHES!
KOKU (NOD)
KOKU
KOKU
KOKU
!!
WHICH WOULD YOU LIKE?
I CAN'T DECIDE!
IF I CHOOSE ONE, I WON'T BE ABLE TO EAT THE OTHER...
KOKU
KOKU
PAAAAA (BEEEEEAM)
WOW. SHE HAS QUITE THE APPETITE...
THAT'S GOOD.
KOKU
KOKU
...WANT BOTH?

TEARING HER MAIDEN'S HEART APART

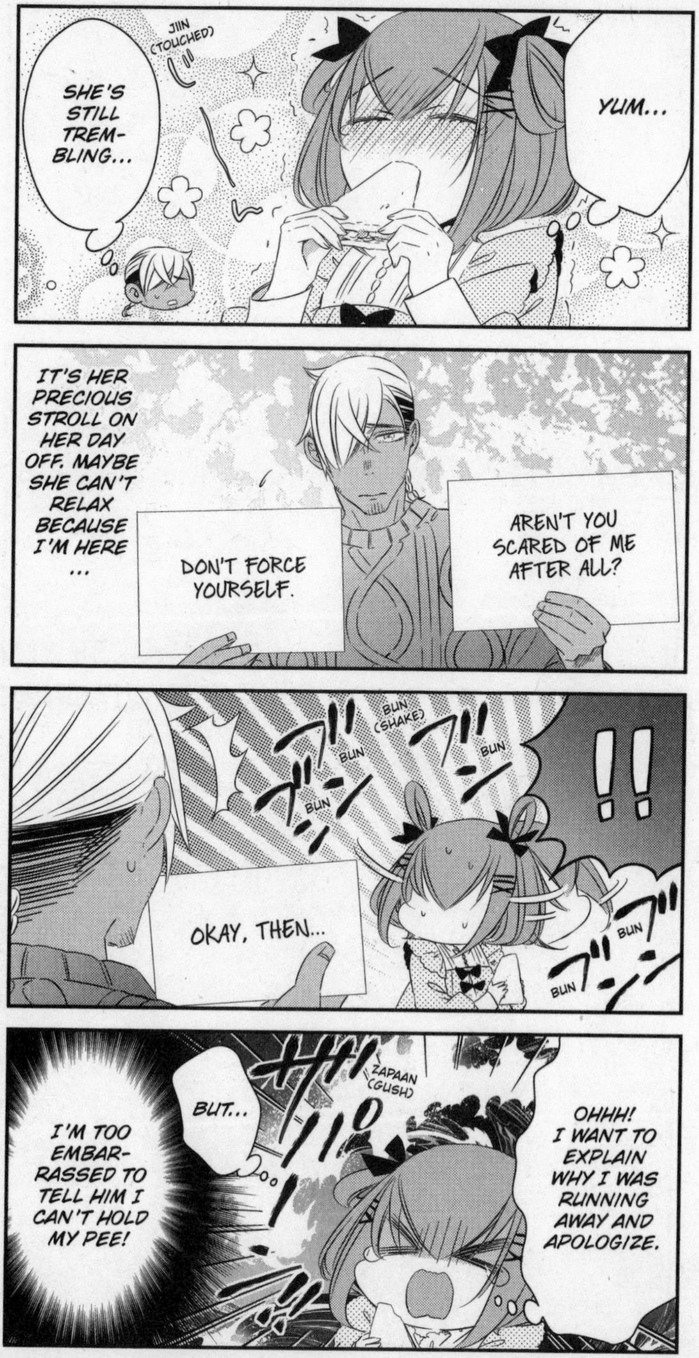
YUM...
JIIN (TOUCHED)
SHE'S STILL TREM-BLING...
AREN'T YOU SCARED OF ME AFTER ALL?
DON'T FORCE YOURSELF.
IT'S HER PRECIOUS STROLL ON HER DAY OFF. MAYBE SHE CAN'T RELAX BECAUSE I'M HERE ...
!!
BUN
BUN (SHAKE)
BUN
BUN
OKAY, THEN...
BUN
BUN
OHHH! I WANT TO EXPLAIN WHY I WAS RUNNING AWAY AND APOLOGIZE.
ZAPAAN (GUSH)
BUT...
I'M TOO EMBAR-RASSED TO TELL HIM I CAN'T HOLD MY PEE!

THE SECRET GARDEN

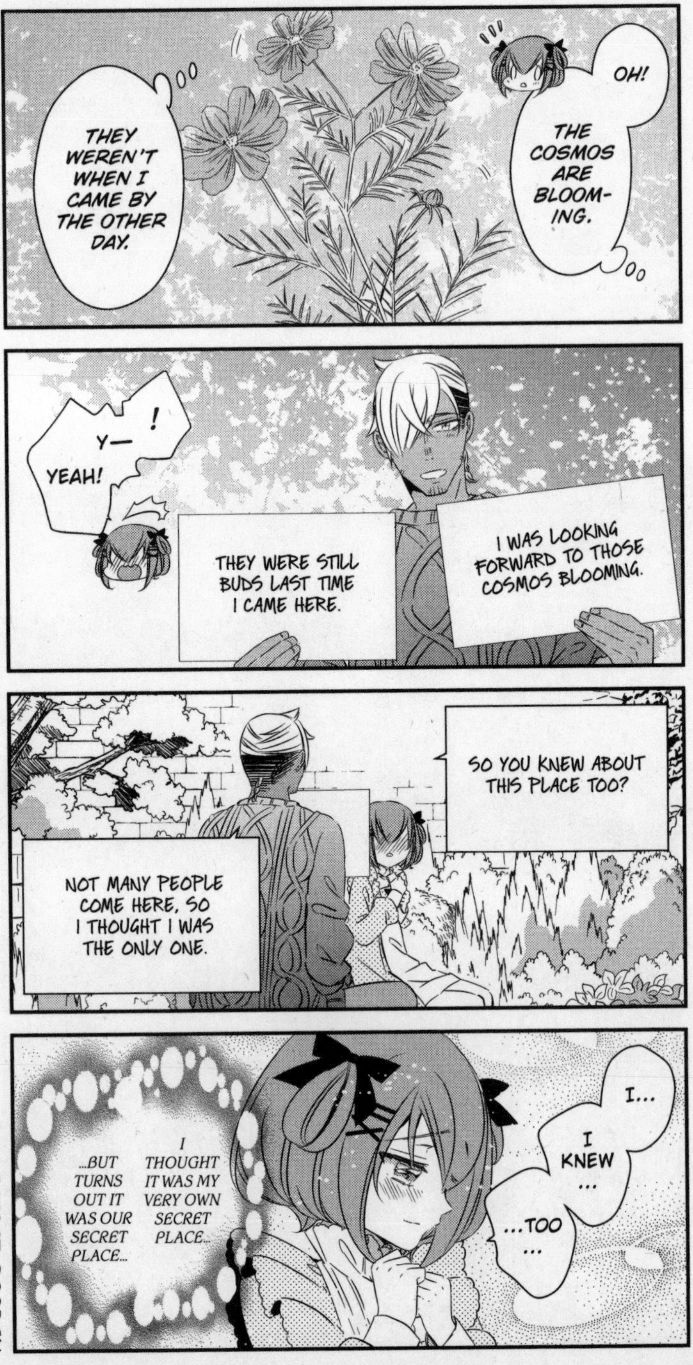

OH!
THE COSMOS ARE BLOOM-ING.
THEY WEREN'T WHEN I CAME BY THE OTHER DAY.
I WAS LOOKING FORWARD TO THOSE COSMOS BLOOMING.
THEY WERE STILL BUDS LAST TIME I CAME HERE.
Y— !
YEAH!
SO YOU KNEW ABOUT THIS PLACE TOO?
NOT MANY PEOPLE COME HERE, SO I THOUGHT I WAS THE ONLY ONE.
I...
I KNEW ...
...TOO ...
I THOUGHT IT WAS MY VERY OWN SECRET PLACE...
...BUT TURNS OUT IT WAS OUR SECRET PLACE...

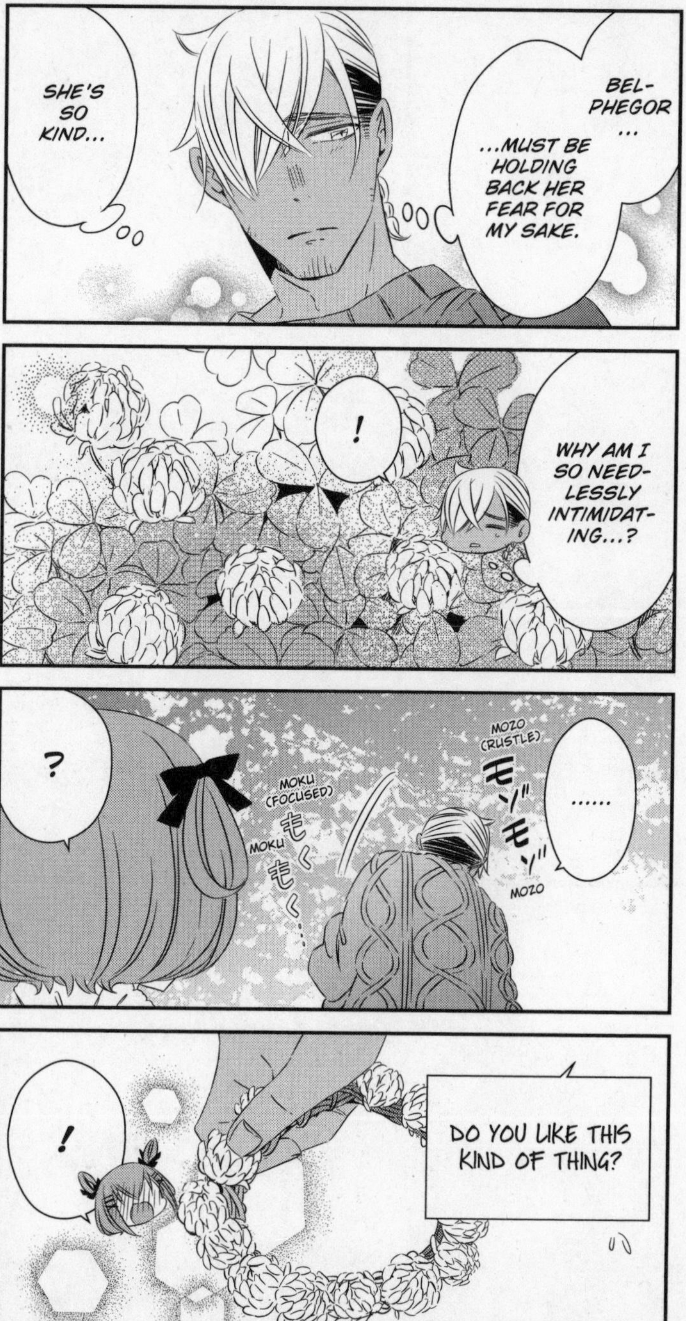
BEL-PHEGOR...
...MUST BE HOLDING BACK HER FEAR FOR MY SAKE.
SHE'S SO KIND...
WHY AM I SO NEED-LESSLY INTIMIDAT-ING...?
!
......
MOZO (RUSTLE)
モゾモゾ
MOZO
MOKU (FOCUSED)
もくもく
MOKU
?
DO YOU LIKE THIS KIND OF THING?
!

A FLOWER CROWN

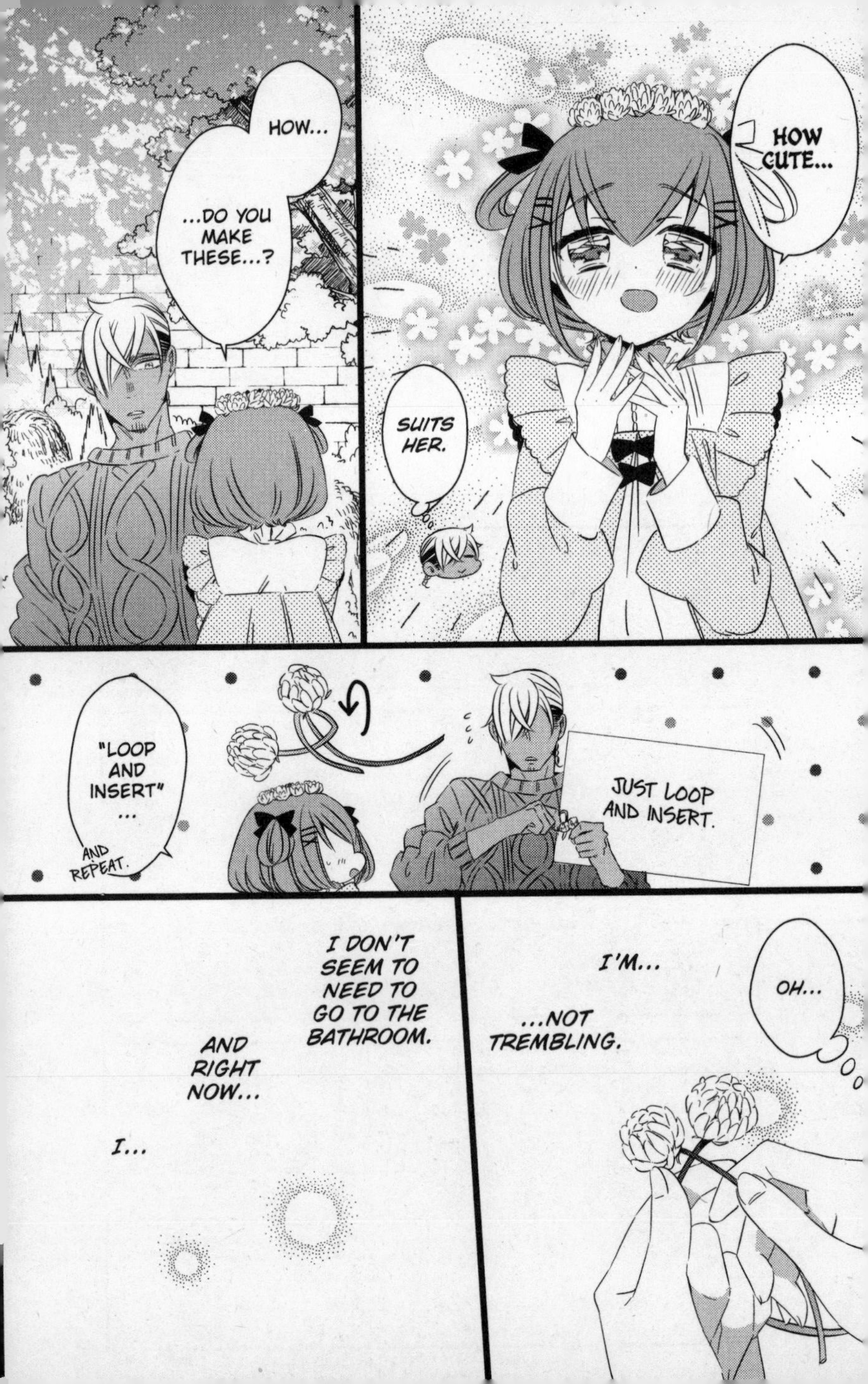
HOW CUTE...
SUITS HER.
HOW...
...DO YOU MAKE THESE...?
JUST LOOP AND INSERT.
"LOOP AND INSERT"...
AND REPEAT.
OH...
I'M...
...NOT TREMBLING.
I DON'T SEEM TO NEED TO GO TO THE BATHROOM.
AND RIGHT NOW...
I...

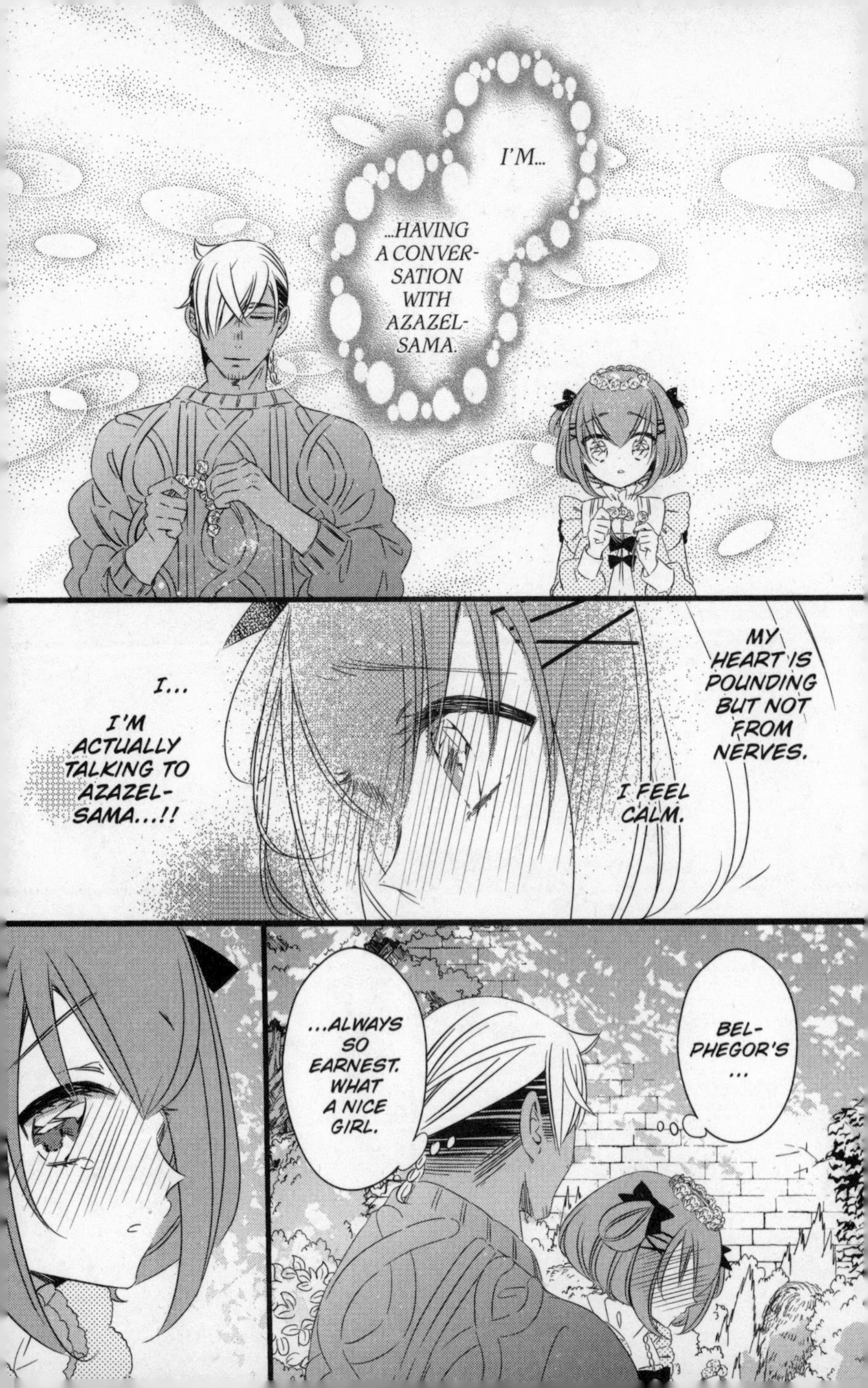
I'M...
...HAVING A CONVER-SATION WITH AZAZEL-SAMA.
MY HEART IS POUNDING BUT NOT FROM NERVES.
I FEEL CALM.
I...
I'M ACTUALLY TALKING TO AZAZEL-SAMA...!!
BEL-PHEGOR'S...
...ALWAYS SO EARNEST. WHAT A NICE GIRL.

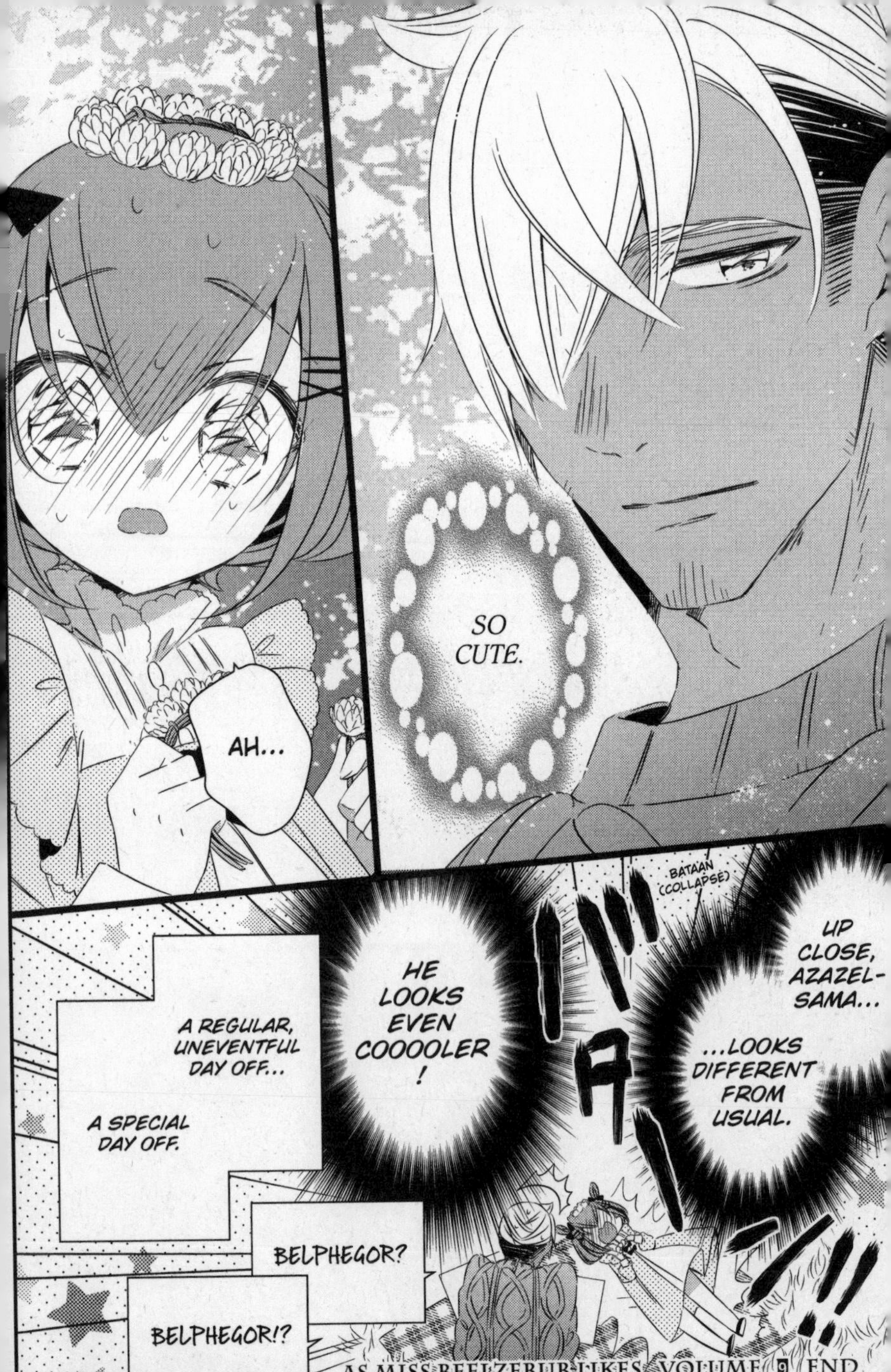
SO CUTE.
AH...
BATAAN (COLLAPSE)
UP CLOSE, AZAZEL-SAMA...
...LOOKS DIFFERENT FROM USUAL.
HE LOOKS EVEN COOOOLER!
A REGULAR, UNEVENTFUL DAY OFF...
A SPECIAL DAY OFF.
BELPHEGOR?
BELPHEGOR!?

AS MISS BEELZEBUB LIKES VOLUME 9 END

As Miss Beelzebub Likes

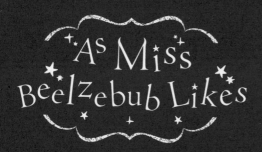

A SNEAK PEEK INTO VOLUME 10 ☆
A SHOCKING DISCOVERY ABOUT THE PANDEMONIUM LIBRARY DUO!?

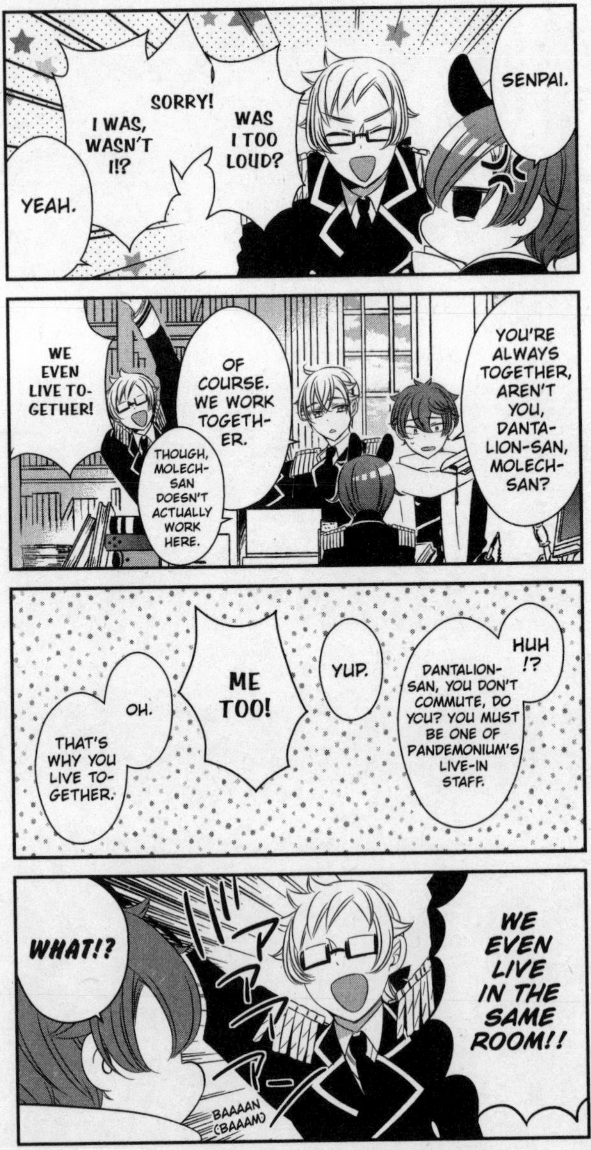
SENPAI.
WAS I TOO LOUD?
SORRY!
I WAS, WASN'T I!?
YEAH.
YOU'RE ALWAYS TOGETHER, AREN'T YOU, DANTALION-SAN, MOLECH-SAN?
OF COURSE. WE WORK TOGETHER.
THOUGH, MOLECH-SAN DOESN'T ACTUALLY WORK HERE.
WE EVEN LIVE TOGETHER!
HUH!?
DANTALION-SAN, YOU DON'T COMMUTE, DO YOU? YOU MUST BE ONE OF PANDEMONIUM'S LIVE-IN STAFF.
YUP.
ME TOO!
OH.
THAT'S WHY YOU LIVE TOGETHER.
WE EVEN LIVE IN THE SAME ROOM!!
BAAAAN (BAAAM)
WHAT!?

SET FOR JULY 2020

THE SECRET BEHIND THEIR LIVING ARRANGEMENTS, REVEALED...!?

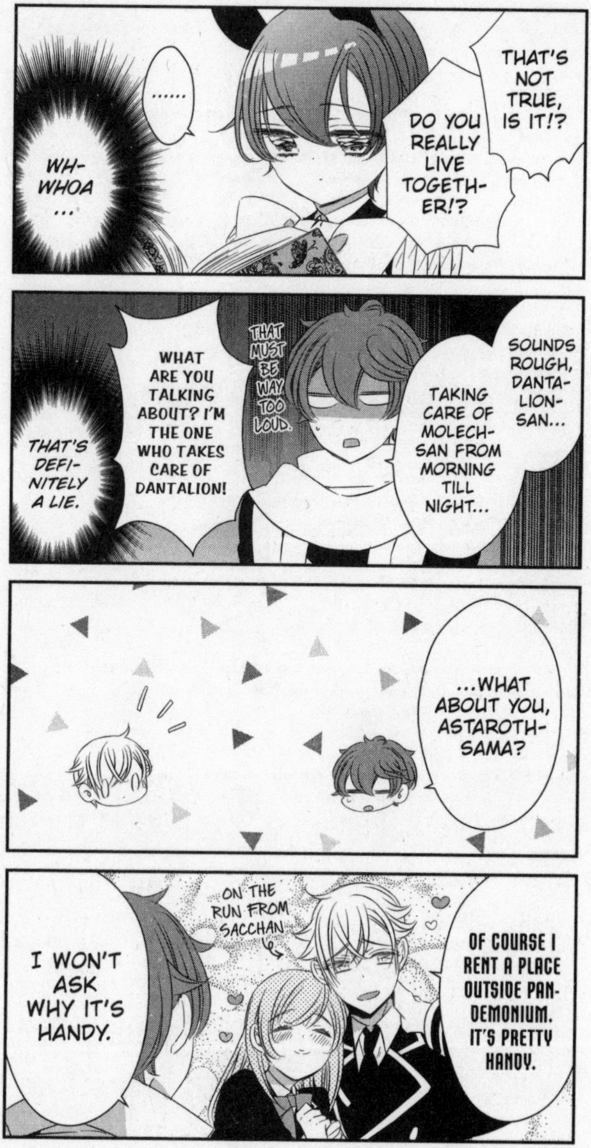
THAT'S NOT TRUE, IS IT!?
DO YOU REALLY LIVE TOGETHER!?
......
WH-WHOA...
SOUNDS ROUGH, DANTALION-SAN...
TAKING CARE OF MOLECH-SAN FROM MORNING TILL NIGHT...
THAT MUST BE WAY TOO LOUD.
WHAT ARE YOU TALKING ABOUT? I'M THE ONE WHO TAKES CARE OF DANTALION!
THAT'S DEFINITELY A LIE.
...WHAT ABOUT YOU, ASTAROTH-SAMA?
OF COURSE I RENT A PLACE OUTSIDE PANDEMONIUM. IT'S PRETTY HANDY.
ON THE RUN FROM SACCHAN
I WON'T ASK WHY IT'S HANDY.

Translation Notes

COMMON HONORIFICS

no honorific: Indicates familiarity or closeness; if used without permission or reason, addressing someone in this manner would constitute an insult.

-san: The Japanese equivalent of Mr./Mrs./Miss. If a situation calls for politeness, this is the fail-safe honorific.

-sama: Conveys great respect; may also indicate that the social status of the speaker is lower than that of the addressee.

-shi: An impersonal honorific used in formal speech or writing, e.g. legal documents.

-dono: Roughly equivalent to "master" or "milord."

-kun: Used most often when referring to boys, this indicates affection or familiarity. Occasionally used by older men among their peers, but it may also be used by anyone referring to a person of lower standing.

-chan: An affectionate honorific indicating familiarity used mostly in reference to girls; also used in reference to cute persons or animals of either gender.

-tan: A cutesy version of *-chan*.

-(o)nii/(o)nee: Meaning "big brother"/ "big sister," it can also refer to those older but relatively close in age to the speaker. It is typically followed by *-san*, *-chan*, or *-sama*.

-senpai: An honorific for one's senior classmate, colleague, etc., although not as senior or respected as a *sensei* ("teacher").

100 yen = approximately 1 USD.

PAGE 4

The Japanese version uses "*juugoya*," which was translated to "**full moon**" in the English version. However, "*juugoya*" holds other meanings; such as the "fifteenth night of the lunar month" or the "mid-autumn moon-viewing time," also called the "harvest moon."

PAGE 12

According to Japanese folklore, the rabbit who lives on the moon pounds rice to make rice cakes. The first panel directly references this story.

PAGE 15

Shotacon, or "*shota* complex," is what Japanese call an attraction to (typically fictional) young boys—the counterpart to *lolicon*. *Lolicon*, derived from "Lolita complex," is what Japanese call an attraction to (typically fictional) young girls.

PAGE 48

Beach Flags is a popular sport in Australia and New Zealand, especially among surf lifesavers. The game is somewhat similar to musical chairs—a competitor must obtain a flag during the round, or they will be eliminated. The number of flags decreases in each round until someone wins.

PAGE 75

Soumen is a type of thin wheat flour noodle.

PAGE 78

The difference between regular *soumen* and ***nagashi soumen*** is presentation. *Nagashi soumen* is served by sending the noodles in icy water down a bamboo chute.

PAGE 85

Tempura refers to the practice of deep-frying food such as vegetables, seafood, or meat in a thin batter. The crunchy parts of the batter that fall off during the cooking process are referred to as "*tenkasu*."

Wasabi is a condiment often used in Japanese cooking. It sometimes is called "Japanese horseradish" and is typically paired with foods like sushi to add a little bit of spice to the dish.

PAGE 89

Tokoroten is a gelatinous Japanese dish made from agarophytes. Agarophytes are a type of seaweed more commonly thought of as red algae.

PAGE 91

Flooring in traditional Japanese homes usually consists of mats woven from straw. These mats are known as *tatami*.

PAGE 95

The Japanese version of the mafia is the *yakuza*.

PAGE 110

In Japan, the distinction between the face you present to other people and your true thoughts is extremely important. Often, people in Japan are expected to behave according to specific rules and customs, regardless of their true feelings. The phrase "*honne*," which can be roughly translated as "true sound," is often used in contrast with the term "*tatemae*," or "built in front," to express this distinction between inner thoughts and your public face. It was translated into English as "*Her real thoughts!!*"

PAGE 116

Moji is a reference to a popular chocolate manufacturer in Japan known as Meiji. The company was founded in 1918 and currently enjoys global success in the chocolate industry.

7619 7937

As Miss Beelzebub Likes

matoba

volume 9

Translation: Lisa Coffman
Lettering: Lorina Mapa

This book is a work of fiction. Names, characters, places, and incidents are the product of the author's imagination or are used fictitiously. Any resemblance to actual events, locales, or persons, living or dead, is coincidental.

BEELZEBUB-JO NO OKINIMESU MAMA. Vol. 9
©2018 matoba/SQUARE ENIX CO., LTD.
First published in Japan in 2018 by SQUARE ENIX CO., LTD. English translation rights arranged with SQUARE ENIX CO., LTD. and Yen Press, LLC through Tuttle-Mori Agency, Inc., Tokyo.

English translation ©2020 by SQUARE ENIX CO., LTD.

Yen Press, LLC supports the right to free expression and the value of copyright. The purpose of copyright is to encourage writers and artists to produce the creative works that enrich our culture.

The scanning, uploading, and distribution of this book without permission is a theft of the author's intellectual property. If you would like permission to use material from the book (other than for review purposes), please contact the publisher. Thank you for your support of the author's rights.

Yen Press
150 West 30th Street, 19th Floor
New York, NY 10001

Visit us at yenpress.com
facebook.com/yenpress ★ yenpress.tumblr.com
twitter.com/yenpress instagram.com/yenpress

First Yen Press Edition: April 2020

Yen Press is an imprint of Yen Press, LLC.
The Yen Press name and logo are trademarks of Yen Press, LLC.

The publisher is not responsible for websites (or their content) that are not owned by the publisher.

Library of Congress Control Number: 2017963582

ISBNs: 978-1-9753-0928-2 (paperback)
978-1-9753-0927-5 (ebook)

10 9 8 7 6 5 4 3 2 1

WOR

Printed in the United States of America